Dominic's Ghosts

Dominic's Ghosts

Michael Williams

 SEVENTH STAR PRESS

Cover art and design: Enggar Adirasa

Cover art in this book copyright © 2018 Enggar Adirasa & Seventh Star Press, LLC.

Editor: Karen M. Leet

Published by Seventh Star Press, LLC.

ISBN Number:

Seventh Star Press

www.seventhstarpress.com

info@seventhstarpress.com

Publisher's Note:

Dominic's Ghosts is a work of fiction. All names, characters, and places are the product of the author's imagination, used in fictitious manner. Any resemblances to actual persons, places, locales, events, etc. are purely coincidental.

Printed in the United States of America

First Edition

For Ben Creech

There comes a time, Vasettha, when, sooner or later after a long period, this world contracts. At a time of contraction, beings are mostly born in the Abhassara Brahma world. And there they dwell, mind-made, feeding on delight, self-luminous, moving through the air, glorious—and they stay like that for—what might seem an eternity. But sooner or later this world begins to expand again. At a time of expansion, the beings from the Abhassara Brahma world, having passed away from there, are mostly reborn in this world. Here they dwell, mind-made, feeding on delight, self-luminous, moving through the air, glorious, and they stay like that for a very long time.
    -The Agganna Sutta

Prologue

On his tenth birthday, three years before his father vanished in the abandoned basement, Dominic went to see the newest Indiana Jones movie, the one about the Holy Grail. His father claimed to have chosen it for its Nazis and Templar Knights, but Dominic was old enough to understand that the father/son reunion was in the house, that the film was another of his vague gestures at bonding.

The boy sat in the cool dark and soaked in *The Last Crusade*, its subterranean floods and attendant rats. Gabriel bought him Jujubes, which stuck to his fillings, and Dominic probed his back teeth with his finger as Indy and the blonde lady were chased in speedboats through Venice by some Secret Society people. But the whole pursuit was a mistake all around, everyone in the chase was a good guy except for the German blonde lady, it turned out.

The film tricked him early, setting up supposes and misdirections. Twenty years later, returning to the town for what might be an extended stay, Dominic was hard pressed to distinguish between what he had seen that afternoon and what he had imagined or dreamed. He remembered laughing when Indy first saw the soldiers in the castle and said to the blonde lady, "Nazis. I hate those guys." He remembered laughing harder when his dad leaned toward him and whispered, "God damn it, so do I!"

When Indy and his dad set the castle on fire and barely escaped a screenful of Nazis, Dominic rested his head on his own dad's shoulder. Here with the film underway, his gums already sore with the sugary candy and his thoughts drifting in and out of some strange Turkish subplot, he again believed his mother was mistaken, that she had to be wrong. His dad was a good guy, after all. Maybe his dad was like the men in the speedboats, where you had to find out more about them in order to know they were all right.

But the scene in Berlin would haunt him the most in the years that followed. The Hitler scene, even more than the end of the movie. Indy is walking through a colonnade in the midst of a big Nazi crowd gathered for a book-burning. He comes face to face with Hitler, and that was creepy enough, with the Fuehrer all glistening in the torchlight, so sallow he was almost green. But it was the crowd around them—the cast of extras—that bothered Dominic the most. Among the Nazis one face peered back at him—a young man, handsome and Nordic, whom he thought he recognized or remembered. The camera passed through the crowd, and the young Nazi looked straight at Dominic, an odd, lonely sympathy in his blue eyes.

Then immediately the camera cut away, focused on Hitler 's autographing Indy's book—in was actually old Henry's journal. It was all done in a brief flurry of what Dominic would know later as reverse angle shots—Indy to Hitler and back to Indy—and the man in the background had vanished by the time the camera came back to his spot.

For years Dominic would trouble himself with that man, that moment. With why he never could locate the man in the film, no matter how many times he saw it again, stopped the VCR tape, the DVD. Later he would see restored footage, but still no mysterious man, and he came to the conclusion, sometime in his early thirties, that he had imagined the figure there. Then he troubled himself with why he had imagined a sympathetic Nazi, a storm trooper looking right through him, until the worry changed to acceptance and then to indifference, until it emerged in the nightmares he would have three years later.

But on that long-ago day the lights went up, Indy and his crew riding off into some Middle Eastern sunset and the credits racing over the screen so quickly Dominic couldn't read them. He and his father sat there a while longer, blinking in recovered brightness and quiet. Dominic guessed, for the first time, that they would know one another in brief visits like this one. Gabriel probably left the theater feeling that a movie about fathers and sons relearning each other had been a silly thing to do, a thing sprung too early on a ten-year-old. But Dominic understood the edges of it, and liked its veiled and awkward messages.

"We should get out of here, buddy," his dad whispered, and Dominic stood up, and then the other thing happened, the grains tumbling onto the theater floor and scattering under the seats in front of them with a kind of hissing rattle. Bewildered, he bent down and picked up two of them—hard, white little pebbles that would go by the word "pearlescent" when he learned that word years later. For right now, they seemed simply bizarre and unexplainable and a little unpleasant, as though all his baby teeth had dropped to the floor in front of him.

Perhaps he should have thought about this oddity instead of the vanishing Nazi, should have told his father or at least reckoned that something about pearls or teeth in a well-lit theater was something he should remember. But he forgot it almost immediately, let it pass from his mind until that Christmas three years later when he stood at the top of cellar stairs, when the topmost step glittered with the banked light from a kitchen window and he saw the pearls again, scattered at his feet, and he recalled that birthday afternoon as his father began the long descent into shadow.

∞

What Dominic did not know was this:

That as the lights in the theater lifted to rows of sad blue chairs and the smell of stale butter and mildew, the last fluttering lights pooled on the surface of the screen gave birth to a receding shadow. Out of a stylized LucasFilm Berlin colonnade a young man walked in restive shade, away from the screen and the theater, back into a darkness that defined itself as he moved through it, back to the furthermost and darkest arch, beyond the last light the camera could capture. Through cables and scaffolding he walked, past a dolly parked carelessly athwart a narrow passageway between sets, and all color faded from him as he moved slowly back and inward, the grey and black of his uniform joined by greyness and blackness implicit in the light. The young man's skin darkened suddenly, the death's head on his collar blanched white like the cables on the floor, and he passed over and through the back wall of the studio, suddenly immaterial, almost invisible, shifting at last into a thin tongue of black flame at the very edge of formlessness, joining the others.

Six tendrils of flame awaited him above the fractured pavement. They gave off no heat, and cast a gray, muffled light over buildings that were more shard than structure, crooked blades drooping like wilted leaves, the flames glowing faintly, rippling like oil pooled on the surface of dark water.

They did not scare him. They were not supposed to.

You are one of us? one of them asked in German, its voice a melodious contralto worthy of Wagner's norns. *Why don't we know you?*

And he, *You do. Or will.*

The cool fires surrounded him, embracing and monochromic, as though they sought to swallow and absorb him. His was the advantage: as they circled him he knew who they were, he knew their names.

He stood at parade rest, shooting his cuffs and folding his

hands in front of him, the gesture a blend, he hoped, of repose and menace. He assured them it was almost their time. That someone had been found, and the wait was nearly over. That soon the weariness would end, and this extravagant spotlit drama would head toward pure light.

So they say. This voice deeper, masculine, comic but weary. *So we were told eons ago.*

Ah, hardly eons, he said. *Seventy, seventy-five years? I know. Believe me. Not even a century, Ombrade. I have endured the time with you. And I had to stay longer.*

Now the shadows fell silent. They pulsed and glittered, circling him as though on the edge of discovery, bending compliantly under his focused gaze.

He would pretend they knew him.

1.

Dry Salvages Book Store was the poor man's university, a place for readers in a non-reading town. John Bulwer ran the premises like a dissipated Buddha, handing out insight and cigarettes to his clientele. It was where a customary magic ruled, where the talk ranged leftward in current events, and where Dominic Rackett had just started work.

It was named Dry Salvages after the Eliot poem. John had told him the first day. Something about *the way up is the way down, the way forward is the way back*. It had sounded to Dominic suspiciously like self-help, like *let go and let God*, a saying he believed in theory but was too embarrassed and too hip to put into practice.

Dominic considered himself a book man, even more than movies and television. Every time he moved (and this was the sixth time in four years, the sixth time since grad school) he would first find the used book store to ask for a job. It had never worked until Salvages: the operations were one-person deals, an overwrought owner doubling as a clerk in a kind of suicidal multi-task—sometimes death for the owner, but almost always death for the store.

It had surprised him when Grandma Mary suggested that Dry Salvages might be hiring. Said at least she knew the owner from her theater days. Nice man, bit of an old hippie, but that wouldn't bother Dominic, now would it? And of course Bulwer had remembered Mary, had taken on Dominic at a dollar above minimum wage and footed the monthly premium on a fairly decent health plan that Dominic figured he wouldn't need, but why not? He had no idea how Bulwer was making do, but it didn't seem to trouble the old man.

John Bulwer seemed, all said and done, troubled by very little. He liked Marlboros and coffee, had given up drinking whiskey "the same night I gave up White Castles, you do the math," and carried himself with a certain amount of grace and vigor for a man in his middle seventies. He had met Kerouac and Ginsberg, had known Ferlinghetti, all names that ranged through Dominic's mythology, though to be honest, he hadn't read their work. And of this, Bulwer was aware, and not above needling him.

"So, no Eliot. No Ginsberg. I thought you had a poetry degree." This said through a billow of smoke, as the space around Bulwer's desk dappled in the beam of an old 1960s tensor lamp, making him look like a vintage photo colorized on somebody's mild mescaline trip.

"Told you it was creative writing, not literature," Dominic replied. He was getting the rhythm of the place, the back-and-forth in which the old man could come off as simultaneously cranky and hip. To this routine, Dominic was the straight man, and he'd worked at Salvages for two weeks without its getting old.

"So, the only poetry you've read was your own?"

"That's about right, John." Dominic squinted in the shadowy aisle, seeking the spot to shelve a book on woodworking. "Here's one on carpentry. Maybe there's a section on how to repair gaping holes in the floor."

It was a standing joke. Not a month before Dominic was hired, boards in the Fantasy/SF aisle of the store had given way under a heavy customer, who fortunately had escaped with only minor abrasions and no threat of lawsuit. The crevice yawned in the middle of the aisle, like a doorway to somewhere else. While it awaited repair, the aisle was cordoned off with crime scene tape and the ominous warning, scrawled in pencil on a piece of typing paper stapled to the tape: *Beware: Here Lurketh Great Nyarlathotep.* Yet another allusion he was forced to explain to Dominic. Lovecraft and the primordial alien monsters hidden under the surfaces of things.

"You can hammer a nail as well as I can, Dom. But for now, you're in the wrong aisle to shelve repair books. Next one over and near the back."

"Too dark to see back there."

"Then change the bulb. And incandescent, not one of those goddamned CFL corkscrews you can't read shit by."

Dominic grinned. His grandmother's recommendation had been enough to get him hired, but he was pretty sure that Bulwer was beginning to like him, though the old man swore that his was the only business in town that set the bar low enough to allow a *haiku* poet on the resume.

"So what brought you back here, Dominic?" Bulwer asked. "You've never really said. Or is it just too dull a story to tell?"

"No, John. It's all kinds of fascinating. Where you keeping the incandescent bulbs these days?"

"At the hardware store," Bulwer boomed merrily. "Sending you there once I hear the story. So, what is it?"

"Well, remember I told you I was in Italy?"

Dominic was always dodgy about the how and why of the Italian trip, financed by his stepfather and supposedly geared toward the vague destination of "finding himself." It had started with the standard tourist's itinerary, which held his interest until he stood on the Campo San Barnaba in the June fetor of Venice, looking up at the church from *The Last Crusade.* For years he had troubled himself with that German officer, that moment in a studio in Berlin. But there in Venice he gave in to the long suspicion that he had imagined the figure there, though for what reason he still had no idea. All that remained was the troubling question why, at ten years old, he had dreamed up a sympathetic Nazi, a storm trooper looking right through him.

So thinking he was giving up the quest, he ran from it once again. He went rogue, off the itinerary and west, all the way to Turin and up into the Italian Alps, where he lingered for a month. And there he received the apprehensive phone call from Ben, who, next to his grandmother, was his closest brush with surviving family, a stepfather still throwing around his dead wife's Boston money in exchange for a say in Dominic's life.

It was Grandma Mary, Ben told him. He "feared this might be it," using that oily psychiatrist's tone he'd duped Dominic with more than once. But you couldn't take a chance, could you? So Dominic buckled and used the card which had lain untouched in his backpack for two months. He had returned on a sudden and steeply expensive flight from Milan, not concerned about the cost because it felt like more Ben's dime than his own inheritance, a reminder of his prolonged adolescence where, at thirty-four, his money was still in the hands of grownups. On his connecting flight south from Chicago, he tried to piece together memories of his grandmother from his fourteenth birthday on, and drawing blanks even though he knew he had spoken with her, that he had even visited several times—arrived and departed, it seemed, without leaving a mark.

When he reached the city and took a cab to his grandmother's apartment, he had found her riding a stationary bike, drinking a gin and tonic, and arguing with her soap opera, *Realm of Desire*, her Galway brogue more audible when she was well-oiled and angry. She confessed, then, with very little guilt, that she might have embroidered her ailments to Ben for the sheer pleasure of embroidering. Nor did she care that her maneuvers had brought Dominic nearly five thousand miles, back to a city he had avoided for two decades: it was high time he visited her, she announced between sips and pedals, and he knew he could stay with her as long as he liked.

Bulwer laughed at the story—that high and wheezy smoker's

ratchet—and called Grandma Mary a conniving old heifer. He could get away with it, had known her since the Sixties, and Dominic was hardly protective after the old girl had tricked him over half the globe to kneel at the shrine of her ego.

But why at this time, Dominic had to wonder, and this time out loud. Why, after all these years, would she stage-manage a visit?

Stage manage was the name for it, Bulwer guessed. From what he knew of Mary, she could go without high drama for weeks, sometimes months, but the time always came when her world dilated, she remembered there were others in the vicinity, and she called on them to pay her homage. Or it could be simpler, kinder and less devious. She could just want Dominic to come home.

"But this isn't home," Dominic insisted. "Never has been, never will be. I came here only a half-dozen times growing up. Sure, it was my father's home, though, but after him I don't remember ever coming back. Except for now."

He placed the repair book between two others of roughly the same size, sorting by guesswork in the shadows. "Maybe this repair book has something about shelving, as well," he called out, as Bulwer put some Coltrane on the old turntable.

"Well, for now," the old man insisted, "we'll stick with the light bulb. There has to be a joke about how many college men it takes to screw one in. Come here, I'll give you a ten and an errand at the hardware shop. Incandescent, remember. Like God wanted the light bulb to be.

"And while you're at it, bring me back a hamburger. Buddha won't mind."

∞

By the time Dominic got back to Salvages, the boy from the movie theater had dropped in, was pretending to talk jazz with Bulwer. Young guy—early twenties, Dominic guessed. Red-headed and with skin so extraordinarily pale that you probably couldn't find its equal on a creature above ground. Far too eager to please, especially since, to Max Winter, pleasing seemed pretty much to mean impressing, and nothing else. Dominic found himself liking Max anyway, enjoying the disapproving glance he gave the hamburger plopped down beside Bulwer's turntable.

Vegan, probably. And probably some specifically irritating kind of vegan, one who had adopted the way of life in order to bring it up all the time and inconvenience others. Dominic knew the type. Had been vegetarian himself during the long defeat of his twenties. But the good thing about Max seemed to be a kind of untapped intelligence under all that earnestness, the sense that when he came out of it, he was going to be fine.

But right now, Max was talking about *Miles and Trane* like he knew them, how *before he died, wasn't Jimi moving out of rock and into jazz?* and Bulwer, who had known Miles Davis a little, was never too comfortable with that kind of familiarity. So before Max went on about other things he didn't really know, Bulwer took the occasion to blow Dominic's cover.

"This young man, Mad Max, has a celebrity in the family," Bulwer announced. "Only son of a native son nobody talks about."

Dominic blushed and said it sounded like a country song. He dreaded when people brought up his father's writing career—not because the book was bad but because nobody ever understood. The tremble of interest when they found out Gabriel had been a novelist almost always receded when they discovered that *Dacia* was fantasy. Then the best of them told him how they had read *The Hobbit* or *Harry Potter* or *Dragonlance,* or how they had tried reading *Game of Thrones*, but they always ended up with how they had outgrown the books, that they had been relics of childhood or adolescence, left behind when real and more meaningful life intervened.

And the same kind of vague disappointment settled on Max, as Bulwer and Dominic told him about Gabriel Rackett's book. "Why doesn't anyone talk about him?" Max asked ultimately. "I mean...fantasy's popular stuff. It still sells, doesn't it?"

And before Dominic could respond and alienate someone else with a kind of muted testiness, Bulwer mentioned that he believed Max Winter could find out for himself, that there was a copy of *Dacia* shelved on the premises. It was news to Dominic, whose first stop in any used book store involved a quick look of the sf/fantasy shelves for his father's novel, but when Bulwer told Max to *look under local authors*, the oversight was clear.

And there it was: the orange cover Dominic's father always claimed he would have done anything to avoid, the cartoonish hill and castle, the young man (far younger than the one in the book) struggling up through a wasteland of trees and rocks toward the castle walls, and a monster (who never appeared in Gabriel's book) regarding the whole scene hungrily from behind a cemetery monument. Max thumbed the pages, feigning interest, and Dominic silently swore to say nothing apologetic, nothing explanatory. Meanwhile, Bulwer went on about how the town was like the Church in how it waited until its artists were safely dead before it canonized them, always with half an eye on what Chicago or Cincinnati or (God save us!) Lexington was thinking of the work. Hunter had gone through the same trial here, John said, said as well that it was like something out of the Bardo Thodol, the Tibetan Book of the Dead, where the soul wanders through monsters in the afterlife. "It's better for the writers, though," he confided, "if someone makes the book into a film, so the home town doesn't have to read to call the writer theirs."

Max derailed the conversation, then, asking Bulwer whether he knew Hunter and whether that was Hunter *Thompson*, and Bulwer, easily tempted to reminisce, owned to running across Hunter now and then in the Highlands, to being vaguely afraid of the older boy. And the anecdotes began, giving Max an opportunity to slide the copy of *Dacia* along the counter and leave it there when he left the store.

Dominic frowned as he picked up the book. It happened like this more often than not: people like Max liked the whiff of celebrity without the work. He wondered if Max had even read Hunter Thompson, or whether the whole conversation was simply a prelude to being on a first-name basis with a dead artist.

Miles. Jimi. Hunter.

Dominic waited until the boy was gone before picking up the novel.

"Oh, you didn't think our Max was going to read it, much less buy it, did you?" Bulwer asked with a sigh. "Occupational hazard at Dry Salvages. I'm but a gardener of good intentions."

Dominic smiled. "I like that it's on the Local Authors shelf, though."

John lit another cigarette and slipped *Kind of Blue* back into the album jacket. "My own copy used to belong to an ex-girlfriend of mine who knew him some back in the day. She gave it to me. Signed copy. Bubble in a stream kind of thing. Well, this one doesn't have to have a permanent home, either, Dominic. I mean, don't break your neck trying to shelve it under fantasy. Beware Nyarlathotep. But take the book with you, if you like. Read it again. Go looking for your father."

2.

Beneath the gilded vault and the bas-relief plaster masks of immortals, the lobby mural seemed modest, out of place.

It was a replica of the Edward Hicks painting of *The Peaceable Kingdom*. Max knew that much.

Lion and Lamb on a high embankment, two sides of the world, led by the Little Child, like in the old Bible story. The painting was simple, primitive, the lion smiling and facing the viewer like a creature from the headboard of a child's bed, in the distance people dancing in a circle. Above, the strange other world of plaster masks—Beethovens, Buster Keatons, and Dantes—looked down from the elaborate ceiling.

The mural was the first thing you saw when you surfaced in the lobby after the films—a way-station of stillness between the flickering images on the screen and those of Fourth Street outside the Shangri-La Theater. They called that lobby the Peaceable Kingdom, before Leni Zauber showed up at the door. And more importantly, before Dominic came to disrupt it all.

∞

Max Winter had worked at the Shangri-La for almost a year. The weekday evenings and weekend screenings were perfect for his borderline schedule. Like many recent graduates in a sluggish economy, he was patching together a living from retail and service, siphoning income from the city's always-dying arts scene. So the Shangri-La was a good waystation, a place to work until a real job came.

It was one of those Baroque throwbacks built in the early 20th century, a maze of balconies and grottoes, reds and golds and cavernous ceilings over a tiered lobby. From the ceiling, the faces stared down at the milling spectators, imitation deathmasks of the great artists mingled with those of the stars at the time the old theater went up. Max could not tell Homer from Aristotle, but the laurel wreaths around their heads assured him they were both Greeks. Some of the others were easier to identify, though. Chaplin shouldered against Milton, D.W. Griffith (who was a hometown boy) up against Shakespeare (who was not), so that you thought they might descend from the ceiling for whatever purposes they were contriving. Their eyes followed you, of course, the hovering faces an audience to the audience, so that, when you looked up, you could not tell whether you were the observer or the thing observed.

Max remembered from college Art History that the Baroque is an art of illusion, built of false ceilings, *trompe l'oeil*, and mirrors trapped in mirrors—all things calling in question the borders where the day leaves off and fantasies begin. He also remembered from college Art History that Shangri-La's Baroque was pretty much considered bad art, but he liked it: there was something serendipitous and right about a place named for a Buddhist holy land, plopped down in middle America, gilded with excess, where the faces of great artists looked down on lines of hefty customers carrying outsized and overpriced cartons of popcorn away from the concession stands. It was an odd amalgam. It crossed boundaries. And that was only one of the reasons that it was an interesting place to work, and one of the reasons Max Winter knew that his time here would never last.

But at least he had dibs on one of the Dante masks. That is, when they held the estate sale.

The manager was George Castille, a well-dressed older dude pushing seventy? Seventy-five? He had been on stage in local and regional productions, had even played Hamlet down at the Park, though it made him mad if you brought up that performance, which apparently had involved experimental mirrors and horrendous reviews. George had the voice of a bad actor, reedy and over-precise in pronunciations, and Max had seen how his eyes followed the boys who worked for him. But it was cool, the old guy was a gentleman and a good, if talkative boss.

George supervised a handful of regular employees who maintained the theater and working the weekend matinees of vintage films. Sometimes a larger crew would come in on Saturday evenings, work for hire employed by the corporation that owned the Shangri-La. Those people would set up lights for the plays and sound for the concerts, but by day there were only five people on the premises: George and Max, the custodian Jerry Jeff, and the twins Todd and Eleanor Vitale.

Ellie's presence made Max want to stay. She was two years younger than he was (she had just turned twenty-one) and a part-time student at the university. Out of that olive-skinned, Northern Italian stock, blue eyes and blonde hair that caught a halo under the false torches when George put her on door, which he did often because she was so disruptively beautiful. Ellie had her moods and dramas, a slight incline toward reefer and melancholy, and Max had noted each mood over the last ten months, wondering all the time whether she had noticed him in return. He had orbited her at great distance, while, like a good film actress in front of the camera, she went on about her anguishes and duties as though no eye were watching.

Sometimes Max felt as though he had imagined her, pieced her together from other workplace romances that had scared him off before: the Asian girl at the front desk of the university library, the Irish theater student he'd plied with Southern charm until he asked her to go for coffee and she turned him down. Those two were sketchy memories now, a blurring of desire and embarrassment, and Ellie was the one he looked at, that mix of unhappiness and perfection that girls roughly his age occasionally drew forth to the heartbreak of all present and watching.

It did not help, though, that her twin brother Todd was a walking creep-show of need and secrecy. Ellie's exquisite coloring looked pale and grim on him, and of course it had to be Todd who approached Max, trying to manufacture friendship out of a shared job and the near-empty venues of the daytime theater.

Nevertheless, despite Max's yearning and the occasional drama from the twins, Shangri-la was his refuge, his time out of time. Work here was informal under Castille's quiet hand. On Friday afternoons, the four of them gathered sometime between two and three and went about the leisurely task of readying the theater for early arrivals, who generally started trailing in thirty minutes before the eight o'clock evening shows. Usually Jerry Jeff Pfeiffer—the janitor Max rather liked despite occasional and uncool thumps on the Bible—was finishing his morning's work; sometimes he would linger at the counter, or even stay for the Saturday matinee. Jerry Jeff was distant but civil, and there was a good in that, for Max had come to appreciate the arm's-length politeness of those around him, a casual respect that was better than the intrusions of friendship when you came down to it.

In fact, he preferred all of life at the arm's length. Liked friendly, unassuming banter and chat. Liked imagining the doings of his co-workers without having to bother with real details. It was pleasant and calm to watch the spectacle: it took little time from his walks and reveries, no time from his visits to Salvages and his main calling as a barrista down at the 3rd Street Starbucks, cobbled jobs that kept him in cigarettes and occasional weed while giving him a front row to Ellie Vitale and decent movies every weekend. Max had thought and hoped that the whole undemanding deal would stretch ahead of him for a couple of years. Give him time to get his sea legs and direction while he prepared to move into a career, to grow up and settle into responsibility and the money he was sure would come eventually. But now they were shutting down the Shangri-La. One last festival, a month or two of cleaning out the place, and then the doors closing at the turn of the year, the building converted into corporate offices, the outside deceptively quaint, masking shiny-new, efficient interiors.

Until the end of this year, though, Max liked his place. He liked Ellie especially, but also George and Jerry Jeff, and some of the time even Todd. He had liked the movies, enjoyed the tail end of the Spring Film Series: Paul Newman in *Judge Roy Bean, The Verdict,* and *The Color of Money*—a variety, but all sit-down fun and no uncomfortable edges—the perfect thing for weekends in the city, even if the audience was small.

But by the same token, he didn't trust the subject of the final season—German silent films, for cryin' out loud! All expressionism, dark makeup, black and white and modern anguish. When he first heard of the series, Max was afraid that a tendency toward artiness had finally caught up to old George. In April, though, George had confessed that the selection wasn't his, that ChemCon and the theater's governing board had chosen the subject, along with bringing in some kind of expert, old and German herself, to mastermind the dog and pony show. Max didn't think it would sell, didn't like George's obvious and rising discomfort, but maybe there was poetic justice in going out with an out-of-style series. And finally, what could you do? he figured. Could it really be that bad?

He was good at calming himself, good at placing things on the back burner. And in the mild summer of that year, the community lay docile and expectant around the Shangri-La Theater. If they knew where to look, they could have seen it coming: Dr. Leni Zauber arriving in a cab on the first Saturday of August, as the Shangri-La crew swept up after *Road to Perdition,* then later that day, Dominic Rackett dumped at the theater entrance like a foundling.

∞

Dr. Zauber arrived in a fashion they would recognize later, emerging from a cab and bursting through the front theater door like a season pass holder, heavy with luggage and the stale whiff of Gauloises. Her meticulously groomed helmet of hair was a red passing into burgundy, a look that George Castille would later call *purple Louise Brooks* when he started to dislike her and knew she wasn't listening. But for now, she gathered balance and vitality, even substance, as she was helped from the taxi, shrugged away Todd Vitale's bracing hand, and stalked across the lobby toward George's office door as if she already knew the lay of the place.

"The trunk, boys," she commanded of Max and Todd, as they all shrank like shadows in her elevated light.

For a while, that was all the Shangri-La's young people would see or hear from her. She vanished with George, and the others gossiped about possible scenarios until the two in charge emerged an hour later with a document. Zauber spread it on the concessions counter after brushing off the glass with a gloved hand.

George told them later that she was all German and all business in the office, marveling at the energy of a woman who "just had to be *my* age, children...I mean, those books of hers came out in the *sixties*". And yet she didn't look a day over fifty, though the light was deceptive around her, and Max caught a moment, as they all leaned across the manuscript, where Leni Zauber looked no older than Ellen Vitale.

A moment that vanished as the old girl produced a cigarette, the masquerade of neatness vanishing in a billow of blue smoke.

"*Caligari* first," she proclaimed, "because...*Caligari*. Then *Nosferatu*." And on through the brief list, stopping only to bicker with Todd Vitale about *Waxworks*. Todd fancied himself a cineaste, lording his knowledge over his sister and especially over Max Winter, but when he dropped the names of Conrad Veidt and Werner Krauss, Leni waved her gloved hand dismissively in his face.

"Florian Geist is the genius of that film," she insisted, vowels blurred by her marked Germanic accent. "The others are merely avatars, vehicles for light and movement, nothing more. Such an ordinary way it is to define the film by its actors. So *alltäglich*."

Max looked dolefully at the sulking Todd, trying to apologize for the insult in the old scholar's tone of voice, though he didn't know the German for *mundane*. There was a part of him that took responsibility for the misbehavior of others. It was in his gene pool.

Meanwhile, Milton and Homer regarded the transactions from the ceiling, their plaster faces impassive. Max was glad the old poets were blind, because the scene below them was irritating, uncomfortable. Todd drew back while the old scholar scanned her commandeered crew as though she needed or even cared about their approval. Her tone softened momentarily, as she made clear that there was a design in the films' choice, that the order would produce *the desired effect*.

Max would remember later how readily he bought into the rationale without its being explained. How he left that day with no real understanding of Leni Zauber's intentions.

He would also remember that this more agreeable moment was just a lull between minor storms.

Seduced by the smoke wafting around Leni Zauber, George withdrew from its pack one of the three Salems he allowed himself a day, tamping it on the counter when Zauber insisted that she be allowed sole access to the theater's projection room. George disagreed calmly, explaining the way things had always been done at the Shangri-La, until he realized that the woman was talking not only a change in duties but also a change in the whole chain of command.

It was the first and most bizarre of the demands she would make. George's voice trembled as he went through the obvious questions: whether the Board was comfortable with a change, whether Zauber's access "could be considered primary rather than sole," and finally, with a scarcely masked anger, what was so secret about the whole series that only one person could be in control of its showing.

It was because of the last film, she answered, her eyes darting over the assembly she had both charmed and intimidated. Because of *Walpurgisnacht*. In this great film, she told them—and they all were to trust her that it was great, perhaps the greatest of all German silent films, of all silent films, one of the greatest in history—the intent of the artist comes across at last in this exclusive printing. The film would strike the audience as altogether new, as fresh and flawless as it would have appeared to them on screen in 1930s Berlin. It would be, she said, as though the time between then and now had altogether vanished.

Zauber had been in Bologna for the process of digitizing the film, she said. This was three years ago, and at the time what she had of the movie was just enough to suggest at its brilliance—a beginning, it seemed, and traces of a fragmentary middle, but the last half of the film a series of fragments connected only by her best guesses, what she remembered from conversations with Geist and other, more speculative supposes. It had been like writing the film herself, like fumbling for keys in a darkened doorway, until a call from an associate in Prague had announced the incredible discovery of a near-faultless print, hidden from the Russian advances of 1945 and stored in a cellar, at low temperatures and in the original canister. Nobody could explain its pristine condition, but there it was, nitrate-based film containing almost an hour of unseen footage she had only imagined and anticipated. Leni Zauber was the only living soul, or so she claimed, to have seen this print when it was used to fill out the film in Bologna. The digitized version that emerged from the Italian laboratories was glorious, or so she claimed, her accented Germano-English rapturous as she described Geist's masterwork. The only thing better would have been the nitrate film, she maintained, and she had been halfway tempted to bring that along, to show *it* instead.

"Nitrate film!" George exclaimed. "My God, didn't you

see *Cinema Paradiso?* Where the film blows up and blinds poor rugged Philippe Noirel?"

He was always doing that, Max thought. Calling a character by the name of the actor who played him, as though Humphrey Bogart had left the girl at the Casablanca airport or that Paul Newman had eaten fifty boiled eggs on a prison dare. But Dr. Zauber was unmoved by the drama, having stored away, it seemed, enough of her own to face down a stagy theater manager. She argued it would have *recreated the original experience,* at which George coughed. Living under the threat of Spanish flu was part of *the original experience,* he said. As was economic chaos and the rise of the Nazis. There were some original experiences you didn't want to recreate, he insisted, but by this time Zauber smoothed the waters by conceding that the board, the Congressman's staff, and ChemCon Corporation had prohibited anything but the digital versions.

But they had also insisted that she alone would occupy the projection booth.

Everyone knew Dr. Zauber had raised the issue for some reason. Everyone knew she was hiding something. George went on about fire hazards, though they were no longer the question, while Max and the twins collaborated with silence out of laziness, uncertainty, fear to confront. At some level it must have been obvious where things were headed now: the plot points of the summer were falling into place, and Max and Todd and Ellie, and finally George, pushed back the inevitability, because it was second nature in a theater after all. Instead, they would ride illusion through August and September, and when all things had come to pass, some of them would leave the theater and blink at the light outside, as the last matinee left them staring into the slanted smolder of early evening, oblique in that hour before the streetlights went on.

But for now, George was skating over non-issues, claiming the Board must have its own reasons for limiting access to the projection booth, but it was by-god right on prohibiting the old nitrate film because could you imagine? and Dr. Zauber in agreement, with that perfunctory, European *of course* that always seems to American ears to be saying, *why bring it up? I've thought of that already.*

Then Todd Vitale said, "'Flammable.' Isn't the word 'flammable', Mr. Castille?"

George shrugged. "*Flammable inflammable.* Same thing, Todd. One of those curiosities of English. Do you have that in German, Dr. Zauber?"

"We have *heimlich unheimlich,* Mr. George," replied Leni Zauber, her eyes fixed idly on the door to the auditorium.

∞

Then she moved through the dark among the tiered seats. She sat in the front row, stretched out her legs like a gangly young man, and looked up at the ceiling where, in the old days, the designers had installed pinpoint lights so that the Shangri-La seemed to have stars overhead. Only now did Leni Zauber exhale, her eyes constellating the false sky's illuminations.

Heimlich and *unheimlich.* Freud had written about it somewhere. *Homelike* and *unhomelike,* but words that had both ended up meaning *uncanny* to the German ear. *Homelike* and *unhomelike* was how the theater had always felt to her. And this one was no different, its canopy of manufactured sky as close to the outdoors as she liked to get. Faint light in the vaulted darkness, and she remembered—or thought she remembered— the Catholic gloom of her Potsdam childhood, after the masquerade began.

A scene almost cinematic, a small girl stepping into alien shade with her father and brothers. Leni always thought of church in a theater, because she had suspected in her earliest days that God was light: the way the stained glass caught the sun was the way the old stories filled with His presence.

They had attended Mass surrounded by illumined conquests. Of Midian, of the Amalekites, of Jericho and Bashan, all in the cathedral windows. Mostly Joshua's great rousting battles, shedding their light on the bare floors, on the altar, on the kneeling girl who remembered the stories long after she had forgotten God. Leni wasn't even sure that the church was in Potsdam, now in the long recollection of years, but the sun glowing behind the glass, the projection of beams over the nave, crossing in front of them as they approached the transept— those were the kinds of things she remembered, or thought she remembered, or might have remembered from a film, having decided long ago that the birthplace of the memory probably didn't matter.

Because if anything was holy to her, it was this convergence of light and transparency and movement—remembered in black and white, oddly, but remembered vividly, like the films she had seen restored while she was in Bologna. The church was where sound dissolved, the Latin of the Mass receding into her young and unschooled awareness. Her father had forced her to attend, but these transactions with the images, with the Bible in a mosaic of glass—these became her own quiet spaces, the stories she chose above the incense and chant. She would kneel between Wolfgang and Helmut, and as they awaited the fracture of the bread, the Host dispensing, she would watch the windows, awaiting the crash of glass, the tumble of the walls of Jericho into fragmented light. Leni thought she remembered how, if you gazed long enough and thought hard enough, the light would gather on the other side of that window, gray and seething, waiting for something, and the stained-glass Jericho walls would shudder, as sentries, distant and minuscule, barely distinguishable from sun-dazzled dust motes, would appear on its battlements, like the saints on the clock in Prague, in the square where she and Florian had walked nights in an occupied city.

And like the saints, the angels would begin to move, life breathed into them from a distant origin. Leni wondered if her drowsing brothers had noticed, had seen the Amorites tumbling from the walls of glass, or the more famous Goliath felled by the sling of a beautiful David, luminously blonde. Defeated giants whose roots lifted from the ground as the walls collapsed around them, the window vanishing to reveal a cold and steady sun.

Leni knew there was something in this spectacle that changed things. That if her family had seen it, they would have emerged from the church transformed. But she walked back with them back into ordinary light, still the least favored of her siblings because she was still the girl and still the youngest. She walked back into a world in which she tended pampered brothers and obeyed an arbitrary and moody father.

None of whose faces she remembered. They were part of a cloudy, impermanent past.

But the world of glass and light was vivid, as were the figures who had moved, struggled, and died within the Gothic frames of the church windows. Leni no longer believed in the God of the Jews, but she believed in the illumination of fragmented glass, in the stories she had watched unfold while the long-forgotten Mass droned on.

It was no great step from the shadow plays of Amorite and Philistine to the first films she remembered. The golem films of Paul Wegener—Florian had called him "the Jew Wegener"—she had seen at the Thalia, in the years before the War. She had seen all three of them, she believed: the one the Shangri-La would show, where the creature saved the Prague ghetto, but also the earlier lost ones, where the antiques dealer resurrects the creature, only to have it pursue his sultry wife, and the funny one where Wegener plays himself disguised as a golem to frighten a dancing girl.

All of them took place in the world of cities: their tumultuous streets, the elegance of their iron suspension bridges, the gasometers hanging in mountains of whitish cloud, the roaring colors of buses and the railway trains, the surging telephone wires (did they not sing too?), the buffoonery of advertising columns, and the night ...the night of the metropolis ...

And soon the drama of a well-painted factory chimney moved her more deeply than any Gideon or Joshua, more than any number of Poussins or Raphaels.

Sometimes lost films would play out in her dreams, and she would glide toward wakefulness and the threshold of full remembrance. At the last moment, though, her reverie would take her to a rocky hillside, to Tibetan *rogyapas* bent above a corpse, to the birds descending, and everything vanishing into the blankness of wakefulness and light. In her rapt attentions, she would lose sight of Geist, certainly of the girl, and even this moment from her life she glimpsed as light and shadow, in grayscale, like she was watching it from the seats of a theater like this one, like the Shangri-La.

But from those early days at the Thalia to the latter days here, the movies had schooled her. Whether it was Emil Jannings crowing in humiliation at Dietrich's dinner table, Louise Brooks running through a nest of besotted men, Riefenstähl's brilliant processions, or Ernst Schäfer measuring with calipers the face of a smiling Tibetan woman, the actors rose into roles, becoming more than who they were by becoming what they were destined to be, and the process of this transformation always taught her things.

Now, in the old and young Shangri-La, where the stage lights played obliquely on her old and young face, Leni Zauber looked up at the artificial stars and focused on one, thinking of the young man sent her way.

Though manufactured, set in the ceiling by heedless hands, the star had become auspicious, guiding him toward her. Something was slowly shifting in him, she had been told, starlight replacing the shadow of his immaturities. She would meet him soon, she knew, having seen him, summoned him from a distance, having helped bring to the theater the one they would not expect, not at first.

Why this one, even she had no idea. But she knew the truth of it as she watched the one film, the secret and anointed film, and Florian Geist danced in the air along the Charles Bridge, staring straight into the camera, breaking the fourth wall, making things clear with his gaze, to which Leni Zauber submitted lovingly.

Florian had approved the boy. Leni had chosen him not just in the happy accident of knowing his grandmother, but for who he was, for qualities of his own: the charm, the intelligence, the slow drift of his late youth, and his continual search for a place, a connection, a calling. And he was already here, this most unusual of suspects.

So she thought as Dominic Rackett set his bags in the lobby to the puzzled looks of Todd and Ellie Vitale. Jerry Jeff Pfeiffer, ascending the stairs from the basement bathrooms, mop over his shoulder like a marching trooper, was staring, too.

Leni closed her eyes, reclined, and watched from rooms away as George Castille brushed the front of his shirt, fingered his gray hair back over his ear, and introduced Dominic to his new co-workers and prospective friends.

Leni breathed in the image of the dark caller, his singed jacket and his old lady's borrowed carpetbag projected on the inside of her eyes like the after-image of light when you come in from the snow.

Like Joshua from long ago. Like a golden man on a steep, recollected mountainside.

She would go into the lobby soon. Would see him in the flesh. But as for now she would receive that likeness in her imagining, shaping it into form until it would match the boy she would meet in the Peaceable Kingdom.

He was shorter than she had figured, darker and older— about Florian's age when she had first met *him,* in the flower of young manhood. Mary had mentioned with a whisper that this one's other grandmother had been Chinese, but such things were reconcilable, even appropriate, and Eurasian men could be quite attractive. That, too, would be helpful, she thought. All in all, she approved. She was glad he had passed through the fire hale and uninjured, was glad she was about to get a look at him.

3.

r. Castille told him that Dr. Zauber was already on the premises, and Dominic, with the sure sense of a freeloader, prepared himself to impress the old girl. Before Leni's entrance, he sized up the others, calculating the best ways to keep the fragile peace that he figured his arrival might threaten.

Dominic had already met Castille at one of Grandma Mary's soirees. He had been looking to move out by then, and a shabby but inexpensive apartment over on 9th Street seemed like the best of prospects, but he knew that the combined income from Salvages and what he had saved from working at the video store up in Vermont would be only enough to float him for a couple of months. Unaccustomed to steady work as he might be, he was also accustomed to some degree of financial comfort, of relying on others to keep him solvent. So when George Castille placed a rough hand on his knee after a couple of martinis, letting the hand linger a bit too long as he inquired whether Dominic would like to work at the Shangri-La Theater in town, a complex series of possibilities came into play.

No, Dominic wasn't too concerned with where the hand

was. He'd had a lifetime of reasonably good looks, attractive to all kinds of people, and he'd come to discover that it seldom played out, that if you smiled and nodded and responded no more than that, flirtation had a kind of arc that settled back into pleasantry. If you "failed to notice", the flirting party assumed you were dense: nobody was rejected, no harm and no foul.

George said that Mary had suggested her grandson might be looking for more work. And if it wasn't just the gin talking—hers or his, how could you tell?—he might have work for that grandson. The upcoming season at Shangri-La—the final one, regrettably—would feature old German silent films, and Mary had mentioned Dominic's attraction to things old and silent.

"That's baffling," Dominic had said, genuinely puzzled. "Do you think she meant herself?"

And George had covered his mouth, stifling a small shriek of laughter. "Good Lord, dear! She'd never think of herself as *old!*"

It was then Dominic decided he could work at Shangri-La. Even after the mysterious prelude George provided over a third martini. This was not only a silent film series, but what was more, an old friend of Mary's, a film scholar of some renown, was scheduled to arrive in town next month, and for some reason Mary wanted Dominic and her to meet.

Dominic figured that it was simply another of his grandmother's attempts to order his life from the outside. It was not unfamiliar territory, after all. He told George he would think about it, and as he tended to do with anything remotely connected to business, he let matters slide until mid-May, when in a surprise to all involved, a letter had arrived, a substantial sum in Euros that impressed Dominic even more when he did the exchange at the airport. Apparently, this friend of Grandma Mary's had work for him, though why he was chosen—why Leni Zauber had come to this city, even—remained a mystery to him as he rented a furnished room near the intersection of Kentucky and Ninth, putting together his belongings, and waited, like the angels and the derelicts, for Dr. Zauber's arrival. Shangri-

La might be good, if temporary, work, and the place on 9th Street beckoned, a way out of his grandmother's apartment and clutches. Furthermore, when it came to clutches, George's had been removed, and the older man had proven to be a decent and professional sort after all.

A new job offered possibilities. And what had become possible—what was indeed quite likely after the Euros came in—was that the mishaps of the last month or so might slowly be set to right.

But in order for things to work, he had to reconnoiter. Win friends and influence people. Then came survival and floating. Good looks, a quick wit, and his father's charm. Ben had called it *his best Ted Bundy*, but even Dominic's mother had found that a little harsh: it was more the scouting of terrain, a casing of the cultural joint. And it was odd that so much energy would arise from his chronic laziness.

But it did, and almost immediately he began the process.

Max would be the hardest sell. For some reason, the boy regarded him warily, the simple *'sup?* and the hipster's upward nod. It was the same look those graduate students had given him—the look that said you may be our genus, but you're not our species. Maybe Max thought his job was threatened, that Dom had been brought in to replace him. Maybe he just didn't like the shift in power at Salvages. Whatever the case, Max was at arm's length, and Dominic would have to curry favor with him.

The janitor, on the other hand—*Billy Bob? Jimmy Jack?*— was friendly and open and a little too earnest: Dom guessed religion, and congratulated himself when *Jerry Jeff* returned to work, wishing everyone present *a blessed day*.

At last he took in the twins with one quick glance. The boy was eager to please and a bit creepy, beginning some string of handshakes, then breaking off when it was apparent that Dominic didn't know the routine. The girl, on the other hand, was lovely, one of those people who absorbs attention in a strange photosynthesis of beauty.

"You two are...uhm...twins?" Dominic began, stating the obvious because it was safe.

Ellie nodded. "Fraternal twins." To which her brother chimed in, "obviously!" She continued, revealing that she was the older by five minutes, that it meant Todd had to respect his elders. The twins fell into an awkward back-and-forth banter, practiced if not rehearsed over a lifetime. Dominic's eyes never left Ellen Vitale during the routine, and he watched as she blossomed under his gaze.

Too young for him, he told himself. What was she? Nineteen? Twenty? Nevertheless, it wasn't like she was sixteen or something. College-aged kids can be surprisingly mature, especially the girls, and so he found himself in reverie, where she leaned across the counter, fixing him with those blue eyes, Magnetic Zeroes t-shirt stretched over her small breasts...

"So, what will you do here?" Max interrupted, more mild interrogation than question.

"Here? Oh, at the theater? Apparently I'm writing the flyers for the film series. Dr. Zauber knows my grandmother, and this and that..."

"Ah, a film buff," Todd observed, attempting irony but settling for sarcasm. "So you're an expert in silent film?"

Dominick laughed softly. "Well, hardly. I barely know why I was chosen, but I did a little writing in college and grad school, and I'll do my best for Dr. Zauber and the theater."

It drew silence from the others. Dom couldn't tell whether it was his mention of grad school or his optimism that was giving him such a bad start.

"Well," Todd drawled at last, "if your best ever needs some input, I'm kind of the film expert around here. No offense, Mr. Castille, but you're mainly a stage kind of guy, we all know. Meanwhile, I hope Rackett's best includes a trust fund kind of supplement, because I can't imagine the theater paying a living wage for flyers. Again, no offense, Mr. Castille."

"None taken, Todd, dear," Castille sighed, in his best long-suffering-mother voice, as he slipped out the back door of the theater, headed for a furtive smoke, but not before announcing that someone should tell Dr. Zauber that Mr. Rackett was here.

∞

Dominic had moved back in with Grandma Mary after walking home from Salvages to find his apartment gutted by fire.

He had heard the sirens from the store. Thought little of it until returning to find Kentucky Street and St. Catherine still blocked by cleanup crews. Even then a trip on foot could get him through the cordons of tape and sawhorses, and it was only when he reached his street corner that the event sunk in, that he saw smoke-damaged furniture being hauled out of the place, that a fireman stopped him and suggested, politely but firmly, that he go somewhere else until things had cleared.

Wiring, they claimed at first. Plague and hazard of older, ill-kept buildings. It was lucky that the fire had started in the middle of the day, when most of the tenants were at work, off the premises, or at least awake enough to leave the building.

It turned out, of course, that some dumbass yap was cooking meth two apartments over, the flame spreading until half the block was engulfed. Dominic had been helping Bulwer with the inventory when it all went down, and at least that part was good, because slowly the news emerged that, like almost any meth fire, this one had come with explosions, and two people were dead, one in the apartment building next to his own. As it was, though, the material damage was complete. All he had to his name was the trunk he had left at Grandma Mary's—roughly a suitcase of winter clothes, a half-dozen books and as many CDs, his brass Buddha and his haiku notebook.

At least those things were salvaged. But he felt as if he was reeling from one mishap to another, and despite his better and more adult suspicions, he somehow blamed his father for where he had ended up.

It turned out, however, that where he was ending up wasn't

so bad this time. Dr. Zauber gave him a long look, sizing him up like she was buying a car. He stifled a giggle, imagining her kicking his tires and checking under his hood. And then she was spelling out his duties, loudly and in front of them all and with more than a hint of condescension. He found himself blushing, though he was really uncertain why, as she explained how he would preview the film, then write an introduction *for the general public*. This would involve seeing the film here, at the Shangri-La, taking into account the wide screen and presence of the theater.

It was all European and artsy, born less of scholarship than of a delight to tell Dominic what to do. He began to have misgivings as Zauber lectured on, but when she told George to *show Mr. Rackett his rooms* the task was suddenly lighter, more interesting. Apparently there was an apartment above the lobby—no more than a couple of rooms and a narrow window to the back overlooking 3rd Street—but it was to be his, rent-free, for the duration of the film series and up to the time renovation of the theater began, if he chose to stay there.

Feeling as though he had been drawn from dangerous waters, now with a place to stay, Dominic understood why Grandma Mary had told him to bring along his belongings. He knew they were staring at him—George and Todd and especially Max—and that the rooms would come at the cost of good graces. But the days ahead would be filled with cutting new deals, he figured: with putting out fires among his co-workers and with getting to know this Dr. Zauber, learning what was expected of him and (because it was not obvious, not at all) why she had chosen him to begin with.

∞

The room was small but not unfriendly. A dormer ceiling tapered to a window overlooking 3rd Street, giving the place a garret look that Dominic had always imagined he'd like, although now, standing at the threshold, seemed a bit more confining and spare than he'd bargained for. The small bath played against his custom of long hot showers, and after the episode in the 9ᵗʰ Street apartment, there was something intimidating and makeshift about the efficiency kitchen.

When he told John Bulwer later that the whole change of circumstance (with its rescue of the burned-out vagrant) felt like something out of Dickens, he could understand when the old man smiled cryptically and added, "or out of Kafka." Not one to question a windfall, Dominic was questioning this one for some reason or the other. Dr. Zauber didn't seem the kind to offer gifts without catches, and she was offering him a deal for which he felt deeply, almost embarrassingly unqualified. He unpacked his belongings and spaced them throughout the room, trying to give the place more of a lived-in feel, but it was still provisional, like one of those motel rooms with huge closets and unnecessary drawers in the dresser. Nobody would ever live here long enough to occupy the flat, so Dominic imagined it as a way station for his belongings more than a home.

Earlier that afternoon he had complained to Bulwer over the gathering downside at the Shangri-La: the Vitale twins were pretty unsettling, he claimed, especially the boy, who seemed unnerved and resentful over taking a back seat to a film writer who knew so little about the history of the art. And if Todd Vitale was unfriendly, then Max Winter (who should have and could have been a friend and ally) was pissed off because he had a crush on Ellie Vitale and so saw Dominic as some kind of rival.

Not that he was interested, mind you. The girl was too young for him.

But what was even creepier about that whole dynamic was that Todd seemed to be party to the same jealousy, the same fierce obstruction of anything Dominic had to say to his sister. Perhaps it was a brother thing—especially since they were twins. It was one of those times when being an only child was a great disadvantage, Dominic allowed, because you couldn't understand the layers of sibling bonds.

John Bulwer, who had two sisters, assured him that those

kinds of things worked themselves out over time. That those hostilities would soften the longer Dominic worked at Shangri-La. The real question lay in how the work was. What was Leni Zauber like, anyway? A couple of her books passed through the store a few years back, and they were so dense and German that Bulwer hadn't bothered much with them.

She's German, all right, Dominic said. But hardly dense. The word he would use was "calculating": Zauber was up all night, doing whatever she did in the theater and the projection room. He could hear it through the floor, a dark tremor just below his awareness, the faint recollection of an unsettling dream. It was like a bad gothic movie, the grumbling in German and the intermittent fluttering of the film through the old-style projector. In fact, George Castille, who had made Dominic uneasy at first, seemed now the most stable one of the bunch.

It was a strange little hive of drama, and Dominic was more than half inclined to leave it.

Bulwer suggested he let it slide. That the creepy would pass, because creepy tends to settle once it is part of custom. He re-emphasized the small luxuries of Dominic's situation, not the least of which was a place of his own, away from grandmothers, long commutes, and meth labs. It was Dominic's choice, of course, but in his shoes, Bulwer would make the best of it.

Dominic quickly decided to stay. Bulwer had given words to the choice he had wanted to make all along. And after all, odd circumstances—misinformation mixed with that *indiscernible karmic shift* that Bulwer was always talking about—had brought him to town in the youth of the year. Maybe it was something more, who knew? A design and pattern he could get his thoughts around.

∞

You must become Caligari, Leni Zauber told him.

That was the slogan when the film was released. *Du musst*

Caligari werden.

Dominic figured he would have to do it quickly and soon. The film's first showing—a "sneak preview" for a number of the jewelry-patrons of the arts—was only a week away, and he had not even begun to think about the article he was assigned to write. Once again he questioned the wisdom of Zauber's choice. Figured Grandma Mary was calling in some kind of favor from the 1940s, when the two had supposedly met (though under what circumstances was no more clear than anything about the old German film scholar).

Nor did the questioning stop when Dr. Zauber called him into the theater to see the film. Dominic found her midway back, seated midpoint in a middle row, almost at the mathematical center of the house. She was holding a DVD remote, incongruous with her vintage pant suit, he thought, like Marlene Dietrich holding a *Star Wars* light saber. Zauber motioned him to sit beside her, as though there was a button on the remote that guided his movement and behavior. He joined her, and with a melodramatic gesture, she started the film.

No prelude, no foretaste. He slid directly into the world of Caligari.

Two figures on a bench, framed by the circular iris of the camera. Their faces were blurred, riddled with light. Dominic recalled that the film was a century old, that at least one of the men on camera was alive in the time of Lincoln, then silently scolded himself for the superficial thought. He wanted his first reactions to be more insightful, more profound, like those of Todd Vitale's cineaste rather than those of a novice. For Dominic, a film was a tangible world, the actors were the people they played, the story a history of substance and genuine event: his professors had left him sophisticated enough to know the people in books were assemblies of words, but those on the screen as gatherings of shadow and light—that was a harder leap without the training. His own innocence unsettled him, renewed his doubts that Zauber had chosen wisely.

"Now watch," Zauber whispered. "Within seconds, you

see *Caligari's* first crucial moment, when Franzis and the old man exchange the first words of the film."

The screen filled with the initial intertitle, as the old man told Franzis, *'Everywhere there are spirits … They are all around us … They have driven me from hearth and home, from my wife and children.'*

And of course Franzis would answer, would tell the tale that trumped the old man's haunting with a whole batch of crazy. Dominic watched as the story unfolded on the screen: the small town of Holstenwall, a distorted cityscape glimpsed through a kind of black-and-white kaleidoscope of triangles and rhomboids, peaked roofs wavering like frozen blades of gray flame against a painted sky, In Holstenwall, a fair visited by the mysterious Dr. Caligari, who carries with him the sleepwalker Cesare— *"Cesare, the miraculous, twenty-three years of age, who has for these three-and-twenty years been sleeping -- night and day -- without a break."* Together, the two perform a kind of mentalist side-show act, in which Caligari wakens Cesare, and the sleepwalker predicts the future, foretelling the death of Franzis' friend Alan.

Now Franzis and Alan are rivals for the affection of Jane— played, Leni whispered, by *the Weimar siren, Lil Dagover*—a young woman whose sunken eyes and butterfly-bow of a mouth conjured images of his Grandma Mary's porcelain dolls, abstract and a little unsettling. They make a completely implausible vow, a kind of 1919 "bros before hos" arrangement that insists they will remain friends no matter which of them Jane chooses. The vow becomes academic almost at once, when someone breaks into Alan's room and stabs him to death, a murder of shadows in which a figure stands above Alan's bed, wielding a large, triangular shard like a fragment of glass from the town's distorted windows.

The film promises a kind of procedural mystery, as Franzis turns from the incompetent police to solitary detection, following clues and intuitions back to the carnival, where a suspicious Caligari is hiding something, something to do with the sleepwalker. Of course, the film left no doubt that Cesare did the stabbing, as the shadow cast on Alan's wall is clearly the tall, gaunt figure of the actor Conrad Veidt.

Dominic leaned back in his seat, drawn into the film's dynamic. If this were just a whodunit, it would be over already, but the film was not about the killing as much as the strange dance of control between Caligari and the somnambulist. Werner Krauss, the old Nazi actor, waddled toward the camera as the mysterious doctor, staring into the camera lens as the iris closed around him, his eyes widened, comical, but hypnotic: Dominic could see why the first audience, still shell-shocked from the Great War, would have been taken in by the madman.

Entranced by Caligari's more powerful will, Cesare abducts poor Jane, and the film moves to a chase over rooftops, Veidt holding a self-evident mannequin instead of the rather substantial Lil Dagover. But realism was not the standard here: the story progressed in a series of lurching, dream-like episodes, with Franzis closing in gradually on Caligari as the spider at the center of the web—in the insane asylum, where the "mad doctor" is no inmate, but in fact, the director. Franzis discovers that the director, influenced by an occult medieval manuscript, had long yearned to find a somnambulist and place him under a hypnotic spell. The book that inspired him was a history of an earlier Caligari and Cesare who, two centuries ago, had cut a swath of serial killings through communities in Italy. Franzis links the Caligari of old with the Caligari at the Holstenwall Fair, and sees to it that the sinister doctor is confined to the very asylum that he ran beforehand.

And it would have been one thing had the film ended here. The triumph of sanity over madness, the young romantic over the cynical old doctor, the basic good over a subtle and manipulative evil. But the film returns to the bench, to Franzis' wandering through the asylum courtyard, where he sees Jane and Cesare as inmates. And then, in a moment you could predict but that was still shocking because it violates almost everything you assumed or wanted to assume about the story, the doors to the asylum open, and the Director walks out into the courtyard, surrounded by respectful staff. Franzis cries out, *You all believe I am mad.*

That is not true. It is the Director who is mad. He is Caligari, Caligari, Caligari.

The lights rose. Dominic blinked, shielding his eyes from the sudden change. "Once again," Zauber announced, and the theater plunged back into darkness, the film restarted.

It was disorienting, like being caught in a searchlight. Again Franzis and the older man sat on the bench, and this time Dominic's attention was drawn far more to Lil Dagover, Jane, afloat wraith-like through a ruined garden, damaged by light exposure and the edge of the camera's resolution.

"Notice that he calls her his fiancée," Zauber commented over the eerie jazz-like stretch and tumble of the music. "And where did she accept a proposal?"

"It's implicit," Dominic began. And then, "Well, no it isn't....I see..."

"Mad from the start," Zauber announced. "The signs are there."

She paused the film in the first scenes of Holstenwall. She asked Dominic to take in the sets, the buildings that were little more than pen-and-ink sketches, backdrops that surrendered their realism to a general feeling, as though they hovered over the actors, pressed in on them. And the composite sets, the town squares fashioned of model and painting, intruded on the streets, squat, geometrical tendrils invading the walkways like aggressive plant life.

"Now this," Zauber told him, and paused the film on an iris shot of Caligari staring into the camera, the scene encircling and closing on his face. The cartoonish face of Werner Krausse, top-hatted, owlish glasses perched on his forehead and not the bridge of his nose, peered through the aperture as though he were standing tiptoe to watch those who watched him.

"What do you think?" Zauber asked, in a tone that anticipated one answer only.

"Standard frame-breaking," Dominic replied, at once ashamed of a reply that smacked of graduate school. "I mean, here we are, ready to be comfortable in the audience, and the film tells us that the drama extends beyond the screen. That there is no safety. But it's commonplace, Dr. Zauber. Perhaps it was new in its time, but now…."

"It's more than what you think, *liebchen,*" Zauber said, the German endearment uncomfortable, more condescension than fondness. "Watch it again, as the actor approaches and the lens contracts on the eye." She touched the remote, and the lens began to close over the round face of Werner Krausse, until only the eyes remained on screen.

And when Zauber paused the film, there they were, looking back at the audience, piercing into Dominic Rackett, finding him out. Dominic tried to turn away and failed, tried to close his eyes but found himself riveted to the screen. He wanted the eyes to vanish, to go away, to stop this horrible unmasking. He remembered the terrible, guilt-riddled time of watching Peri undress through her apartment window, the shock of seeing the walls and the little alcove in front of her bedroom as they showed through the near transparency of her body, the image of someone behind her, ill-formed of light and shadow like a tendril of gray flame, and how he knew he had seen what he'd come to see, a phantom lover disrobing to bed her and enter her…

Leni was saying something. Something about the architecture, the design of Hermann Warm and the painted sets of Reimann and Röhrig—names Dominic would have to Google later, much to his chagrin. For now, he sat in the middle row of the Shangri-la house, clammy with sweat, having fought off something, dropping his pen and feeling for it with his foot, desperately trying to track the old scholar's commentary about set design as character, how the landscape breathed and schemed as much as the sleepwalker, as the good doctor himself.

∞

And on the screen Dominic kept seeing an afterimage, as Zauber lectured him about cityscape and sleepwalking, as she guided the film over the scenes that followed, pausing it at Alan's murder, the abduction of Jane, the moment of apparent victory in which Franzis exposes the director as Caligari, and then the last framing scenes, amber-tinted and desolate, when it is revealed Franzis is or is not insane. There was a circle about the face of the leering Caligari—bristling with borrowed light. It shouldn't happen, he told himself, still trying to attend to what Zauber was saying about the film's crazy ending, how the director had inserted Franzis' madness over the objection of the screenwriters, how it might have something to say about a time in Germany when the world was beginning to turn toward madness. The face of Caligari could well be imprinted on the back of his eyelids, he told himself, like the reversal of color and light he remembered from snowy childhood days, when he would seek shelter from drifts and makeshift igloos and brilliant, icy sunlight, the spectral swimming glow before his eyes like motes of stained glass. And his mother, scolding him for the in-and-out, complaining of the tracks he left for the housekeeper, the doors ajar that ballooned the heating bill. And his mother glared at him again, her disapproval as brilliant as winter sun.

And then Zauber prodding him, insisting that he listen and take notes. A sudden lurch back to attentiveness, to the musty house of Shangri-La, to the task of writing about this complicated, alien film. It felt like college, when assignments were due. He wondered what he'd signed on for.

∞

His first memory of life in Boston was his stepfather's office.

Ben Mountolive was at the height of his career when Dominic came to live with him. He had moved east, back to the city that had produced him, and had set up a profitable psychiatric practice. Connected with two of Boston's more eminent hospitals, Mountolive also taught the occasional classes at medical schools. His research stood at the respectable borders of the eccentric, in the uneasy truce that Jungians often strike with the academy. Nobody liked that Mountolive was widely published, nobody liked his appearances on talk shows, but his name drew attention, and as money for higher education contracted in the Reagan years, Mountolive's mild celebrity was a commodity. After all, if Phil Donahue or Oprah Winfrey gave stamp of approval to a psychiatrist, who were college administrators to argue?

By the time Dominic arrived in the city, Ben Mountolive was living his wealth in a spacious, high-ceilinged townhouse. The office was so neat that a four-year-old was wary to enter, its walls arrayed with Leonard Baskin prints and poems of Ted Hughes and W.S. Merwin in tight calligraphy, each piece signed by the artist or author. Dominic had thought at first it was an art museum and looked for the children's wing where he could fingerpaint, but soon he was corrected. It became apparent early on that the house was not for children: his own room was furnished with a geometrical, modernist bed and desk, and no amount of mock enthusiasm from his mother (*look! a big boy room for a big boy!*) could soften his discomfort.

Dominic would awaken at night from disturbing dreams. He would want to run downstairs and crawl in bed with his mother, but the man was there, and she wasn't too welcoming even when the man was out of town, so he learned to watch the light shift across the white walls of his room, to imagine crows, feral dogs, cave paintings from the shadows. He was sure these creatures had crawled in through the windows to inhabit the dark spaces of his alien bedroom, and his mother frowned when he told her the news, said that he was too big for such foolishness.

Then came one of the nights that Mountolive was out of town. Dominic was alone with his mother and the housekeeper, both of whom stayed in the downstairs bedrooms, and that night a thunderstorm swept in off the Atlantic, and lightning crackled out on the bay. It was like the darkness fluttered, and a huge roar of thunder awakened him not long after he had fallen asleep. He called out for his daddy, then remembered they had moved, they were in Boston now, and Ben was his daddy who was out of town. Nor did his mother hear him when he cried out a second time, so Dominic climbed out of bed and padded across the smooth, hard floor, down the steps toward the bedrooms on the ground floor.

He turned the wrong way at the steps, baffled by the dark and his fear and surroundings that were still new to him. The door was ajar, and Dominic walked into Mountolive's office before he found his bearings. There, alive in a flash of lightning, a Baskin crow hulked over his stepfather's desk, and it moved in the stirring light, and Dominic screamed as it pushed its way out of the frame, pressing against the glass and the black wood, its maw open, screaming a soundless cry.

His mother had scolded the housekeeper for reaching him first. The woman, unsteady in English, undocumented, and nervous in cold climate, said nothing, but held the boy tighter for a moment, despite his mother's disapproval, as the light in the room settled and the storm grew suddenly faint, sweeping north up the coast toward Maine.

Solo un cuervo pintado, she had whispered, and he calmed against her warmth, almost understanding what she said.

∞

They all settled behind Caligari, the flames that spoke and the ones still silent. Around them the light collapsed into the heart of the slow, smokeless burning, and a dark corona cupped each flickering blade. They were whispering to each other now, the flames, and if they could see (for the jury is out on whether such creatures are eyeless like Norns or Fates, or whether they bear some rudimentary sight that translates past the screen into the world of flesh and desire) they would see the tiered seats of the theater, two figures seated at the center of a web of shadow and light. And perhaps, if the lens permitted, into the lobby, past the Peaceable Kingdom painted in tired stasis, into the sun or lamp of the city streets. Here was the country that called them, not made up of tonal values, but something which bombarded the eye with sizzling rows of windows and humming beams of light dancing amidst vehicles of all kinds, a thousand undulating globes, the shreds and fragments of individuals, the signboards, the roaring tumult of amorphous masses of color.

It was country on the move, the canvas of film rather than painting or even photography, roiling with spark and violence. And yet, despite its power, in the mild summer of that year, the community lay docile and expectant around the Shangri-La Theater. A brokered peace spread south to Broadway, once a main city thoroughfare but now, except for a few blocks in the center of town around the theater, a bleak passage of warehouses, hospitals, and fast food drive-throughs from its western end at the river to its eastern end at the Cave Hill Cemetery, where, on evenings in late July, expectancy spread like a soft summer rain, and the tombstone angels turned in the last light, their blank eyes belying their sweet and mournful smiles, a summer wind whistling through them until the winding drives of the cemetery trembled in a ruined chorus, waking a tattered old man asleep behind a mausoleum, who smiled benignly and still a little drunk as his day of vagrancy began.

I supposed they would come, he thought, finger-combing his hair into a makeshift pompadour. *I supposed so, but you never know until the lights dim and the curtain parts.*

New at the Shangri-La: A Festival of Silent Film

For almost two decades, the Shangri-La Theater has been the city's showplace for vintage movies. Situated in what was once our premier shopping district, now a mecca for nightlife and entertainment, this beautiful old theater has almost always been an island of elegance, a place for escape and remembrance, and a home for fine films.

From its opening in 1917 to the late 1970s, the theater was known as the Horizon. *Gone with the Wind* made its regional debut here, as did *Lawrence of Arabia* and *The Godfather*. Many children of the '40s, '50s, and '60s remember the Horizon as their first movie experience, or as part of their first trip to the city—an adventure that might have included shopping at Grant's or Stewart's, a meal at Huntington's or the Blue Boar, but always a walk down Louisville's Fourth Street, a walk that would usually end at this theater, watching a film that would crown their day in town.

Restored in the 1980s, when it was renamed the Shangri-La in honor of the celebrated Chicago film venue destroyed in a 1940 fire, our theater is a treasury of memory and nostalgia. That is why, aided by the generous contributions of local benefactors, we began to stage performances of time-honored drama, music and film. ChemCon, the local corporation whose innovation and dynamic look to the future makes the familiar fantastic, has sponsored a variety of entertainments—from Scoot Tamblyn's Big Band Sounds to the Eagles Reunion Tour, from LaShanté Terry's dynamic play, *Ain't Gonna Suffer No Triflin' Man* to the beloved actor Wade Abner's final one-man show, *An Evening with the Gipper*. In recent years, the theater has offered afternoons of film, not unlike those "long-ago but not forgotten" times of Fourth Street's heyday. Each summer weekend from 2001 has featured classics like the patriotic John Wayne Series of 2002, 2007's *Singin' in*

Michael Williams

the Rain Musical Series, or 2014's "I'm Also Just A Girl": A Julia Roberts Retrospective.

But this year, sadly, marks the curtain call for this beloved institution. In January, renovation will begin on our elegant old building. The traditional exterior will be preserved as much as possible, while the interiors will be converted to friendly and comfortable office space for the ChemCon executive board—those same people who have brought you quality entertainment for so many years, and who will continue to direct their charitable and creative vision toward the city's thriving suburbs, as we try to bring arts and entertainment to venues throughout the metropolitan Area.

So, as a grand finale and a new beginning, the Shangri-La will reach way back to the infancy of film. Thanks to the generosity of former Congressman Roy Rausch and our generous ChemCon stockholders, we present "The Haunted Castle: German Film before 1939". The series will be a wonderful selection of early celluloid, chosen and arranged by Doctor Leni Zauber, internationally renowned as an expert on the subject.

"What a way to go out!" exclaims George Castille, the manager of the Shangri-La. "If you know only one German silent film, it is probably Fritz Lang's epic *Metropolis*—a film that ends with all kinds of high drama. A flooded undercity. A workers' revolt. Mad scientists scuffling with heroes on the rooftops. Boy gets good girl while the bad girl gets what's coming to her, if you like that kind of thing. Of course we're showing *Metropolis*! Who'd miss the chance? But I'd like to think it represents the whole series in a nutshell: a fabulous weaving of time-honored stories and themes, ending with a magnificent bang!"

Now before you object to brushing the dust off of ancient silent movies, consider this: these films are the forerunners of our great cinematic traditions, grandparents of the horror and science fiction films, the very films that the Duke and Bogie grew up on, and in which great stars as different as Greta Garbo and Bela Lugosi began their careers. All the drama of the last century begins here, and there is a poetry in the silence of these stories, as your humble correspondent will attempt to explain in the Movie Guides available for free in the Shangri-La lobby before and after each screening.

Late this summer, time will stand still in our city and our theater. Stars will rise in the Shangri-La of your recollection, as faces forgotten or barely remembered will emerge from the silent past and once again flicker across a screen where they once performed, glowed, and delighted thousands of viewers. As the past recedes into shadow and the future approaches in all its promise but all its uncertainty, we can share this short month of films and memories.

One of the great early films, 1919's *Cabinet of Dr. Caligari,* will begin the festival, and the schedule will proceed as follows:

Friday, August 17, 8 pm; Saturday, August 18, 2 and 8 pm; Sunday, August 19, 2 pm: *Cabinet of Dr. Caligari* (1919). Dir. Robert Wiene. Starring Werner Krauss, Conrad Veidt. A mysterious Doctor, his somnambulist (sleepwalker), and a series of unexplained murders during a surreal carnival. **Special preview showing for Theater Partners, Thursday, August 16, 8 pm.**

Friday, August 24, 8 pm; Saturday, August 25, 2 and 8 pm; Sunday, August 26, 2 pm: *The Golem* (1920). Dir. Paul Wegener. Starring Paul Wegener, Albert Steinruck. In 16th-century Prague, a Jewish rabbi creates a creature from clay to protect his people from persecution.

Friday, August 31, 8 pm; Saturday, September 1, 2 and 8 pm; Sunday, September 2, 2 pm: *Nosferatu* (1922). Dir. F.W. Murnau. Starring Max Schreck, Greta Schröder, Gustav von Wangenheim.

The grandfather of all vampire films, to this day living up to its subtitle, "A Symphony of Horror".

Friday, September 7, 8 pm; Saturday, September 8, 2 and 8 pm; Sunday, September 9, 2 pm: *Waxworks* (1924), Dir. Paul Leni. Starring Emil Jannings, Conrad Veidt, Werner Krauss. A young poet receives the assignment of writing stories to accompany the figures of Haroun al-Raschid, Ivan the Terrible, and Jack the Ripper in a traveling wax museum. The result is a series of framed stories ranging from the comic to the horrifying.

Friday, September 14, 8 pm, Saturday, September 15, 2 and 8pm, and Sunday, September 16, 2 pm:

Metropolis (1927), Dir. Fritz Lang. Starring Alfred Abel, Brigitte Helm. The most famous film in the series. Fritz

Lang's dystopian tale of a city oppressed by its own diabolical machinery. A lavish, spectacular epic, to some the ultimate film of the silent era.

Friday, September 21, 8 pm, Saturday, September 22, 2 and 8 pm, and Sunday, September 23, 2 pm: *Walpurgisnacht* (1936), Dir. Florian Geist. Starring Emil Jannings, Hermann Braun, Hannes Stelzer, Lil Dagover, Tsering Pema. Based on a World War I German/Czech novel, Walpurgisnacht is set in the castle district of Prague during that disastrous conflict. The aristocratic inhabitants of the district are oblivious to the brewing civil unrest and the collapse of the political order around them. To this setting, the director adds an apocalyptic horror/ fantasy sensibility: an ancestor possesses her descendent through a painted portrait, a one-eyed general returns from the grave, and the devil visits the dreams of a retired court physician.

Unscreened as of this printing, it is described by its restorer, Ms. Leni Zauber, as "grand and magnificent chaos. The technique of *aweysha*, or magical domination of the personality, is important to the plot of the film, but *aweysha* is a strange and deceptive force. Are those manipulating others themselves psychic puppets? The film raises the question, and gives a number of answers. "

Dr. Zauber says that *Walpurgisnacht* is the ideal film of the period, embodying all its obsessions and concerns. Magic and mayhem mesh perfectly with Geist's images of stagnant social custom and the violent revolution that will shake a culture to its foundations.

We are honored to host this film's long-postponed premiere, and Dr. Zauber is more than eager for this story to be shown. "Monsters, ghosts, demons, mesmerism and the end of the world!" she says. "I promise it all!" And all we can do is wait for them eagerly.

Sunday, September 16th, 5 p.m. Gala reception in the lobby.

So there it is—a month of retrospection and nostalgia. Of doppelgangers and monsters, machinery and romance. The Shangri-La Theater stands at the cutting edge of entertainment by simply looking back through history, at past images that tempt us, allure us, and haunt us as we leave the theater for good.
  --Dominic Rackett

∞

There is a time in most movies, Dominic had noticed, when the hero, bound on a quest of his own making, discovers that there is a larger story underneath his story, or that there was a side road better than the one he had been on. He begins what he *thinks* will be his tale, only to find out that perhaps the quest was about something else all along.

This was what he thought, as after a decade of oversight, he settled into bed with a copy of his father's book.

It had been a rough day at the office. Dr. Zauber had taken him to the woodshed over all the first three drafts of the introductory flyer. Nothing had been right: his attempt to make the series sound appealing had been dismissed as pandering. American ad copy, she had called it, filled with cliché and corporate pitches. They had closed the day not with a finished revision as much as giving up, settling for a kind of ceasefire. And all the business about *aweysha*. What was it, anyway? Magic or inspiration? Insinuation or possession? Zauber insisted on including it, said that the film would make it clear.

Dominic had the *Caligari* article still to write. Perhaps the film had a bit of *aweysha* in it as well: after all, Caligari controls Cesare through hypnosis, suggestion, the power of will. Perhaps it was for that reason that Zauber was so insistent.

It was too much to think on for now. Dominic drew the copy of his father's book from his backpack, lay his head on the pillow, and began to read at arm's length.

∞

Published in Dominic's infancy, the book had also marked the time of his parents' divorce. He remembered nothing of his father from back then, only from the scattered visits of childhood and adolescence, always planned with his mother's quiet reluctance and always uncomfortable once they were underway, as he and his father would spend the first half of the stay relearning each other. So it turned out that, when he was old enough to read it, the book became his substitute for a vanished Gabriel Rackett. Or at least that was what Ben Mountolive, stepfather and unethical psychologist, had claimed during the terrible long stay on the analyst's couch that took up almost twenty years of Dominic's youth.

Oh, Gabriel had written other things. There were a number of short stories, some of which he had never quite completed and which were, as far as Dominic could tell, somewhere in Mountolive's papers. But *Dacia* was the published novel, the work that was out there. It was the thing that Gabriel formed and licked into shape, like the old legends claimed the lioness does at the birth of her cubs.

Dominic and the book were contemporaries, twinned in the last hopes of a crumbling marriage. Which was probably why had he never liked looking through the thing, why his own copy was still with Peri Bathgate in Vermont, who, like Mountolive before her, would no doubt make all kinds of evidence out of his father's writing. *Mulian Rescues His Mother* was what she had called it, making a connection from an Asian Lit class that had been one of her university whims back then. Dominic didn't know the play back then, never saw a solid connection when he learned about it. And even after a decade there was part of him that had not forgiven her.

If Peri had commented, as one reviewer did, that *Dacia* was "a fairy tale writ large," or mentioned a little bit of Rumpelstiltskin in the fabric of things, Dominic would have better understood. But the novel was and was not its own creature: an heroic epic fantasy about three sons pursuing a girl in a land of ghosts. It contained rivals and apparitions, sometimes the rivals as cloudy as the ghosts. Which made the book even more Dominic's twin, because rivalries and pursuits had come to seem like his calling. His father's strange vanishing and his own presence when it happened had haunted him for years, though he had been only thirteen at the time and remembered little to nothing of what went on.

He did remember the aftermath, though—the tag end of what everyone soon referred to as "the incident". Dominic had awakened on a landing to the smell of stale cooked cabbage and the tattered filaments of cobwebs across his face. He had tried to cry out, but it was like the air had fled his lungs and there was no breath left for crying. He stood, almost slipping in the rattle of small hard grains underfoot, and picking one up, he drew it into the light and examined it.

Pearlescent. This time he remembered the word.

But Dominic remembered little else of that Christmas: the not unkind questioning of a Metro PD detective, Grandma Mary's restlessness with him, something about a phone call to his mother. But things obeyed the original holiday schedule: he landed back at Logan on Boxing Day, wrapped in Gabriel's parka and sleepless since the ordeal at the top of the stairs in the old Bell house. Bone weary and irritable, he had stumbled straight into his mother's and stepfather's interrogating presence. Dominic had assured them he was all right, had almost persuaded his stepfather until his mother intervened.

His long analysis began almost immediately, first with several of Ben Mountolive's colleagues, all of whom sought to uncover the time Dominic had lost in the abandoned house. He caught on to the script early, realized it was supposed to end in a huge outpouring of recovered memory, after which he would be drained and stable and saved by their ingenuity. So of course he resisted them. He decided quickly (whether it was true or not) that the analyst should be as smart or smarter than he was, and from where he stood, that seemed doubtful.

Ben Mountolive must have reached the same conclusion, because he took up the process again, five years after his colleagues had failed. Mountolive took over the therapy like he was coming to the rescue. Dominic knew it was because his mother had insisted, because Ben's role of stepfather had trumped that of the psychiatrist, at which he was better and far more comfortable. Dom had never liked Ben that much, but this intervention made him even more distant. Dominic knew the tricks, the shifts and dodges of avoidance, knew as well the words you could say to mimic progress, healing, and growth; he also knew that Ben would fasten on to those words because the whole thing was about pleasing Jasmine Mountolive and, as Dominic would discover later to his rage, about publishing an article called "Orfeo: A Study in Depressive Behavior" that was every bit as fictional as *Dacia*, and ten times as unethical.

From those psychiatric sessions had begun the long estrangement. Dominic had seen his mother only once since then. Mountolive became a name at the bottom of a check, because Jasmine saw to it that her son was provided with enough money to complete his education. At first Dominic had resisted school as well. He had retreated to Vermont, where he clerked in a bookstore and ducked all kinds of coaxing by his mother and stepfather to "make something" of himself. He spent his time reading, watching old movies at the college theater not far from where he stayed. He had even made a foray into college himself, doing two years of a degree in psychology financed by his parents, then switching his major to religious studies, and by the time he graduated, secretly switching again, this time to creative writing. And on, to the chagrin of his parents, to an MFA program in poetry, which they continued to finance despite no real evidence of (or belief in) his talent. There he endured a bad romance, then dropped out of the university, vowing never to return.

. The trip to Italy had been on his stepfather's dime: after Jasmine's death, Dominic had a small trust fund, a yearly income that stretched in his style for about ten months. Ben Mountolive however, had a desperation of money, and felt guilty about not liking his stepson. So he would tide Dominic over in the lean weeks, had even sent Dominic away on the tour of Rome and Florence, packed with train tickets, a lump sum of money, a MasterCard for emergency, and a cheap European mobile phone, which Dominic turned off in the Da Vinci Airport, intent on dropping off the grid immediately.

Neither Ben nor Dominic had an idea of what might be

found, or, for that matter, why you'd be more likely to find it in central Italy. Drawn by the Roman ruins, the expansive haunted wastes of the Palatine Hill, Dominic lingered in atmosphere and wine, discovering after two weeks in the expensive city that he could already glimpse the bottom of his bottomless funds. Now "dropping off the grid" seemed less appealing, when he had less money to cushion the fall.

Up to Florence he went, with much the same experience. There Dominic regarded the great art of the Renaissance with a mild discomfort, knowing that his money would not last much longer. So, within a week, Tuscany and Dominic parted paths, and he found himself on a train headed north out of Torino Porta Nuova, rising steadily into the sun-bedazzled foothills of the Italian Alps. The stops on the journey had ceased to be recognizable names for him: Torino changing to Chivasso, Ivrea, Nus…until he arrived in a small place, nestled in the mountains, a town that two thousand years before had been a Roman outpost on the borders of the wild. There he stayed for a comfortable spell, baked in Italian sunlight, holing up in a nearby hostel, taking in the ruins—a bridge, an arch commemorative of Augustus. Most impressively a theater whose enormous interior wall was eroded by two millennia of wind and rain and time, but still towered over the surrounding rubble as almost the tallest structure in the town.

Ben's message about Grandma Mary reached him in the second week of his stay, after he emerged from what they called the cryptoporticus. It was a covered arcade, one that had bordered and contained the old Roman forum of the town, but was now half-buried by years of soil accretion, its windows either sealed or boarded, providing a fractured light from outside . Now it was only a slim tunnel brushing the crypt of the nearby cathedral, so close that Dominic leaned against the wall, pressed his ear against the cold Roman concrete and puddingstone, and thought he heard the vanished heartbeat of the saint buried next door among her relics.

It was as though voices—the muted sound of breathing,

Latin and Italian and the muddled Transalpine French—filtered through walls and transfixed him, sound as fitful and fragmentary as the light through boarded cloister windows. For the first time Dominic saw his movement through space as a long passage uncertainly lit. It seemed as though the arches trembled above him, that they were letting in more light, but at the cost of crumbling and collapse and great danger.

He climbed the steps into the hot Italian sun, gasping for open air. He was unmoored, disconnected in a country six hours ahead of comfortable time, where they spoke a barely comprehensible Romance language and the mountains looked down on him with indifference. For the first time in months he missed the States, if only for a conversation in English, and his hopes rose when he turned on the phone and a short text message came up on its screen.

Your grandmother ill. Could be the time. Use the card for ticket if you're coming. Sincerely, B Mountolive

Dominic took the news more with relief than bereavement. After all, he didn't really know Grandma Mary, and the crisis offered an excuse to get Stateside while still saving face. He knew it was self-centered, felt bad about it on the flight from Turin the next day: with a knapsack full of dirty clothes and a half-dozen books stored overhead, he could have passed for the college student he was ten years too old to be.

Dominic arrived at his grandmother's place, finding her as he had described to Bulwer—drinking gin and pedaling a stationary bike to the heightened dialogue of her television soap operas. He had almost spoken harshly to her, before conceding, silently and passively, that he was getting what he wanted out of the whole return. And then, when Mary offered him a place to stay, a room for as long as he liked, righteousness took a back seat to convenience, and he began to unpack his belongings.

It turned out he had gathered little over a month's journey. And after several days, his grandmother went on with her daily life as though Dominic wasn't even around, with a kind of tranquillized routine of telephone calls and theater events, always capped off by sherry parties with former actors, where people drank too much and reminisced about careers that seemed to be wheel-spinning, at best, but usually had never gained traction to begin with.

It was not a home for a young man with huge, indefinite ambitions. After Bulwer took him on at Salvages, Dominic began to look toward moving from Grandma Mary's. Still, it was the time of year when his trust fund entered the lean months. He was several paychecks shy of an apartment, and he refused to go to Mountolive resources. It took George Castille's tipsy grip on his knee, along with the conspiracy of old folks—Castille, Grandma Mary, and (as it turned out now) Leni Zauber—to set the resources in front of Dominic. The money gave him the last push toward the doomed 9th Street apartment; the writing gig had followed, and when the apartment burned, a room above the lobby. It was a run of luck that now seemed insecure, because Dr. Zauber hated the writing he had done, smelled the ad copy between the lines and (Dominic just knew it) regretted ever having made a promise to Mary Conroy.

By now, the cryptoporticus and its shadow-cramped subterranean passage was beginning to resemble a refuge. That night he dreamed back to Italy, to cool winds off the Alps, the dry and fruity savor of Torrette, and the long, eventless weeks of his detachment.

The Cabinet of Dr. Caligari (1919)

This is one of the films that started it all, so it seems only fitting that our series begins with Robert Wiene's *The Cabinet of Dr. Caligari.*

Before *Caligari* it was all novelty and mostly throwaway, at least in German cinema. The short films that experimented with what the medium could do—"Look! A man running!" or marvels of time lapse and early camera tricks—had given way to historical epics, pornography, and filmed stage dramas, with only a few films we bother to watch today outside of a film studies class, and these were mostly American (Chaplin and hometown D.W. Griffith come to mind).

Caligari changed those things. But its story is rather simple, and goes like this: The film begins with a scene in which our hero, Franzis, is relating a memory from his past. In his story, a traveling fair comes to town, its main attraction being Dr. Caligari and his prophetic somnambulist—or sleepwalker—Cesare. Soon after the fair arrives in town, the town clerk is murdered, the first in a string of odd homicides. Franzis and Alan, two best friends competing for the heart of Jane (Lil Dagover), go to the fair and see the sleepwalker, who tells Alan he will die before dawn.

That night, Alan is murdered by a mysterious figure, and Franzis, remembering Cesare's prediction, relays it to the police the next morning. Franzis and Jane's father, Dr. Olsen, decide to visit Dr. Caligari and Cesare. Jane goes to look for them later, only to find Caligari instead, who leads her to have a strange encounter with the sleepwalker. At sundown the suspicious Franzis waits outside Dr. Caligari's trailer, while the killer Cesare somehow manages to slip away and kidnap Jane. After a rooftop pursuit, Jane is recovered unharmed, but the lifeless Cesare is found. The police search Dr. Caligari's trailer and find a mannequin sleepwalker in Cesare's coffin-like bed. Meanwhile Caligari escapes. Franzis, seeking revenge and justice, goes to a nearby insane asylum in hopes of locating the mad doctor. He discovers that Caligari is head of the institution, and flees in panic.

That night Franzis returns with the hospital staff and police to examine Dr. Caligari's documents. He discovers that Caligari has assumed the identity of a traveling monk named Caligari who controlled a homicidal sleepwalker in 1803. In this role, he has used Cesare to kill others as part of an experiment on hypnosis and domination of the will. The asylum authorities wrestle Dr. Caligari into a strait jacket and confine him to the asylum. It seems that Franzis has won the day, but the film isn't over. It returns to the framing story, where Franzis concludes his tale. But the surprises are not over.

Screenwriters Carl Mayer and Hans Janowitz were veterans of the Great War, tuned to the trauma and paranoia that troubled Germany in its aftermath. Hiring director Robert Wiene and the Expressionist artist Hermann Warm, the pair wanted a film that set forth all the anxiety of their time, and in many ways they got it: the distorted buildings, shaped more like wavering flames than recognizable geometry, the eerie, carnivalesque atmosphere of the fair, the strange sleepwalker Cesare (played by the silent film icon Conrad Veidt in his first major role), and above all, Caligari himself (Werner Krauss), the ominous, shifty authority figure—unreliable father to the sleepwalker—who takes on villainy for the first hour of the film, only to switch to an even creepier kindness in the last five minutes.

And that is the controversy about Caligari. It seems that Wiene tacked the frame around the film—one that in ways reverses what you see in the main story. But I'll keep quiet about that, if only for spoilers' sake. I will say, though, that what happens to Franzis happens at times to the best of us—though we would certainly hope not with such horrific results. We labor along, make assumptions, and reckon that our lives are going to unfold in a way that is familiar and foreseeable. But behind our easy plans,

61

sometimes, there are designs and plots—maybe even conspiracies, who knows?—that persist in silence until the moment they emerge from the shadows and change everything.

That's no great wisdom. Lives are filled with sudden changes, and film stories very often reflect that things happen in such surprising fashion. But keep in mind that when it comes to plot twists and turns, you'll have seen many of them before, mainly because *Caligari* has set the pattern for films to follow. Its main unsettling magic lies in the odd and vicious Caligari, or in the questions surrounding Cesare (an actual sleepwalker? Caligari's own creation breaking terribly free from his control? his double or doppelganger?). And most of all, it is the sets: the menacing buildings, distorted and bent, that suggest that, despite what we assume, we walk through a world gone mad.

--Dominic Rackett

∞

The Preview Night, Dominic understood, was a thing they would not do again. Only three weeks after his arrival, his *Caligari* copy written and printed, he joined his co-workers at a Thursday event, the night before the festival began.

At Leni's insistence, George Castille hosted an event in which the Shangri-La doors were thrown open and the movie would be free to all comers. George announced it to the staff cautiously, explaining without conviction that the Shangri-La had its own charm, that people would return for the venue itself. Not to worry, he claimed: a free house would pay for itself through the course of the series.

Dominic knew what was afoot. George was justifying Leni's demands, giving them a marketing turn, a language that probably translated to only a trickle at the box office. Because he was discovering that this was a free-sample town, customers pocketing syrup-flavored sausages at the groceries, toothbrushes and travel-sized shampoo at health fairs, on up to Florida weekend trips advertising time-share properties where you could recreate your own neighborhoods among other time-sharers with whom you had gone to high school. People in this town gathered things for the freeness of them and forgot them the next week for the familiar basketball and high school events, for a huge, gaudy spring display of fireworks they were already talking about although it was only August, for auto parts and tanning beds and smokeless tobacco. Dominic figured a few would attend a silent film if it was free, but he was still uncertain they would hand over five dollars for the experience.

Which, incredibly, was all a ticket would cost. A film for five bucks, when in the suburbs you were paying ten, twelve, fifteen for the next installment of *Twilight* or some rocketing car-chase/special-effects extravaganza interrupted by snarky dialogue that passed for plot and character development. Though he had not imagined he would much like silent movies, suspected that it might have been a passing fancy much like graduate school, Dominic found himself drawn to them, on their side as he watched *The Cabinet of Doctor Caligari* one last time before the preview.

Alone in the theater, making notes for the introduction he was afraid Dr. Zauber would hate, Dominic wondered what it was that he found compelling about silent films.

The poetry outside language. That was kind of what it was— the thing you sensed before the iridescent screen, but when you tried to talk about, it found its way back into shadows, receding from your words. Lights, camera, action, as the cliché announced, but these were part of that poetry. The script had been images and story, he understood, but when it came to dialogue, the actors improvised before the camera, their lips mouthing words that would be impossible to translate for this audience, unschooled in either German or lip-reading, but ended up being universal, he guessed, because the story crossed boundaries of language. And when the actors improvised, they would speak from their hearts or imaginations about the situation, the turn of the plot as it was recorded by the old stationary camera, words that were lost in the long, effacing quiet of time. The result was a kind of spontaneous magic of gesture, where the face revealed worlds as the actors danced in their own inaudible conversation, created a script out of movement and expression, their unprepared speech a kind of free will across the determinism of the screenplay. It could be far more expressive, he figured, than speaking someone else's words.

Though all of that had a whiff of graduate school about it, though the ideas would never make their way into his little essays, Dominic kept the thoughts for days, sat down with them on the Preview Night, when the lobby was abuzz with muddled conversations and the ear guessed at what was being said.

Perhaps fifty people filed into the seats, mostly George's Old Louisville neighbors and associates from the theater community. Todd whispered something about *gay men everywhere you look,* but by now Dominic had enough of Todd, knew how to ignore him politely and not risk the favor of his twin. To his dismay, Ellie had seated herself by Max Winter as the lights lowered. Sighing, Dominic settled into the row behind George Castille and three middle-aged men as the film began. He glanced around the house, but could not locate Leni Zauber, so he assumed she was in the projection booth, that all staff and residents were accounted for.

Now Dominic settled in to watch the opening of *Caligari* for the fifth time this week. It was now familiar to him but suddenly made strange again by the presence of an audience—a handful of people watching two actors miming in a circle of darkness. The prelude to the action, the notorious frame of the story, made more ominous to him because he now knew where the film was headed. It was the moment before the story began, and *the poetry of silence* that had seemed romantic in words felt off and grainy inside the blurred camera's iris of shadows and light. Less than a minute into the showing, Lil Dagover lurched across the garden, entranced and remote like some beautiful specter, and the iris blinked, closing and opening to reveal the painted town of Holstenwall, its buildings rippling skyward in a pyramid of flame, its population cycling up and down the center-stage stairwell to give the illusion of a big crowd. You could notice as the same extras reached the top of the stairs, circled and returned, like Holstenwall itself was a town of doubles.

And then Dr. Caligari came on screen. That old Nazi Werner Krauss shuffled across the stage, scruffy and aged disproportionately for his role as diabolical scientist (or the concerned psychologist, depending on the version of the story you ended up believing). And as he shuffled, as the camera framed and focused on him and the iris closed on his leering face, a whoop erupted from the balcony Dominic was sure had been roped off for the screening.

"Oh, Jesus," George whispered. "Someone's upstairs. Go up and investigate."

Dominic met Max on the landing, bound on the same errand. The two of them entered the balcony, where a solitary figure stood at the railing, leaning heavily over the seated audience. The stir was already over, as the people below had decided it was one of those simple disruptions, too loud a conversation or someone talking back to the screen, but Max and Dominic approached the man and drew him gently into the lobby.

Dominic had a jacket like that. Gray tweed with elbow patches, like an assistant professor's. He hoped his wasn't that soiled, knew it wasn't as tattered. It was too old and unfit for an August night, but so was the man who wore it, a bearded, crusty type, pompadoured and stubbled and approaching seventy, smelling of stale muscatel. Max and Dominic seated the old fellow on one of the lobby benches, where a plaster Dante glared infernally down upon them all, as though something in the outer circle of Hell was unfolding once again.

Max spoke to the man as Dominic went to get him coffee.

Dominic hadn't liked Max all that much on first meeting— still didn't like him, if truth be told—but he admired the way the younger man handled the tramp. He disliked homeless people himself, feeling that he'd brushed against vagrancy too often himself, and not wanting to admit he'd been retrieved only by his well-off family. And though Dominic thought he could see through Max, right down to the condescension and the posturing, the old man seemed rather grateful for the attention.

By the time Dominic returned, Max and T. Tommy Briscoe had become confidantes if not friends. It seemed they shared a story by now—how that afternoon, in the crawl space of a hipster landmark, T. Tommy had been shot in the ass.

∞

As far as Dominic could tell, the old man was undamaged by alleged gunplay. No holes in the back of his trousers, and when T. Tommy dropped his pants in the lobby despite the laughter and protests from the two young men, there seemed to be no holes on his person, either. And yet his gaudy account made the facts not matter so much. At one unsettled moment mid-story, Dominic locked gazes with the old man, noticing they had the same color eyes, a brown sparked ever so slightly toward hazel. In that instant a dark patch stirred in Dominic's memory and a musty, mildewed smell seemed to rise in the lobby, something soon crowded out by the murk of sweat and stale wine.

T. Tommy was, by most descriptions, a tramp. Not romantic enough for a hobo, he feared, but not sorry enough for a derelict. He preferred above all terms that of the *flâneur*, the idler, the man of leisure who wanders and observes city life. The crowd, he told the boys, was his element, his home the ebb and flow of movement, the fugitive and the infinite. He was a prince rejoicing in his incognito, or so he claimed, like that king in *The Arabian Nights*.

Just that morning he had been south of the cemeteries, where he had awakened under angels, never imagining the violent turn of the day. By afternoon wandering in back of the bohemian business district of guitar shops, designer cafes, antiqueries and book stores. Tommy had to admit that his purposes were not of a lawful bent, for he was shopping for an adit to the mineral wealth of the stores. Because sometimes comes the occasion, Tommy explained, when grace fails, and, down on pragmatic luck, even the most insightful *flâneur* might try to steal copper.

Copper, the boys surely knew, was the currency of meth and crack, traded by addicts to pay for their substances, but Tommy was a traditionalist who surmised that copper would trade well for liquor, too. In a familiar back alley, he had seen the opportunity at last. He had not taken into account, however, the gaunt mobility of crack and meth addicts, the thinness that would let them negotiate tight passages.

Indeed, for a moment, with the late afternoon light just right, Tommy thought he had seen another in the crawl space— someone moving toward him, angular, scuttling like a crab, mirroring his movement in the shadows underneath the house, bound toward the copper.

Not that Tommy was stuck. Nor that he was scared. But he

was compressed enough and startled enough by this intruder to make noise, to cry out. Which of course aroused the proprietor of the establishment, who of course came outside and exercised Second Amendment rights in rock salt upon a poor man's backside. God bless him for the lenience of no further pursuit, and God bless the crawl space with two entries, T. Tommy declared, for he squeezed into light, it seemed, up Second Street and away from there.

He had heard about the preview at the Shangri-La. Remembered the theater had a balcony, and figured it as a high, air-conditioned retreat where he could sit in darkness for a couple of hours and lick his wounds. That was a figure of speech, of course.

He had been to the Shangri-La before, in the company of his old man back in the fifties, when it was the Horizon. Together they had seen *The Ten Commandments*, Heston puffing and posturing and brandishing the Tablets over a cast of thousands. Back then Tommy's clothing and spirit had been cleaner, and he had been provided for. But this time the theater housed the strange world of *Caligari*, with its thwarted buildings and eerie somnambulists. It was like T. Tommy's own world framed in light, he said, like he could step outside onto Fourth Street and watch as the carnival came to town. He could sit at a distance, safe in the balcony where he'd sat with his old man nearly sixty years ago. Where he could gather his breath, recline, and escape pursuit.

But that night Tommy had sat in the balcony and watched old Werner Krauss duckwalk through a tilted city street, and Werner was Caligari, if he remembered correctly, or a crazy man who thought he was Caligari, an inmate of the madhouse or the keeper of the asylum, one or the other. But that was a minor concern to T. Tommy, because something was wrong because something *wasn't* wrong, if you boys know what he was saying, and it took him a few seconds to recognize that his backside was no longer hurting.

He thought perhaps he was called to Jesus or even *by*

Jesus, that he had lost all sense in his extremities and that death was creeping up the somatic ladder like the hemlock done on Socrates, rising through chakras while the great philosopher arranged his estate, but danged if the back of T. Tommy's pants weren't stitched together whole when he groped it, and danged if he couldn't take up his bed and walk.

And begging their pardon, he stood again, and once again turned the backside in question toward Max and Dominic, who still saw nothing wrong with his trousers beyond the scuff and soil of wear. Now Dom made the sign of the cross over the old *flaneur,* and intoned, *Behold, thou art made whole: sin no more, lest a worse thing come unto thee.* And as Tommy strode youthfully down the steps and into the lobby, peering carefully out of the theater door before taking off down Fourth Street, Dominic looked out of the corner of his eye, at Max, who looked back at him, like linked faces in a distorted mirror.

∞

But there was something else he had not told the boys. Something about the intertitles.

Tommy had noticed it from the start, as the first scene opened with the actors sitting in a garden, their images drained and commingled with light, so that the first thing he thought of was how long those actors had been dead—the strange, morbid haze of their appearances.

Then the older one spoke, his account a litany of leave-taking and regret, the words up in English first. *There are spirits everywhere,* he said. *They are all around us...they drive me from hearth and home, from wife and child...*

And let that be a lesson to you, T. Tommy thought, but he knew already, and as he mouthed each word of the intertitle, it swiftly blurred into the original, the cartoonish script looking sinister in German:

Es gibt Geister—Überall sind sie um uns her...

He found himself reciting it, a language he didn't know, and as the iris closed on Franzis and his nameless older companion, the world of the movie unfolded, the characters speaking to T. Tommy directly, the intertitles informing him, advising him, cajoling him.

And at the end warning him. For Franzis's story ends in an asylum, his pursuit of the mad Caligari and the sleepwalker Cesare turned suddenly on its ear, as we come to suspect that Franzis himself has been the madman all along. Sehen Sie…das is Cesare, he warned T. Tommy. Lassen Sie sich niemals von ihm wahrsagen…

See? That is Cesare. If you let him tell your fortune…

Tommy knew how it ended.

If you let him tell your fortune, you will be dead.

So Tommy had whooped then, raised the authorities. But before the boys came to get him from the balcony, before the Man crashed down on him (or rescued him, he was no longer sure), he watched Franzis stalking wild-eyed through the asylum, saw Caligari approach, all cleaned up and renamed and respectable now as Herr Direktor of the Madhouse.

Ihr glaubt alle ich sei wahnsinnig! Franzis warns. You all think I am mad, but it is the director who is mad! He is Caligari!

And wrestled away in the stronger hands of young orderlies, Franzis is dragged off into madness, and the Direktor spouts platitudes about *diagnosis* and *cure* to the camera in the final scene. But T. Tommy was no longer listening, no longer reading the intertitles, because he was seized by the stare of Werner Krauss (the Direktor, Caligari, in real life an actor in the most terrible asylum in history)…

And the screen seemed to erupt, a silent, glittering explosion that sent its shock wave hurtling over the balcony, and Tommy had seen a courtyard hemmed in with geometrical barbed wire, lit by shadowy gas flames. The images gained substance and weight, rushing thick against him until he shrieked, then gasped for air, drowning in tidal light. Something pushed down his throat, slowly at first, but then with speed and insistence, and something else followed in its wake, and his heart beat quickly and he was smothering. He felt suddenly *inhabited,* something from outside lodging and roiling inside him, breathing as he breathed, gaining purchase. He fell back against the chair, panicking, struggling for air, and hands clutched his shoulder and something took hold of him, the light around him spangling and striating, and he could breathe again.

Escorted into light by his own latter-day orderlies, seated in the cool lobby, plied with coffee and interrogated mildly, Tommy regained his bearings. Things looked different as he told his story to the young men—the light on the red walls, the mural, the faces looking down on the three of them in silent audience. He left out some of the story and made some up, but it was mostly the truth. And the red-headed boy was the friendlier, but light pooled against him and he was opaque. The darker kid was deeper, and Tommy recognized something in the boy that was coded and obscure but finally familiar. Something told him had known the boy once, perhaps before the drink set in, though the kid did not look old enough for that to be true. Whatever the case, Tommy was not afraid of either as they sat with him, listened, and sent him off into the city night, shook free of his wounds and his healing. Just outside the theater he turned and looked back through the glass door. The red-haired boy had vanished, but the other stood by the gate and regarded him, arms folded and a stance that mirrored his own.

5.

"**I** still think your attitude is elitist, Dominic. Elitist and just a little bit mercenary."

Once again Max was on about T. Tommy in the lobby, and how Dominic had treated a vagrant like a vagrant.

The two of them stood in the back alley with the twins, as the Shangri-La staff passed around a joint before the 8:00 show. Inside, Jerry Jeff was policing the house aisles in a rushed pickup before the theater opened to the official debut of *Caligari*. George had warned them not to lose their edge, that tonight's showing promised a number of local dignitaries, some of whom had sponsored the series to begin with. That advice was enough to encourage the cannabis, but Dominic had slipped outside more for the conversation than for the supplementary weed.

Dom found himself in that curious middle age of recreational drugs: past the time of college and grad school where it was the social lubricant like his dad's whiskey or Grandma Mary's gin, but not old enough to return to it for rejuvenation, for recovered youth. He was the one who wasn't smoking, inhaling instead the sheer good looks of Eleanor Vitale. It was as though all of them—Dominic himself, Max Winter, even George (undrawn by women) and Todd (who was her brother)—opened and blossomed in Ellie Vitale's muted light, almost as though they made a community around her.

And yet at moments like this, passing a joint in the alley, you could see how frail that community was, that desire was already dismantling it.

"Elitist? Well, I'm sorry you think so, Max. Why am I an elitist?"

Max shook his head, looking to Ellie for approval. "I didn't say *you* were elitist. I said your *attitude*. It's different."

Dominic saw very little difference, but begged off saying so. The argument would become collegiate, filled with student rhetoric, and he would lose out because Max knew the slogans. Ellie was already nodding in agreement, her short blonde hair luminous, the joint between her lips aglow.

Dominic sighed. College had changed even since his time up in New York. It seemed to him that a lot of energy was spent in taking offense these days. Every resentment—every axe to grind—turned into a field of study, and Dominic wondered if you could major in butthurt and lament. He figured he would be compared to Hitler soon enough. Or at least to Goebbels.

"I'm an assistant here and an assistant there, Max," he said at last. "Burned out of an apartment and holding two marginal jobs, actually, since I'm working at Salvages. Hard to get up any elitism behind a gig like that. No captain of industry here, no cultural giant."

They all knew Dominic was explaining too much. Max shrugged and looked down the alley, where the January light was tilting over the tall shadows of the Fourth Street buildings. "Well, you should of at least treated him with some human dignity and all."

Dominic laughed, unable at last to help himself. "Oh, come on, Max. The man was making a case that Bulwer shot him. John freakin' Bulwer, for God's sake! Do you really think Bulwer has a shotgun stashed on the premises just for salting the ass of an occasional hobo? I mean, I knew there'd been break-ins, but I figured with Buddha on the premises…"

Max sighed, and Ellie, in the first rush of cannabis, giggled at the image of the two old men in pitched gun battle. Dominic stifled a laugh, and Max grinned despite himself, glancing alertly to the stage door because they could catch hell even from a lenient boss like Castille. Nobody knew what to say next.

"You know," Todd said, after a silence in which the joint quickly circled. "Here's the thing I never understood about *Caligari*. Franzis and Alan."

"Franzis is the hero. Alan's the friend who gets murdered so Franzis has a case to solve," his sister explained. "You shouldn't make a deal of this stuff, Todd."

"But it's the whole red herringness of things, Ellie. You have Franzis and Alan making this deal that they will stay friends no matter which of them wins over Jane, and then it isn't five minutes until they kill off Alan. So you wonder, why bring up the deal in the first place?"

"It gives Franzis a reason to go after the murderer, Todd," Max insisted. "It's really that simple."

"But see, he would have a reason just being Alan's friend!" Todd insisted. "Why bring in the extra layer if you aren't going to do anything with it? That's all I'm asking. "

Ellie tamped the roach and slipped the last sliver of marijuana into her pocket. "So it's another conspiracy, Todd? Franzis was in on it? In league with Caligari and the sleepwalker so it's one-eighty-seven on Alan and Franzis can be all heroical with Jane?"

Dominic chuckled. "*Franzis is in on it.* That's your T-shirt, people."

All but Todd laughed, Max's laughter wavering when he saw that Ellie couldn't stop giggling.

"Oh, it's just the dope, Max," she explained. "And Todd, I don't mean *you!*"

A silly comment as she sputtered the last of the smoke and coughed, her breath misting in the fickle January air now suddenly gone cold. *Franzis is in on it*, she whispered, and started to laugh again. Dominic opened the door for her, guiding her with a grand, dramatic wave of his hand back into the warmth and light of the Shangri-La.

∞

Max made to follow, but Todd grabbed his arm and drew him back into the alley.

"I can take care of this, Max," he whispered, his eyes reddened, the pupils dilated like a scene opening on darkness.

"What do you mean, Todd?"

"I can…restore things. I mean, to their earlier state. I can bring back the peace, Max. It's what we both want, own up to it."

"But you can't be thinking…" Max's words balked, unable to frame the idea.

For a moment, their gazes mirrored in the shadowy alley. Max tried to pull away from the thought, and Dominic called them both again from the exit.

He frowned at Todd, who laughed softly.

"Oh, not in *that* way, Max. Ohmygod, not *that.*"

They both giggled, the dope in a second rush over them as they shared a cigarette.

Max coughed and sputtered, "*Jesus!* I thought you were offering to whack him, and I was thinking how *Goodfellas* of you, how Pesci…"

Todd collected himself into a serious stare. "But I do have ways with Ell. She's my sister, my twin. Our instincts are bonded in our cells, dude. And I can put him out of the picture, because he's cold and treacherous and too old for our girl."

Max nodded, just wanting to get away. The alley righted itself, the buildings brought back to plumb as Todd's grip loosened on his arm.

"I can put in a word, Max," he urged. "That's all I'm sayin'. What did you think I was sayin'?"

∞

A little buzzed and giddy from the weed and the back and forth, Ellie Vitale watched as the boys spread out over the ground floor of the theater.

August was going to be no-reprieve river valley summer: hot, dry and heavy humidity. The air anticipated the reprieve of summer rain, but it wasn't coming soon, the Weather Channel warned, just getting dryer and dryer until what grass there was in the desiccated city crackled like hay underfoot. Inside the theater was a blessing, however, and the first guests arriving were sweaty and relieved in the first embrace of the Shangri-La's overworked AC.

Ellie had no idea what Todd and Max had been talking about. Didn't care much, because Max wouldn't put up with her brother's creepy side, even though he could be kind of smothering himself when it came to her attentions. As the one girl present in the Shangri-La's pack of characters, she was used to being center stage, aware that even George played toward her audience. She would bask comfortably for a while in the regard, until it became too much for her, became relentless and the principal subject. Then she would dress down, leave her hair unwashed and come to work in jeans and a grunge flannel shirt, would brood and take umbrage when George would say she should clean up, for god's sake.

You couldn't talk about beauty. People resented if you complained. And yet it made you lazy, as it made them lazy as well, everyone resting in the evident, underestimating her and letting her get by. She felt more complicated than they allowed; her thoughts tunneled and undermined each other, but the simplicity of weed and wine was a kind of reprieve. And when she would think she had overestimated her looks—was *filled with herself*, as her mother would say—the regarding eyes of men (and even of some girls) would remind her that, for now, it was a factor, and it made things easy and difficult.

The new man was nice, she thought, her gaze turning to Dominic, who was talking to George and another middle-aged man over by the stairway to the mezzanine. Dominic had helped her lift things, had spelled her at the door and at the counter the night of the preview. He wasn't as tall as Max, but he was polished—so much so that she had suspected at first some chemistry between him and George. That is, until she saw where his eyes settled in the conversation. Perhaps it was just maturity: she knew he was older by a few years from his talk and his music, though Dominic looked about their age, because you know Asians.

Speaking of which, there was something Zen, she guessed, in the way Dominic put up with Todd. Or what she imagined Zen might look like—that kind of calm bemusement you saw in old martial arts mentors, at least the way they came across on film. She'd been to his room above the lobby once, to say hello and to borrow a corkscrew which he did not have, and though she barely stuck her head in the door, she saw the books on the makeshift cinderblock shelf—a couple dozen of them, some of them paperbacks in Buddhist yellows and oranges, though he would claim later that it was more Bulwer's spiking his interest than an actual spiritual leaning.

But Dominic wrote haiku as well, had showed her one about the city,

> dreamed from the field's edge
> shadows on the cobblestones
> the blades of rooftops

to which she wanted to say, *and?* like she always did with haiku. But that was it. She remembered there was a syllable limit to them. Something about nature. She didn't know whether Dominic had gotten the rules right, but he was cute and attentive, and interesting in the give and take. So she had read the haiku and nodded sagely, told him it was good. She was relieved when he hadn't pressed her reaction.

Now the Republicans pressed toward the bar, where Max stood and dispensed beer and wine and marginal conversation. She'd asked once how they were telling Republicans from Democrats in the Shangri-La, and George had told her it was never a sure thing, but Republicans would come early for the bar, while the Democrats came late, drinking at home because the theater over-priced its alcohol.

But don't overthink it, darling, Castille had said, rolling his eyes. *Democrats in this town are basically Eisenhower Republicans.*

Ellie was a Democrat, but she liked the celebrity of these Republicans. She knew Representative Rausch by reputation (they called him Reprehensible Rausch around here), and she knew that Mr. Trabue—who made her laugh with his foul mouth and when his bald head sprouted veins of aggravation— had worked for the party for years. She figured Mr. Trabue was having to behave himself with Peter Koenig, who wasn't drinking because he was a preacher, but was probably Republican for the same reason he wasn't drinking.

Max had his hands full, to be sure, but he was smiling and working the crowd, and the old men in suits liked him as their sort of resident hipster, their safe brush with the youth culture. He poured the drinks stiff, and everyone liked that, but there was also that attitude, temperate and pacific, that made you at home in his presence.

At first, Ellie had mistaken Max's quiet for charm. But now things were falling into the typical pattern of her dating years—the choice between the steady, passive bartender and the possibility of the charismatic haiku poet. She would pick the wrong one as usual, like she did with Cowboy. But for now, the dilemma wasn't far enough along to know exactly who the wrong one was to pick.

∞

George Castille paced in the lobby, greeting the groomed men and a trinity of wealthy liberal ladies in their costly and morally unfashionable furs. Max recognized the bunch of them from other film series. Castille's circle of friends.

There was another crowd here, too, of course. George had pointed them out: the big money behind the theater and the series, whom George insisted on calling *the suits,* barely aware that, owing to his age and the generational tides, he was simply a suit with a cooler tie.

Max watched the mingling begin, as the bar opened in the Shangri-La cellar and the dignitaries convened to drink and to talk about anything but film. Max poured bourbon and listened. Such things usually amused and fascinated him, but the encounter with Todd in the alley was troubling. Even more so as the adrenalin of being several places at once was wearing at the cannabis buzz.

And it wasn't just the general creepiness of Todd Vitale, but the specific creepiness of his offered friendship. Max had seen the dance of eyes between Ellie and Dominic, how she had pushed him playfully when he joked and how her hand rested a second too long on his shoulder. It was frustrating to have surmounted his shyness around girls, to have built on months of friendship and confidence, only to have it all take a back seat to a fresh attraction. And yeah, Dominic was handsome enough, not that Max noticed these things, and the whole part-Asian thing made him kind of glamorous and exotic, but he was probably fifteen years older, and nomadic, and set to stay on the move. No wonder Todd had it in for him, and Todd's friendship for Max was, admittedly, not much more than taking sides against Dominic.

The press was here, or at least the number and kind of press that you could expect at a silent film series in a small city. Wade Abner was there, and you had to keep half an eye that the city's most renowned arts critic crossed no path with George, because nothing said drama like when an aging gay actor ran into his aging gay detractor. The Peaceable Kingdom was in jeopardy, though Max knew in his heart that, no matter how you looked at it, the mural had been fading for days.

George sailed like an impeccable galley above the potential conflict, a glass of champagne in one hand and Dominic's flyer in the other. Max had to hand it to them both: George kept an actor's cool under a version of opening night jitters, and Dominic's writing, though not Roger Ebert's, was lively and passable. He hated the rumor that Leni had despised the *Caligari* article, had called it *postmodernist quatsch,* a judgment he thought was a compliment until George had told him that *quatsch* was a German term for *bullshit.*

Leni, Max had decided, was a film dominatrix. Her rejection of Dominic almost made the new guy likeable. But not quite.

In the far corner, sequestered from gays and hipsters and the scattering of rich liberals, the suits with the financial wherewithal gathered and drank. Todd had pointed them out to Max: like any good hipster of his time, Todd both hated Republicans and lacked the energy to vote against them.

They were arrayed against the wall like the docile animals in the facing mural. The horrendous Roy Rausch, who, in his brief three terms in the Indiana State House had outraged conservatives with his philandering, moderates with his policies, and the four liberals in his district with his complete disregard. Beside him, the pompadoured Peter Koenig, pastor of Antioch Church, leaned toward his wife Maraleese and whispered something amusing and no doubt cautionary, as the little woman covered her mouth and laughed.

Bucky Trabue stood between Koenig and Rausch, frowning at the overall festivities.

Though Max's politics were reflexively liberal, he rather liked Mr. Trabue, whose scowl, explosive temper, and sustained rant reminded him of a human Donald Duck. Smoker-lean and balding, Trabue had managed four campaigns for Rausch, winning three of them, but his political savvy was less of a factor here on the south side of the river. In fact, the district's sitting Congressman had said not long ago that "Bucky Trabue may be a gift to the Democratic Party."

Right now that glowering gift leaned back against the lobby wall, the bas-relief face of Buster Keaton drooping sadness and flaking plaster above him. Bucky Trabue was casing the crowd as well, and wishing he could enjoy the proceedings.

∞

At least the old girl smokes, Bucky Trabue thought, as Leni passed by him in a whiff of Gauloises, and the house lights flickered to signal that *Caligari* was fixing to start.

By the smell, she was a pack-a-day girl. At least the goddamned Germans had the sense to enjoy their economic decline and humorless movies.

Bucky filed into the aisle behind Maraleese Koenig, looked toward the screen framed by plaster putti and Apollos. He wished he could sit by himself when *Caligari* began: Rausch and the Koenigs would no doubt find something to take umbrage with instead of trying to enjoy the movie, and Bucky was guessing that it would be hard enough to buy into these films without the Puritans.

He'd seen *Nosferatu* back in college. Nursed a hip flask of Jack till the vampire almost got scary. But it wasn't the Coppola Dracula, or even Lugosi. For Bucky Trabue, it was words that were the contours of things: he knew he was no film buff because he had no reverence for the *mise en scène*, savoring the dialogue, the cool, aggressive bouts of conversations he wished he had with the people he wished he could have them with. When Rausch had bad-mouthed last year's Paul Newman series, calling the feature actor a *salad-dressing Maoist,* Bucky had kept silent. He had loved the Newman series. Especially Butch and Sundance, the whole road-picture-meets-Western business of it, and their frontier dying in that strange, unexplainable sadness that came, he guessed, with being born a generation too late.

He didn't share his party's contempt for Hollywood, though

he knew how to say the right things in the right surroundings. After all, Hollywood had brought America the Reagan years, and Bucky would have thrived then, would have walked the gold-paved streets of the City on the Hill, aware of its ironies even as he breathed its mythic air. Of course that pavement led to a place where you had to listen to every goddamned preacher in the Republic, where you couldn't openly believe in the basic fucking science they taught you in the fifth grade. His people talked in a code that Bucky had deciphered to mean that you said the same thing about Hollywood that you wanted to say about the preachers—that they dispensed the bullshit that most everyone bought, and if you couldn't beat them, you could use them to carry a district.

At least tonight it could have been worse. Peter Koenig was less a Bible-thumper than an ad man, bright and blow-dried, running a big old mega-church south of the city. The guy had read some things other than St. Paul and Leviticus, he listened to Dylan and Metallica unthreatened, and best of all he liked the movies and would stand you a beer in the Shangri-La's downstairs bar, though he wouldn't by theology drink one himself.

Bucky could have got behind Koenig as a candidate. Koenig was like a smart Reagan. But what Bucky got instead these days were two-faced throwbacks like Roy Rausch, who bucked up to run for something new every year and had trouble winning it because even the respectable right-wingers hated the two-faced bible-thumpers and oh, for the Old West, when they ran such motherfuckers out of town in tar and feathers.

Thinking apoplectic thoughts, he took his seat by the Maraleese Koenig and soothed himself in the shadows. He didn't understand why he operated at a low-grade rage when it came to just about everything. He wished he could smoke in here, and he bet that Leni Zauber could: she had the right carriage to do forbidden things in public and pass it off as charm. She'd have made a great maverick Senator or a dance-hall girl in a John Wayne movie. He wished he could cast things otherwise, wished this was the John Wayne series again, or a string of westerns,

Newman's or even that tinhorn Costner's. The silent films were overdramatic: everyone always looked dirty, like they were up to something. Bucky would try to read their lips, to determine their agendas, but it never worked, and what's more, this bunch would be mouthing things in German so he would be shit out of luck to begin with.

No. Give him the westerns any time. Except for the brokeback kind, which he'd never seen anything like, goddamn it. Them people didn't bother him like they were supposed to—in fact, he was amused as much as horrified by George Castille, and had come to like the old bird, though he couldn't own up to it in party circles. But Castille was no cowboy, and cowboys should not be homos. They should be rugged and free and everything the Duke and Paul Newman stood for on screen, not banging each other in a pup tent.

He wished he had a smoke. He knew Leni Zauber was packing tobacco, and wished he was sitting by her in the front row. Away from Rausch and the Koenigs and all of the faithful. Away from the world and in some silent-movie city.

Caligari began, and he got the first crazy tilting glimpse of the town. The old man in front of the carnival tent, opening the coffin in which the somnambulist has slept for twenty-five years. Bucky stood as Roy Rausch slipped out past his seat, wondered if there had been something in the first ten minutes of the movie to offend a Tea Party Republican. But with Koenig and Maraleese still seated, no doubt the Congressman was simply headed for the john.

Ten minutes in and the prostate beckons. They were all getting old. Bucky felt as though he'd slept for twenty-five years himself. A blink of the eye and damned if you don't wake up to a time disenchanted and post-Gipper. The world had never made sense, but he remembered a time when it was *headed* toward making sense, before, like the song said, Jesus took the wheel.

Well, Jesus might have taken the wheel, and the car might be turned in the right direction, though Bucky'd be damned if he saw it. What he *did* see was that Jesus drove the party into a ditch, and it was going to take a tow truck of magnitude to get them out.

∞

Dominic loitered in the lobby, still smarting from Leni's review of his article. They didn't come here to read, she had told him. More art, less matter, please. Don't over-analyze the films, for God's sake. Write to them as though you're speaking to them. Pretend to respect their intelligence and tell them how discerning they are, how sophisticated. But play down the cultural history, don't give the plot away, and major on the star lore. Give them the same kind of gossip about Conrad Veidt and Lil Dagover that they expect over Brad Pitt and Jennifer Aniston, because that's what they want, they just want a bunch of old Germans to talk about so they can look like cinephiles, look *à la mode* and well informed.

Dominic carried the advice with him and headed toward the bathroom, standing nervously at the top of the steps like he always did, enduring the mix of vertigo and fear, just glad that the lights were on leading down. He opened the door to the men's room.

Roy Rausch, as pale as a silent actor, was lying on the enameled floor.

It was as though Dominic had expected this, had foreseen a body sprawled. Rausch was sweating, clutching his shoulder. Dom spoke the man's name, crouched over him, extended his hand, withdrew it, then shouted for help into the deserted basement. Shouted again, his panic rising...

As Jerry Jeff Pfeiffer sprang through the door.

For a moment the janitor stood there, too. Then gathered himself.

"You got a cell phone, right?"

Dominic nodded, surfacing toward words.

"Call an ambulance, man," Jerry urged calmly. He knelt,

loosened Rausch's collar, hoisted him gently to a sitting position. "Find aspirin, if you can. I'll pray with him."

Dominic obeyed, the man's voice galvanizing him. He spun, bumped against a gaping Todd, who had followed him down and was standing behind him, and headed up the stairs with a last look back.

6.

ater, as memory collected, Dominic would recall the
look over his shoulder, Pfeiffer kneeling beside Roy
Rausch, hand on the Assemblyman's chest, speaking in
hushed, consolatory tongues as Todd Vitale stood above them
helplessly. On the phone to 911, Dominic ran into George
Castille, who sprinted downstairs as fast as seventy-year-old legs
could take him, bearing aspirin and encouragement. The theater
lay only blocks from a good hospital, and Dom was certain the
ambulance would arrive immediately, not taking into account
that it might be out on a run, that a number of things could add
up to delay.

When EMS arrived, twenty minutes later, they met Roy
Rausch walking up the stairs, straightening his tie, Jerry Jeff
Pfeiffer beside him, arm wrapped around Rausch's shoulders as
if they shared a bond of old and sacred friendship. A false alarm,
Jerry assured the med techs. A touch of indigestion, no more.

And though they would carry Roy Rausch to the hospital,
though they would give him blood tests and cardiograms and a
thorough working over, the drama had left the building. Few of
the audience beyond the Koenigs and Bucky Fuller even knew an

episode had taken place, and by the time Rausch was loaded into the ambulance, Fuller was inwardly grumbling that he would have to accompany the congressman to the hospital and miss the rest of the movie. Indeed, on arrival, the doctors would find the janitor's diagnosis was correct after all—that there was no evidence of heart attack or even an "episode", though George Castille asserted later that God only knew the whole business just about gave *him* one.

But Dominic Rackett knew what he had seen, and knew that Jerry Jeff Pfeiffer had laid on hands.

∞

They could not have been further apart, Todd Vitale and Jerry Jeff Pfeiffer. They had nothing in common until that moment at the *Caligari* preview.

Now Todd was all antennae and inquiry. Pfeiffer had risen into his line of sight, the conduit for some kind of healing grace—whether religious or magical or the product of pure chance, Todd found it hard to tell. He hovered near Pfeiffer into the late hours, eavesdropping as the janitor talked to EMS and the police and to George.

The story was always that Jesus had done it, that a surge of energy and of unsuppressed will had passed through his hands, through the agency of prayer. Todd was tempted to ask him if he believed that—*really* believed it—but he knew that Jerry would be offended and the conversation would stop. So he sat and listened as Jerry reflected on how he had walked with such mystery since he was old enough to remember. How signs and wonders had always been his companion, even unto now, when the times were at their worst, as everyone and everything was for sale.

You just look around you, he told Todd, waving away the cigarette that the young man offered him. Look at these films, for instance. You look at what they are about—these monsters and demonic creatures that might be out there and might be inside us, the films never come down one way or another, like it makes a difference where the evil settles in. And we're supposed to think, Jerry said, that if some director can show us that the monster is inside us, well, that's the first step in fixing things, in healing what ails us. But what that director really wants to do is show us a monster: he doesn't care what we make of it. Only what he makes *from* it. Because, Jerry said, it's not about the monsters as much as the money.

And how much different is it today, do you think? Our monsters are car crashes and full nakedness and pretty people dodging bullets at a different frame rates. Frame rate—did he have that right?

Todd nodded. Yes. Pretty much so.

There was this time, Jerry said, when his own people were baptizing folks at the river's edge down by Brandenburg. It was a country way of doing it—an old-school thing—but his family done it that way, and it wasn't like it was the only right way, but it was a good one.

He was ten and had already been baptized—by water and by the Holy Ghost—so he felt like this was old hat. He knew it was awful to think so, but that was what he was feeling, sitting there bare-footed on the river bank, the red clay pressing between his toes. And out in mid-current, out on the oily-black surface of the river, the water began to split and fork around something. A towhead, maybe, or somehow a branch lodged and stationary against the flow of the river. He should have suspected something then, he allowed: it was too deep out there for anything to hook or anchor or lodge.

He told Todd that he wanted to call attention to it. But more important things were happening near the banks. People were being born again, submerged in the water and cleansed and brought up new. It was trivial, the nature at mid-river, and for a moment he suspected it was a distraction, the Enemy's way of diverting his mind from folks being saved, from seeing the whole picture of redemption.

The world turned gray as he thought on these things. Perhaps a cloud passed over the sun, perhaps his eyes or thoughts clouded only. But then the air above the ripples began to fork and darken, and the crossbeam breasted the rushing water and the cross itself rose and hovered, black and huge and dagger-shaped at its cloudy base, like it had a single, powerful taproot that burrowed to the riverbed and below it into the heart of the world.

A cry rose up from the people on the banks surrounding. And for a moment, Todd, he had thought that others had seen the sign, that the wonder in mid-river was for all of them, but no, he looked around and nobody else seemed to notice. And no, he did not tell his father that evening, afraid he would be suspected or even punished for a vision, not so much because he seen it as because he was not sure it was real.

It was that kind of seeing, Jerry said, that took him below the surfaces of things. And he would of thought, Todd, that below the surface was where the truth lay, but it was like that strong dark rush of river out there north of Brandenburg, on the day he saw the cross hover over the water: something might have bent the current, might have hooked onto things as they floated past, but then something might have not. You might dive deep below the surface, down to the riverbed, and there you might find relics, or wreckage, or something solid and older than man-made. If you went deep enough, you might find a place to stand against the current. Or you might find something else.

Todd thought about this story as he drove home in the dark hours, back to his parents' house in the Highlands where he planned to sleep late into the morning. Jerry Jeff Pfeiffer had disturbed him, had set a huge undertow against his passage. Like many artistic young people, Todd was intently anti-religious, so the healing had undermined the way he liked to see things. He wanted to ask the obvious questions…

If you're a man of faith, how come you don't believe what you saw? If you're so anointed, why does it bring you grief?
He hated to think that he and Jerry Jeff Pfeiffer just might

be seeing the same world.

Instead, it was better to reside in the popular serious films of the here and now, Todd told himself. None of the silence of *Caligari*, its ambiguities and art house sets. Tonight give him the harsh, manic genius of Tarentino, whose world stopped at the edge of the screen, who made movies that were about movies, wild and brilliant and empty. It was the world in which Todd Vitale was most comfortable. Alone in his room, he kicked off his shoes, sprawled prone on the bed, and aimed his remote at a paused blu ray of *Inglourious Basterds*.

∞

Two healings in a weekend.

Dominic lay back on his cot and stared up at the ceiling. The article on Wegener's *Golem* needed to be finished by tomorrow morning, and here he was only halfway through, lost at what to say after a pretty listless plot summary.

The mended heart of Roy Rausch could be explained away by all the medical reasons, and T. Tommy's closed wounds by the simple rationale that the old drunk was probably lying in the first place. In the aftermath of Thursday night's preview, George had owned up to the staff that he had known Tommy back in the day. Claimed that the old bum had been a part of some disastrous Greek tragedy production over at the Central Park stage, had been a chorus leader in the play, and that you would be downright astonished at what an unreliable workforce winos tended to make. But whether or not Tommy was lying and whether or not Rausch's heart attack was a bad burrito, the weekend had shaken Dominic's science.

So now his week lay before him, blocked out with strange creatures and mysteries. Dominic wondered if some impulse in his paternal DNA had not dropped him in the midst of uncanny imaginings. His dad, after all, had written fiction about this shit.

He laughed and lit a cigarette stolen from George, who

was downstairs filling out insurance forms as Max did the evening inventory. These snatched moments of his own solitude were relished as much as the narcotic inhale of menthol and tobacco—he had claimed to quit smoking five years ago, but nobody ever does. For this had become paranormal territory, its strangeness spreading like ripples in an unsettled pond, from the working-class suburbs where his father had vanished to this spare apartment above the theater lobby, where Dominic sat on his bed now, in his lap his father's book—perhaps the one testimony to eternity that Gabriel Rackett had existed at all

What Dominic remembered about his father was sketchy now, fast becoming indistinguishable from what he imagined or invented. When he was only three years old, his mother had taken him off to Boston to be with the man that would be his new stepfather, and as far as he could remember, contact with his dad had been those sporadic, awkward weeks like the one in which they saw *The Last Crusade* or that darker holiday when, together like Henry Jones and his son Indy, they stood at the threshold of Trajan Bell's cellar as though it were the edge of some perilous subterranean adventure...

...which, beyond his expectations, it had turned out to be...

His father looking up at him. Dominic's last memory of the night, standing upon the landing, his feet shuffling through an army of small, pearlescent beads, as though an indifferent heaven had rained hail on the whole nocturnal enterprise, the rattling sound fading into silence along with the color of the light behind him, Gabriel vanishing into the shadow below, then nothing else for days.

Dominic remembered the intervening span of years, visits to what seemed like a new apartment every summer, though he knew it probably wasn't. Visits that were cut short by calls from his mother, by summonses back home. There had never been, at least to his knowledge, another woman. Gabriel had claimed that Dominic's mother had been enough for a lifetime, and the entanglement of irony and love in a comment like that was too intricate for a boy to unravel. But of all the things he would imagine in the years before the incident, he never thought his parents would reconcile.

Dominic tried to summon his father from distances. At seven, he switched his handedness, shifting his fork from right to left and throwing a baseball awkwardly because he had heard Gabriel was left-handed. He had thought that becoming a southpaw would declare some kind of genetic connection. His mother and stepfather had ignored it as a phase, until writing assignments in school had failed for illegibility. Then Dominic returned to his right-hand script, which never returned to the old Palmer clarity his Grandmother Bowers had spanked into him. To this day, though, he did everything else left-handed, as though a yearning for his father had permanently jumbled his hemispheres.

As the stepson (and, for a while, the subject) of a then-eminent Boston psychiatrist, Dominic wondered what was up with memory, with how it worked and what he had done to disrupt his recollections. He had read his own case history, knew that Mountolive had broken all kinds of ethical rules in counseling and writing about his own stepson, but Dominic was past most ethical concerns by now, or at least past getting outraged at injustices. He simply wanted the memories straight.

His father's manuscript, found in Grandma Mary's house after the vanishing, told a different story, or at least a different version of the story, leading right up to that Christmas night when the two of them bundled up and walked across the dark suburban street to the old house. It was a variation on the theme, in which Dominic took on the instigator's role, had urged his old man on the adventure. It was not the way he remembered it, but he was as far beyond blaming as he was beyond ethics now. Again, he just wanted the memories straight.

They all claimed—the papers, the police, his mother and stepfather—that Gabriel had left his son in the abandoned basement, had slipped out of the house and away for good. It was too simple and weird, that story. It didn't take into account what Dominic had seen in the house, and how the premises seemed to dilate as they passed through it, the hallways and the stairwell to the basement stretching in front of them, like one of those Hitchcock shots from *Vertigo*. It did not take in the cobwebs and the cabbage, the hard, smooth grains underfoot.

The two of them, father and son, had been headed for a place where senses didn't apply. It was like Dominic told Ben Mountolive later, forced into that long and irritating consultation in the aftermath of years. He wondered if it was like that in all those sensory deprivation experiments, where they put you in the Lilly Tank and after a while you start making things up, or having visions, or whatever you'd call it once you start seeing, hearing, and smelling things.

That description had haunted him after the consultation. After all, it was ten years after the fact, and his mother had demanded the sessions because he wasn't doing well, he was sliding to the edges of things. And of course the sessions were a search party into his soul, and he kept them both out—his mother and his wicked stepfather, like some strange version of a fairy tale family. But by that time he had read Gabriel's manuscript, he was primed with another back story.

His father's side of things. Which had not brought him back south, but just might be keeping him here so he could work some things out. For Dominic had come to wonder if his mother's accusation wasn't right after all.

If he wasn't, all said and done, just like his father.

∞

That night after the film, as the audience rose and filed out into the lobby, the screen again fluttered briefly, then went dark for the evening. And while the small crowd milled under the plaster death masks of Western artistry, some gathering a last bourbon for the road, all pretending to like the film more than some of them did, Caligari, Cesare, and Jane took shape in a small pocket of space between the screen and the wall behind the screen, invisible to the audience but gaining solidity and substance, as the Inside expanded around them and they began to move through it. Three fictions of light receding In, through a Holstenwall the camera had not bothered to film, they passed through geometric flames until the city gave way to camera and cable, and for a moment they became solid, almost fleshly, adopting street clothes of greyscale shadows. Then Caligari shed years, Cesare shed pallor, Jane her abstracting makeup, so that Krauss and Veidt and Dagover left the studio, instead of the characters they had played, slowly losing shape and definition as they traveled the dark corridor to the foot of the mountain.

There lay the jetsam of a hundred filmings. Two castles like sentinels framing a passage winding steeply through a necropolis littered with stone angels and monuments, both moated in a litter of gutted cars, Ferris wheels, capsized onion domes and turbans. All of it like a curiosity shop as the three figures caught cold fire, changing shape and names.

Now they were gray flames climbing through the foothills. Condensed thought, manifold illusion, passing around and through the headstones, they floated over foil and costume jewelry, papier-mâché and feathers. The country expanded around them. The others waited, blades of ashen light that dissolved and commingled, rising in a titanic column of speaking flame.

Well done, Maria proclaimed, rising almost oracular from the column. As usual, Marie echoed her, the low voice melodious under the pure coloratura. But the one they called Ombrade— meaty and saturnine, speaking from the heart of the heart of the fire—was not having it.

The first night, it cautioned. *He was in the balcony. He is not the one we want.*

Is and is not, the arriving flame argued. *He was there, but perhaps not as you imagine. Yes, by accident, but accident that falls into a greater plan. What escaped the screen must be tended to, rounded up, but better yet, must be made our instrument, our servant in a larger design*

Fair enough, Kapitan, Marie conceded. *. After all, he was unforeseen in the balcony. You remember what he was like—vulnerable, a screen of nerve and vision, permeable by light and intention. He is far too exposed. His life in the cemetery has opened a lane to the land of the dead.*

And the dead travel fast, agreed Ombrade.

But the gods are slow, dear, said Marie, her low flame entangling Ombrade's until the two of them blended in the enveloping grey light, and the set around them was outlined in painted mountains and tripods and dollies and the stumps of papier-mâché trees, their annual rings molded by a forgotten set design into small castles, the walls crenellated and the towers peaked with flame-like tendrils. Above them, stage lights rolled across imagined horizons, blue light for the moon and bald white light for the sun.

The gods are slow, and remember that I was there as well.

Yes you were there, another voice answered, at first from inside the wooden castle as though it were a genie trapped in a lamp. Then a cloud played over the little battlements, and a face emerged, conjured of spotlight and smoke. A uniformed young man, Totenkopf on his collar tab. *You were there, Marie,* he said. *But you are not the one to tell this story.*

The story that is underway now, he continued *And over the span of twenty-five years, I have summoned the boy as its principal actor.*

Why this one? asked Maria, her flame commingling with Marie's and Magdelein's, the three of them indistinguishable now, as close in substance as their names in sound and symmetry. Then separate again, the tendrils of dark fire forking and branching, recovering autonomy and balance. *Why this one over all of the possible others?*

Because this one looked in, the young man replied. *Because this one returned my gaze.*

7.

She walked after the Sunday matinee, just like she always did after the screenings.

Like she had done in Germany, like when she came stateside.

It was a way to unwind and gather traction. To get to the next step in a larger scheme of things.

The so-called scandal was in the air now. The expected call from the reporter. The outrage, genuine and manufactured, from the Flannery woman and from the Board. But the news had broken just in time. Any later and the furor might have dampened the series; any sooner, and there might not have been a series to begin with.

Leni Zauber crossed Broadway dutifully at the signal. Walked down Fourth Street past the small Catholic university, its origins not unlike the girls' school she thought she had attended in Danzig, though she might have imagined her stay there. Her walk took her past nursing homes and abandoned groceries. She crossed a notorious intersection the townspeople called Fourth and Fellini because of its almost cinematic strangeness, then followed the sidewalk down to the park and its geometrical outdoor theater, closed two years ago, after a disaster involving a riot at a dress rehearsal of *The Bacchae.*

Small-city America was the place things came to pass, she thought. Any smaller was too insular, any larger too devouring. When someone rose from the masses in a small city, it was the perfect balance of attention and ambition—a place you could be recognized without wanting to stay. Leni had intuited this, sensed it on her nerve endings, experienced it in Stuttgart, Genoa, Dublin. You could have vintage film festivals there—such cities were large enough for a passable crowd—and yet things that happened in such places slipped beneath the radar of the Berlins, the Romes, the Londons of the world, and took their own veiled or subterranean paths toward sudden, brilliant emergence, when the larger venues would ask, *Where did that come from?* before they seized on the enterprise, took credit for it, and brought it to global fame.

So Leni had gone through a list, a cluster of small American cities roughly the same size as Genoa or Dublin or Stuttgart. Milwaukee was too educated, Portland too hip, and Las Vegas too rich and spotlighted. An accidental glance at theater reviews had uncovered the name of the Shangri-La in yet another city, and she thought of how apt that was, of the Younghusbands, Roerichs and Schäfers who had crossed a continent in search of that city in the Himalayas, and thought about her own long and often mountainous journey, about the figuring of Tibet in the imagined and remembered history of her youth.

It seemed only fitting that her path would lead to another Shangri-La, especially when she discovered that the Mary Conroy Lull, who had performed at this ramshackle amphitheater she approached now in the warm midsummer twilight, was the Mary Conrad she had known from Galway over seventy years before. Opportunistically, Leni had contacted last spring,

Mary had been astonished that Leni was still alive.

Leni assured her that the difference between their ages had been less than she could possibly have imagined.

Back then Mary was but a child, and her people were still

listening to the Blueshirts and Eoin O'Duffy. It was a time when a little girl might find a heroine in a young film actress from the Continent. The girl had begged Leni to take her to Germany, her heart set on Berlin, Neubabelsberg Studios, and *becoming the next Marlene Dietrich.*

Dietrich, who had left for the States already, an opponent of the Reich.

To this day, whenever Leni saw *The Prime of Miss Jean Brodie,* Maggie Smith prissing as the misguided and misguiding teacher, she thought of Mary McGregor, the poor stupid schoolgirl in the film. Inspired by Miss Brodie's rapturous rhetoric, Mary McGregor had trooped off to Spain, to join her brother fighting for Franco, only to be killed after discovering he had joined the other side. The world was vexed and at odds, back then: whenever Leni thought of Mary McGregor, she thought of the other Mary—Celtic and idealistic and dim in Galway. She had saved the girl's life, and Mary Conway had owed her a life in return.

Leni knew when she passed York Street and the library that she was being followed. He tailed her at a safe distance, his presence tangible enough that she knew she had not imagined him out of the city's humid inertia and diesel fumes. For a while he flitted between buildings, close to the walls, like Cesare the somnambulist, but only half a block assured her he was not dangerous, was if anything leery of her and of being recognized.

It was Todd Vitale. She had seen that coming from a safe distance as well. The fascination at Shangri-La, the blue eyes glaring right through her as though he was reading a kind of translucency in her face. For a while she had been concerned, a little menaced, but when she saw that the others did not take him seriously, at least not that much, she figured he was harmless to her as well.

Leni slowed down at Fourth and Fellini, waited for him as a southbound bus passed, its doors hissing open for her before the driver realized she was walking, *a silly old woman on a dodgy street, didn't she see that weird boy following her, best slow down just in case…*

    Ah, but she knows he's there. They know each other, not that there would be time if they didn't. Next stop is Ormsby.

∞

She turned and stared him down in the intervening block. Watched him slip behind an abandoned bank building and knew he didn't want to meet her, certainly didn't want to talk. She figured their time would come, figured he might even prove instrumental in what she had in mind as the series of films made its way through the month.

For right now, though, the other boy was far more interesting. The Eurasian, the grandson of Mary Conroy. The grandson was handsome, taller than many of his racial mixture. His appearance had bothered her at first, but she decided that these days it just might be more asset than liability. After all, good looks were everything in America, like they were on screen, and the young man did have a certain Irish charm like some of the old actors—Crosby, Kelly, O'Toole, Richard Harris—but from what she could see he was dreaming and wandering it away. Once you reached a certain age, there was a charm that generally receded from you, starting to fade in your mid-thirties, usually vanishing by forty-five or fifty and unrecognizable after that, like film deteriorating into rusty powder, or like that acrid vinegar smell of the later safety stock that replaced the dangerous, volatile nitrate film of her youth

Preservation was crucial, she thought, crossing to the park's edge and taking a sidewalk toward the amphitheater, its abstract, jagged outline brown through the skeletal webbing of trees. This was the stage where Castille had his undoing, she thought with a kind of harsh delight, a *schadenfreude* at the old invert's staged humiliation.

Castille's *Hamlet* was intended to leave his stamp on a city he obviously both loved and hated. Instead, owing to the cracked and pretentious set design of mirrors, not to mention his own cracked and pretentious acting, George Castille had given a performance that Wade Abner, with whom he had been feuding for years, had described in print as "histrionic, from its arm-waving Danish Prince down to the funhouse looking glass in which he seemed to have misplaced himself and his dignity."

Leni Zauber settled among the tiered wooden benches and wrapped her shawl more tightly around her shoulders, looking her age briefly before recovering, gathering vigor and substance out of the cooler breezes of approaching night. The stage was like something out of *Caligari*, its jagged chaos spread across a house of litter-strewn gravel, and she was glad she had worked in studios, where this kind of desolation was intentional, no accident of nature and neglect. She preferred the arranged disorder of the film sets, the angular streets of Holstenwall in the film she had just seen, the more rounded and cushioned set of Jane's chamber, womblike and inviting down to the rose tinting of the frames where the actress sat and swooned.

That actress had been Lil Dagover, of course. In the last screening, Leni had seen Dagover take on new life as *Caligari's* Jane, almost as though new forces traveled through the film stock onto the screen. Leni had seen the story a hundred times before, but this time she noticed a moment when the light shimmered around Jane's head, when the actress seemed to turn from the action on the screen and look straight at her. It was then Leni knew it was working, that the *aweysha* and Eastern ventures of the years between the wars had paid off. Their eyes met, Dagover's magnified by the huge Shangri-La screen, Zauber's by the scholarly round-framed glasses she wore to watch films, and at that instant an understanding passed between them.

There was no telling what the screen image, the Lil Dagover vitalized by light and attention, made of the older woman seated in the audience. But Leni Zauber looked into the screen, to where the light pooled like sun behind glass. She saw Lil Dagover move through shapes on screen, transform, almost solidify. And now, a mile from the Shangri-La and in the open-aired park theater, *Caligari's* Holstenwall took shape on the stage, the rusted angularity of the sets draining of color, as twilight blanched its ruddy colors completely into grayscale.

Now Leni braced herself against the bench, rising, ascending the stage, embracing the air's torpor. Suddenly many Lil Dagovers peopled the theater, passed through the old scholar, revitalizing her, dwelling in her bones and charging them with suppleness and life. Not just the heroine of *Caligari,* though Leni began there, slipping first into that role, back arched and hand cupped like sweet beleaguered Jane listening for inaudible dangers, dreading the sleepwalking Cesare. And now Leni narrowed her eyes as all the Lil Dagovers ascended the stage— serene, even regal older women, no longer the nervous girl on Expressionist streets.

Like a shot back-and-forth of filmed dialogue, Leni Zauber saw herself seated in the late summer dusk, then these women— every role that Dagover had played, from Jane in *Caligari* to Helene in *Vienna Woods* sixty years later—perched in the alcoves and the balconies of the set, in the sloping amphitheater seats, park promenade behind them. The pillars and stone lions bent toward Leni, toward the curtains of a theater interior, one she recognized from a long-ago Vienna.

Slowly, the illumined ghosts faded from sight, and Leni sat on the balcony stairs in an elegant baroque manteau. Then at mid-stage in an even more sumptuous imperial gown, then a sleek twenties knee-length skirt and tunic top, cameras and lights flickering in and out of view from the promenade and the smell of Marlboros, "mild as May" in the close, dry studio air.

All of these were glimpses of a life Leni had heard about, that her own life had brushed against now and then during Lil Dagover's long span of years. Leni had not expected it to be like this, these brief illumined flickers of history—studio, candle-lit dining room, theater, the dining room again, a Hollywood backlot, the dining room again, Harold Lloyd's location ranch, a cobblestoned street at Neubabelsberg.

Then a dining room, with its decorative Swiss cembra pine

paneling, resolved from the dark sienna of the sets. The host seated across from her, back to the famous window and the view of the Untersberg Mountains. He had wanted her attendance and attention, like the impresario he was, maintaining that, *for the majority of our guests, the constraint imposed by protocol is a genuine martyrdom. Wouldn't it be better to offer them the company of some pretty women who speak their language fluently? In Berlin, of all cities, we have the luck to number amongst our actresses women like Lili Dagover, Olga Tschechowa and Tiana Lemnitz.*

She had accepted because what else could she do, and dinner was at eight. While this was the main meal, it was as simple as one could imagine. Vegetable stew, followed by stewed fruit as dessert. This the host topped with a single glass of beer, all the while eating rapidly, mechanically. In the course of a few minutes he was finished, but the entire meal lasted two hours, the other guests allowed to dine leisurely as the host held forth.

He wasn't one for chitchat, Leni remembered, or remembered hearing. Or was just discovering, because the vision stabilized, and the scene wrested itself from her imagination and took shape as though she watched it on film, knowing the outcome, the cast, but surprised by the nuance of movement as the dinner unfolded through Lil Dagover's eyes: a POV shot, subjective camera. When Lil (or Leni?) or Goebbels talked, the host sat turned to his own thoughts, seemingly without listening to the conversation around him. However, he followed the dialogue vaguely, listening as he listened to the murmur of expectant crowds or a Wagner overture, letting the fluid sound stimulate his thoughts and relax him. He talked in a mellow baritone, without that raucous, unpleasant stridency of his public speeches.

They had just screened *Schatten* again. *Warning Shadows.* The Arthur Robison film, silent and almost twenty years old, where Alexander Granach, the "shadowplayer," kidnaps the shades of aristocratic guests at a dinner party and makes them act out their own masked desires, in a story filled with violence, adultery, and intrigue.

It was pure Freud, Lil knew. Knew better than to bring

up the name in this company, because Goebbels was already on about *Granach the Jew,* how even the aristocracy *rests on compulsion,* and the difference *is only whether the compulsion is a blessing or a curse for the community.* The host listened to the Reich Minister's rhetoric, disapproval growing for a film he had chosen for his guests.

Let the business men weep, said the host at last. *It's part of their trade. I've never met an industrialist without observing how he puts on a careworn expression. Yet it's not difficult to convince each one of them that he has regularly improved his position. One always sees them panting as if they were on the point of giving up their last gasp! Despite all the taxes, there's a lot of money left. Even the average man doesn't succeed in spending what he earns. He spends more money on cinemas, theaters and concerts than he used to, and he saves money into the bargain. One can't deprive people of distractions; they need them, and that's why we cannot reduce the activity of the theaters and studios. The best relaxation is that provided by the theater and the cinema.*

He looked at her, or through her. Watery blue eyes, red-rimmed. Leni knew—though perhaps the Lil Dagover whose role she played did not—that the mistakes had begun, that the world was going wrong on the Russian steppes. But that night he was in his element.

He lifted his fork to proclaim. Remembered where he was, and spoke it quietly.

From time immemorial the Jews have always succeeded in insinuating themselves into positions from which it was possible to influence public opinion; they hold, for example, many key positions both in the press and in the cinema industry. Those who behold them are infused with a projected spirit. But the Jews are not content to exercise a direct, open influence; they know that they will attain their ends more expeditiously if they bring their influence to bear through the so-called Agencies and by other devious methods.

Insinuate. Influence. Like shadows behind the unwitting players. Like *aweysha,* Leni thought, and Lil thought she followed his reasoning. And though in the nights and years that followed, as he lost his grip and the world dissolved, she would remember that dinner.

He talked to and through his guests, and Leni Zauber, seated on a stage nearly five thousand miles and seventy years away, saw through the artifice in this talk as well, though now, from the vantage of decades, she could not tell whether his unmasking was taking place in her eyes or those of Lil Dagover. But it did not matter. Something dark within her was summoned by something darker still, and she could see that all of it was entirely human. Feasible.

Occupational hazard, Leni told herself. Time would come to look this head-on, and stare down the outmoded parts. The old way would no longer work. Unsustainable when everyone was watching. Time to climb the mountain slope toward the light.

The evening air buckled and steamed above the sets. She had been sitting longer than she supposed.

Someone cleared his voice in the row behind her.

"Mr. Vitale," she said without turning. "I saw you over by the college."

A silence, and briefly, even momentarily, the sharp stitch of fear that she might have been mistaken, might have misread. But it was Todd Vitale, after all. Anyone's guess whether he had been sitting there long, had slipped up during her reverie, or whether he had condensed out of the moist winter air. Her senses were too jostled to determine.

"Dr. Zauber," he said quietly. "It's almost dark. This is no place for a lady after sunset."

"How kind of you, *liebchen*, but an old woman such as I no longer draws those attractions."

She knew it would unsettle him. That what she implied was against his schooling, that he had been taught to distinguish sex and assault when it came to old women wandering a dodgy park. And indeed he gave her the slogans, the young man's bookish take on violence against women, which showed her he was tamed in thought.

She rose slowly from the bench. As she hoped, he offered his arm.

"And how long have you been sitting here? Hovering protectively like my guardian angel?"

She pronounced *angel* with the hard "g" and watched his liquid blue eyes soften.

"Not long enough to be stalking you, Dr. Zauber," he replied, his joking layered with timidity. She waved it away, leaned on his arm to embolden him, and asked if he truly thought she was in danger, if he had seen anything in his short vigil...

"Nothing, actually. A drunk asleep by the tennis courts. And Dom Rackett walking west down Park." He laughed at his own accidental pun. "Tennis and Racketts. Go figure."

She laughed as well, and not by accident at all. At twenty, the boy was as nervous and star-struck as the six-year-old Mary Conroy. It was a passion Leni felt she could use, though Todd passed under her notice then and later.

For the time being, his was a chivalrous arm on which she rested. He called her a cab from one of those intricate phones that they all carried, and he stood with her by the curb until the cab arrived, opening the door for her, wishing her *guten Abend* in the worst accented German she could imagine. It was almost flirtatious, though such a prospect was impossible, and Leni would have had no interest even if it was.

On her way home she marveled at his naïveté, at the naïveté of all these cheerful Americans. She looked over her shoulder as the driver turned onto her street, vaguely persuaded that something was following her, but completely unable to position it in her preoccupied and distracted train of thought.

∞

He saw her back to the theater, and, the next morning before work, he drove to the southernmost part of the county and spent an hour at the gun range.

It was not what people thought. Not at all. Let one guy not run with the crowd, and let him like the release and concentration of shooting a pistol, and people jumped to all kinds of crazy conclusions.

Todd Vitale was not a far-right wingnut. He thought different from his sister, from Alex, from Castille and Bulwer and all the bunch that affirmed their own agreement when it came to the theater and the bookstore and the whole independent artsy bunch in town. He figured that Dominic would be more of the same.

And yet Todd voted against the Republicans as much as any of them, hated the whole one-percent America as much as the most leftwing one of the group. And yet they wanted him to march in time. Felt that anyone who picked up a gun was one step away from the Tea Party.

It was why he kept these visits to himself. Like Ellie's weed and Alex's music, like Bulwer's books and the new guy's *om mani padme hum,* it was his way of winding down. He liked the slow pressure on the trigger finger, the holding of breath and following the imagined arc from the barrel to the target, and so what if they shaped them to the human silhouette like a shadow on a screen, it was the range's doing and he simply shot to the spot, intending neither malice nor harm, but simply protection, security, a way of warding those he cared about.

He thought of Ellie and her questionable choices. Too much cannabis and beauty. She needed someone to mind her, to keep her from harm. From men like that grad student her freshman year, or worse like that bastard Copass. Or maybe like Alex, it was too soon to tell. Or like Rackett, who seemed used to having things fall into his lap.

And Professor Zauber. He needed to stand on guard for her. It was hard to believe she was over seventy, but even if she didn't look it she would still be physically frail, in need of protection and mindfulness. After all, she had been friendly to him. Almost motherly or grandmotherly. She couldn't say anything, of course, but Todd was certain she regretted her choice of Dominic to write the articles, or perhaps the board had insisted on him, who could tell?

He loaded the gun and aimed at the target. He was told his grip was too tight on the pistol, that he still pulled the trigger instead of a steady, mindful squeeze, so he took those things into account and the first shot struck the target to the right of the shadowy head and the second closer and the third struck home.

He lowered the gun, fully mindful of all the safety lessons he had received, intent on playing by the rules, observing the regulations to the letter. It worked here, because he had begun to gather respect from the other shooters, the occasional nod, the passing *howdy*. And when Dr. Zauber saw how he played by the rules, no doubt she would rearrange things, would talk to someone. She would need someone to have her back, because the news about this Florian Geist was about to hit the press, and he had the arts community figured in this town, a bunch of self-righteous rich people who would comfortably rail against people like Geist while not doing jack shit to keep them out of political power, where they could do greater harm than they did in films.

He lifted the pistol and the world condensed to the space between his hand and the target. There was something wrong in his technique, he was still sure, but practice and focus and time solved everything, didn't they?

Five more shots, three of them squarely in the heart's inner circles on the target, the other two ranging farther wide. Not bad: he had kept on task. He hoped he could learn to repeat it.

Film Series Controversy at Shangri-La Theater

Historic venue hosts Weimar, "Nazi" film

As part of a Silent Film Month at Louisville's Shangri-La Theater, a rarity of early German cinema will debut in a restored version here in the city. Director Florian Geist's 1936 *Walpurgisnacht,* a silent movie made years after the industry switched to the "talkies", was unusual on a number of counts: it employed a cast and crew of unknowns; though it was produced by UFA Films, the principal German studio, unlike so many of their productions, it was shot in Prague rather than at the Babelsburg Studios outside of Berlin; it was presumed lost until recently, when a damaged print surfaced in Austria and was restored in Bologna by noted film scholar Dr. Leni Zauber.

And it has caused furor and controversy because of its director, a known member of Adolf Hitler's SS.

According to Dr. Zauber, Florian Geist (1900?-1945) was a little-known but influential figure in pre-World War II German films. "He was involved in a number of the films we are showing at the Haunted Castle Film Festival, though his contributions are largely uncredited. His association with the SS is based on circumstantial evidence, but even if he was a member of that unfortunate unit, his role was minor and inconsequential."

Not according to a number of community activists, who see the showing of the film as "culturally insensitive—a slap in the face of Louisville's proud Jewish community and conscientious citizens of all races, colors, and creeds." So it is characterized by Citizens for Justice Chairperson Molly Flannery, whose organization registered a formal complaint with the theater's board of directors and with ChemCon, the local corporation that is noted for sponsoring this and other "vintage film" events through the Shangri-La.

When reached for comment former Congressman Roy Rausch, a member of the ChemCon advisory committee and head of the Theater Board, insisted that the controversy was "more smoke than fire, as they say. The film is seventy to eighty years old. And anybody who knows me knows that my reading about the history of the Nazis is the main thing that made me fear big government as I was growing up. It was a reprehensible time in history, but a film by one of the participants is like a film in the 60s made by a Hollywood Communist, or for that matter, by one of today's left-wing producers or directors. They all have First Amendment rights, and after all, it's just a film, isn't it?"

A spokesman for Representative Rausch, W. Buckminster Trabue, later clarified that First Amendment rights "certainly apply only to American citizens and not to dead Storm Troopers. The Congressman knows the law, but he also believes that the film is interesting as history. We come to the Shangri-La so that we will not repeat the past mistakes of others."

∞

Tommy folded the article and slipped it under his head, then removed it at once, vaguely superstitious that the scandal of Florian Geist—the memories of Nazis and discord—might creep through the newsprint and settle in his sleep. Cautiously he slid the morning edition of the *Courier* down the park bench until it nestled under the ragged bottom of his trousers.

Though the wounds were gone—effaced, he believed, by Dr. Caligari's therapy in the balcony of the Shangri-La—Tommy still felt the sting implicit, subliminal, slated to return with new heat and pain at some unforeseen time. Like shingles, or more like a memory pushed into obscurity.

The world had a knack for returning to nettle you. Of those returns he was a veteran. And the Shangri-La had been a kind of field hospital last Thursday night, a dressing station after the fact. There the two boys—the one who had talked to him and the other, both foreign and familiar, who had gone to get him coffee—both tended to his spirit in the lobby and had left him restored and lifted.

Why had he told his story to one and teetered at the edge of tears before the other? Tommy pondered these questions as he watched the weathered, geometric stage of the park amphitheater. He saw the old woman approach, saw her joined by the strange boy from the movie house. For some reason he connected the woman to the Shangri-La as well, but he would be switched as to why that was. Perhaps it was simply fancy, a Richards Wild Irish dream, but the notion brushed against him that theaters everywhere, stage or screen or what have you, connected behind the curtain in a vast labyrinth of illusion. After all, it could happen, he told himself, always buying into film fantasies where a character steps out of the movie or the audience steps in. Oh yes, a cliché that even a drunk was inclined to reject, but like most clichés, it just might cover a truth we no longer knew. Because the Shangri-La was following him. He was seeing Holstenwall everywhere, and the characters on the screen were becoming, slowly, the inmates in his own asylum.

Tommy lay back, drowsed, awaited the oncoming night. He needed to be mindful: after sunset, a man of his station always had to be vigilant and wary. He tilted toward restless sleep, descended toward a restful darkness until, at the bottom of his downward path, he looked up toward wakefulness and light. He thought he saw the boys there, the ones who had tended him kindly in the lobby. For a moment their faces hovered among a great cloud of witnesses: alabaster Shakespeares and Keatons, Homers and Pickfords. And a wistful regret rushed over him: he wished them all well, the bards and buskers, blind poets and muted clowns.

Especially the one who, from the depths of a memory damaged by wine and weather, stood on a landing above him, part of the pantheon, covered in winter light.

8.

They had declared a truce by the time *The Golem* showed at the Shangri-La.

But at first it was touch and go. After the film's second showing—the matinee on Saturday afternoon--Max and Dominic had trudged out together into a gray and humid August evening, bound for the haven of Dry Salvages. Submerged resentments boiled on the surface of their conversation.

It started with the business of Florian Geist. Max believed it was time to call in the dogs and piss on the fire: the series was over and done with, stamped with its own dismay and shame by Nazi associations. "For God's sake, Dominic!" he maintained, his pale, soft hands virtuously slicing the air with his passion. "How could Citizens for Justice or the ADL *not* be right on this one? Geist was a fuckin' Nazi—game, set match."

Dominic listened calmly. Nodded, though Max could see he was preparing to disagree. There was a maddening calm about the dude, as though he leaned with comfort against a decade's advantage of living and passing through drama. Dominic looked like a kid, but thought like an adult—or so Max assumed, out of his irritation and jealousy.

"I dunno, Max," Dominic said at last. "People like Ezra Pound and Yeats ended up on the wrong side of the issues. Yeats died before it became a problem, but Pound was even arrested for broadcasting for Mussolini. Went to jail, to an asylum. Still ended up revered as the big gun of Modernism."

Max resented the lecture instantly. He gathered himself as the two of them passed the cemetery, figured if Dominic could be civil, so could he. But it felt as though a pack of resentful ghosts lurked behind the curtains, itching to burst forth and haunt the place. He knew the two of them had to settle this Ellie business, but the maddening part was that he didn't know Dominic's intentions, whether he was even interested in her.

So instead, he made a point or two about art and morality—good points, he thought, ones he had heard in school. Dominic seemed to brush them away. He claimed that the jury was still out. That they'd have to see *Walpurgisnacht* to know what to make of Geist. Or of Leni Zauber and the series, for that matter.

It was almost impossible to argue with that. So there on the sidewalk, the line of boutiques and cafes becoming a little shabbier as they walked away from town, the two struck a silent armistice, and the conversation shifted to the second film.

Dominic made Max laugh with how he had Leni's accent down. And Max's feathers smoothed as he looked forward to visiting the bookstore, to John Bulwer's cool, shifty ironies, the hip crowd, the shelves of twentieth-century fiction, and the jazz vinyl. Miles and Coltrane, of course, but others like Yusef Lateef, Charlie Mingus, Anthony Braxton.

Despite himself, Max had liked Dominic's new article on *The Golem*. He was intrigued by the missing father angle, and even more by the idea Dom called his "Frankenstein concept." As a peace offering, he asked about it as the two of them approached the notorious corner of Fourth and Fellini, the epicenter of the city's extensive chaos magic.

A thoroughgoing skeptic, Max was nonetheless sentient to ambiances. He had passed the intersection once on his bicycle, seen a pair of missionaries from Heart Ministries Outreach saving a transvestite in front of a CVS pharmacy—a convergence of everything about the neighborhood and much of the prevailing strangeness of the city. It seemed the right place to hear tell of monsters, but when Dominic began with something about Tibetan Buddhism, it immediately killed the buzz.

Dominic's reputation for a kind of rock star's undigested Eastern religion had preceded him. They said he couldn't help himself once he was onto the subject, that he was quiet about it until you coaxed him into talking, but then his thoughts lurched forward untrammeled, and so he was off to explain whatever concept is was, knowing that as he did it, he was probably lecturing again.

It was even more irritating to Max because of Ellie. He could tell that she was allured by Dominic's Asian ancestry, caught a whiff of the exotic in the new arrival, something that brought him closer to the nirvana imagined in her suburban white-girl dreams.

"The tulpa," Dominic began, is kind of like the golem or Frankenstein's creature…"

"Then let's talk about the golem and Frankenstein," Max said, a little too quickly.

"Frankenstein's *creature*," Dominic corrected, then retraced his steps. "Victor Frankenstein creates his Adam, then leaves the creature on his own. I don't think he ever takes into account that his creation will think for itself. Rabbi Löw is supposedly wise and well-meaning, and Frankenstein is all scientifically brilliant and unscrupulous. But if you look at the two of them together, they end up doing the same thing. They let loose of the reins. All that invention and creation, only to let go of their offspring.

"But here's the thing, Max," Dominic continued. "There are always cases, like the birth of some babies, in which the thing is born without forethought, almost by accident. Those are dangerous. The ones the creator makes without much thought. We see it every day in our schools and on our streets. But worse still are the ones that are made, then just let drop. So even if some are experienced in the matter, like Rabbi Löw in *The Golem*, or simply gifted and reckless like Victor Frankenstein, it's not so much creation as abandonment that comes back to haunt them. The yearning that the creature has for the source of his making. Just like all hearts incline to God."

Max nodded. Tried to appear attentive as Dominic sought to reel him in.

"Like how a child inclines to his father. Like you'd feel if your father left you."

Max fumbled in his jacket pocket, produced a cigarette pack. "My old man's at the military base. A bird colonel. Enough of an asshole to rise up the echelon, not smart enough to be a general."

Dominic accepted an offered smoke. "You're lucky."

"Nah. We don't talk."

"My dad and I don't either," Dominic said. "Hard to, when he's been missing for twenty years."

The two turned left onto Ormsby toward that part of the street that was obscured—a small half-block dogleg off of First Street, where the sounds of the city hushed, and you could believe that a century had not passed, that these houses were still almost as new as the "photoplays" being screened at the Shangri-La, or the Horizon, as they called it back in the day.

Max loved this little square of houses. Loved knowing where he was headed, and that Dominic had to follow him through the alley.

"So, this tulpa you were talking about?"

"For another time, Max," Dominic said. "We're almost there."

The Golem: How He Came into the World (1920)

This is one of the early achievements of the great silent film actor and director, Paul Wegener, and considered by many to be his greatest work. Of the three films Wegener did that related to the ancient Jewish legend of the golem, this is the only one to survive. The 1915 version, *The Golem* (Galeen and Wegener, 1915), a tale about a golem's modern day re-animation, and the satire *The Golem and the Dancing Girl* (Gliese and Wegener, 1917), are both considered lost.

This one is set in Prague in the sixteenth century. Emperor Rudolf II (Otto Gebühr) has ordered the Jewish community to be expelled from the city. In order to protect his people, Rabbi Loew (Albert Steinrück) magically animates a clay figure: the golem (played by Wegener himself). The animation employs some of the most inventive special effects of the time: remember that Wegener had far less technology at his call than do the film directors of today, so he was forced to improvise, to invent, and to trust in the imaginations of his viewers to a degree that a 21st century audience can hardly imagine. The famous conjuring scenes were a triumph of early 20th century set design and engineering. The stage was built on scaffolding, and Wegener lit fires beneath it to create a smoky, eerie under-lighting (crew members under stage worked in gas masks). When the summoned demon floats across the stage, it is a creature made in the editing room from three superimposed negatives. And in a scene that is hard to believe possible even to this day, the crew replaces the clay statue (pre-animation golem) with Paul Wegener (as the animated creature) literally while the camera is running.

The story, on the other hand, is fairly familiar. The golem, who possesses enormous physical strength, is a forerunner of perhaps the most famous of film monsters, the iconic creature played by Boris Karloff in the Frankenstein films produced almost two decades later. And Wegener's golem starts out much like the famous Karloff character: hovering between the animate and inanimate, the human and the monstrous, the golem yearns to make contact with the people of Prague.

In one scene, he accepts a flower from the young, lovely Greta Schröder (uncredited in this film, but soon to be the beleaguered heroine of F.W. Murnau's Nosferatu and, after that, possibly even more beleaguered as Wegener's fourth wife). Perhaps the golem yearns for romance as well, for the Rabbi's lusty daughter (played by Wegener's third—and sixth!—wife, the raw-boned Weimar sex symbol Lyda Salmonova)? Meanwhile the people around him seem taken up with trivial, scheming, and petty concerns.

At Rabbi Loew's audience with Rudolf II, the golem saves the emperor's life as a roof collapses. He is the good guy for now, holding up the roof of the palace and preventing even greater catastrophe.

In gratitude the emperor lets the Jewish community remain in the city, though of course they remain in a ghetto. Only now do we discover the double edge in the golem's making: that the stars that had to be exactly right in order to bring him to life will change, become malign, and cause him to become increasingly violent. Alarmed at the creature's dangerousness, Rabbi Loew deactivates the golem.

Unfortunately, unrequited love steps in to cause all kinds of problems. The Rabbi's assistant Famulus, in love with his employer's daughter Miriam, reanimates the golem in order to wreak vengeance on a rival. The golem now becomes a rampaging monster for real, and the conclusion to this tale is... well, you will just have to see.

So when the golem acts, does he act for the one who made him? For others? Does he, eventually, act out his own will? Critics have a number of interpretations, but the one that unsettles this writer the most is the possibility that the creature acts upon the darker, more suppressed desires of those who control him.

Speaking of darkness, It is nearly impossible to watch a 1920 film set in the Prague ghetto—even if the ghetto has been exaggerated and fantasized by Wegener's art director, Hans Poelzig—without thinking of the horrors that would befall Europe's Jews within the next two decades. And the verdict is still out whether the film helped stoke the flames of holocaust. Certainly part of the film's great uneasiness lies in its suggestion of a completely alien presence within the modern city, the foreign in the midst of us, and perhaps even the foreign within ourselves.

--Dominic Rackett

∞

Max had always thought a bookstore was safe haven. Not in the sense that people usually sentimentalized them—all the tired expressions about "worlds of wonder" or "all the knowledge between covers".

Dominic had escaped into bookstores, too. Had worked as a clerk in what Max's bird colonel dad had called "slacker heavens"—in a small bookstore in Vermont, and now at Salvages—and it was on premises like these, by different paths and histories, that both Max and his precariously new friend had grown to believe that almost better than doing something was reading about doing something.

Because that was the thing about readers these days, the Colonel had told him. There had been an age in which there were a few who wrangled with a book, who opened its intentions like a mystery, read its codes and veiled directions, and learned by the last page the gifts of strenuous travel. It was strange and fitting that an army man would beat two would-be sages in enlightenment, would come to the heart of the issue: that they read like boys rather than the men they wanted to be.

Nevertheless, it was a thing they had in common, recognized in their recesses and better than not reading at all, at least at the level they were doing it. And Max wanted to like Dominic Rackett. They had other things in common, as well, and maybe almost better than liking someone was wanting to like someone. But Dom had interloped the Peaceable Kingdom: he was a know-it-all—what was all this bullshit about tulpas anyway?—and he was way too old for Ellie Vitale. Seeing him come to work at Salvages was another small defeat, because who was to say but that Dom would take over here as well, use that Sino-Irish charm to win over John Bulwer and make this a place in his johnny-come-lately orbit.

But not yet. Max figured that Salvages was still his by squatters' rights. And if Dominic pissed away the job—as his history seemed to indicate he might just do—then the haven reverted to the one who saw it first. It was, after all, a rule in the social ramble.

Bulwer sat behind a paper-cluttered desk, a 1970s-style stereo playing some subtle jazz Max wished he knew.

"Back from the theater, boys?" John teased. "When you bringing the girl by?" Saw the subject was a bit delicate, and backed away.

"So how's the series going, fellas? *The Golem* a box office hit again?"

Max had always called John's humor *sarcasm,* though he had been corrected a number of times to see it as *only irony.* Todd hated the old man cordially: on one occasion he had followed Max to Salvages, where John had teased him a little about his tattoo, telling poor Todd that from the Chinese he had studied with Arthur Waley and Willis Barnstone, that the character Todd's tattoo artist had sworn meant *resolute strength* meant *dumbass* instead. It had Todd going for a nightmarish, panic-stricken half-minute, had him swearing vengeance against all body art. Then Bulwer had assured him that, no, it probably meant exactly what the man told him. He confessed that his own Chinese was but a random phrase or two which had come from reading Luo Guanzhong, another name Max had not known, but, in search of approval, nodded as though he had.

So the two of them—Max and Bulwer—talked about *The Golem,* while Dominic straightened the high shelves of the Salvages back room, where books tilted and towered like mountains over the wanderer. Amid the talk of Paul Wegener's genius (Bulwer) and the cool fire near the film's end (Max), the two heard exclamations from Dom as he roamed from aisle to aisle discovering things.

The conversation passed to the incident with T. Tommy Briscoe. Max had dismissed the old vagrant's claim that he'd been shot under the book store until Bulwer assured him that, indeed, he had shot a vagrant, peppered him with rock salt. He confessed that, given it all to do over again, he would not have shot at the intruder, especially over copper, but that the break-in had just unsettled his natural *ahinsa*, that he hoped the man was well.

Dominic emerged from the shelves then, delightedly holding a pair of tattered paperbacks. Two of the *Dragonlance* novels he had read, apparently, in his teens, and which Bulwer gave him readily, confiding that copies of the series came in and out of Salvages like a lending library. With a faint tremor of embarrassment Max recalled that he had been offered a copy of Gabriel Rackett's novel and had intentionally forgotten it on the counter. It was too late to ask after it, so he smiled and tried to join into the goodwill that followed.

∞

That night, *The Golem* showed to a good-sized audience, minus the celebrity and hoopla.

Todd and Max were the ushers, for Castile had decided to use them in a time-honored but now unaccustomed duty. Flashlights guided the latecomers to their seats, and it was all '20s and '30s elegance, or something still done perhaps in the larger cities, though here the audience usually trailed into seats lugging popcorn and oversized drinks.

Todd liked the ushering, had made a joke that he and Max were "The House of Usher"—something Max didn't get. He was sulking a little as he waited at the top of the tiered seats, following the opening of the film abstractly. With the aid of his assistant Famulus, Rabbi Loew prepared to create the golem in a shadowy study that looked like the sets of *Caligari*, only less edged and more crumbling.

Figuring the film was underway, at least enough that he could sit and watch, Todd slid into the back row and watched. He had read Dominic's essay and thought little of it. Instead, he was drawn to the romance between Miriam and a rather feminine Sir Florian—and yes, he wondered at the man's name, given last week's news article. But for the most part, he watched the unfortunate Famulus, mooning outside Miriam's door as the girl carried on with her lover.

Cowboy Copass. He hated to think of the Cowboy.

Seven or eight years older than the twins, a high school basketball star that had fallen on hard times at the university an hour down the road, Copass returned to the city with that strange tarnish on celebrity that still showed the celebrity underneath. He appeared at university undergraduate events, and at one of them he met Ellie, whom he dated for about six months before setting her aside for another girl—one who was, as far as Todd could see, neither prettier nor more interesting than his sister, just someone new for Cowboy to go after.

By that time, Ellie's brother had hated the man cordially. When she had brought Copass in after a date, Todd (who was always still awake) glared at a movie or video game on the television and ignored all greetings and pleasantries until the couple simply passed by him down the hall to Ellie's room. On occasion, when they closed the door, Todd would follow them quietly and peer through the keyhole like Famulus in The Golem. He was sure, more or less, that nothing would go on while their parents were home, but the couple always returned in the early hours when the older Vitales were asleep, and who could tell what a man like Cowboy would try in a veiled situation.

It was a night about a month after El's first date with the Cowboy that suspicions were confirmed. Crouched at the doorway, the arcade sounds of his abandoned video game loud behind him, Todd peeked through the keyhole again, this time to see her smooth, olive-skinned legs wrapped around the thick, pale waist, the two of them moving slowly, erratically, his sister shushing Cowboy with panting, shallow breath until soon they rocked in a swift, fluid unison and Todd was panting himself, reaching inside his trousers in the shadowy hallway.

The house lights fluttered and rose to the bald, disorienting glare of the real world after a film. Todd flushed with embarrassment, and scrambled from his seat to the door just as the first of the audience were stepping into the aisle. His farewells were quiet, almost furtive: Dominic passed him and nodded, then his old friends, Apache Downs and Billy Shepard, passed him without speaking, still in the residue of a two-year-old dispute over a Dungeons and Dragons campaign, he guessed. He said goodnight to all of them, and after the last person filed into the lobby, he started down the aisle, picking up discarded popcorn boxes, crumpled copies of Dominic's essay, and, when he leaned over to snatch up an empty Jujube box, found an odd, hard white kernel inside it—not popcorn, but soon forgotten as he shoveled the refuse into the trash can.

∞

And she watched the boy approach down the lamplit aisle, sometimes losing form, sometimes reassembling in his yellow jacket uniform, arms laden with little boxes and oily bags.

Quietly Magdelein receded from his view, though she knew he could not see her, the others had told her so. She stepped back into the shadows, the tangling cables and the stilled studio lights, as the screen became opaque in front of her and she turned from it, her own shape unsteady now, wavering between cloud and dark flame.

In her arms she carried roses, as he carried scraps of litter in his. She did not look back, but headed toward the mountain now a darker shadow in the fog ahead of her, where the others would wait and she would take her place by a window, holding a flower aloft in the artifice of floodlight and dream.

∞

A circle of shades, a ring of shadows.

It was how Bucky thought of the day that had transpired.

Or a *cloud of witnesses,* because Bucky was a Christian, too, goddamnit, and what they were supposed to be up to here was the bringing back of virtue, the restoration of goodness.

Which is why this gathering took him nearly out of his comfortable seething and into a downright overflow of rage.

Late at night, after Max and Dominic had apparently returned to their respective homes and beds and slumbers, three men gathered at the Antioch Baptist Church, demesne of the Reverend Peter Koenig, and the "local church home" of Bucky Trabue and his erstwhile employer, former Congressman Roy Rausch.

Oh, and over nine thousand other people, who traded pastoral attention and community for the chance to gawk at local celebrities in the pews and "Christian interest groups" that confirmed what they believed about themselves.

Bucky had joined Rausch and Koenig for a special, more secular occasion tonight. They gathered to celebrate the demise of DeMoyne Troubles, the old, corrupt, and thoroughly wily Democratic Councilman who had been caught at last in the scandal that might derail his campaign for a fourth term.

Famous for hiring his relatives, for cobbling sweetheart deals with minority contractors, and suspected of stealing his two primary elections by what one of his campaign spokesmen had called *ballot adjustments,* Troubles had nonetheless lifted his district, finding ways to bring forth prosperity via slush funds and laundered PAC contributions, until an enterprising reporter, heavily financed by Roy Rausch (who had always despised Troubles), had discovered the fifteen-year-old girl who had in turn been financed by discretionary funds so discreet that Marquetta Troubles, the Councilman's loud and insightful wife, had known nothing of her presence under sheets in the district and the things she did with the body politic. DeMoyne Troubles had dropped the ball on the penis issue, and once again Bucky marveled how they did it—Democrat, Republican, Troubles and Roy Rausch himself years back, goddamn it, with that Vietnamese girl who worked on his campaign over in Jeff, the episode Bucky had covered up and deep-sixed until his own head almost exploded. They couldn't keep it in their pants, these public servants, and sometimes it was great evil, but sometimes that evil converged with a general and long-term good.

Which was this, as he saw it: the Democrats could still win the election, but it might be embarrassing beyond repair for DeMoyne Troubles to serve another four-year term while he served one to five for statutory rape. It was the first (and possibly the last) chance to make the Council seat Republican. It was a long shot, because the winner would likely be whoever unseated Troubles in the primary, but a long shot was a shot, and the former Congressman had a notion.

"But you've just cottoned to him because he saved your life!" Bucky objected.

Rausch was of the opinion that it was a pretty good reason for gratitude.

But not a reason for mounting a campaign, god damn it, Bucky countered, drawing a glare from the Reverend for his language and a combative grin from Rausch. And after all, this Pfeiffer was a *janitor*, for the love of Jesus, and surely there had to be *credentials*, a sense that he'd thought about the *fuckin' body politic* (again a pastoral glare) instead of how to clean a bathroom, and forgive me, Reverend, but religion, the last I checked, was not the sole qualification of a candidate for anything except sainthood, and as far as I can tell, the Baptists ain't big on canonization, at least not yet.

It was a surprise to Bucky when Koenig agreed with him. After some throat-clearing where the Reverend owned up to his admiration, to suspecting that Jerry Jeff had a gift for laying on hands, for healing, that was remarkable in these latter-day times, he wondered whether that wouldn't be more useful in the ministry rather than in politics.

Roy Rausch sniffed at such wondering. Said there was absolutely no difference. That the task was to set a GOP ass in the Council seat, to get that black bastard Troubles out of influence, and to play it by ear from there. Which was why Jerry Jeff.

Not for the first time, Bucky Trabue rankled at his lot in life. He believed in hard work for a day's pay, and that Americans should get first crack at American jobs. He believed that every decent person should have a gun or several to defend his family, that socialism was the thief in the night, and that Democrats like DeMoyne Troubles were socialists, not to mention chickenhawks. Bucky believed in Jesus. He believed all these things—good things, he thought, and right things—and he ended up like someone who made monsters.

He thought about Caligari and Rabbi Löew. One was crazy and malign, a mad scientist sending a sleep-walking murderer through a sleepy, geometrical German village, and doing it because he could, and the other was a good guy, sending a clay murderer through a smoky, geometrical Prague to save the Jewish people. Both of them ended up murderers, because there was a vanishing point where intentions converged, a dark spot on the horizon.

Or maybe not. It seemed to make sense right now. He leaned back in his chair, withdrew a pack of Marlboros from his shirt pocket before he recalled that Koenig didn't allow smoking in the office.

There were worse things, though. Worse things than the preacher allowed. Pfeiffer was a nice man but a political mistake: a sleep-walking clay monster with a knack for laying on of hands like something out of the fuckin' *Green Mile.* They were going to place a sideshow act in nomination, and Bucky would smile and comply and have a hand in it.

9.

ucky wasn't smiling, though, when he backed out of the parking lot at Antioch. The evening had gone long and tedious, Rausch planning the demise of Democrats everywhere, but more specifically that of DeMoyne Troubles. It went way back with Rausch: was deep and ideological and racial and altogether personal, and even Bucky, estranged politico and conservative to his utter heart, was put off by the venom in the room he left, the venom that followed him to the car as he began the long drive over the river, taking the Congressman home.

He wished he could have told Roy Rausch otherwise. Wished that someone in the whole fuckin' Republican Party would listen to some sense when it came to candidates, that they didn't have to nominate Jesus down here but just another good Republican. One with a sexual track record that was more respectable than Troubles'. Or Rausch's, for that matter.

Because the city was falling apart. It was decadent and frivolous and nasty. Just go up Fourth some night, north of the theater, and see what awaited you in bars and preciously named restaurants. Walk past the corner of Fourth and Liberty, still empty from where the one goddamned book store in the downtown had closed two years ago—no, he did not count Bulwer's bastion of Buddho-Marxism south of the cemetery, Dry Salvages (which he and his buddies called "Dry-Hump Salvages" out of the respect it was due). The town was rotting, while underage girls flashed their titties in the RockHard Restaurant, or Bowling for Boobies, or Rabbi Löw's Beer Emporium and Hoocherama, or whatever the fuck the places were going by this week before people lost interest, they closed down, and got replaced by another cute little bar with little outdoor plazas where frat boys could vomit al fresco.

Jesus, it was a roaring mess. He hated to be part of it.

Which was why they needed someone to make things decent. Not silly and frivolous and stupid like downtown was now, but not some kind of Evangelical version of Salt Lake where the bars were closed, either. Bucky had lost the sense of what he wanted. It was something back there in the past, something like the world he had yearned for, had imagined his friends living in when he sat on the bleachers at the Little League park after practice forty years ago, watching as parents in station wagons picked up the infielders and took them home to suburban ranch houses with lawns you could lie down in safely at night, and look up into a whole vault of heavenly stars. Not the place your own folks took you in that flower-decaled VW bus, closer to the city and smelling of patchouli and parsnips…

His thoughts lurched as a form passed through the headlights. A white form sliding from darkness to light to darkness again, like a ghost on screen.

Bucky hit the brakes and veered to the curb, the tires slinging gravel and the car bucking as it skidded onto the sidewalk and off, coming to a stop at the edge of the road, as whoever it was staggered on out of sight.

"What the *fuck* was that, Roy?"

Rausch floundered to attention and peered into the dark. "What was *what?*" Because whoever or whatever it was had shambled off, and the road lay empty before them.

Rausch kept asking as they pulled onto the interstate, but

lost interest and was drowsing by the time Bucky's old car passed over the river and into the next state, waking up as they neared his house in time to hear, in full and florid detail, Bucky's misgivings about the candidacy of Jerry Jeff Pfeiffer.

It wouldn't be the first time, Rausch countered, that they'd run a preacher. Not even the first in that district. Because when things get bad, people look to messiahs, or ones that walk the walk.

Waving off Bucky's insistence that he was Christian goddamnit, more Christian than Roy himself would ever be, the former Congressman laid out the map of the city's death. It was like decadent Berlin, Rausch claimed, scolding Bucky for not knowing his history. The streets were sexually charged. It was all out in the open. Prostitution, transvestism and drugs, just like here and now. Cocaine out in the open. Cabaret boys, in sailor suits, greeted patrons at the doors of clubs, enticing tourists who came to Berlin to gawk at its display of licentiousness, extremity and exaggeration that had not been seen since the Caesars.

And it was the same near-apocalyptic decadence Bucky had thought about, they agreed that the city was bad, was falling into shambles, but Rausch's solution was patching problems with a preacher, and nothing Bucky could say would change his mind once the Congressman had fixed on Jerry Jeff Pfeiffer, and Bucky was shaken anyway because damn it, he had nearly run someone over a block or so from Antioch Baptist and the movement in front of the headlight had unnerved him and set his deeper thoughts onto the past.

There had been this time when he was eleven, after Little League practice when his parents' hippie van had not shown at the ball diamond. It was two hours after the last of his teammates had been picked up, the mother calling out the window with concern, *you need a ride, Buckminster?* and obviously relieved that he waved her away, that no, he would be fine, his father would be there soon.

At dusk he began to walk. It was two miles, was all, and he'd only been sticking around so as not to worry them if they pulled up and found him missing from the bleachers and thought he'd been abducted or something.

Not that they ever would. Nor that they would be worried until he was not there come morning.

Bucky spun this story out, unsure of the line between memory and an eleven-year-old's desolate inventions, as he crossed into a subdivision—*his* subdivision—rows of sad little ranch houses that were not much more than anchored trailers. The sun had set by then, and he quickened his pace.

He saw the man emerge from between two houses. Approach him slowly on the sidewalk, shambling like something wounded. Bucky stepped off the sidewalk to give way, as the man moved nearer, barefoot and indefinite in a wife-beater and cutoff denims.

He stared directly at Bucky, his eyes red-rimmed and focused on distances.

Bucky had frozen on the easement as the man passed. Caught the smell of vinegar and something sweet and decomposed.

Recalling it now as he neared the Congressman's home— *the compound,* as Rausch's campaign workers had always called it, since the house lay among a half-dozen or so Rausch-owned properties—he remembered how wild his thoughts had been as the man stumbled away. That he had thought, *someday that man will come for me someday it will be different and that day will mark my death.*

Nearly forty years ago, and he still shivered as he remembered that twilit encounter, still shivered as he pulled into the huge circular driveway where Rausches in four residences parked their cars on less menacing curbs. Nearly forty years of reprieve and haunting.

∞

It was all haunting and no reprieve late that night at the Shangri-La. Seated in the projection booth at 3 a.m., her forbidden

Gaulois alight and the images of *Nosferatu* fading to the stark tower at the end of the film, Leni Zauber took stock of what lay ahead. By now the series was well underway. Two films they had screened and the third one was Murnau's classic of subdued sexuality and vampirism—the film she was reviewing one last time before she talked to the boy later on. Dominic would join her tomorrow evening—or at least that was the plan—and they would map out *Nosferatu* together, consider what should be said and not said.

Leni was glad the whole Nazi affair had emerged from the shadows. It was as though a formless fear had been set aside, a kind of implicit tension when the series was announced, when she was hired to travel to the Midwest, to leave behind the expected venues. From the coast she had embarked, knowing that Florian Geist and his connection with the SS would eventually emerge, take shape, like the light that received embodiment through the old films.

It was all a matter of biding time. Things were converging now, the thin disparate lines of story among those gathered at the Shangri-La were starting to tangle and intersect, and like a director, she watched from the high booth, guiding the action with a subtle hand. Now Leni rose, still holding the cigarette, and shuffled to the lobby door, where she took a deep drag as the acrid smoke bristled in her throat and billowed out, wafting over the eyeless, expectant faces in bas-relief above, clouding the mutual vision as she sat on a lobby bench, her thoughts almost a century away.

Meanwhile, back in the house, in the darkness of the front row, Todd Vitale awoke with a whimper, his knees scuffed and his eyes tearful and disoriented. How had he found his way from his bed, over half the town through the brindled, abject dark, to lie here in the Shangri-La, dressed only in his stained underwear, sweaty, his palms blooded and his thoughts capsized, afloat between vampires and golems and his sister's legs. Sobbing, he crawled toward the back exit and down the stairs to the storeroom, where old productions had kept a tiring room and he could find thin, ill-made trousers and a refuge from the crashing chaos of his recent dreams.

$$\infty$$

As Bucky Trabue sat in the conclave with powerful men and Todd Vitale stirred in troubled sleep in the recesses of the Shangri-La Theater, Dominic dreamed that he stood on a sloping foothill, where the soil was rocky and bare. A solitary tree in front of him, its branches wavering in a strong wind he could not feel, that he could only see as it swept across the incline, scattering dried leaves and rubble before it. And the roots of that tree, wrenched partly from the ground by the dry, hostile weathers, arched over a darkness that looked like the mouth of a tunnel, drawing his gaze forward and down.

He moved through ragged darkness into a close room filled with smoke. The walls tilted here, careening into depths he could only imagine, and it was like standing on the threshold of a cellar that branched out into infinite caverns. He had been here before. Here, deep enough that he could no longer hear the wind above him.

She was at a table, smoking, perched atop a high, uncomfortable stool, her sharp features as angular as the walls that framed her. She gestured, and he sat across from her.

For months he had wondered about Leni Zauber, why she was here and not elsewhere—in Europe or along an American coast. What could have brought her to a small Midwestern town, to a festival few attended. And here in his dream he wondered again for a moment, until she spoke and his thoughts tunneled into shadow.

You know this place, she said. It was not a question, so he nodded in agreement. Strangely passive, even for a Gen-X stoner, he waited for her guidance, for what she would tell him.

Is the cellar, Dominic, she announced, her lips moving in German, he suspected, while the words trailed inaudibly into his thoughts and gathered meaning. *The cellar that brought you back to the backwater.*

He tried to speak, but her words anticipated his, and in the cavernous shade of his dream she spoke to him in a veiled language—something about *father* and *wandering* and something untranslatable, something called *sensucht,* which, as he began to marshal thoughts, to ask for meanings, she scoffed and waved away, a translucent cigarette between her fingers.

Only a yearning, liebchen. A yearning that you alone are brought here to fulfill.

He certainly knew about yearning, and for a moment the old woman's face softened and transformed, free of the creases of age, and young, and radiant, and he thought of Elaine Vitale, and remembered from somewhere that in dreams a person was not who she appeared to be, was not even one person but a strange recombinant of many faces, many figures, and his wandering thoughts were slowly brought back to the Leni of his dreams, who was saying something about his father, about Ellie Vitale, was bringing those memories and images together in a way that was beyond his grasp and hearing, and he regretted having veered away in thought, having missed some insight that the dream was offering.

Something in you making you look for him, nicht wahr? Leni asked, and he understood she was speaking in German, remembered that he did not know German. *Nor do you know what it is, because you do not know yourself, young man, nor the yearning that guides your return and your being.*

And *sensucht,* she said again. *Conrad Veidt and the Countess. Oh yes, there was a film about it. A film by Murnau. Poor Conrad, the sleepwalker of Caligari. He plays Ivan, a young Russian dancer, who falls in love with a Countess. Gussy Holl plays her, I am thinking. Well, the dancer is arrested. And when he emerges from prison, she is nowhere to be found. A lengthy search ends when he discovers she has died while he was in jail. A sad story, no? Sadder still when you think of poor Murnau, arcane in his desires. You do not like boys, do you, Dominic Rackett? You don't like boys, as*

Murnau liked boys? As Veidt liked boys?

He shook his head. Not in that way.

I supposed as much. It is that Elaine Vitale you like, yes? Your countess? Ah, but too young for you. A girl, barely a woman. Women have been harsh to you, so is girls instead?

Yes. No.

What would you do for her, Dominic? Would you do anything?

No. Then yes, because it was a dream, where you could uncover the inner promptings of the heart. Something there was in that strange, directionless sense that had brought him back to town, that *sensucht*, that yearning after something he could not pin down, could not name. He was the dancer in search of the countess.

So yes. Yes, he would do anything. And was surprised at his own confession.

And *Very well*, Leni Zauber said. *So anything is just what you will do.*

Dominic lurched to wakefulness, and dark and cold. The rush of traffic uncomfortably near, the blare of horns and shouting as an auto filled with black kids raced by not ten feet away. He was standing near the curb on Ninth Street, bewildered and a mile from his theater room, in front of his fire-gutted last residence, the apartments boarded up half-heartedly, burned furniture in the front yards and parking lot, prey to scavengers before the quarterly Large Item Pickup the city so proudly advertised.

Shivering in his underwear, far from home, he collected his bearings. For some reason—perhaps continuity and the peace it brings—he picked up a mirror from the chaos of furniture. It had been the one above his dresser, he told himself. Or one just like it. It was easy to carry, and it covered him to oncoming traffic as he angled through back lots and crossed Broadway just north of the Catholic college, slid into an alley and found, as he thought he would find, the back door to the theater open, where he had unlocked it in his sleep and wandered off into the dreamy subterranean night.

∞

Not long after the analysis ended, his mother had her first bout with the cancer that, after lengthy treatments and two remissions, would kill her years later.

Ben called him on the phone. The dormitory was full and raucous that winter evening, and Dominic had to wave two hall wrestlers to silence, motioning the boys toward the other end of the corridor.

Dominic heard, for the first time, that condescending urgency he would come to associate with the stages of his mother's illness. Ben would intone—his best impersonation of a distraught husband—while instructing Dominic as to what the next proper and prudent step might be. By the first year of college, Dominic despised his stepfather, but he negotiated politeness on his mother's behalf.

And now, according to the voice on the other end of the phone, his mother was gravely ill. Ben thought he should know. Dominic agreed, said he would be on the road back to Boston by morning, and then the other end of the phone went quiet, whispered conversations, hissed urgencies, and his mother was on the phone, telling him there was time for this, that she had months assured by her doctors, and his true devotion, she said, would be to finish the term and join them over the winter break.

Like nothing had happened, she said. *After all, you're up there to study, Dominic. The best psychology program in New England. The doctors are optimistic, and you should be, too. Ben can handle anything on this end, believe me. I have enough to do without attending to more sentimental things.*

Later Dominic walked through the icy Vermont night toward the Congregationalist cemetery at the edge of the campus, the cold air bristling in his nostrils and bringing upon it the faint smell of burning leaves, rising somewhere out of the dark. He wondered why they had called if they didn't want him by his mother's bedside. He thought that perhaps he should take initiative, then. Should hop a bus and head down there, should be at her bedside whether she wanted him there or not. The recesses of the night gave him no answers, and he decided to wait until the next day, and then the next, obedient but all the while suspecting that such obedience, when it came down to it, might be read as a sign that he just didn't care.

∞

For some reason, as he settled into sleep, Dominic thought about Peri Bathgate. Whom he had thought, for a year, he had loved, and who had dismissed his father's book as *Mulian Rescues his Mother.*

The two of them had met in graduate school, when instead of his particular studies, Dominic had focused on an impromptu writers' group led by Reynaldo Rosa, a charismatic man a little older than his father would have been, who, strange as it may seem, claimed to have known Gabriel back in graduate school. Rosa had been encouraging when it came to Gabriel's writing, but Dominic suspected it was because the professor had liked his old man back in the day, so he held little stock in the praise. And furthermore, even stranger than the fact that the two had connected sometime in the past—perhaps in Dominic's infancy, perhaps shortly before his birth—Rosa had mentioned the acquaintance and nothing more, and all questions made the history more vague, as though the facts were receding under layers of time and memory.

At the time Dominic had been working on a long narrative poem called *Anagoge.* About a bluegrass musician who fell in love with a saint in a Russian icon. It was based on an unfinished story by his father, a scattered twelve pages or so that had come down to him as Gabriel's sole and unwitting heir. Dominic took it upon himself to finish the arc of the story, but in another form: if his father had written prose, then by God he would write poetry, and haiku to boot—brief, evocative images that would gather themselves into story so that they were no longer haiku but a telling from frame to frame.

Dr. Rosa had thought it was a decent enough idea, though he claimed that the haiku form of the piece was *arbitrary and a little silly*. He had invited Dominic to visit his bachelor's digs to discuss his work. Two weeks after the invitation, Peri joined the group, and to Dominic's disappointment, Rosa turned his attention and encouragement to a coming-of-age novel by a slender teenaged German boy who took pages of notes at each meeting.

But by then, Peri was a fan of *Anagoge*. And of Dominic. Or so he believed.

Peri's journey to that place and time had been as roundabout as his: at 22, English was her sixth major and she had already been married and divorced twice. It had all the warning signs, which made Dominic fall more readily into what he thought was love.

Not beautiful, thin to the point of gauntness, blonde and beak-nosed, she was physically not that attractive to him from the beginning. Yet she seemed the right woman for the right time, sharing his interests, smart and strong-willed. From the start the sex had been listless: Dominic was drawn to her because she was a woman, but there was nothing specific to intensify a kind of clandestine bump-and-run.

The initial charm faded, and soon the romance became a kind of power struggle. By the end of their first month together, Peri Bathgate had started to fade as well.

It was weird to remember, and he had shielded himself with comparisons. Said it *was like she was fading and almost as though she was becoming transparent*, but it was more than that. She moved in with him after the third week, and the next Thursday night, she passed in front of the lamp by his desk and he could see her bones, her skin turning pink to crimson as the light passed through it. It was scarcely a month more until, when she stood in front of the window, he could see the grid of the panes behind and through her.

He was reading his father's novel for the fourth time when they were together. It was then that Peri had said that thing about *only Mulian,* and it was a whole year before he could visit *Dacia* again. She had spoiled something at the heart of his imagining, but the poem changed as well, shifted as she read it and commented. And as she became more and more transparent, her enthusiasm for the poem faded as well, until in their sixth month together, she called it pretentious. After all, it was a narrative written in haiku, for God's sake. Who would read that? She said he must work on something else, he just had to, he was squandering his talent.

So he worked on something else. Behind a counter at Starbucks, not on his writing. He dropped out of graduate school as well, abandoning both scholarship and art for the daily, tidal reliability of things. After all, the poem was no longer close to what he had imagined: he saw through its language to Peri's expressions, even her point of view, and realized that he had surrendered a part of himself out of sheer passivity. The early drafts, written before he met her, were now as unrecognizable as the woman who had set up residence in his territory. He threw the papers away, deleted the files. Then left his own apartment.

After all, nothing held him in the small New England town anymore, except his job at the coffee shop, which he abandoned as well. Off he went toward Boston, to a mother whose mortal cancer had yet to be discovered and to a stepfather whose distaste for him had been evident for some time. Peri's calls to his mother's house went unanswered, and then, two months after he left, Dominic began receiving the threatening letters from his landlord. Ben Mountolive—a good stepfather only when it gave him a chance to display power—paid the balance of the lease, then shamed Dominic into returning to recover his belongings. Somehow it had seemed that leaving it all behind was the best way to end both romance and graduate school—a kind of indoor illegal dumping—but Ben had argued otherwise, persuading him by saying he couldn't trouble his mother like that again.

Dominic guessed he would never see Peri Bathgate again.

He heard from Rosa that she was holed up in a place in the burbs. That within a month of his leaving, she had found an older and wealthier man. He told himself he wished her well, and one time in his last week in town, he had taken a bus out to the subdivision where she lived, stood on the sidewalk at night, knowing it was creepy, that he ran a risk of being run off or even arrested. He watched through the front picture window of her house, saw the man in question talking to someone, gesturing to someone, holding a cigarette lighter in the lamplit air, its flame igniting something. The glowing dog end of the smoke and the smoke itself curling in front of the man, emerging from a ripple in the air. Or from a ripple in the glass, like the house had old Victorian windows though it obviously had been built sometime in the seventies.

He saw the smoldering end of the cigarette dip and waver in the room, like a huge, swollen firefly drawing its mate across a hot and predatory night. He wondered what the man saw.

Two years later, Peri's book was published by a rather prominent university press in the Midwest. A narrative poem, written in haiku, chronicling the love of a Russian Orthodox icon for a mortal human—how that mortal changed, and indeed how the icon had discovered that the only thing about him worth loving was his capacity for change. How he never lived up to the still and silent perfections of lacquer and gold leaf and eternity.

Some of Dominic's lines were in the poem. But by then, he had to admit, most of it was hers.

Nosferatu (1922)

Nosferatu , the signature (though perhaps not the greatest) film of Germany's iconic director, F.W. Murnau, is the father of all vampire movies. Shot in 1921 and released in 1922, it was an unauthorized adaptation of Bram Stoker's Dracula, with names and other details changed because the studio could not obtain the rights to the novel (for instance, "vampire" became "Nosferatu" and "Count Dracula" became "Count Orlock"). Nevertheless, the widow Stoker won a lawsuit over Murnau's and Henrik Galeen's script, thieved and ghosted as it was from the original.

The story is uncomfortably familiar to anyone who knows Stoker's novel. Thomas Hutter lives in the fictitious German city of Wisborg. His employer, Knock, sends Hutter to Transylvania to visit a new client named Count Orlock. Leaving behind his wife Ellen, the carefree (and a little silly) Hutter takes off toward the Carpathian Mountains and the "land of thieves and ghosts." Hutter is welcomed to the castle by Count Orlock, and a number of eerie events occur. Even on the first night of his stay, Hutter accidentally cuts his thumb: when Orlok tries to suck the blood, the repulsed guest pulls his hand away.

Such is the beginning of Hutter's harrowing stay in the castle. Indeed, his work for Knock is successful, as Orlok signs the documents to purchase the house across from Hutter's own home. But gradually Hutter begins to suspect that Orlok is Nosferatu. Eventually, through a series of scenes that still manage to horrify after almost a century, Hutter's suspicions are confirmed. He is trapped in Orlock's castle while the creature embarks for Wisborg, but manages his escape and races Orlock home. What ensues are a series of scenes that mark the antagonists' journey and arrival, and most especially how, from afar, Orlock begins to influence and finally dominate the psyche of Hutter's young wife Ellen.

There are many deaths in the town upon Orlock's arrival, and it is curiously Ellen who may well have found the key to defeating the monster in a book on vampires her husband has forbidden her to read.

All in all, the film still taps into some primal terror in all of us. Gustav von Wangenheim is amiably dim-witted and naïve as Hutter, and Greta Schröder (the flower girl from The Golem, remember?) is poignant in her first starring role as the beleaguered Ellen. But it is Max Schreck who steals the show, unnervingly inhuman as the vampiric Orlock, commanding the screen in all his grotesque, rat-like charisma.

Germans of the 1920s—indeed, people everywhere in that momentous time—were first being schooled by Freud to the idea that dark, often sexualized forces and impulses may guide our lives in ways larger than we think. At the very least, they lurk under our calm, respectable, Hutteresque surfaces like ghosts in the cellar of an old and unsteady house.

--Dominic Rackett

∞

Back at the theater, the disc paused and lurched in the projector, and Leni Zauber, drowsing after an afternoon at the Steenbeck, surfaced into new mindfulness and turned from editing a sequence in *Walpurgisnacht* to the screen where, only a moment before, she had been letting *Nosferatu* run through unheeded for a last time.

She had met with Dominic, had discussed his article and returned to her veiled work in the booth. But suddenly it was no longer *Nosferatu* on screen, the sequence shifted in locale from Orlock's castle, the familiar setting in which the action of the film took place. Now Leni watched another hillside, steeply sloped and even more desolate. The body on a stone platform, wrapped in linen, readied for the approaching *Tomden*, who stood above it now, cleaver in hand.

The *Tomden* was the *yogin*-butcher, the corpse cutter. Florian had told her when they watched the funerary rites in Tibet.

Now they unwrapped the body. The camera was stationary, a wide shot taking in the body, platform, the rubble and monks. The cleaver flashed through the air, the light on its descending blade for the first hacking cut, for the second, then the body expertly, impassively dismembered. Black gobbets spattered the rocks, one small dark blot on the camera lens, as the cleaver rhythmically severed limb from torso, the companions of the *Tomden* warding away a pair of vultures already descending to the spot. The birds approached cautiously, the grotesque bob and tiptoe Leni remembered, as though they were treading softly to keep the silence of the film.

A low-angle shot, her eye level at the time she had first seen this, when she was very young or very new, a shadow lingering at the right of the frame.

The shadow was Florian. And she was the only girl on the mountainside. This she also remembered. And remembered

145

his hand on her shoulder, and the words meant to console, to explain:

It is a funeral. They honor their dead in this fashion.

Now the monks calling *shey, shey* (she did not hear it, of course, because Florian's work was always silent, but she remembered it, reconstructed the sound as she watched the screen). They were urging the birds to approach, stepping away as a frenzy of wings covered the body, as the naked, wattled heads of the vultures rose from the black boil of the feast, their craws engorged with the already-turning meat, their wings flapping like blades of dark flame.

The way of the world, Maus. That was what she remembered, did not hear. Florian Geist's world black and white, tooth and claw.

And as the monks waded among the glittering wings, removing flesh from the carcass, tossing it to the birds, the frame speed seemed to slow, she remembered the wind picking up, the smell of the body and its devourers, and Leni thought she remembered regret, wanting to be elsewhere. But she also remembered desire, and comfort, and a strange terrible joy in standing with Florian on Tibetan slopes, on receiving his instruction, his hand heavy on her shoulder, clutching her girlish bones a little too firmly, so that part of the joy was that he could crush her at any moment, scatter her to the winds and vultures.

For this was Florian Geist, no ordinary man. Bourgeois but dashing, one model for a synthetic aristocracy "of soul and blood". Explorer, adventurer, maker of documentary films and that great crowning fiction, his feature-length *Walpurgisnacht,* grand in scope and silent by choice in the first diminished decade of talking films, and lost in the rubble of the Reich…

Until now, she told herself, her eyes on the screen.

∞

In Tibet she had longed for his stature, for his features and blonde hair. Longed for a pair of Meissen blue eyes. But these she had not been given.

Years later, old but not showing the intervening three generations of age, Leni Zauber had long lost interest in the romance of Aryan beauty. That myth had died in the rubble of Berlin. What she longed for now instead was a clear, unmitigated image of Florian Geist. What she had instead was scattered—a recollection cobbled from her own, unreliable memories and also from the second-hand accounts she had gathered for years.

Born in Potsdam to a nouveau riche family, his mother a cousin of a manufacturer of artificial flowers and cheap novelties. He was named "Florian" as a family gesture.

In 1912, the cousin sold an abandoned factory to Bioscop Pictures, who had been forced by fire marshals out of their makeshift apartment studio, and what would become the famous Neubabelsberg Studios were born. When he came of age to be useful there, the boy Florian took on menial jobs at the studio, but eventually apprenticed to a cinematographer, who introduced him to Willy Hameister and Fritz Arno Wagner, two of the greatest cameramen in the German film industry.

Geist always claimed his rapid rise was without his cousin's influence, that nobody knew because they did not share surnames, that he had simply offered suggestions in framing a sequence of shots. That his mentor, Lothar Lieber, had been impressed by his cinematic eye, and that a career was born at that moment.

The evidence seemed otherwise. From beginnings in extraordinary youth, Florian Geist rose, talented but rich and entitled, through the ranks of Weimar films, until by the mid-1920s he was a second-tier cinematographer, stretched to the limits of his talents but not his ambitions. Family money and a good deal of Aryan blue-eyed charm attached him as Lieber's assistant. What this meant Geist rarely talked about, and Leni remembered Lieber in scattered images, a man in his sixties but already doddering from what people would recognize today as early Alzheimer's, doting nearly as much on the flash and rhetoric of Germany's new regime as he did on his young protégé.

At any rate, it was Lieber who arranged, with some reluctance, Geist's presence on the little-known Tibetan expedition of the strange Nicholas Roerich party. It was the young man's fascination with the story of Shambhala, the Spiritualist lure of a place in the remote Himalayan region, that inspired him to join the bizarre Russian painter, his family and followers, on a journey that raised all kinds of controversy, that in secrecy began to promote a fantastical alliance between Buddhism and the Bolsheviks.

At that time, Geist was strikingly apolitical. He shared half of Mitteleuropa's antisemitism, but cared little to put it into practice. The Bolsheviks, however, were neither here nor there in his estimation, but Roerich's grab for a kind of world power, as ill-starred and naïve as it was, offended him. His ambitions trumped his sense of adventure, and so he returned from Asia in secrecy, during that period in which the Roerich expedition was lost, presumed annihilated.

Upon Geist's homecoming, an elated Lieber enlisted him as a photographer's assistant, and they dropped from sight for years, more or less, resurfacing in the 30s to document cultural and historical studies surrounding the Teutoberg Forest, site of an ancient Germanic victory over the Romans. Geist filmed the scenery, some archaeological excavation, and early recreations of "authentic Teutonic ritual," all cast in a dodging, mythic light that, unlike the startling cinematography of his contemporaries, simply blurred the edges of things. One Hollywood director called Lieber's work "history through the Vaseline lens of tittie shots", but Geist had made the right connections, maintaining close friendship with Lieber, who in turn had friends in the Wewelsburg Castle of Heinrich Himmler.

Florian Geist joined the SS in 1933, one of the "March Violets" who signed up as the Fuhrer entered office and, by 1939, when the famous Ernst Schäfer expedition to Tibet—the strange harbinger of invented "Nazi science"—arrived in Lhasa, Geist, then just shy of his fortieth birthday, was there to greet them. What he had seen in the years since his last visit to the Lost Kingdom was nothing short of astonishing, but it had begun in the Himalayas, years ago, when he first saw the magic lantern.

∞

Pema, his young traveling companion, first showed him the lanterns. She claimed they were brought north by Chinese wizards.

How Leni knew these things about Pema she did not know or could not remember. She had no recollection of meeting the girl, would have disputed her very existence were it not for the evidence on film. Geist was quite taken with the little thing, enough to feature her in *Walpurgisnacht*. Perhaps he had recounted her story—in Tibet or in Potsdam or Prague—because Leni had put it together from fragments and cuts, employing her gifts as an amateur film editor to the long, obscure reels of Geist's recollected history.

Pema was only a girl, scarcely thirteen when their association began, so Geist first marked down her talk of magic lanterns as Tibetan superstition. Until he saw the devices, candles in small cages of translucent paper under thin-bladed little fans that turned with the heat of the candle flame. On the blades were silhouetted black figures, cut from paper as well, representing dancing men, horseback riders, moons and constellated stars. *Pi ying*, they called them, and they were like the characters of the Shadowplayer in the old Arthur Robison film, the one Fritz Wagner shot with the Jew Granach in the role. And Pema claimed they were like his moving pictures, marveling at Chinese magic as they lay in bed after sex and he made shadow puppets with his hands to amuse her.

Oh yes, she agreed. *Your images are more real, if what is real is what we see. But the Pi ying are only shadows next to our more solid creations.*

He encouraged her, but his indulgent smile quickly faded as she told him about the tulpa.

The tulpa, Pema explained, were called *thought forms* or *phantoms* by the old Tibetans, but she claimed they had more solidity, more substance than the ghosts that Westerners conjured or imagined. In some cases, tulpa are created on purpose, either by a long process of meditating and visualizing, or, if the magician is powerful enough—as were some of her family and ancestors, she claimed—almost instantaneously.

The tulpa would gather life, Pema said. Then came a point in its formation, a kind of decisive moment when it could play the part of a real being. Others could see it—others beyond its creator. Sometimes, indeed more often than her people cared to admit, the tulpa would then free itself from its maker's control, just as a child, when his body is completed and able to live apart, leaves his mother's womb, or an adolescent comes of age and leaves his parents' home. Sometimes the phantom becomes a rebellious son: Pema had heard of uncanny struggles taking place between tulpas and their creators. Sometimes the offspring would injure or even kill its maker.

Leni had little idea how she knew this conversation. Each time her imagined memory of the incident—the night, the candles, the puppets, and the girl's account—unfolded in the same way, so fantasy merged with recollection, until Leni could no longer distinguish history from fiction. So she found herself refusing to think about it, becoming confused and unsettled when it crossed her mind and took up residence. Leni knew this much, though: that after the night of the *Pi ying* puppets, Geist no longer believed that Pema was only thirteen, for her inner essence, he said, seemed ancient at that moment. She smelled of juniper and smoke, and in the right light she was insubstantial, even translucent. Yet he was glad her body was smooth and supple and oh so young, her breasts scarcely formed, her brown face free of the drawn lineaments of hardship so characteristic of a people in bleak and weathered country.

He wanted to keep Pema as she was, or so he told Leni

in the first days of their acquaintance, when Leni was new and Florian Geist was the wisest and most handsome creature of her world. But of course young girls do not stay young girls—in short, young girls do not stay—and by 1939, when Florian, now a film director of visionary if not financial success, had returned to Tibet in the vanguard of the notorious Nazi expeditions, Pema had vanished somewhere in the rocky maze of the Himalayas, like a creature from one of those "lost world" films or novels.

Florian had told Leni, there on the steep steps of the Potala Palace, that a man could dream a daughter. Leni was never sure if that meant her or Pema, but she delighted in the presence of the older man, basked in his company, and vowed to be the daughter he wanted and needed.

Now Geist had become his name, a ghost in the flickering frames of his 1936 *Walpurgisnacht,* and a daughter's duty, Leni told herself, was to preserve the ghost, to clarify and guide the images he had put on the screen almost eighty years before. She had gathered the prints from Berlin, Austria, and Paraguay—one, not surprisingly, from Voronezh, where it had drifted into the hands of a former Red Army lieutenant, who let her have the film for a pittance. This Russian copy, in her hands three years ago, was the longest, a damaged, grainy print punctuated by scrawled, near-illegible intertitles. She had taken her work to Bologna, where the tedious process of editing and restoration began, aided by moonlighting technicians and starving but ardent graduate students. They, of course, had urged Leni toward a digital copy, but then she had received the call from Prague, where the Grail of her quest had been discovered in deep archival recesses: the near-flawless print of the film, well preserved narratively, marred only by scrawled intertitles in almost illegible German. The Prague copy, the one Geist had told her would *assure his immortality,* became her original document. She patched it with fragments from the others, editing delicately the film that, though impeccably preserved, was after all old and fragile.

There were stages in this process that went beyond a clear

and complete copy of *Walpurgisnacht* as Florian had intended it. There was something that a generation before her had not understood, not well: the scholar and critic are as involved in the *creation* of the film as the director or the actors or the cinematographer. They do *not* discover or uncover it as much as make it what it was intended to be, perhaps not by the director, the actor, the camera, but by the subliminal pressure of the film itself.

Leni felt that her hand, her eye, her thoughts were guided. Which is why she retranslated the intertitles, shaping the words on screen to fit the dialogue, the cleansing *grand guignol* of *Walpurgisnacht*, and the threefold bargains with the devil made by Dr. Halberd in the film. She felt that she had fulfilled Geist's intention and will, as she edited the print and packed it, almost complete, for her destination in the States. Of course Geist was long dead by then, killed outside his beloved Prague in the closing days of the war, the subtle mind leaving the body, bound, as Leni figured he believed, for the realm of the *preta*, the land of thieves and hungry ghosts.

He must have passed through a kind of bardo into a kind of rebirth, Leni thought—one fashioned of light and nitrate. And where Leni was once his creation, his daughter, perhaps his lover, she began the process of closing the circle: laboring over the film entrusted to her by accident and death and indefinite love, she became, in a monstrous passage, the mother of Florian Geist.

∞

Nosferatu, of course, drew a larger and younger crowd than the two previous films the Shangri-La had shown in the series. Old goth kids mingled with the standard horror crowd, *Rocky Horror* meets *Blair Witch* meets *Annabelle*.

Dr. Zauber had said they would all be disappointed. That *Nosferatu* was more the "Symphony of Horror" it professed to be than anything watched by contemporary audiences.

Ellie didn't like Zauber much. Found her pushy and overbearing. But surely if the old professor was right about one thing, it was the old films. *Caligari, Nosferatu,* and *Metropolis* were the ones Ellie had heard of. She'd always liked the old Universal *Dracula,* if only for its campy residue. So on Sunday afternoon she switched assignments with her brother, left him creepy and eager at the gate, while she ushered until the lights lowered, then took an aisle seat about midway up in the near-abandoned house.

The opening scenes were so obviously a calm-before-storm kind of setting, Hutter romping through the outdoors like some overenergetic pre-teen, bringing flowers to his wife Ellen, a stock character played by Greta Schröder, who according to Dom had handed flowers to the golem in the previous film. So the circle had gone full circle, Ellie concluded, and Schröder's role in *Nosferatu* so far seemed uncomfortably like an expanded cameo. More compelling was Orlock the vampire, who appeared early on at the reins of a coach, and slowly, almost seductively, takes in the juvenile Hutter.

The vampire hunger must be a kind of insanity, Ellie thought. Otherwise who would want a boy like that? Orlock was sexier by far, though he seemed a strange combination of rat and insect and John Hurt. It seemed that the drama would take place between Orlock and Hutter—a little bit mentor and pupil, a huge bit homoerotic—nothing she hadn't seen before. But after Hutter reads the book about Nosferatu, after he passes through what must be a dozen arches on way to his descent into the cellar where Orlock's body sleeps in its coffin, after his imprisonment, when he watches Orlock's departure from the castle, the story goes back to Wisborg, to Ellen.

Who, in the depth of night, tightropes on a balcony railing, her arms extended toward the rising moon, as if she was trying to embrace someone from afar.

Ellie sat back, pressed herself into the back of the chair. For a moment the light passed through Ellen Hutter and seemed to ripple across the breast of Ellie Vitale. Watching Ellen Hutter dance on the railing, she thought of the time she took up Todd's dare.

They must have been twelve, thirteen. At their grandmother's house, with its own balcony, its precarious railing, its drop into taxus bushes and mystery. Seated in lawn chairs, the twins had surveyed the long roll of the lawn up to the road in front of the house, the red dirt of the embankment greened over with the last of high spring.

They had fought not thirty minutes before, she and Todd. And while her brother sat in his chair brooding, enduring a scratch on his left cheekbone that she had inflicted, was pretty proud of, Ellie stood up, stretched, and leaned lazily over the railing, peering into the blue-green sea of bushes.

That's right, butthole, Todd murmured behind her. *Hope you fall.*

She could have told on him for that. Not only was he mad, but at that moment he was wishing her ill.

Instead, she leaned over the railing, wondering how Todd would react to such recklessness. Felt the blood rush to her head and peered back through the balusters at her brother, who was or was not absorbed by the comic he was reading or pretending to read. She leaned farther, lifting her legs from the ground as he looked up and she reached back to smooth down her dress, to cover her thighs.

Suddenly she rocked over the railing, the floor behind her lurching high, the cornice passing though eyesight as her legs kicked up, she lost her bearing, tipped and tumbled...

...the bunched waist of her dress catching on a nail protruding from the bottom rail as she fell, the fabric ripped...

...and Todd grabbed her ankle in the bright green vertigo, tugging her back to safety, where he held her and cried and apologized and promised to do better.

And even then, after a decade the excitement returned to her, there in the brindled darkness of the Shangri-La, as Schröder faints and tumbles into the arms of Georg Schnell, who calls for his wife and the doctor. Ellie sat there, the light at play over her parted lips, her eyes half-lidded, as the scene shifted back to the vampire on his way to Wisborg by boat and coffin, then to Hutter on horseback, trying to overtake his seducer.

11.

By the time he visited his mother's deathbed, Dominic had thought of seeking refuge, of becoming Buddhist rather than thinking about Buddhism.

His first guide in the process had been Reynaldo Rosa. Rosa was a Filipino cradle Catholic, but in the writers' group, with Dominic and Peri attentive and curious, he talked about becoming Buddhist through *avenues intensely personal.* Peri had guessed that Rosa's suspected sexuality, unwelcome in his native church, had led him to the Buddha, the dharma, and the sangha, but neither she nor Dominic ever really asked. Dominic's own search was less complicated in private matters and more to do with an unmoored yearning, a spiritual discomfort, for which his father's unsteady Catholicism and mother's fierce secularism had never provided answer.

Rosa had steered Dominic toward a mentor, a monk south of the college. Nguyen Van Yen had schooled him in basic meditation, the counting of breath and the focused third eye, listened intently and with acceptance to his questions, and guided Dominic's reading and exploration toward a more traditional understanding of the beliefs, stripped of patchouli and flaky West

Coast associations. So, though he still felt like a novice to the whole process—though he still really *was* a novice—Dominic was set upon a sound path, and after six months of instruction, could look back and notice he had passed into new country, though he still lacked the words and the thoughts to frame it.

It was Nguyen Van Yen who guided him on his conduct as he prepared for the Boston hospital and for what he knew would be his last visit with his mother. Calm, no strife. The moments in which the dying pass into the bardo are crucial, peace in the last breath enabling higher return.

Dominic held desperately to that peace in the cancer ward, his mother a ragged after-image of her former loveliness dark and cool. He was unprepared for how Jasmine Mountolive looked in her last days, the swollen wreckage of her body and the gasping, almost convulsive swallowing, her throat narrowed and constricted by pain and pain-killer, the residue of chemo and radiation, as though she was a convergence of the disease and the treatments that were killing her just as rapidly.

Ben had warned him how his mother slipped in and out of lucidity, so Dominic had thought he was prepared for that as well. And yet when she could focus, could ask to be left alone with him, he could not elude a feeling of being trapped and cornered—one he would identify after her death as something a good deal more than the deathbed and the edge of bereavement. He was afraid to sit vigil in her dying, afraid of what she would reveal.

It was odd how someone as nontheistic as his mother would recognize this as a time of confession. It gave credence to the old laws of deathbed testimony, to a certain authenticity in last goodbyes, but in the months that followed Dominic had trouble remembering what was said exactly, piecing the truth as recollection or the drug decide, parsing what was genuine atonement and what was a last power grab, her notion of how much she meant to her son derived and distilled from how much she was able to wound him.

Jasmine told him about the winding down of her first marriage, how by the time she had made clear to Gabriel Rackett that she had been a long time in Ben Mountolive's bed, the first betrayal was ancient history: she had been out of love with him since not long after they married, and all actions that followed the heart's estrangement had been a logical progression to the moment she had driven off toward Boston and Ben and her new home and Dominic, barely three years old, had looked in the rear window, she said, and waved to the diminishing image of his father.

What was more, his mother told him, she had strayed with Mountolive far before she had previously let on, though there was no chance that Ben was Dominic's father, really not, because at some point the calendar itself was a testimony to fact, at some point numbers were inarguable.

At first Dominic thought he knew why she was telling him these things. Soon after he would wonder if he had deciphered it all, whether something was coded deep within their last private conversation. It was a suspicion that came hours later when, on departing the hospital, he felt as though he was being followed.

∞

Mary Lull lived in Old Louisville now. Widowed and eighty, she had outlived three husbands, annulling the first, divorcing the second, and surviving the third.

It was not the house Dominic remembered from his childhood, the one that lay across the street from the spot where his father vanished. But it was his father he was seeking anyway, here on foreign premises in his grandmother's new old house.

There was a door on the stairway landing that opened to a brick wall. A circular alcove that had once lodged a window but was now walled in as well, as though some stealthy contractor had sought to close the place in through a series of slow, effacing steps. And Mary had trouble with memory, though it was not Alzheimer's she assured him, and frankly it wasn't that bad for eighty.

Still, her recollections of Dominic's father were not helpful. Mostly scraps and fragments sentimentalized by her Irishness and dramatic training, by her suppressed fear that she had wronged her son those years ago. Dominic wondered if she had confused her memories of Gabriel with scenes she had played on stage or had watched in movies, the pure wholesomeness of her recovered mother-son memories a contrast to what he had gathered second-hand as he grew up.

On Leni Zauber, though, Mary Lull was effusive but strange.

"I met her in Galway, Dommie. Back when all that tension was brewing over Eoin O'Duffy and the Blueshirts."

Dominic nodded, having no clue, expecting this was some pop band from the 1950s. He soon discovered it was older, somehow political and scary.

"So…they were like *subversives*, Grandma?"

Mary nodded gravely. "Oh, we all were stuck on 'em for a while, Dommie. All that Christian Ireland and Crusade in Spain business. All romantic, like Miss Jean Brodie's student heading off to join the conflict opposite her brother."

Dominic frowned. "Yes, ma'am."

"I wasn't but a child then. Six or seven. Sure looked up to her. The film star looks and the exotic accent. She wasn't a member. Wasn't Irish, for one. But she attended the speeches and talked to us girls about Spain and the Red Menace. I thought she was wonderful, wanted to go to Germany with her and be the next Marlene Dietrich, but she would have none of it, of course. Even that moment stood out in grace and clarity, Dommie: I couldn't refuse her when she come into town and wanted to take you under her wing, like she would of done me had things been different. After all, who knows but that she might have inspired me to the stage meself, and all the glory and ruination that come of that?"

Dominic masked a smile. Whenever Grandma Mary talked about her acting career, the brogue thickened.

But it troubled him, the story.

"That would have been...the late thirties, Grandma? The Spanish Civil War and all? Then...Leni Zauber must be older than you?"

"By some deal, Gabriel," she replied, forgetting who she was talking to, and his guard dropped a little at her blurred vulnerability. "By some deal, but don't be reminding a woman of her age, especially one who out of her kindness got you the job at the theater."

And she was back. To his relief and confusion.

"I don't recall you thanking me for that job, Dominic," she offered.

He smiled. "I don't think I have this week, Grandma Mary."

"But there's one thing troubling me, darlin'," she said, cocking her head curiously, her eyes half-lidded, losing even their dwindling focus. "Well, two things. What brought you over here in the late hours the other night, and seeing my light on, why didn't you pay a call?"

"'Over here,' Grandma?"

She nodded, and he listened to an account of how he had passed through her shallow yard, dressed in white, she said, and scantily against the cold of early spring. He would have insisted that he hadn't been there, but for two things. He knew Grandma Mary's defensiveness when told she hadn't seen or remembered right. But this time, given his episode of sleepwalking, his appearance on the steps of his burned-out apartment, there were also odds in her favor.

Shaken, vaguely embarrassed, he humored her with apologies and prepared to leave. She walked him to the door, talking about nothing as he opened it, then stopped in the center of the foyer and sat on the stairs. She grabbed the thought out of the dark, motioned back over her shoulder.

"Dommie, there's some papers of your father's I put in your old room. In a big manila envelope with his name on it, under the table by the window. I'm trying to clear the place, and since you come here askin' about him, you might find something of interest. He packed them himself. I labeled the box the New

Year's after you had gone back up east to your mother's, and clean forgot about them till Shimmy and Mark was helping me gather up things for the large item disposal. You can have the box if you're inclined. It's takin' up painful space."

Dominic knew better. Knew his grandmother's indifference when it came to those parts of his father that had little to do with her, how she cared little for his writing after his novel fell on mixed to bad reviews. How, after all, did a manila envelope take up space?

As he ascended the stairs he pushed back the resentment, thought of its karmic consequence, how none of it helped his father anyway. What was left was his own coming to terms, he figured, as he lifted two boxes to get at the envelope Grandma Mary had offered, her Irish schoolgirl's script bold and dismissive *Gabriel* across the front of the envelope.

Out of curiosity he opened it, skimmed the surface of its contents. Half-begun letters to his mother, sent letters to Grandma Mary, discarded along with the rest of the papers. Legal pads with the old man's bold and vertical handwriting—a draft of "And Yet They, Too, Break Hearts," the story on which his own poem was based. Drafts of his father's poetry, as well. The beginning of an essay on childhood friendship, something called "Ere Babylon was Dust", and letters to Barry Green, Gabriel's old agent, negotiating deadline extensions and pleading for royalty advances.

Sighing, he took the package with him, kissed his grandmother's cheek at the door, and set out into the cold March morning, the envelope clamped under his arm, his hands in his jacket pockets against the abiding wind.

∞

At Huntington's, the Peaceable Kingdom assembled of a Monday night.

There the staff of the Shangri-La would post-mortem

the weekends, planning for the next film, for arrangements of everything from the artistic to the logistical. This time, they returned to old subjects, as the talk centered again on drama at the premises and the heroism of Jerry Jeff Pfeiffer.

"I don't follow how it's *heroism*, Max," Ellie insisted, dolloping ketchup for her fries at the corner of the plate. Her enthusiasm had bloodied the formica table, and all but Max had sidled away from the mess she was making.

Todd agreed with his sister. Whether or not Jerry Jeff had saved the Congressman's life, nothing was done at risk, after all. It wasn't like he had braved gunfire or faced down Frankenstein, for God's sake. Furthermore, the doctors maintained that Rausch was not near a heart attack, not even near an episode. Jerry Jeff had set out on faith, laid on hands, and tumbled into incredible luck when he became a local celebrity. Perhaps even more luck for the Congressman, though they all doubted as much.

"Luck's what Dom calls 'low art'," Ellie added out of nowhere, in her voice a kind of reverence that made Max sniff and mutter, his mouth filled with Huntington's Famous Fish Sandwich.

"So that's probably what the dharma says, then, Ellie," he grumbled—ironically or sarcastically, he no longer knew the difference. "God, this fish is overrated. Rock Star Dharma. John Bulwer on the rocks, *por favor*, without the research. Dominic Rackett is fuckin' up *my* Buddha nature."

"Children, children," George intoned, stirring a third packet of sweetener into his coffee. "The boy's a haunted figure. Let's show some charity to Leni Zauber's protege."

All heads turned, as George held forth on the circumstances. That Dominic was sweet and charming. Perhaps not so bright, and certainly feckless, but certainly more of a pleasure to be around than *some*.

And he had come through rough times. They just didn't know.

George's knowing glance took in the whole table, and each member of the Kingdom took the comment personally.

"One would think you rather fancied Dominic," Todd said, not without malice, at which George hooted and scoffed.

"I've told you before, dears, I like my men the way I like my coffee."

They awaited the line they had all heard, but were not surprised when he followed through:

"Scalded. And in a mug. No, darling Todd, the serpent in the garden is Ms. Zauber."

He Germanicized the pronunciation to Ellie's amusement. Max hid a smile and looked through the window over George's shoulder, where a familiar, shambling figure paced in front of the Shangri-La, apparently talking to himself.

"No, Dominic is haunted by his father. Rackett *père* was an erstwhile novelist who disappeared into our southwest suburbs. As so many have, you might say, but this vanishing was altogether literal…."

"George."

"And so the dear lad—I know his grandmother Mary Lull from the local theater, she understudied under the late, unlamented Muriel Thorne—the dear lad is on pilgrimage. In search of the father in natal ground. Even now he's atop the theater in his dank, patchouli-smelling digs, reading from that envelope Mary gave him. I don't envy—"

"*George.*"

"What *is* it, Max?"

"That man over by the marquee. Do you know him?"

Sighing, interrupted in mid-story, George turned and exclaimed in falsetto. "T. Tommy Briscoe. Chorus leader in our strapped and ill-fated *Bacchae*."

"Jesus, I sense another story coming," Todd muttered, then poked at his fish under George's dramatic glare.

"For another time, dearest. Let it just be said that the man has history in the theater world. I'd heard he was dead. That, of course, is highly unlikely, considering he's wandering the premises as we sit here."

"And was in the theater for the sneak preview of *Caligari*.

The disruption in the balcony."

"Do tell! The one, then, who thought he was being courted by Lil Dagover? It only makes sense. And Johnny Bulwer shot dear Tommy? My God, but it's a small world when guns are involved! But now it makes sense. After the disaster at the production, Tommy sank back to obscurity. Alcohol-induced psychosis, I had heard. Capgras Syndrome, as well."

Ellie brightened. "Which is…?"

"See?" Todd grumbled. "A story coming."

"Well, it's actually pretty interesting," George continued, providing voice-over as the four of them watched Tommy out the window. "Caused by schizophrenia, I've heard. You believe that a friend or family member has been replaced by an identical-looking impostor."

"My brother's been replaced by aliens," Ellie announced.

"Fuck you, too," Todd muttered, nose to the window. But all of them were listening.

"That may account for Tommy's ill-starred Lil Dagover romance," George went on. "He was never too attached to begin with, sleeping in the park by the theater, hanging at Fourth and Fellini. Stealing copper, it turns out. They say that some people with Capgras talk about time being warped or substituted, too."

"How does that happen, George?" Max asked, and the older man rolled his eyes.

"For God's sake, honey, I'm not a physicist. And it doesn't *happen*. Someone *thinks* it happens.

"'There is nothing either good or bad, but thinking makes it so,'" Todd announced, and George recoiled at the *Hamlet* quote.

"Lunch is on me, Max," the old man proclaimed. "Get thirty from the till to cover the damages."

As he stood, Max caught the glance of Ellie Vitale. She held her plate toward him, offering the last gory huddle of fries with a sweet smile. He dropped into her eyes readily, unabashedly, sure this time that there was flirtation in the air, and wondering if time and identity were working right for him, if they had passed the point of disruption, where someone had come along, changing the girl and the venue in order to get under his increasingly thin skin.

If at last he was one up on Dominic Rackett.

Who was somewhere above the theater, reading.

∞

So who is this Jerry Jeff Pfeiffer, and what can be done with him?

Bucky Trabue steered to the edge of the city, the county, the Metro area, veering out of his lane once as he checked the directions on the paper in the passenger seat beside him. Another one of these little charismatic churches, smelling of sweat and spoiled tomato soup, loud with tongue-talking, which was one of the things Bucky hated most about the whole goddamned business of taking on every religious quirk because the bearer of the quirk would vote for the fucking party.

You couldn't find these places by steeples or huge parking lots. They were glorified Quonset huts, usually. The husks of funeral homes or drive-in banks. Bucky considered this weird shift in his lifetime—what happened when the buildings changed.

Time was when the small chapels that dotted the state—Presbyterian or Episcopal or Methodist, denominations you could recognize, with steeples and bells and pseudo-gothic windows—had commenced losing their energy, then their congregations. Then the buildings themselves would follow a slow decline until they became insurance offices, or realtors, or private residences renovated by gay couples. Bucky had seen it happening as a kid, not that Desmond and Floral Trabue had seen the inside of a church, but that Buckminster Fuller Trabue himself had caught the lament of secularizing, the *shift of the state into the 20th century*, they were calling it before Reagan.

But then came the promise of his early teens, the Gipper in the White House and the delight of living with parents who cordially hated the 40th President. Desmond and Floral were baffled by a changeling son, and the tide was turning. As Reagan said, it was morning in America, and almost morning everywhere, so now the buildings changed again. Insurance offices and realtors left their squat little orange-bricked headquarters for offices in geometric towers, tinted windows east of the city, while little splinter churches took up more prominent shop, with literal Bibles and seminary-free preachers and always the talking in tongues.

God damn it, Bucky hated the tongues, but he had to pretend to believe something was happening when somebody jabbered and someone else "interpreted": "I am the Lord your God, and you was my people afore you knowed me," for the sake of ungrammatical God. But you had to subscribe to the attention-grabbing bullshit because they were votes, just like every Democrat had to take seriously some black preacher who praised Arafat or Hugo Chavez because they brought the votes in, too.

And there was the place. He saw the sign and pulled into the pocked gravel parking lot. Heart Ministries Outreach, unfortunately acronymed so that it was called "HMO" by its detractors and even in private by the Congressman. The lot no longer filled with pickup trucks alone but SUVs and upscale foreign cars and bumper stickers announcing SARAH!, I AM NRA AND I VOTE, SANTORUM 2012, IMPEACH OBAMA. His kind of crowd, he observed with a sad resignation.

He could feel the hammer of the bass drum as he approached the building where Jerry Jeff Pfeiffer served every Sunday, Wednesday, and Friday night as a Spirit Deacon and Prayer Warrior. Taking off his fisherman's cap, the cool spring wind gusting through the sparse hair the cap tried to hide, Bucky stepped into the church and slipped into the back pew beside a mulleted "deacon" who smelled of stale cigarettes and Brut.

The man introduced himself as Aldo Wooters, and Bucky smiled and shook hands, barely listening to the whispered welcome, his eyes panning the tabernacle. Thank God there were no snakes, no rapturous flock writhing in the aisles consumed by the Holyghost: you could campaign on Biblical literalism because the country club crowd didn't pay attention to theology, but theatrics would embarrass them, would lose votes among the sensible.

Bucky seated himself as the HMO congregation sang a pretty fair version of "I'll Fly Away".

"Brother Pfeiffer's doing the preaching today," the deacon whispered, and Bucky was suddenly attentive.

He would know what he had to work with. God damn it, he hoped Jerry Jeff wasn't a fucking idiot like the last goober they got to run against DeMoyne Troubles, a mulleted nincompoop named Clayton Crowe, who had denied evolution, climate change, and the Holocaust in one meltdown of an October speech: he had been ten points behind before the disaster, and afterwards was outpolled by a drag queen named Stella Artois, campaigning as performance art on the Drinks All Around party ticket.

The tongues began as they passed the plate, a big old woman lifted her hands to Jesus. *SHAMbala!* she proclaimed. *Ha sham da ka ba la mesa la!*

Bucky dropped a five in the collection, noticing his was the highest denomination of bill, that the plate was filled with ones and change, with scrawled notes and what looked like a pair of earrings. For a moment his sight blurred as he passed the plate along to the deacon.

Bless them, he thought. *It'd be about time.*

And Jerry Jeff Pfeiffer stepped in front of the pews.

He began, "'I have loved you,' says the Lord."

Affirmations and assent from those assembled. The snake-rattle of a tambourine.

"But what does *that* mean?" Jerry asked, eyes scanning his expectant audience. "Because the Lord *also* says, 'Yet I have loved Jacob, but Esau I have hated, and I have turned his mountains into a wasteland and left his inheritance to the desert jackals.'

More affirmations, but Jerry Jeff raised his hand, stilled them. "They was twins, you may recall. Rebekah's twin sons, from the same father Isaac. The one his father liked to sacrifice until the Lord stayed his hand."

Fewer assents and *yes, Lords* now. The same people who brought you *the Bible is the literal word of God* did not recognize that Jerry Jeff was talking about Abraham.

Not the first time, Bucky wished himself elsewhere.

"Before the twins was born or done anything good or bad—in order that God's purpose in election might stand: not by works but by Him who calls—God told Rebekah, 'The older will serve the younger.' When they emerged from the womb, Jacob clutching onto his older-by-seconds brother's ankle."

"*Yet I loved Jacob, but Esau I hated.* Why would the Lord say that? Why would He love Jacob and hate Esau?"

The fellowship stirred uncomfortably.

"It has to do with choosing one man and his descendants and rejecting another man and his descendants. Not loving one more than the other. But choosing.

"How do you think the chosen Jews felt in Hitler's ovens? They was chosen as God's people. Not loved more than any of the others. Just chosen. Preferred."

Bucky fidgeted in the pew. Have to keep him off of the Holocaust.

"And in Isaac's old age and blindness, he couldn't tell the boys apart. You know the story. Esau was hungry and come back from the fields, and he begged Jacob to give him a bowl of stew. And Jacob agreed to it, in exchange for Esau's birthright. That is, his right to be regarded as the first-born, because back in the olden days, the first-born inherited everything. He must not of thought much of his birthright, his inheritance, to trade it away for a bowl of stew. And Jacob was his opposite, I guess. His smooth and shifty double, who come at the gifts of the spirit in the opposite manner.

"For the gifts of the spirit are hazardous, brothers and sisters in Jesus. Some are like Esau, who receive them as a birthright and hold them at no account. Others, like Jacob, do anything to have them, and lose them by doing anything. Two sides of the double-edged sword, people of Heart Ministries. A blade that cuts the wielder and the foe."

∞

Double edges bothered the thoughts of Dominic Rackett, as well, when Ellie offered to drive him to the South End.

He was coming down the steps from his room above the theater when they met on the landing. Exchanged pleasantries, as he discovered she wasn't doing anything, not much, and that he was catching the 18 bus to his father's old neighborhood, for reasons he couldn't pin down on a day that threatened rain.

So she offered to drive him there. Hadn't been in that part of town, it turned out, which only confirmed Todd Vitale's claim that his sister was sheltered, had hung around a nice East End neighborhood until it was time for college and rebellion. Still, she was showing gumption for having moved west of the interstate, to an apartment not far from Grandma Mary's, where apparently she took an occasional class at the university, lived off her parents' money and didn't do much except cultivate her demeanor.

Oh, Dominic knew about her blues. He didn't need her brother to tell him. She was smoking too much reefer, stringing Max (and occasionally him) like an old-school Southern belle, and reading Hunter Thompson at the suggestion of John Bulwer, because, like her brother, she was eager to impress the guru of Old Louisville by reading the stoner bard of the city.

Dominic liked her when she drove her car up onto the sidewalk while texting or high, but he knew it didn't bode well for passengers. But that wasn't the reason that he declined her offer.

There was something he needed to settle with Gabriel Rackett alone. It was the purpose of moving here, after all—the whole rationale.

When Dominic had screened *Nosferatu,* notepad in hand and prepared to write the flyer, the film had unnerved him. He got up and left as the vampire's shadow ascended the stairs toward the room of poor innocent Ellen Hutter. Count Orlok was always rising up out of darkness: out of the cellars of his castle, out of the ship's hold on his voyage to Germany, up the last stairwell to Ellen's room, where his shadow loomed unnaturally large, its fingers lengthened by slanted light as they reached for the latch of her door. And now Count Orlok had risen into Dominic's thoughts, connected, in some way, with Gabriel's vanishing into subterranean shadow, and encouraging Dominic to travel those suburban streets once more, to locate, if he could, the abiding source of his uneasiness.

"I should go by myself, Ellie," he had said with a smile. *"Bound for the land of thieves and ghosts."*

"Don't, Dominic," she said, and he remembered her confession that *Nosferatu* had upset her as well, more than she liked to let on.

And that, too, was why Ellie Vitale could not come along. Two allegiances wrangled with each other in his thoughts, as unsettled business ran up against this new attraction, this pretty, half-stoned balance of brilliance and heartbreak that he figured he had no chance with, not really. No, best settle the past before taking on the present, he told himself, pretty much certain as he thought so that it was the nature of the past to remained unsettled, that the lovely girl he left on the landing with a baffled look on her face was unsettled as well, uncertain how to behave when a man didn't do exactly as she had expected and wished.

12.

The place looked the same, as far as he could tell.

Grandma Mary had lived here as a single mother, raising her only son after Tom Rackett left her for a girl in her late teens. Mary had annulled Dom's grandfather, hitched herself to a science teacher named Billy Hume, who had turned out to be crazy even by her forgiving standards. Then she had married to the third husband, a benign man twenty years her senior, who had passed away when Dominic was sixteen. Not believing in divorce, at least on paper like a good traditional Irish girl, Mary annulled Dom's grandfather, disbelieved the short marriage to Billy Hume, then married Andy Lull several years later when Hume had divorced her for his own religious reasons. Still, Gabriel said she had been strangely relieved when old Tom Rackett had died, as though if he'd returned from Detroit and the recesses of her past, she'd be bound to take him back by some mythological constraint.

The only grandfather Dominic remembered was the third husband, Andy Lull, and he mourned the old man a while on the sidewalks next to his house. He remembered only hot weather, the grill in the driveway, the summer struggles with the lawn mower, and Grandpa Andy's loving inability to make sense of the changeling that stood in his yard and watched him season and turn the steaks.

The house across the street, where he had been headed all along, was a disappointment now. It had been entirely renovated a few years back, his grandmother had told him, by a young couple from Tennessee who were, she confided in a whisper, living out of wedlock. Dominic didn't remember much about the Bell place beyond a wooden incline leading up to the front door, but that had been taken down, and the attached garage had become a side room of sorts. He could only imagine how the basement of the place had changed, but then his recollections were so hazy, so distorted by that Christmas night two decades past, that the basement he remembered was probably not there to begin with.

Recalled or misremembered or even hallucinated out of trauma and loss, the Bell basement was where Dominic's long aimlessness had begun. That was still how he figured it, in part because that was what they told him. His mother and stepfather majored on his indirection, his changing schools and callings ("like he changes shirts," his mother had said), but years of counseling had made him superficially whole, smoothing his surfaces to the point that everyone decided he wasn't damaged at all, just shiftless like his father.

Now he stood in front of the Bell house and squinted at the picture window. It seemed as though something moved in the recesses of the house, something that caught his eye through the reflecting surface of the glass, but he wasn't going to be taken in, refused to be lured by the place he only imagined had swallowed his father.

For it was only imagination, wasn't it? What was it the doctor had said in *Nosferatu,* when the girl had heard the call of the vampire, over the miles and in the dead of the German night?

A sudden fever, and mild blood congestion.

But Dominic's own fever had not ended well, and his imagination was often unkind. On that night he had awakened on the floor in Vermont, babbling nonsense about *the old man* and *Dacia* and *Christmas,* it was a dream that had unseated him, a dream of his father, pale and drained of life and substance, rising to meet him at the head of a stairwell into darkness. Perhaps it was a deep psychic tremor, or perhaps he had conjured it from years of Jungian analysis and bong duty. Whatever the case, it was his specter, the trailer to his own film: it had always been behind him, a haunted past and afterthought that had shaped his aimlessness. Sometimes people got to know about Bell House and Gabriel's vanishing after they had become Dominic's friend: he would talk about it after a couple of drinks or a pipe, but he just as often kept silent, as he had done pretty much in his time in New England. Now, though, he was back in his father's country: the history was moving ahead of him, beginning to shape all acquaintance as he passed by the people he met in order to follow it into shadows.

Something he thought he noticed, standing in the yard in front of the Bell House, as the wind dropped suddenly and the world around him hushed, the far-off approaching thunder (or perhaps guns testing miles away at the army base) rumbling through the air and dissolving into silence, and something pale, indefinite in the branches of the water maple that towered behind the house, the summer sunset dappled by its dark, turning leaves.

$$\infty$$

He took the 18 back to Broadway, passing down a long section of highway littered with shops that featured auto parts, tanning beds, smokeless tobacco. A half dozen men, no older than he was, wearing camo and collared by their chest-length beards, got on and off the bus, regarding him warily for the three or four miles they rode.

It was hardly a life-affirming trip. Dominic saw as much, smiled bleakly at a young woman who wedged into the seat across the aisle, a brace of equally heavy (but jelly-smudged) toddlers in tow. He was met with a glare, and decided it was best to look straight ahead, to count the stoplights and the strip malls, as the buildings loomed taller and more derelict.

Dominic's thoughts raced back through Gabriel's account of this route. How, as a child, he and Grandma Mary had taken a Greyhound (no city buses traveled that far into the 'burbs back then) to the old station on 5th and Broadway, then south a few blocks, by cab or on foot, to the big conservative Catholic church in the middle of the old city. Dominic imagined that rigid Catholicism mixed with Grandma Mary's gin-and-tonics, her entourage of old gay men, serial marriages, and her chronic embroidery of the facts regarding any of these.

Quietly he traced a circle on the bus window, watching the world pass and darken with the prospect of rain. The bus route bent past the racetrack, under an overpass where, according to his friends, eighteen-wheelers crashed incessantly, their drivers lured by a possible time-saving short cut into trying to negotiate in deceptively narrow space. Now, passing the university, the strip mall of eateries rarely visited because the students were mostly commuters at heart, rushing out of the neighborhood before dark, headed toward restaurants with cuter names, trendy menus, and wall-to-wall white people. Melancholy store fronts, staffed by sleepy, underemployed students, switched on their outside lighting, and Dominic was surprised to be overtaken by dusk.

His stomach rumbled, and shadows deepened in the alley. Dominic thought of the Hungry Ghosts, the *preta*, spirits too well-behaved for hell, too anguished for even the lowest of heavens. Cast into a vexed and grasping country, condemned to desirous streets. Sitting outside the walls and at crossroads, slinking back to the homes they had occupied while alive, in death fed only by offerings from their survivors.

It was a long trip from his father's old haunts. Disembarking at Broadway, Dominic walked the several blocks toward the rubble of his old apartment, this time awake and with enough light to see by. Sifting through ash and garbage for any belonging surviving the explosion and fire, he could retrieve little beyond a standing mirror, a housewarming gift from his grandmother, who had mirrors aplenty and could not imagine an apartment without at least one. Shouldering it onto the bus, he thought that he must have looked like a looter to the driver, who stared at him through the mirror as the bus wound its way back downtown, to a stop within sight of the Shangri-La.

∞

Dominic was still thinking of the strange side-trip and salvage as he hauled the mirror up the theater steps toward the top-floor apartment, staggering a little on the same landing until the cumbersome load was steadied out of nowhere, and Jerry Jeff Pfeiffer asked, "Can I give you a hand with that, Dominic?"

The janitor stood behind him on the stairs, not a big man but sinewy and solid, an earnest look in his eyes as he reached out to catch the base of the mirror.

It startled Dominic. This time of evening, he was seldom aware of Jerry Jeff, who went quietly about custodial business, so unobtrusive that any noise from downstairs was almost always Leni Zauber, thundering around the projection room and bristling the air with whistling, singing, and muttered German. To *see* someone was unnerving, especially for someone used to the routines of the old building.

"It's not that heavy," Dominic stammered, "just a bulky old mirror," shifting part of its weight into Jerry's arms as the two of them climbed to the apartment door. Jerry Jeff allowed that bulky was certainly the case, and that it didn't help none that the weather had got so very *hot* this weekend, that Dominic must be glad to have an air-conditioned place to stay, even if it didn't have a mirror in it to begin with.

Dominic explained that how it was more sentiment than vanity, that the mirror was about the only item salvaged from his apartment fire—and see? Look at the blackened edges of the glass, how the scrolling at the top was seared—and that he got it because, oddly enough, he had felt sorry for the mirror, felt like it was orphaned and homeless and needed a place in a room.

Jerry Jeff didn't know about feeling sorry for inanimate things, but he said that the good thing was that us guys really don't have to look all that pretty, though you might not be able to tell that from the way some fellas preen and groom themselves before a date. And a tremor of embarrassment passed through Dominic as they set the mirror up in a corner, facing the door and away from the one window and the natural light. He opened the window to the muted sound of traffic on 3rd Street, as if to show Jerry Jeff that it wasn't that easy being Dominic Rackett, that the AC was spotty and the top room stored the heat. No reason for envy, but as he thought about it, the janitor hadn't seemed envious at all, the negative emotions all brought to the room by Dominic himself, stoked by the heat and the long bus journey.

The next morning he preened and groomed himself in front of the mirror. He had a meeting with Dr. Zauber later that day, and he figured he should look presentable. With second thoughts, he tilted the mirror toward the window, and things suddenly changed.

The attic room was stuffy, and he had opened the door. Through the mirror appeared the cloudy incline of the stairs leading to the lobby. The stairs descended to the landing, where the bas-relief faces of Dante and Virgil stood half-framed in amber-tinted light, like in a night interior from *Caligari* or the shadowy flight of steps the vampire ascends in *Nosferatu*. But Dominic was here in broad daylight, and the faces seemed to turn, to look up the stairwell, gaping at him, their gaze meeting his in the depths of the mirror as though they were looking through him, beckoning. *Jesus,* he whispered, his legs giving way as for a moment he lurched forward through the glass and into the reflected landing.

Translucent, a creature of light and shadow only, he took the first step down as the walls and banister, the newel post and the rug at the foot of the stairs all resolved around and below him. It was like walking in the fog of dreams as his descent yawned into the shadows and, for a moment someone breathed behind him, gibberish syllables in his father's voice and inflection, stripping away all his senses but hearing. In a dense and manufactured darkness he stopped on a step he could no longer see, tried to gather his breath, but the shadows were drowning him, filling his lungs like water. He gasped and flailed and the world went away as the far-off basement swallowed him.

For a moment the death masks appeared at the foot of the slowly resolving stairs, their eyes fixed on him in sluggish astonishment, gaping, becoming gray, translucent flames at first and then slowly transparent, until they dissolved into the darkness, revealing a man who had been standing behind them all along, whose shadow took on familiar shape from his past.

And *I see through a glass darkly*, Dominic thought to himself, until his imaginings steadied and he knelt mystified in his theater apartment returned to breathing and swaddled in light.

∞

Shaken, Dominic lay down on the cot, attending the cracks and water stains on the ceiling—anything to distract him from the strange voyage through the looking glass.

What the fuck just happened? he whispered, his fingers trembling as he lit a cigarette.

The theater was silent. Nothing stirred on the floors below.

It was like Resourceful Jack, Dominic told himself, the narcotic inhale of tobacco smoke bristling in his lungs. Resourceful Jack, the hero of his father's novel *Dacia*. That was a boy used to looking down into darkness and carrying on nonetheless.

He thumbed through the recently acquired books, setting aside the *Dragonlance* and the Rilke and the Alan Watts, picking up the spine-creased copy of *Dacia* and opening it to the first chapter, because it seemed like a good place for his jostled thoughts to settle. He read his father's words, then, over the years and miles and out of the Realm of Hungry Ghosts:

∞

Only Jack could hear the voices of the cemetery angels.

Gabriel, Michael, and Raphael. An angel for Jack, and one for each of his brothers.

The statues had told him how everything faced the light. The sparse plants, the stones and cenotaphs, even their own marbled eyes turned toward the palace at the height of the steeply sloping necropolis.

Orlando and Valentine were older. They assured Jack that no angel spoke, most especially none made of stone. That perhaps it was an unmoored sadness in his blood, their inheritance: after all, they had lost the family fortunes three generations back, their father had moved to far more humble quarters in a ramshackle manor among the tombstones, and not long ago, their mother had gone to her own narrow last home in a grave at the borders of their demesne. It was a long and sad migration, one that could no doubt give a young man visions, make him hear things.

Jack had become a scavenger there. It was ignoble business, the pawning of grave offerings, and the traditions of wine and beans offered to the hungry dead had been the dinner for a quite-living boy more than once. A little more shameful was the hocking of the things left to memorialize children: dolls, beads, tops, and lead soldiers found their way back into the hands of the merchants who had sold them, no questions asked. The mounded earth that the tombstones marked was warmer at night. No doubt it bristled with worms, with the slow, smokeless burning of decay, and it was a refuge of sorts, asylum from the scrutiny of the Dacian police, their nets and gisarmes.

And Jack was the one who heard the voices. Like an only child, much different in age from his brothers, he had grown up in the care of servants and the bewilderment of his widowed father.

He had long since ceased to believe in the god of Dacia. The angels, however, traditional messengers of His Ineffable and Inscrutable Will, continued to prompt him with subliminal voices, whispers just below the surface of hearing. They spoke in memories and desires and ghostly yearning, and on occasion you could see them, spilled light weaving through the dark slopes of the cemetery as though the tombstones were ablaze with shadowy fire.

So when a decree had come down from the King of Dacia, proclaiming a search for a consort—a husband for his daughter, the Princess Anamchara, whose beauty was famous among those who lived along the cemetery slopes, none of whom had ever seen her— it was the angels' voices that discouraged Jack. Let Orlando and Valentine seek their fortunes, the whispers seemed to say.

You go about your own business as terzo, they would tell him. The Dacian term for the third son, which is how Jack was referred to, by his brothers, and, it seemed, by the angels themselves. Take into account your plot of ground, they all said, your role as vagrant and pickpocket, family chronicler and keeper of the ancestral graves. Let your brothers decide on rule, on marriage, on dominion, on respectable callings.

And never the third son of fable and tale, never showing particular talent or gumption, Jack was content to obey those voices. Until the tune of the angels changed that spring of his seventeenth year.

A fortnight after the decree, as Orlando and Valentine prepared themselves for ascent to the Dacian Heights, for the charges and contests that traditionally led to the choosing of a Royal Consort, an unmoored disquiet troubled the promptings of one of the angels— Gabriel, of course, Who is the Bearer of Tidings. This whisper slowly overwhelmed the others, and soon the sound of the angel's voice was accompanied by portentous dreams, in which the Princess Anamchara appeared at the summit of the Necropolitan Hill, framed in the glow of the twin moons and attended by small companies of shades— ghostly creatures, but none whom Jack could recognize.

Slowly, then, the voice of Raphael intertwined with the vision—a song of health and encouragement.

Rise up, the angel told him. Rise up and find your way to your inheritance.

Never mind that the road is dark and that your inclination is to give up. That you are so inclined to give up, so wearied by the whole prospect of beginning a lifelong search, a search you have put off until you have almost forgotten that there is something left to find…

Turn your eyes to the foothills, Resourceful Jack. To the shadowy depths. In your descent is your rising, and the rising of your line and your family. And for every obstacle that lies before you, there will be someone at your side to lift and encourage you.

Mine is but the first of these voices.

∞

Dominic was drowsing, the book gabled on his chest, when Leni Zauber knocked at his door. Hastily, almost embarrassed, he cleared the bed of books, setting them in a tilted tower on his table and offering the old woman the only comfortable seat in the room.

She was all questions this afternoon. How was he getting on with George Castille? With Todd? With the janitor and the other one? He responded with brief, discouraging *just fine, thank yous* as she stayed too long, sat on the bed, looked at the books, the little tensor lamp, the brass Buddha and his bare coat rack.

He hoped she wasn't feeling sorry for him. He doubted she was. It didn't seem to be a sentiment she was good at.

Instead, he suspected she was interviewing. Tapping his depths with her long and angular insight. At last she touched on the subject of Eleanor Vitale, and Dominic knew she was leading him onward and inward, beckoning like the drowned poets in the mirror.

13.

Seven flames at the foot of the mountain, gathering light from each other, each blending with the next until they were four, then one, then three, then seven again, each returning to unsteady separation, the stone of the mountain behind them occluded by their brilliance.

For a moment, as his flame gathered solidity and substance, the twinned death's heads flickered in its midst, as though he were becoming a monster wearing a collar of skulls. But he knew this image and the others were illusion, dreams and projections of his disembodied intellect, steps on the journey he was taking. Convinced he was coming home, he watched the others commingle—a gaunt male figure transforming and gathering weight to become a stocky, geometrical shape, seemingly made of the same stuff as the mountain behind it. Then softening, becoming rounded, less angular, taking on female form, the eyes slightly asymmetrical, the nose and hands a bit outsized, all lending her credibility and a familiar beauty he remembered from film and from in person.

In this form of flawed and fluid loveliness she began to speak to him in German. The time had passed for that, at least for the moment, so he steered her into accented English and she followed, competently if not gracefully, asking him if the man beyond the light had yet been chosen. Draping herself on his shoulder, enabling conversation but stopping short of affection, she drew him out, her pale flame fluttering nervously as he delivered the news.

Yes, the man has been chosen, Maria, he told her. *And he is drawn to the girl out there, which was what I have been hoping all along.* The death's heads glittered like eyes in his flame now, intent on the supple apparition of the woman beside him. He spoke to her beneath human language, human knowing, their flames commingling like the mating angels in Milton's heaven, but this was the light of intellect and information they were sharing, here at the foot of the mountain that marked the center of all things.

Are you willing? he asked her in all but speech. *Willing to cross and mingle with the girl, your alien flame entering the warm blood of a vital creature? Or are you homeward bound, the job unfinished, the world unredeemed?*

For a moment her pale flame bent toward the questions. Two of the others drew near as well, their smoky tendrils curling like hooks through the eyes of the death's heads as though they sought to latch onto him, to follow him out. He blossomed like a gray flower under their urgent attentions, but he pulled back from where they hovered.

And yet Maria refused to follow. She told him that a light more brilliant and uncompromised called her from up the mountain slope. Already she felt herself dissolving, she told him, old angers and envies fading and the light sifting her. Soon, she believed, they would all be headed toward that higher and purer place.

The flames around the two of them were receding now, taking form in recognizable shape—the meaty, comical Ombrade and elegant Marie. And the lovely, flawed flame of Maria told him that soon they would be moving, it would be soon, she knew, that they would gladly lose themselves in a realm of light.

For a moment, improper anger surged through him again. He did not act upon it, did not voice it, though he suspected that Maria's preparing for the world up the mountain was far too premature. Anger, too, that she would not accompany him, that instead he would seek the journey's end alone, relying on a humbler vessel. The old scholar, resourceful and ruthless as ever, but still flushed and confused by breath and the heart's insistent pounding.

Through the gray twilight of the borderland an auto rushed by, taking shape from the mist and passing intermittently from shadow into slanted light, as though a camera was catching sight of it through a nest of baffles and blinds. He remembered the cautionary words of the lamas, not to be seduced by illusions of power and movement, but nonetheless he followed the impulse, alert now in the passenger seat of a sleek Mercedes, there and never there, the Reichsprotektor beside him as they took the hairpin curve by the Troja Bridge, the whole panorama of the city visible, Hradcany in a spring mist at the southwestern edge of sight.

Then nothing. The world collapsing. Breathless he stood again at the foot of the mountain, the car and the road it traveled, Maria and Marie and Ombrade all vanished. It was as though, like the young poet in the film, he had awakened to a landscape stripped of spirits. And quickly he, too, began to dissolve, the fire of his passing as faint and indeterminate as memories of a former life.

But it was not that way. He had come here by other roads.

∞

It wasn't long before Leni brought up at last the reason she had taken Dominic on, had chosen him for an odd, unnecessary job, housed him in the theater, and paid him above the minimum wage.

It had to do with the last film. Dominic had come to

suspect that, but he wondered why it was so important. Why it was here.

"The debut of this *Walpurgisnacht*," she said, "must be successful. Must be acclaimed and celebrated. It is why I chose who and where, Dominic."

"This is a relatively small town, Dr. Zauber. I…have found myself wondering why this venue. There are beautiful old theaters all over the country, in larger cities."

"You think like a *Drogenhändler*, Dominic. Like how you say? 'A dealer'? Just because this is not your New York or Chicago or Los Angeles—the big shimmering locations that Americans always distrust. You love the small towns, you Americans, because they express the way you like to regard yourselves, your own best self-image. Oh, I am not saying it is all illusion, mind you. But instead, it is simple small-town living seen through the eyes of complicated people who make money from your vanities of plainness."

Dominic nodded. "I see what you're saying. Happened in our popular music, as well—all the "aw shucks" rock and country hard-sold and commercialized, polished up to sound polished. But weren't these films different? Weren't they all made in Berlin or Vienna, and just about as sophisticated and urban as you could imagine back then?"

Leni lit a cigarette, not stopping for permission, exhaling a billow of blue smoke before she looked directly at Dominic, her voice rising in pitch, her eyes glittering. "And you think this is about these films, Dominic? About the Wegeners and Murnaus and Langs, who are all dead, whose films will be seen by cineastes and aficionados, and occasionally at a little festival such as your own, where people will watch them because you are supposed to, then lose interest within the hour because the celebrities are dead, too, the explosions unenhanced, and most of all because they have to read the dialogue?"

"But then…"

She waved her hand, the Gauloises spiraling plumes of dismissal. "No, *liebchen*. It is all about the last film. About

Walpurgisnacht. And finally, not about that film at all."

A long silence in the little room, as Dominic tried to decode that odd statement. Leni offered him a cigarette, which he took absently, inhaling the first draw before he realized he was smoking it. He looked up, spellbound by her bright gaze, and for a moment he wanted to tell her everything—about the lure of the salvaged mirror, his feelings for Ellie, his roundabout search for his father. After all, she had just opened up to him, hadn't she?

He wanted all kinds of follow-up questions, as well. *If it is and isn't about this film's debut, Dr. Zauber, about this film you've been talking about for days, then what are we here for? What is it all about, this cinematic commotion of yours?*

And of all people, why did you hire me?

But instead he found himself talking about Ellie Vitale, the safest of his revelations. That they had yet to go out together. Why he chose Dr. Zauber as a sounding board he would second-guess later. But there you had it: the young man lamenting, the old woman leaning toward him, portraying concern like the good minor actress they said she had been back in the day.

What she was doing was a form of inveiglement. That listening look he could see through readily, but was drawing him in nonetheless. In that, she was like the fictions she presented on screen, he figured: you knew that the actors were formed out of shadows and light, a series of static images flurried through a projector rather than people living through actual lives, but you sit back and consent to be taken in.

∞

There was a time, of course, when Leni Zauber herself was taken in.

She knew Florian Geist largely from the tales others had told about him, so that her first real recollection of him, standing on a sunlit slope in Tibet, beckoning her to come out of the shadows, was already loaded with associations. She approached him that bright noon like she was seeing him for the first time, and she had hidden beneath his arm that day—the light was deceptive, because the wind was uncannily cold.

It was on that day that her memory began.

Oh, there were images, dreamlike and fragmentary, of the time before, like the filtered sun through her half-recollected cathedral windows. But before and after those moments it was simply story—the hearsay of memory, where the Florian Geist she believed and believed in took the shape that she needed—her mentor, originator, lover of her soul and perhaps of her tentative body.

Geist told her stories of his early life, about his days at Bioscop and Ufa. The romance of the early films, how he had worked on *Caligari* and *Nosferatu,* on all of the golem movies she had loved at first sight. How he had sat in attendance in the filming of *Waxworks,* the very film they were showing at the Shangri-La this week, and that he had a voice in dismissing the character of Rinaldo Rinaldini, the romantic Italian bandit.

Few people tend to notice, Florian told her, but at the start of that film Rinaldini's is among the wax figures whose story the young poet is hired to write. The moody, glamorous outlaw did not fit with the others—Haroun al-Raschid, Ivan the Terrible, and Springheel Jack, all tyrants and monsters in their own ways. Rinaldini was a rebel, a victim of love, the dashing outsider who was more a romantic lead than a rival and foil for the young poet, played so handsomely by Wilhelm Dieterle.

Florian told the story, and Leni believed him. Saw Florian himself as a noble bandit, a hero in his own right. He was a hero like Robin Hood, like Wilhelm Tell.

She did remember asking him, though: if he planned to take the bandit's story from the film, why not take him out entirely? What good was Rinaldini at the beginning of the story, a wax figure stationary and remote, while the caliph, the king, the murderer, act out their comedies and horrors?

People come and go in films, he told her. She knew that. But what she probably didn't know was that people came and went *from* films as well. Spring-Heel Jack was not alone, Florian claimed—not the first character to step from the stage or the screen to inhabit the waking life of his audience. It happened in Shakespeare's time with the Grocer Errant in the old Beaumont play, in Pirandello, in the States in *Hellzapoppin*. And films made by Jews in Hollywood.

In 1941 he wrote to her again about these things, after the disastrous battle at Rostov, the Russian winter bogging the assault on Leningrad, the entry of America into the war. It seemed more plausible, then—in a time when things were stepping out of the collective nightmare and becoming facts on the streets and beaches and steppes—that monsters would break the fourth wall on screens and stages everywhere, that all the customary lines were blurred.

Florian made her believe that the old fictions were still possible, though. His letters came from Potsdam at first, then later in Prague, and by now she was in the mountains again— Switzerland, she thought she remembered, but the details were damnably unclear. She remembered only the letters, the rapturous, triumphant, anti-Semitic poetry having given way to a brittle shrillness she could not match to the romantic bandit of her memory. It was not long until she found the comparison: that all Florian's exuberance, all his idealism, had frozen on screen like the abandoned Rinaldini, and Spring-Heeled Jack had burst forth, stalking the wings of the theater and the self-dismantling carnival around it.

∞

Geist had not told Leni of the events in the spring of 1940, after his return from Tibet and six months following the outbreak of the War. In Prague, in the offices of the Barrendov Studios, he had met with Rudolf Vesely, whose recent developments with cellulose triacetate had led to a film stock the young chemist promised would be flame-resistant and long lived. The research was secretive, even more so since the occupation of Prague in March of the previous year, as the Reich pirated Czech art and science to serve its own ambitions.

Some things were even more secretive. Geist had it on good authority that Vesely's grandfather had changed his name from Veischelis in the wave of antisemitism following the Hilsner Affair. Vesely scarcely showed his fear when Geist brought up the genealogy and suggested that it might be healthier for all involved if Vesely simply handed the research over to the Geist family in exchange for protection.

Vesely had two young daughters, and the family was respectable, was safe for the moment. It showed Geist's confidence, his belief that in the rising Reich there was money to be made from more durable film. After all, hadn't the Reich Ministry of Propaganda shown that the cinema would be the art of Germany's future, the herald of the new age? Not that he set top priority for the vision of Goebbels and his lot: as long as it advanced film careers, the ideology was fine with Florian Geist.

Fine and convenient, for of course Vesely, terrified at the prospect of relocation, complied to the letter with Geist's demands. The research was handed over, and Vesely handed over not long after, bound on a train for Theresienstadt when the camp opened and the years of its killing began. From nightmare to nightmare the young chemist ranged until he vanished into the silent maw of the Holocaust.

Waxworks (1924)

Directed by Paul Leni, who sadly would not survive the decade, *Waxworks* is one of the first anthology-piece movies—an honorable genre that includes films from *Hotel* (1931) through the Scorsese/Coppola/Woody Allen *New York Stories* and beyond. The trick of such films is in the connections of the stories—that a world is revealed in which everything is connected, like the Buddhists and the scientists tell us. The imagination of the viewer discovers a universe as it links one story, one setting, one situation with the next. It isn't your usual form of storytelling, but give it a chance.

Also, it's like the weather around here: if you don't like what you get at first, just wait a while and something different comes along.

The premise of *Waxworks* is a simple one: a young poet (Wilhelm Dieterle) is hired by the owner of a wax museum to write tales to go with the principal figures at the display: Haroun al Raschid, Ivan the Terrible and Spring-Heel Jack (a slightly camouflaged Jack the Ripper).

These figures are played by three of Germany's best actors—Conrad Veidt, Emil Jannings and Werner Krauss (remember Veidt and Krauss from The Cabinet of Dr. Caligari?)—each of whom opposes, somehow, the budding romance of the poet and the young daughter of the wax museum's owner.

Or is it their characters who are thwarted by these formidable tyrants? The film blurs lines between the actors and the characters they play, between the fictional worlds of the poet's fantasies and the "real world" (you tend to forget that it is fiction as well) that frames the story. It's one of the first films to "break the fourth wall," and sometimes it's hard to remember that such a thing wasn't a cinematic cliché back in 1924.

The scenario was Henrik Galeen's, who was also in on the writing of The Golem and Nosferatu. It reflected German filmmakers' fascination with power, which in some

ways is the common theme
of the stories.

The story goes
like this: a young poet
arrives at a carnival in
response to a newspaper
advertisement. After
being given a tour of the
waxworks, and noticing
that the proprietor's
daughter (Olga Belajeff)
is quite pretty, he accepts
the job.

Noticing as well
that Haroun Al-Raschid's
statue is missing an arm,
the author is inspired,
the waxworks fade into
an exotic Arabian Nights
setting, and we see the
young poet in the role of
Assad, a poor baker, and
the girl as his lovely wife
Maimune.

Haroun Al-Raschid
(played broadly and
with meaty lust by Emil
Jannings) is drawn by
Maimune's beauty, and
comes to the bakery
to have his way with
her. What follows is
a complicated story of
intrigue, a counterfeit
sultan made of wax, whose
arm Assad amputates
in bravado, trying to
persuade his wife that
he is a manly, worthy
husband, and the magic
ring he takes from the
severed wax hand.

The episode
devolves into a chase
and a bedroom farce, but
needless to say, it ends
happily for the young
couple, who are reconciled
by magic and love.

The next story is
darker, as Czar Ivan the
Terrible (played manically
by Conrad Veidt) and his
astrologer are in the cellars
of the Kremlin, where the
Czar's poisoner has just
finished administering
a dose to a prisoner. To
Ivan's delight, the prisoner
dies just as the last grains
fall to the bottom of a
large hour glass, which is
central to this tale.

Ivan is pleased, but
the astrologer warns that
the man may pose a threat
to the Czar himself. Things
follow as you'd expect with
a tyrant, but before the
poisoner dies, he writes
Ivan's name on the hour
glass and turns it over,
and the urgency of the plot
begins.

What follows is a
creepy account of Ivan's
intention of what was
called droit de seigneur,
the unsettling medieval
tradition in which a
monarch can precede the
husband in the wedding
bed. The marrying couple
are, of course, the young

poet and the girl of his dreams, and though they would appear powerless against the tyrant, the good news is that the hourglass is slowly draining.

As the poet begins the third story about Spring Heeled Jack (a kind of Central European recasting of Jack the Ripper), Jack himself (played by Werner Krauss) comes to life in the tent to pursue the young couple through a nightmarish version of the carnival, in perhaps the film's most frightening sequence. Instead of entering the world of the story, the story enters his world, and the line between fictions blurs disturbingly, so that this audience member, leaving the theater, found himself looking over his shoulder, in case something from the screen world of *Waxworks* was in pursuit.

Technically and conceptually advanced for its time—the set design,

cinematography, and daring blending of the world of films with the world of the people who watch them—*Waxworks* is a brilliant addition to our series. What makes it fun, though, is the presence of its stars: Jannings' Haroun is pathetically funny in his grotesque pursuit of the much younger baker's wife; Veidt is suitably obsessive, discomforting, and preoccupied as the monstrous Ivan; Krauss, in a surprisingly short appearance, may be the most frightening of the three, emerging from the screen to pursue the innocent young couple calmly, his stately gait in contrast to the fact that, wherever they run, he is right behind them. No world is sealed from Springheel Jack, it seems, nor is any form of refuge safe. It was a feeling that would no doubt be pervasive in the Germany of the next two decades.

--Dominic Rackett

∞

Slumped low in a back-row seat, Max watched the preliminary screening of Waxworks.

Sullen and loudly slurping a Coke, his feet propped on the back of the chair in front of him, defying all of George Castille's warnings about decorum and neatness, he was unaware that as he watched the actors flutter among the lights of the filmed carnival, he was being watched as well.

Gathering and dissolving in the shadows behind the screen, three tongues of gray flame mingled and forked. Intelligence passed among them—something beyond language and gesture, borne out of an insubstantial fusion.

Is this the one? they asked in a chorus, in chorus answering themselves, as if it was all ordained, the story all told, no character able to change the narrative nor bow out.

But *no*, they answered, *not this one*. As though the answer was foregone, as though it involved no discovery, but was more a rehearsed call and response, a behavior unfolding according to a silent script.

Max watched as Assad the young baker, played by the handsome poet played by Wilhelm Dieterle, sneaked into the house of Haroun al-Rashid, Caliph of Baghdad. Assad was clearly the hero, for who didn't love the poor young man, striving to please his beautiful wife and smooth the edges of her discontent?

Max knew this story, knew its conflict and its world. The boy was not worthy of her, had married far above his station and talents. It was fairytale stuff, so much that you knew how it would end. But when Assad cut the wax arm off the statue of the Caliph to steal what he supposed was Al-Rashid's "wishing ring," Max was swept with a sudden tearfulness, his gloom of minutes before rushing toward something stronger, less passive.

He gripped the arms of the theater chair, felt cool grit on his palms. The story resolved in a mutual embrace, blessed by the smirking Caliph, and Max watched impatiently as the baker became the young poet once again, became Dieterle staring apprehensively at the menacing statue of Ivan the Terrible, tall and attenuated like an icon, like a shrine to paranoia.

And when Ivan entered the second story, intervening in the wedding of a young pair of aristocrats, abducting the young woman and imprisoning Wilhelm Dieterle (who was again the beleaguered suitor), Max fought down fears of his own—rising fears, unnatural. There was no way out, he told himself: how could this one end happily, how could Jack have Jill? It was only Ivan's sudden insanity that saved the couple, the story's ending with mad king's turning and turning the hourglass as its sand ran out in a nightmarish eternity, having been promised by his court poisoner that he would die of an assassin's dosage once the glass was empty. It was a crazy scene and haunting, but strangely distressing, in that there was nothing the couple could have done to save themselves, that their fate lay wrapped in the whims and the chances of an all-powerful monarch.

He thought of El and himself. This time it made him nervous. Max was glad no evil king stood between them. For despite whatever he thought, he could not bend Dominic Rackett into such a role. Again, and not for the last time, he chided himself for making it a fight over a girl: El was an adult and had her own mind, and she would end up with whichever one of them showed he understood such things.

The thought reassured him. He only had to try. But with that comfort came a sense of something having withdrawn like a tide receding, leaving him feeling safer but vacated, as if the film was already over and all that remained on screen was a play of light and shadow.

The last section of the movie was brief, and Dominic's essay had promised it to be the most disturbing of them all. Just when you thought the story was over, Springheel Jack—the film's calm and frightening Jack the Ripper—stepped out of the poet's story to chase him and his beloved through the carnival that housed the wax museum, as lights and Ferris wheels and sideshow booths became the stage for a swift and relentless pursuit. Again, it was only accident that saved the couple: the poet awakes from a nightmarish dream, his stalker a figment of imagination, and Max wondered why he had ever expected anything more from a simple movie as the segment ended too suddenly and the lights went up.

∞

At the switch was Jerry Jeff Pfeiffer.

The screen glared in the wake of the film, and he had cleaning to do before the debut of *Waxworks*, so he turned on the lights, picked up a small trash can, and made for the front of the house. He passed the Winter boy, saw him blink and recoil like someone had got up in his face and swatted him. Jerry liked Max, liked the whole bunch of them, but of late it seemed like they were on hooks, that something was circling their camp. It concerned him in the midst of his other concerns.

He had seen Max's startled look before. Not here, not now, but as he had grown up. On the faces of the newly baptized, arising from the full immersion of creek and river, as they blinked at light for the first time, drenched in the flow of the Spirit. It was maybe that look of survival, he thought, as he passed by the alcove with its statues of the Greek gods to the little broom closet by the exit to the alley.

There was more, though. He paused at the alley door, broom and dustpan in hand, and remembered his mammaw's small and country church, how they handled snakes up in the mountains and he had been taken to a revival there when he was five? six? And there he had seen a look comparable—when he was but a child, unused to the movement of the Spirit and frightened easily by how grownups courted the things that undone them. Frightened as well by the face of a startled deacon when he drew the cottonmouth from the crate and the snake wrestled his grip and struck like a lash against his shoulder. All of this happened slowly as he remembered it, the congregation continuing its ecstatic dance, the tambourine and bass line, the smell of sweat and tobacco, the deacon dancing with them until he couldn't dance no more and the other Brothers lifted him and helped him off to a fate Jerry Jeff never heard of and never asked about. It must have happened so quickly, but the frame speed of memory changing it like the film students talked about around here, that something shown in more frames, if he remembered it right, slowed down the action. Turned the moment into momentous.

The moment into momentous. Jerry Jeff liked the phrase. Knew he could work it into his next sermon. Wasn't that, after all, how the Spirit often descends?

Carrying the trash can, he stepped into the alley. Did that last check of his belt for the side door key and found it there with the strange combination of relief and of knowing it would be there all along. Emptied the can in the dumpster, turned to reenter the theater…

And saw the rats lying to the side of the door.

What in the world? he thought, sweeping them with disgust into the dustpan. They were lighter than he expected: there was no smell, though the night was warm after a string of hot days. And the bodies—two of them Norway rats, two a strange dappled version Jerry Jeff couldn't recall seeing outside a pet store—were crusted with a translucent salt that clung to the dustpan and glittered in the light of the lamp over the stage door.

14.

The ticket booth outside the Shangri-La was a dusty throwback to its first heyday in the '20s. Octagonal, its window still the original watery glass despite the fact that, at some time or another, almost every pane on the street had been broken, it had straddled the ground between curiosity and eyesore until, as a last gesture toward the old films in the series, George Castille had decided to touch it up for use on the last hurrah of the theater. He had assigned Todd Vitale the task of making it presentable in any way short of painting or renovating it. Because, after all, it was set for demolition (or salvage at best) when the building gave way to the ChemCon offices.

"Just clean it up with some elbow grease, dear," George had suggested, his hand brushing the air vaguely as though he were starting the cleaning from a distance. "After all, it's only a short run for the poor thing, alas."

So on that Friday afternoon, as they began to prepare the theater for the first showing of *Waxworks,* Todd dutifully stepped out into the stifling September air, the summer that would not leave the city, into the booth which was even more stifling. For a moment he had trouble breathing—not so much from the heat as the confinement, a sudden stir of panic in his stomach and chest--but when he parted the ancient red velour curtains to look at the open street, he recovered balance.

Now he opened the bottle of wood polish, and the stringent chemical smell reminded him of huffing days in high school. Giddy, he pressed his forehead to the rippling glass and watched the heat buckle across the sidewalk, where shoppers and tourists sauntered by in shorts and tank tops. Why this kind of heat didn't thin the crowd he had no idea, but from inside the taut little casket of a booth it was like watching a film in surround, looking up and down the street, getting a little high from the fumes, dragging his thoughts back to the simple task at hand as he began to rub the counter wood, slowly reviving its original glow.

A young family passed by on the opposite side of the street, under Huntington's awning, where they stopped for a moment to look into the restaurant's window. A boy of six or seven, whom Todd took to be the oldest son, turned and peered at the booth, regarding it through distance and relentless sunlight.

On a whim, Todd stood mannequin-still, expressionless. He thought of the old carnival fortune-telling booths, staffed by turbaned wax figures who waved their hands over a fan of cards as the machine sent a neatly rolled little paper prophecy out to the wide-eyed yokel who had dropped a dime into the slot. He felt like something from a Ray Bradbury story, or some dummy-faced plot device from a *Twilight Zone*—the cool ones in black and white, the ones Rod Serling introduced as he smoked and squinted into the camera like the boy was squinting over there...

And the boy approached, hands behind his back, shifting from foot to foot as he stared almost obsessively through the glass at Todd, who was now as still as he could be, like Conrad Veidt as the sleepwalker, upright in a Caligari coffin. He wouldn't even blink, and his eyes began to smart from the pungent hot air, and it was becoming a contest now, who would flinch first. He couldn't even return his adversary's stare—he'd have to move his eyes and it would be a giveaway, a tell, a defeat.

But the mother called from across the street, barely audible through the glass—some Brandon or Brendan or Braden, he couldn't quite make it out—and the light shifted at the very edge of his frontward stare, and still looking ahead, he saw the boy rejoin the family. Only then could Todd relax, at last victorious.

That was when Ellie and Dominic passed between the family and the booth, bound toward the restaurant. Todd exhaled with a shiver and frowned, watching Dom open the door for her as she stopped briefly outside the building and turned toward the theater.

The two of them were talking softly. He could tell by the incline of her head, her genetically Italian shrug and gesture at something Dominic must have been saying. Todd wished she'd pick better men—her track record was lousy, from the older boys in high school through the Cowboy up to this clown—and even Max, whom he could tell adored his sister, would be a better choice than some dark-eyed charmer who was probably a dozen years older than El, from what he was hearing. Frustrated, sidling close to anger, Max watched as his sister pointed to something on the marquis above the booth, stretching as though she had to stand on tiptoe to point even higher, Dominic aligning his head too familiarly behind her shoulder to watch the angle of her slim arm, as he said something and they both laughed.

Ellie stayed in that posture a few seconds too long for Todd's liking, her stretched back hoisting her blouse until it ever-so-slightly cleared the waistband of her jeans. And the summer light set the fabric aglow, and her slim curves a faintly detectable shadow under the sheer drop of the garment.

Todd rubbed the little counter in the booth more intently, more rapidly.

Older guys took advantage of young girls much too often. He was no fan of Max, but maybe Max should know what was happening, since he, too, was supposed to have a date with El— tomorrow, when they were both off work, at the matinee of *Waxworks*. Max needed to know, because something or someone needed to take the wind out of Dominic's sails.

And as he thought so, the booth's interiors rising to a soft, recovered glow beneath his hand, Todd's sister and her suitor-come-lately vanished inside Huntington's, and the door closed behind them in a blaze of reflected sunlight.

∞

Dominic thought it was strange how, when she was away from Max and her brother, Elaine Vitale became more playful, more irreverent and satiric. When they were alone, she delighted in the roadhouse drama of what was afoot at Shangri-La—the campy feud between Leni Zauber and George Castille, the odd ascendancy of a janitor to celebrity simply by seeming to be at the right place at the right time.

"So what's all the fuss about Mr. Pfeiffer?" Ellie asked.

"The *Reverend* Pfeiffer," Dom corrected mock-seriously, handing her a menu.

"Yes, yes, the *Right* Reverend Pfeiffer. I've worked with him almost two years, Dominic, and had no idea he was a preacher or something. I mean, I suppose I shoulda guessed in that he was always polite and never checked out my boobs. But then, that would go just as well for Mr. Castille, wouldn't it?"

"I allow it would, Ellie. You know Pfeiffer's being primed for a City Council seat."

"For real? Jerry Jeff?" She shook her head, and they ordered politely as Marlene, the oldest of the world-weary Huntington's waitresses, gave the two of them a look ironic enough to wither irony itself and walked away shaking her head over a skinny girl like that asking for only French fries, then taking up the whole goddamned half of the booth to eat them.

"The cute fella at #7 wants the portabella sandwich," she announced to the cook just a little too loudly. "And a small fries for Mizz Nervosa over there."

"I think she hates us," Dominic confided in a stage whisper.

Ellie laughed. "Nah. It's *me* she hates. So really with Jerry

Jeff? This place has to be the weirdest I've ever worked in."

Dominic started to reply, then stopped himself.

Ellie rolled her eyes. "It's ok. I know what comes next, how Todd and I don't seem like twins, not at all, and then the questions about was he always this weird."

"That wasn't coming next," Dominic lied, twirling the ice in his glass, his eyes on how the cubes bobbed in the water's gentle spirals.

But Jesus, look at him, she insisted, and sure enough he was still across the street in the ticket booth, head down, about some kind of odd business and seemingly oblivious to everything around him.

Yes, Todd was a strange one, Dominic conceded inwardly. Though he held off saying since this might very well be a date he was on with Ellie.

∞

He had told her before that he had an ex up East, but not that Peri Bathgate was fast approaching fame and transparency. He said nothing about the riddles, about the stolen poetry and strange transparency.

Instead, he let Ellie linger in guesses and suppositions, no doubt fashioning a mystery woman from what she knew of Dominic and his sketchy past. He gave the general account— the one his mother and stepfather had heard when the romance faltered. He tried to frame it so that it would look like he was trying to be fair, to own up for his own failings. After all, he had mentioned the cannabis and the free float over jobs and residences, the fact that he reached thirty without a goal or grasp (or bank account, for that matter). The shortcomings carefully chosen to hint at poetry in the hopes that someone Ellie's age might still mistake shiftlessness for a romantic refusal to sell out. Better to dwell on imagined ghosts, he told himself, changing the subject, trying to sound brave when the bravery was actually avoidance, which was in fact more cowardly than meeting his history head on.

In return, Dominic had to listen to her excuses for Todd. It was part of the display of courtship, this guarded display of weaknesses, of the things that will come up if the romance starts and progresses. So he looked out the window as Ellie went on about her brother. Something about how he'd always been that way, that despite what everyone said about twins, Todd had always been opaque to her, like some changeling a family of aliens had dropped into the nest. Dominic feigned interest in Todd's chronic oddity, but his eyes strayed toward the front of the theater where the ticket booth was empty now and the pavement shimmered in front of the marquis.

"Toddie did a lot of drugs back in high school, Dom," she continued. "Our whole family's prone to substance. My dad still drinks too much, and my mother had a bout with prescriptions a couple of years back. And I confess my fondness for weed, as I'm sure you noticed."

She laughed uncomfortably, and continued.

"But he did all the crazy school stuff. Glue first, then weed and hash in middle school, hallucinogens in high school. It was too bad, because I think it hit him with leftover damage that will catch up someday, because it was just too much, you know? But I've never known any stoner who just happened to move straight into drugs as a kind of accessory to a perfectly happy life. Perfectly happy kids smoke reefer, and it's no big deal, but it's the ones who are out of step to begin with, the unhappy ones, who take on the drugs as a way of being."

Dominic nodded, pretending he was hearing this social wisdom for the first time and that it wasn't coming from a girl whom he knew to be a pretty convinced pothead. Still nodding, he scanned the street outside the window, the sidewalks blistered by a September sun that gave no sign of conceding to autumn.

That old homeless dude he and Max had discovered in the balcony —Timmy? Tommy?— was taking retreat underneath the Shangri-La awning, there at the edge of the shadows, over-dressed for the withering heat, his mania of only two weeks past having surrendered to the climate. Somewhere Dominic had read that 92° was the point of eruption, where the day was its most violent among those who would fight or felon, that 91° was not quite as volatile while 93° was too hot to move.

Of course, none of that applied to the old dude seated in the shade, slumping now against the wall, his legs splayed and his head bent into the darkness.

For a moment Dominic's eyes blurred and watered. Ellie was still speaking somewhere, but her voice was no more than a background music of pauses and inflections, gliding beneath his own mournful thoughts.

That man out there. Sometimes Dominic thought of the Tommies or Timmies when the first hard frost hit, like they were some kind of hothouse plant left inadvertently outdoors, but wasn't the heat almost as bad? Like Dante's higher circles of hell before they circled down to the core of ice. And here he was, on his own self-seeking and postponed vision quest, like someone half his age in a novel from the 1960s, while old men like the one across the street sweltered and froze, having long forgotten or never known Dominic's indulgence and luxury.

He looked to Ellie when she prodded his arm with her finger. Gazed more or less in her direction, then back to the window, which for a moment filled with light in brilliant opacity. A foolish part of him thought himself on the brink of some kind of insight or knowledge, as the diner's interior reflected on the surface of the glass and he saw the customers, a passing waitress…

And himself seated on a stool at the counter, looking back at him.

Dominic blinked. It was not a reflection.

Ellie continued about Todd, about a year in middle school when her brother simply refused to speak. But Dominic slid away from the other story to regard his other self, who seemed to be regarding him with an impassive gaze, not quite alive but not quite lifeless, either, like a face full on in a silent film. Dominic tried to stand, but his legs gave and he fell forward into a clatter of tableware and Ellie's astonished stare.

"Dom!"

"No, I'm alright," he gasped, waving a hand at Ellie, brushing away her concerns and attentions. The restaurant tilted around him, the light banked, and the man at the counter was gone, replaced by the approaching figure of John Bulwer.

∞

Bulwer, it seemed, had been in the area and decided to drop in for lunch. He noticed the shaking at once, greeted the couple quietly, made as if to leave. But to Dominic's disappointment, Ellie scooted over, offered him space in the booth.

Dominic signaled Marlene for a last warm-up of coffee. The strange apparition of his double had vanished into the afternoon light. He had no clue whether anyone had noticed. He sulked as Bulwer sat down with them, exchanging pleasantries with El and ordering coffee when the waitress arrived.

Ellie continued the conversation, filling Bulwer in on Dominic's career as a poet, his "brilliant" articles for the film series, which everyone at the table knew, at some deep level, to be anything but brilliant. By now the whole thing seemed vaguely embarrassing, unworthy of their new guest, and Dominic regretted bringing up his literary career to impress a girl, regretted having a so-called literary career to begin with.

Decided then and there that it had never been a literary career, not really.

Bulwer's understanding almost made it worse. He listened to Ellie's scenarios, drank coffee as she encouraged Dominic back to the task, to expanding on the narrative poem that she had no idea had found its way into a promising first book by a transparently thin poet up in Vermont. All the while Bulwer listened benignly, almost interested in what the girl was repeating or inventing, until El had exhausted her powers.

"It could be his legacy, Mr. Bulwer," she said, her tone somewhere between triumphant and pleading. "What he leaves behind after he's gone. The sure sign he's been here."

"Not bad," Bulwer said, grinning amiably. "Kind of a Southern Gothic *ringsel*."

"*Ringsel?*" Ellie asked. Dominic waited silently, because he didn't know either.

Bulwer nodded. "Also called *śarīra*. They're kind of leavings from Buddhist holy men—I'm surprised you'd never heard of them, Dominic. Some of the sangha take them to be the signs of sainthood."

Ellie pushed her fries amiably toward Bulwer, and he took one, dabbing it dutifully into the ketchup. "The *sangha?*" she asked.

"What they'd call 'the faithful' in the West, more or less," Bulwer explained. "You see, there are signs among them that indicate spiritual growth in previous lives. Marks on the body, powers of movement, invulnerability to the elements.

"But *ringsel* are some of the strangest and most common of signs," he continued, given this opportunity to hold forth. "They're small spherical relics, usually white though not always, which emerge from the ashes of great teachers after their death or from sacred places such as Buddha statues or stupas. They're like pearls in ashes. Supposedly the devotion of the disciples calls them forth. No disciples, no *ringsel*."

Dominic stared intently at the older man, set down his fork and pushed back the dismal little mushroom sandwich he'd been picking at. *The Last Crusade* rushed back to his memory, the afternoon with his father, then the night years later at the head of the basement steps...

"And here's what's even cooler about *ringsel*," Bulwer continued, staring down into the dark, trembling mirror of his coffee. "There are also cases where they appear after the ashes or bits of bones have been collected and kept for a while. Someone might have some remnants and keep them very devotedly and carefully, and after some time, look at them and they may have turned into *ringsel*. *Ringsel* also reproduce. One of them gets bigger and bumps appear on the side and then the bumps become small *ringsel*.

"There are all kinds of things that Buddhists believe in," Bulwer concluded, "and some of them are as wild as the stories of Christian saints. Images weep or come down from pedestals to dance or speak. Many of the *sangha* have seen showers of blood, heard donkeys braying beneath the ground or other animals speaking like humans, but others consider those kinds of things to be more folktale than spiritual signs."

Ellie grinned. "Where do you draw the line, John?"

"The line?"

"What gives *ringsel* the street cred that showers of blood and underground donkeys don't get?"

Dominic's eyes widened. "El! Don't be…"

But Bulwer waved it away with a laugh. "No. No, that's a good question. The difference is that neither the blood showers nor the donkeys—nor the moving images, for that matter— leave evidence behind. The *ringsel* stay on. People keep them. I've seen them."

Ellie stared at the older man, long and hard, before she nodded.

"I'd like to see one of them," Dominic said.

Ellie nodded, her eyes still fixed on John Bulwer.

"Then come with me this week. To the Varhana Monastery north of the river. It's a good time to go—it's just past the end of the Ghost Month in the Buddhist calendar. And there are *ringsel* there."

15.

Leni Zauber was seated in the projection room of the Shangri-La, feeling brave in drawing a dangerous print of *Walpurgisnacht* through a Steenbeck. Peering over an isolated sequence of the film, she was struck by the jewel at Pema's throat, and paused on the frame where it was most central.

The girl couldn't have been more than fourteen at the time, Leni remembered. Why Florian had indulged himself with a child simply beggared belief. But there she was as a moving face in a painting—Florian's careful effect, borrowed from Fritz Lang's *Metropolis*, that projected a brief clip of her through a translucent screen. It was an outdated technique, clumsy by today's standards, but innovative for ninety years ago, and striking in its detail. Florian had improved on Lang's experiment: that knotted pearl on Pema's necklace, clear in definition, was blistered on one end like a growth from a geode, yet pale and pristine and beautiful, as the girl was pristine and beautiful.

Leni rubbed at the hollow of her throat, feeling a slow, compulsive burning. She laughed bitterly at rediscovering her jealousy after all these years.

Because of the Kuleshov Effect, you old fool.

She had been in the business long enough to know some things as second nature.

She leaned against the projector and lit another forbidden cigarette, stirred as the smoke streamed into her throat.

Lev Kuleshov had been a Soviet filmmaker—a contemporary and acquaintance of Florian's—who revealed in a brief experiment something that people had pretty much suspected for some time. When you tell a story in film, he had showed, visual context was everything.

His original experiment used shots of the face of the old Tsarist actor Ivan Mozzhukhin, in which Mozzhukhin's expression did not change. Kuleshov would show the face, then cut to shots of different items—a bowl of soup, a girl, a coffin. Each time, Mozzhukhin's face seemed to show a different emotion: hunger, lust, grief. And by montage, a director could change the emotions on the screen, shape the meaning of shadow and light not only into a human form, but also combine images to suggest the emotions felt by the invented form. No wonder Joe Stalin had censored the montage in Soviet film. It was misdirection at its best—what Florian had called *beschiss*, but a tactic he had boasted of using in *Walpurgisnacht* and which Leni was trying to recover as she edited the film.

Leni almost didn't hear the knock on the door. As George Castille began to open the door, she lurched to her feet and blocked the entrance.

"Is everything all right, Dr. Zauber?" George asked, trying to peer around her into the projection room. Leni blocked the door: she could sense that the power was only a glance from shifting, that if he saw what was behind her, his first guess might be nitrate film.

And his second guess might be that the Board of Directors would now listen to him over her.

So she let him see the Steenbeck. *Safety film*, she assured him. *So that spool and travel and the noise of the film will make it like it would have looked and sounded had they ever screened it. It deserves that. A recreation of its very moment in place and time.*

And furthermore, why would I risk the old film?

It was a shabby rationale. She knew it. He had caught her unaware, forced her to scramble.

And the old invert wouldn't let well enough alone. *It's a good thing,* he told her, cocking his head and meeting her glance skeptically. *Not just in Cinema Paradiso, you know. My dear, theater history is scarred by nitrate fires. The famous one in Montreal back in the twenties—the Laurier Palace. Seventy children dead. The one at Stanford in 2009, the National Archives, the Eastman House. Just to save space, we could always get Jerry or Max or Dominic to load up the Steenbeck and move it to wherever she was staying.*

And why would we do that? she asked him. *I told you it was safety film.*

And *Dr. Zauber,* he said, trying again to shoulder his way into the projection room, again wedged in the doorframe by a slight, elderly woman. Two hags fighting over nitrate, she would characterize it later, but at the moment it was physical confrontation, and George pushed harder, saying *I may not be in charge around here for long, may not have a say in film choice or order or in those hideous, obscure introductions you have that boy writing, but for now, by God, I am still in the driver's seat, this is my theater as much as anyone's, my raison d'etre, damn it. And if you won't let me in there, it's something other than safety film you are hiding, and if you won't answer to me, I can be in touch with half the ChemCon board within five minutes, and then you will see...*

Leni watched him draw to full height, blink, and realize his anger. Good. The board would hear of his attempt at intimidation, and she would "go old" in their presence, bending a little and trembling, her eyes watering but none of it too much, all of it subdued as though she were holding it back, as though the last thing she wanted was to win this one because of her age.

When in fact, she was younger now, younger than she had ever been.

She told George to watch his step. Reminded him of the American phrase to *pick your battles.* Laughed at him when he insisted that this, indeed, was a battle he had chosen, and

211

promised him that she would ask Max to load the Steenbeck into his car, though it would make the whole process inconvenient and a waste of time, and she despised a waste of time.

As George left for the lobby, Leni offered to join him, offered to help with the gate since they seemed to be the only two in the theater. He brushed away the offer, equally polite and solicitous, as though acknowledging the end of the argument: Dominic and Ellie were just across the street, he said, and they'd be back by 1:15 at the latest. Ellie had a knack for being on time, he reminded her, and took her responsibilities seriously.

Leni sensed a criticism of herself, though for the life of her, she could not determine what for.

∞

It was just like the damn Germans, George decided. A natural knack for walking into a place and taking it over.

He stood at the gate, at the old velvet rope where he had stood when he first began to manage the theater, before the switch to old movies and hiring the kids. Both decisions seemed pretty crazy to the city's business community, at least at first. But they had paved the way toward business grants and attracted the ChemCon Board of Directors, eager to prove that a so-called heartless corporation had a love of art, kids, and the community.

George realized now, of course, that the honeymoon was over. Despite good will and better publicity, the theater kept running in the red, and nothing killed a romance with ChemCon so quickly.

And yet he would call on them now, because the theater, the company reputation, the whole goddamned enterprise stood in jeopardy if what he suspected was indeed true, if up in the projection booth of the Shangri-La, Leni Zauber was playing with fire. His phone roamed oddly, the little circular arrow vexing him from the heart of the screen, and he wished for the days of the dial-up land line, where you could be sure the call would get through.

With rising irritation, he tried Rausch's office. Then Koenig's, then down the list to a couple of more board members he knew. But each time the phone gave him dead air, someone's distant dial tone, a masked and unintelligible conversation where the words became almost audible, then faded back into a blank and maddening silence.

George felt unexplainably old as he set down the phone, unlocked the double doors to the theater, and felt the blast of heat from the outside. Ellie and Dom would be back in an hour, followed closely by Max and Todd. Jerry Jeff would come in after the film and clean up the premises, but for the moment, George was alone.

Though the solitude didn't last long. Almost by reflex, George smiled and greeted the first very early customer through the door, a tall blonde man, unseasonably dressed in a gray suit and wearing a pair of vintage wire-rimmed spectacles. The look was sweltering but charming, as George saw his own reflection off the glint of the man's glasses, saw his own smile, the gaze held just long enough to give a stir that was probably all in his own mind because the tall young fellow was in his early thirties, for God's sake, there could be no chance., he was old enough to be the man's father…

He caught the hint of an accent as he exchanged pleasantries with the young man, as the young man lingered by the rope and George Castille looked over the broad shoulders and saw, with pleasure and a kind of eagerness, that nobody else was arriving, not yet.

∞

Leni lit another cigarette, again defying all theater rules, the city smoking and fire regulations, every sensible warning about nitrate film. The smoke bristled in her throat, and she closed her eyes, dreaming herself back to Tibet.

Florian had insisted that Pema was a dream, conjured by agreement among his fellow travelers. She had told him it was difficult to imagine, which made him laugh.

It was all about imagining, he replied. Difficult or not.

Out of the stream of smoke rose a hint of sandalwood, and for a moment she hovered between waking dream and dreaming wakefulness, in that middle ground of insubstantial Prague. Then the sandalwood prevailed over the tobacco, and she knew that the older, more genuine world had overcome the shallow brilliance that had followed. And despite all reason and better judgment, she knew that Florian Geist was near, and she welcomed his arrival.

Below her, in the dark of the theater, the step lights shone dimly on two figures passing down the aisle toward the alcove to the right of the screen, where a louche reproduction of Praxiteles' Apollo bent over footlights. The walks of both men were familiar, though years apart, like a difference in ages glimpsed in a distorting mirror—like Veidt and Krausse, perhaps, from *Caligari* or from *Waxworks*. Leni could not explain it, not quite, but she knew where it was headed, and as the two of them vanished behind the statue, framed clearly in light for only a moment, Leni relaxed and inhaled again, stubbed out her cigarette and prepared for what would inevitably follow.

∞

Bulwer was surprised when T. Tommy Briscoe walked into Huntington's, but the bookseller had reached an age in which surprise passed into alarm rather slowly. Instead he was curious and a bit repentant.

The two men exchanged glances as the memory registered on Tommy, who buttoned his jacket and nodded uncertainly. The hesitation seemed to wash away, at least most of it, when Bulwer beckoned him over, and he sat down in the booth with a little more confidence, like an employee in front of an inscrutable boss.

T. Tommy smiled. "You kinda popped a cap on my person, sir."

"Indeed I did," Bulwer allowed. "And for that, I have regrets. May I buy you coffee?"

They discovered they had things in common that afternoon. Refugees from the Sixties, readers of Ginsburg and Blake. They had differed politically in those times: Tommy had voted twice for a Nixon who would have hated him and tapped his phone, while Bulwer carried the Red Book of a man who would have exiled and rusticated him in some Cultural Revolution. While Bulwer was down on First Street, beginning Dry Salvages with a small inheritance from his father's estate, Tommy was being struck by lightning after a Doors concert, his vision opened into broader, hallucinatory horizons.

But these days, half a century later, their blood had lost the temperature of passion and reform. Now, like old gunslingers after a range war, they regarded each other over coffee—Tommy's with twelve sugars—and over Ellie's plate, yet to be bussed from the table.

They talked about cause and effect, about the currents of time and place that had brought them to this table. They understood and did not understand each other, both of them too inclined to see one cause for one effect, to see cause uncaused and effect uncausing.

When in fact, they both concluded, it was more complicated than that. Everything, they knew, was a result of multiple causes and conditions. The coffee they drank was the product of a seed sown in a wet season, the wait of three to four years as the tree matured, then the harvesters who picked the coffee cherries, the workers who process and hull and dry them who cull and grade them, who ship the beans and cup and roast them, grinding them into the coffee the two men drink, brewed in the back kitchens of Huntington's and brought to their table by Marlene, who saw to it that his coffee was served quickly and hot because her job depended on it but also because she had bought a copy of Kerouac's *Dharma Bums* from Salvages six years ago and had been treated like an adult whose ideas and reading and spiritual growth were of a mild but real concern to an aging hippie who did his job by running a store...and the web of connections spun out over the city and the state and the country until no strand dangled uncaught in the measureless oceans of space.

Nothing was left out. The cosmos had gathered to bring them this coffee.

∞

How can we know the dancer from the dance? T. Tommy asked, and Bulwer silently scolded himself for being surprised that the question was framed in that famous line poetical. Because somewhere in that rising matrix of causes and effects, his road had diverged from the road of the man who sat across from him, vagrant and probably high. For a moment, John Bulwer felt sorry for T. Tommy Briscoe, and then not so much because nothing had been left out.

He remembered the lines from the Bodhi Sutra:

> *When this is, that is.*
> *From the arising of this comes the arising of that.*
> *When this isn't, that isn't.*
> *From the cessation of this comes the cessation of that.*

Tommy, on the other hand, fought down hazy resentments. The wounds of the shotgun were long past, and he forgave Bulwer for the quick resort to violence, for his knowledge of the streets trumped the Buddhism of the bookstore. And yet there was a residue, something he could not explain, that came to him in a feeling that Bulwer was stealing something of *his*, was walking off with it slowly and in broad daylight. It had to do with the theater as well, with the two boys who had come to help, who had become icons or curious saints in his story of pilgrimage and redemption.

Somehow Tommy's thoughts returned to the older boy—dark and slender, very possibly Eurasian. Tommy's friends had teased him, said he was sweet on the kid, but it wasn't that at all: he simply wanted this one to be safe, attended to in a bleak world filled with the black-and-white flutter of uncovered specters.

But from what Tommy had heard, John Bulwer offered a kind of protection. Literate and mostly wise, kind and brushing against Buddha-nature. Also a pretty good shot, but that was another issue.

His boy would be in safe hands. Or safer than his own.

So the conversation moved then to pilgrimage by a silent and mutual consent, and Tommy explained how he found his way back to the Shangri-La most every other day, because he had been healed in there, in the balcony, by the good physician Dr. Caligari. And waving away Bulwer's sudden burst of laughter, he assured the old bookseller that it was undeniably true, that the rock salt wound he had received in his quest for copper—a wound inflicted by present company—had vanished entirely on the preview night under the gaze of that benevolent doctor. And that he had heard the Shangri-La was a place of further healing, that the janitor therein had laid hands on a man of power and influence, that what promised to be a heart attack had been diverted by a larger power's descending to the basement men's room.

Bulwer had heard the same, because news traveled quickly along the strands of that gossamer web. He knew that Jerry Jeff Pfeiffer had been speaking to crowds, that he had gained a following. Suspected that it was pretty much more of the same right-wing fundy hogwash that made this town hard to live in.

A hogwash for which Congressman Rausch, no doubt, thanks whatever God he worships, T. Tommy replied. For Jerry Jeff Pfeiffer arose out of basis and motive, and was there because he was included in the web and the fabric of things, as much a cause and effect as anything in the world that surrounded him.

Indeed, when Tommy had entered the theater, he had sought and failed to find the janitor, had instead ascended to the balcony, and after the healing of Caligari had rushed over him and the boys had come, looked for Jerry Jeff as they guided him down to the lobby, his panic rising as the stairs in front of them seemed suddenly steeper, darker, and more narrow.

Do not discount Jerry Jeff Pfeiffer, the old vagrant warned, his cup empty now, a faint funk beginning to rise from him as the heat of early September left its smell at the table. I still look for him in the shadows of the theater. Bulwer said he would keep that in mind, promptly forgetting it as the two shook hands and parted, heading out the door together, neither of them realizing that things had turned awful in the shadows across the street.

∞

He couldn't believe he was doing something like this. Not since the Seventies, in that remarkable, liberated breathing space between Stonewall and the Plague, when all had seemed adventurous and possible. But that was over forty years ago, and George was vaguely embarrassed at his behavior now.

Embarrassed but exhilarated. For God's sake, he was too old for this.

The young man who walked in front of him seemed to know the lie of the theater. It was as though he should have been familiar, but he wasn't. And it was that strangeness, that misplacement of context, which was most attractive. He was far too young to show this kind of interest in a man George's age. So what was it? And why did George drop all caution and follow him into the damp recesses of the theater alcove?

∞

Leni watched from the projection room, trying not to gloat.

It was sad, ultimately. Something in inverts was drawn to

the theater. Dietrich, Murnau, James Whale. Florian always claimed that it was simply that homosexuals had performed all their lives, their masquerade of normalcy a prelude to careers on stage and film. And as a result, he claimed, the theater loved them back, indulging and even celebrating their passion for the fantastic, the colorful.

The theater, Leni thought, indulges all kinds of passion. Like Florian's own for underage girls. Coddled by Ufa and then by the SS, he had pampered himself with flesh excessively firm and smooth and young, until Leni had come to wonder whether he had a limit in his affections, just when he had taken her to his bed in the long sequence of trysts. Men were all the same, she had concluded. Whether after boys, young girls, or creatures insubstantial, they pursued desire at the expense of wisdom. And Castille was no different, following a spectral new acquaintance into the consuming shadow.

Over in the alcove, the light was tricky. Above the statue of Apollo, two slim shapes—Prometheus, George had told her once, and Hymenaios—reached toward each other in a sinuous, excessive arch, their extended torches crossed above the god, glowing with a cheap incandescent light where once there might have been the more romantic flutter of gaslight. Only a few feet behind this trio lay impenetrable shade, but she could see at its margins the silhouettes of the two men cast on the alcove wall, the broader, shorter one kneeling as the two blended quickly into a lurid shadow. By now, she guessed, George Castille had tapped into the monstrous error of things.

As the smoke blossomed in her lungs, Leni smiled and watched the one figure emerge from the darkness. Behind the tall suited man, the shadow of two legs dangled under Hymenaios and Prometheus, between the god of marriage and the titan who defied the order of the gods. Somehow it seemed mythic and suitable.

She beckoned the young gentleman in thought. He looked up toward the projectionist's booth, his eyeglass lenses winking briefly with borrowed light as the shade he passed into seemed to diminish him, to darken his hair. By the time he crossed the lobby he would be indistinguishable from the Rackett boy, which was all part of the plan. Were Leni able to draw Dominic hither, it would be perfect. But she could not do so—not yet, her attention exhausted by its focus on the shifting eidolon who stood at the double doors of the house, the figure that, for a brief moment, darkened and diminished as it climbed through the margin of the mural, past the animals of the Peaceable Kingdom, and on to the circle of men in the depth of the painting, standing in frozen accord.

16.

But what of George Castille on that afternoon? What had befallen him in the alcove beside the screen?

Almost instantly, he had drawn back from the encounter. The young man walking ahead of him blended for a moment with the shadows before re-emerging, shorter and more round shouldered, almost recognizable now, when only minutes before he had seemed foreign and alluring.

What am I doing? George had thought again. Had almost gone back up the aisle. Then the man had turned and beckoned, his skin pale and his eyes small and glittering like a raven's. George followed him, the desire of a moment before now transformed into a kind of compulsion, a kind of metaphysical rubbernecking because he knew now that the creature before him was nothing natural.

Silently, with a slow, erratic beckon, the young man had drawn him toward the shadow. George could see through his companion now, the torch of Hymenaios brilliant and vivid through the filmy outline of the youth, and surprised at his own calm, knowing the next few steps were mortally perilous, he had stepped forth anyway, into a gloom that suddenly became darkness visible, forms suggested and writhing in the folds of shadow.

Oh, my, he breathed, to no one listening, because he was alone now in the presence of insubstantial images, setting forth the shadow play of his own past, a parade of what might have been. His one appearance on Broadway as Bardolph in Henry V, then a hopeful but failed audition as Lear's Fool, a handsome older man who left him in the Village, a brief stint off-Broadway as John Proctor in *The Crucible.* Then his mother's lingering illness and a return to his native state, where he had hoped for a comeback over thirty years, blaming his mother, his schooling, his goddamned Kentucky origins for having never risen high enough, certain that each play would be the threshold to a launched autumnal career. He saw his savaged Hamlet reflected in the cracked mirrors of the Ramey Amphitheater, in a kind of imagined intertitle the words of his bête noire, Wade Abner: *histrionic, from its arm-waving Danish Prince down to the funhouse mirrors in which he seemed to have lost himself and his dignity.*

And oh, it was too much mockery, what he had done to himself in four, almost five decades on the stage. After such knowledge, how could he have emerged from the shadows? It was Moliere, wasn't it, who collapsed and died backstage after a performance of his own *Le malade imaginaire?*

I told you so, the old frog must have thought. George had laughed, despite himself, at the prospect. He had reached for the stepladder behind the tabs, upon which one of his staff—Todd sometimes, but Max usually—could reach the ropes that opened and closed the grand drape for the stage shows. Laughing again, he had opened the ladder and climbed to its topmost platform, thinking all the time that he was dreaming, that Freud would certainly have something to say about a dream where an old queen killed himself just to start over. The rope had been thick and difficult to loop, but two generations of all kinds of stage work had left his hands knowing if arthritic, and within seconds he had fashioned a manageable noose.

Moliere and I, he told himself. Bardolph and Proctor and the

Poor Fool.

My poor fool's hanged, he thought, as the noose tightened deftly. He wondered, as he kicked free of the step ladder, how he had not seen this coming from the first act.

∞

Kind of a date, she had said.

Max figured it was better than nothing.

He had asked her several days before, as they stood on the landing of the Shangri-La, in front of all his co-workers: Dominic and her brother were there, and Jerry Jeff sweeping the tiled treads below them, trying not to listen, and George Castille at the foot of the stairs looking up, arching an ironic eyebrow.

And why had he felt that her acceptance was a shootdown?

They would see the movie together, the *Waxworks* debut, the 8 o'clock Friday showing where Todd and Dominic would work the theater. There was something disappointing about a date at work, as though Ellie didn't want to go out of her way or block off a free hour to be with him. And Max had seen the movie already, and it was like she wasn't even considering what would be fun and interesting for him.

Yet it was a start, he figured. So he got a haircut and borrowed one of the Colonel's Oxford shirts when the old man wasn't looking. When he arrived in the theater lobby he was looking smart, if he said so himself, but he had sweated through the shirt by the time Ellie arrived. He had wanted to ask her for coffee over at Huntington's, and asked her if she thought there was still time before the show.

She didn't seem to notice the invitation or the shirt, for that matter. When he asked again she was short with him, said she'd been at Huntington's this afternoon and that Marlene over there hated her, and that there were people in the lobby now, Todd had sold them the tickets and nobody was there to take them. Where was George, after all?

Max tried to remain cheerful. Said he'd take the tickets while she looked, that George couldn't be far because, see? there was his phone on the counter. Try the projection booth, he suggested.

Ellie rolled her eyes and reminded him that the booth was Dr. Zauber's domain, and Dr. Zauber hadn't let George in there since the series began, but whatever. And off she went, just ahead of the first people filing into the auditorium.

Maybe she will get the idea, he thought. Maybe *Waxworks* will put the rescue and romance into her imagining.

The idea cheered him, gave him faint hope. He was able to nod without hostility when Dominic walked in and greeted him, spelled him on taking the tickets.

Max headed into the auditorium, intent on finding Ellie. As he opened the door and stepped into the aisle, a scream rose from behind the statues in the alcove.

∞

It was an odd sermon at Antioch. Jerry Jeff Pfeiffer, in what the Reverend Koenig called "lay testimony," spoke to a congregation of the city's most influential people. His subject danced close to offending everyone. At first he bewailed the collapse of society and morality, receiving grave nods from all the tiers in the cost-effective mega-church.

Bucky had to marvel at all the people who had come to hear Jerry Jeff preach. Some people from his own church, yes, and Deacon Aldo Wooters, and, oddly enough, that strange twin to the pretty girl who worked at Shangri-La. But the audience included about 15,000 others: Bucky scanned the front rows and picked out two coaches from the university, a deputy mayor, the owner of a prominent chain of fast-food hamburger places.

Out of jealousy, the Episcopals and Methodists called Antioch "Six Flags Over Jesus." Bucky had been around enough to know that the disparaging nickname wasn't original. It was one of the reassuring things about the town: nothing surprising was said, very little thought. The mainstream churches just grabbed a convenient label off the internet and used it without taking into account that smallness didn't necessarily make their own churches any less dead to Jesus.

You just said the right things at Antioch. You nodded in agreement. And if you put in money, nobody would ask you to match walk with talk.

But Jerry Jeff could talk a talk that would demand much walking. They had gotten him to stay behind the lectern instead of stalking the stage like a tent revivalist. He had promised no tongues, no offer to lay on hands, though in a way everyone knew such things were part of the usual program. This was his audition with more respectable conservatives, the ones who, after the service was over, would head for the golf course or the Boat rather than to Applebee's.

And the *lay witness* at Antioch was headed to the boat this afternoon, though he didn't know it yet.

Bucky had plans for Jerry Jeff Pfeiffer. The preaching janitor was the perfect candidate for the perfect candidate. Pfeiffer had promised to join him for lunch, but had no idea that a long process of recruitment was underway—one that would end up a few months from now, when Bucky would register him at the Board of Elections to run for City Council against the newly vulnerable DeMoyne Troubles.

Bucky Trabue saw all kinds of merit in the choice. Jerry could speak the language. If you kept the sermon at a general float, the listening ear would transform it into something agreeable. The sins lamented would be the very things you regarded as sin, and you would hear nothing uncomfortable.

Jerry started out respectable, brushing the wealth of America, its economic opportunity for everyone, and the people said *amen*, Bucky noticed, though not like they would of done over at Heart Ministries Outreach, but more with that pillar-of-society kind of *amen*, the nod of assent, the leaning back in the pew, the satisfied arm-folding which told Bucky Trabue that his man was making inroads and not enemies.

But of course, Jerry Jeff Pfeiffer just had to go on. For the next thing he did was ask a question of the congregation. *Since this is the case, he said, let me ask you...*

Bucky steadied himself for the discomfort that would follow. It might be different in the ministry, but at a political speech you should never ask the audience a question that could not be answered by a strangled, even wordless shout, and here it came...

So why are two of the fastest growing businesses nursing homes and private prisons?

"Gottdamn it!" Bucky hissed, then looked around furtively. There was no good answer for this speaker and this group.

And *Simple,* Jerry Jeff said. *On account of we have lost touch with each other. We don't see the connections, how outside relates to inside, how either/or is better off both/and...*

Jesus Christ on a fuckin' pony! Bucky thought. Was the sumbitch gonna torpedo his whole campaign before it began? He longed to rush the stage, to hustle Pfeiffer off the podium, but that would look like the boy preacher was having a breakdown. Or he could stand up and applaud, and pray to God that someone—anyone—would follow suit and drown out the words that would follow, though if that didn't work, they would think *he* was having a breakdown, and before he could think of doing something, Jerry Jeff was continuing:

For wasn't it our Savior who said, 'When you make the two one, and when you make the inside like the outside and the outside like the inside, and the above like the below, and when you make the male and the female one and the same, so that the male not be male nor the female female; and when you fashion eyes in the place of an eye, and a hand in place of a hand, and a foot in place of a foot, and a likeness in place of a likeness; then will you enter the kingdom'.

Bucky wondered where *that* came from, wished that Pfeiffer would shut the fuck up. He was sure this testimony was headed in directions that would please nobody at Antioch, though they would nod soberly in pretended agreement when it came to the words of our Savior, it was bound for that business about the poor. The people here—the "glittering flock at Antioch"—talked a good game when it came to poor people, but you'd get into big trouble if you figured on any of them doing a damn thing to lighten the load. It was the common ground of poverty and Hell, Bucky had decided: we like them both for the sheer pleasure of imagining others in them when we aren't.

And what is the kingdom, brothers in Christ?

Oh, good God, don't start speaking tongues, Bucky screamed internally, the veins on the side of his neck swelling to just this side of apoplexy.

The kingdom is where your parents, declining into age, are still held in respect by children who worship the Lord instead of the next new thing. Where we speak to one another face to face, rather than through the glassy film of our iPhone screens. Where traditional values are strong—and not just the ones that have to do with sex, brothers in Christ, though I agree with you on those, but the others—gentleness and generosity, hospitality to strangers and tolerance and respect for them.

Someone coughed in the great orchestra of Antioch, and Bucky realized he had his work cut out for him.

Pfeiffer had to check himself when it come to business, when it come to anything that would give a crowd of people like these, assembled in a place like this, the notion that they weren't all right. It would not be the easiest thing, since it was pretty evident that Jerry Jeff found a lot of these people to be self-important and useless, and Bucky was inclined to agree with him—up to the point that agreement imperiled votes and contributions. He would start the lessons at the Boat, he decided. It was what his old mentors would call counter-intuitive, a vessel afloat on capitalism and riverboat gambling, its hull suspect and its rudder permanently bent, but it was ultimately the place to set minds right.

He would have brought it up to Jerry Jeff then and there, begun the sales pitch at the little reception of lemonade and cookies that followed the service. After all, Pfeiffer was pretty much alone in the corner, after Peter and Marileese Koenig had introduced him to some of the potentates, then left him on his own to alienate those around him. Jerry didn't seem to care much, sipping out of a Dixie cup and enjoying the distance. Aldo Wooters had joined him, and oddly enough, the Vitale boy—Bucky had at last recalled his name —and Bucky was measuring the time now, setting up to approach Pfeiffer and whisk him away from Antioch on a trip that would school him and set his mind right.

Rifling through all there was to do, Bucky hovered in distraction until a hand on his shoulder—the Reverend Peter Koenig's hand—brought him back.

"Mr. Trabue," Koenig whispered. "There's bad news from the Shangri-La Theater. It seems that old George Castille just hanged himself on the premises."

∞

"I guess I should of seen it coming," Jerry Jeff said, as he stared out the passenger window of Bucky's Volvo, riding west through a soft evening rain on the Indiana side of the river. "I mean, don't they always say that about the homosexual?"

Bucky kept his eyes on the road. "What's that, Jerry?"

"Oh, that the…inversion comes with all kinds of…greater unhappiness. The fear of discovery. Of blackmail."

Bucky snorted. "Oh, son, it wasn't like anyone in the whole world didn't know about George Castille. One look at him. One listen to that voice. You'd have to live under a rock not to notice. What straight man has worn an *ascot* this side of the millennium, for God's sake?"

"Tarquin LaForce does," Jerry offered. "Antioch's music minister? He's a married man, Mr. Trabue."

"That he is," Bucky agreed, masking a smile as the car sped on Highway 111 toward a destination he had yet to reveal to his passenger.

∞

Leni sat in the booth through discoveries and investigation. She feigned well the dismay at George's suicide, assured the weary-eyed detective (and by extension, herself) that she had no hand in the tragedy beyond a kind of benign neglect, letting things pass in the dark of the theater that were not her business. Things unattended, she told the lieutenant, have a way of falling into sorrow, and among the sad things, she allowed, was that we could not attend to everything.

There are among us divisions, she said. Intangible walls that let us know that each is divided from the other. In ways, yes, it is a sad thing. But there is a nobility to it, a grand and melancholy isolation we should respect, since we all share in the loneliness.

All of this said with her back to the projection booth, leaning against the door frame in a masquerade of calm, her slight, spindly form blocking entrance, blocking his sight, she hoped, though it was a good guess that even a police detective would not recognize the nitrate film she was editing on the Steenbeck, in such good shape that to notice it you almost had to be a film scholar who expected to find it. Once he glanced over her shoulder, the somnolent eyes reflecting no interest, and she suspected she was home free.

Her story sounded convincing, as well.

"I was up in the booth, officer. Right where I am now. This project takes the energy of a woman my age…"

She bent appropriately, regarded him with an expression that she recalled had something to do with kindness…

"And so, *wenn ich nur and wenn ich nur*. If only I and if only I."

The detective's eyes had glazed over by now. Leni could see him waiting out of Southern politeness for her to finish.

She rushed, then, toward an empathetic and somber conclusion, knowing that he would not come back for more. Then he left, and she was off the hook and free to re-enter the booth.

Where *Walpurgisnacht* awaited, in all its grainy brilliance.

Based on an old occultist novel by the Meyrink who had written *The Golem* years before, *Walpurgisnacht* was set in Prague, the city that had haunted Florian Geist and she believed had eventually taken his life. Set in the Castle Region of the city, peopled by Meyrink's aristocrats and eccentrics, the book had told of a revolution boiling over west of the Moldau River, the rabble of Bolsheviks, anarchists, and petty criminals inspired by ghosts from the city. Florian himself had played the mad actor Zrcadlo, a figure able to transform himself into the shape and demeanor of innumerable characters. For the romantic leads of Ottokar and Polyxena he had decided to cast unknowns. Just who had played Ottokar remained a mystery. Leni had guessed at a number of possibilities but had noticed through the Steenbeck a gesture of the actor's—something in the roll of his shoulder when he extended his arms quickly. It was unsettlingly familiar.

And if her suspicions were right, it made perfect sense that Pema would play the aristocratic young girl, impelled by the mystical power of *aweysha*.

Aweysha was the word old Meyrink used. The transfer and dwelling of the spirit to someone else, as the soul moves from one creature to another. She had thought at first it was like the transmigrations of the Buddhist afterlife, but Geist had persuaded her that it was altogether different, not the result of karma but of the will, as a powerful entity forced itself on soul and body. *Aweysha* was best performed on the dead, but it could be practiced on living people, provided they were asleep or in a trance when the wandering spirit descended on them. Meyrink believed that those among the dead who had very strong will-power when they were alive, or who had unfinished business among the living, might have power enough to enter living people while they are awake, without them noticing, but usually they, too, used the bodies of sleepers, or of corpses, which became the undead through their ghostly agency.

Florian had chanced upon Meyrink's book in '35. Not a reader by nature, resistant to fictions and drawn only, through his love of Wagner, to writers like Gobineau and Houston Chamberlain, he had read *Walpurgisnacht* at the insistence of one of the young men at Castle Wewelsburg, and immediately afterwards, or so he would tell Leni Zauber, had fallen asleep for two days.

"It was the aftermath of revelation, *Maus*," he insisted, on that weekend in Budapest, in a time that was still happy and halcyon before he rushed the film into production, before the world turned for her and the sorrows began. "Only once before have I fallen into slumber such as this. Back with Roerich in Tibet. Back when I discovered what and why I am."

She had lit his cigarette and retreated to the window: at that time she was still very young, and repelled by the smell of smoke. She looked through the glass, the world outside the window vanishing in the reflection of the lamps behind her, pooled light on the surface of things, masking the enormity of the world elsewhere.

Of course at the time she did not think in metaphors. It was Florian's cold, impressive beauty that preoccupied her, the nagging fear that his soul had never left Tibet and that the movie ahead of him, his first directorial event, would be nothing more nor less than Tibet spilling over into *Mitteleuropa*.

Now, safely across an ocean and a span of decades, she threaded the film through the elaborate maze of wheels in the Steenbeck, sometimes advancing it by scene, by shot, even frame by frame as she peered into the screen, imagining things in the slow passage of weeks, as incident, as a frozen moment, all part of the inscrutable stream of events unreeling before her eyes.

17.

Bucky had to show him the Boat.

It was where half of the region found itself when feeling blue, disenfranchised, or estranged from the means of production. A huge complex with riverboat, casino, hotel, restaurants, shopping arcades, golf course and nature preserve, it was America in several hundred acres. Jerry Jeff should get used to it.

He hadn't let the weird Vitale boy accompany them. Todd had pleaded to go, saying the death of George Castille had upset him, too, and that he needed to get away, needed Jerry's spiritual advice in a time of crisis. But Bucky sent Todd for lemonade and rushed Jerry out one of the many side doors of the Antioch compound, and within two hours they were in the parking garage of Runic Legend Casino, ready to board the Boat despite Jerry's misgivings and mild protests.

"This don't seem right, Mr. Trabue," Jerry said. "I know you mean well, but this is not my thing. I've heard about the casino and I've even preached against it, so I feel kind of two-faced even being here."

"Keep an open mind, Jerry," Bucky urged, as he guided

his companion into the huge lobby of the complex. Very much like he'd done when he first entered the huge reception area at Antioch Baptist, Jerry rocked back on his heels, peered to the ceiling, lifted his dropped jaw.

"Just think," Bucky went on. "These people need the help and guidance of decent folk. Avoiding them is what don't seem right."

Together the two of them took the elevator to the upper stories of the complex, passing by costumed attendants, fur-draped and horn-helmeted like characters in a bad Viking movie. Jerry seemed nervous in the confinement of the elevator cab, watching the buttons light and register. "If you decide to run," Bucky hinted, "Some of these folks will be your constituency. Good to shake some hands and get to know them."

"I'm not so sure on this running business, Mr. Trabue. I don't mind shaking hands and getting to know people, but maybe I should do that in the ministry. The Reverend Koenig was telling me that maybe my calling is still from the pulpit rather than from City Hall, and I kind of been thinking that way myself of late."

Careful now, Bucky told himself. The choppy waters of Republican politics lay ahead of him now, as treacherous as the river and with no big boat to ride the current. You wanted preachers on board because your crew loved or claimed to love Jesus, but sooner or later in even the best managed campaign a preacher would wade in to fuck things up. But you could say nothing against one of them: your tent should be wide enough to include all Protestants and some Catholics.

He closed his eyes and exhaled. God damn me for being so cynical, he thought. I can follow a notion through the gutters of my thought, and there you are.

He thought that, but what he said was, "Jerry, let's think about what you're saying. Don't a ministry usually mean that a man has to get ordained? That you have to go to seminary or something? And all that money and time spent while the world unravels and you have your nose stuck in a book?"

"My church ain't tied to a seminary or those commentaries," Jerry explained. "It's the Holy Spirit that teaches and guides us, and it's through the Spirit that we sew the torn world back together again."

The third floor was Asgard, where the lighting was good and the tables were steep. It was where Bucky wanted to end up. But for the time being, as a kind of test and preliminary, the two of them got off at the second floor. Valhalla was smoke-filled, crowded with slot machines and heavy women in late middle age. Jerry stood by the entrance watching the old birds work the bandits, while Bucky leaned against a wall and took in the ironies.

No doubt it was Sodom and Gomorrah to the preacher. It usually was to his sort, until they soaked in how much money was in play. Bucky inhaled the secondary smoke and basked in his role. He'd light up later, after Jerry went to bed. Get on the outside of a couple shots of bourbon as well. But right now he'd let the preacher take in the pandemonium and realize it wasn't so bad after all.

Bucky figured the bunch at Heart Ministries—maybe even the more educated and worldly folks at Antioch—would cast him in the role of tempter, seeking to corrupt a country boy with big-city gambling ways. He knew how they thought and he bought into maybe half of it. He knew they wouldn't think of him as a good man, but sometimes to fight for good you had to dirty your hands a little. All things considered, Buddy supposed, his was a life more rich in possibilities, in metaphor and poetry, than the whole lot of those who judged him.

Because here they were, all said and done, so wed to the bottom line of day-by-day, of money and consumerism and all those things their religion taught them to set aside if they only looked hard enough. But they didn't have the insight to look: they took their Book literally, which you could never do with any book because, god damn it, someone *wrote* it, and any time anything fell into language it got changed, changed permanently. You couldn't even pin down the words. They didn't mean what they meant an hour ago.

Bucky knew that. He made a living by paying attention to what lay between and behind things. And as Jerry Jeff Pfeiffer began to stroll across the casino floor, as he stopped at last to watch over the shoulder of some henna-haired biddy, Bucky approached him, almost certain that it was about to happen, that he guessed this from afar and seen it coming from nearby.

And the woman hollered ecstatically as the machine spilled a small fortune onto her bony lap. Jerry Jeff looked up, his eyes wide and a broad smile from sideburn to sideburn, standing in the presence of what he surely believed was remarkable coincidence.

Bucky had been in Republican politics for thirty years, and found nothing remarkable, even less coincidental. But this was a sign. Behind that convergence and between that minister and that aging gambler lay the groundwork of miracle. He was sure that something in the banked energy of Jerry Jeff Pfeiffer had stopped the tumblers on a jackpot, and that it would continue past jimcrack proof and reckoning. not the Reagonopalypse they had awaited for over thirty years, but something good and wonderful and close to miraculous, something that would do the city well.

Something Buckminster Fuller Trabue would bring into being.

But in the meantime, he figured, they had the hotel for the next two nights. Time enough for Jerry Jeff to watch over his shoulder at the blackjack table. Might as well work the Prosperity Gospel to his own worldly benefit.

∞

It was in Asgard that Max ran into them, as Bucky rode a wave of divine luck in the company of Jerry Jeff Pfeiffer.

Max had arrived at the Boat with the twins, who as usual, wanted to go to exactly the same place for entirely different reasons. Ellie was distraught over George's death, naturally, so

Max had a double motive, part of it generous, in suggesting a drive on Monday morning. It would get her mind off the tragedy and get him alone with her.

He was not surprised when Ellie urged a trip to the Boat. She was fond of gambling, a leftover from when she helped her father pick horses at Churchill Downs. But her talent in handicapping had never been horse sense as much as intuition set on fire, the distracting thrill of things on the line, and when she could not draw companions into physical risk, she sometimes commandeered financial hazards.

Max was more surprised, and disappointed, that Ellie raised no fuss when her brother invited himself along. Todd jumped at the chance to go to the Runic Legend. Something about Jerry Jeff, though Max was damned if he knew how those two had connected beyond shared theater work. Nevertheless, there Todd was, in the back seat of Max's old Volvo, stealing the conversation and distracting his sister as the three of them sped across the river up a winding state road toward the casino.

When they arrived, Ellie made straight for the elevator, punched the button for Asgard. Not the second floor, she assured him. Too smoky, and just slots anyway, and what was the fun in that? Dutifully Max followed, hoping that when Todd found his buddy it would leave private time with Ellie.

No such luck. Jerry Jeff was with Mr. Trabue there in Asgard, and Bucky motioned them all over. They were at a blackjack table, and Max watched with increasing amazement as the cards found every way possible for Mr. Trabue to win and win again. Jerry and Todd made to leave the table, but Mr. Trabue grabbed Jerry by the arm and held him there, as the dealer dropped a five of hearts over Mr. Trabue's standing sixteen and he won again, laughed, and slapped Jerry on the back.

"Got damn it to hell, Pfeiffer, don't you budge!" he exclaimed, and as Jerry urged him to watch his language, he winked at Max and told the dealer to hit him again. This time a queen of clubs atop the seven and four he held. Then twenty to the dealer's nineteen, then two further twenty-ones, as suited goons began to gather at the table, ear-budded for instructions and looking attentive.

Leaving Todd behind at the edge of trouble, Max guided Ellie toward the elevator. "I'm surprised Jerry's here," he confided, one hand slowly moving to her elbow as the other touched the lobby button.

"He's riding a wave he can't handle," she replied. "Seen it before."

They carded Ellie at the bar a second time. This time, though, Max escaped the bartender's scrutiny. He leaned forward, propped his elbows, and looked into the mirror behind the bar, admiring himself for a seasoned appearance. He felt protective toward his companion, in that condescending way that a man sometimes displays for a much younger woman, though they were really close in age—not as concerned about guarding her as that she will feel guarded, somehow be drawn to his circle of security.

Ellie drank a fruity, elaborate concoction that was the choice of newly legal drinkers, then moved to bourbon on the rocks to show that she knew what was up. At her insistence, they considered the odd pairing of Trabue and Pfeiffer, how even the political agreement seemed skewed and impromptu. They agree on most things, Max told Ellie. But if they thought about each other's reasons, they might disagree.

Ellie stirred her whiskey with the little plastic Thor's hammer and nodded absently. "Jerry's too innocent for Bucky Trabue," she said at last. "He's luring him. Every time I see that old cynic it makes me…lose my love for everything around him. It's because I can't see his love for anything, Max. I wish he'd lay off Jerry, and I wish my brother wasn't getting caught in the undertow."

She was melancholy now. Max didn't want things headed that way. Now it was Bucky Trabue was spoiling things, even in absence. Or Jerry, or Todd—Max could hardly tell any more who was keeping him from Ellie Vitale. Bolstered by a second vodka martini—a drink he had picked to seem all Rat Pack and mature to his pretty companion—he decided to move to the question.

"El, I came with you because it's too much to bear in the city right now. What with George and the funeral arrangements."

Ellie nodded. "There's a sister coming in. I never knew."

"Everyone has a brother or sister, Ellie. My older brother's in Maryland being responsible as we speak."

"Oh, you're responsible enough, Max. At least for now. Your jobs may not be steady, but you work two of them. Don't strike the romantic pose. You're way better than some emo slacker, and you know it."

He didn't know whether he liked that.

"And not everyone has a brother or sister," Ellie continued, intuiting where this was headed. "Dom's an only child."

"Shows."

"What's that supposed to mean, Max?"

He went for it. "Self-absorbed. I mean, he's all right, but he's kind of eat up. Don't you think?"

She nodded again. "The father thing. He's Telemachus."

"Sorry?"

"Remember the *Odyssey*, Max? How the son goes off and looks for the father because the suitors have messed up the palace so much that everything's on the edge of chaos? Well, Dominic's like that. He's haunted by what's missing."

"You sweet on him?" And there it was.

"I wouldn't say that."

"What would you say, then, Ellie? How would you describe what you think of him?"

She fell silent, and with a kind of desperate courage, he pressed further. "For example, would you rather be sitting here drinking with him instead of with me? I mean, just for example."

She lifted the hammer from her drink and regarded it abstractly. "What girl did Telemachus leave behind, Max?"

Max couldn't remember. He signaled the bartender and waited for a second martini.

∞

"It's something you might consider, Jerry. For the good of all of us."

Bucky swirled the bourbon in the glass and looked up at his suitemate.

Of course, Pfeiffer would object to whiskey in the room. It was part of the fundy preacher demeanor. Which was exactly why Bucky had brought a bottle of Maker's onto the premises. Time to secularize the Lamb.

"We're in peril on all sides, my friend. You may not notice it from the shelter of your church, but the whole world's in the balance these days. Just look outside and check the weather. Three years in a row with triple-digit temperature from April till October, and this ain't about to go otherwise."

Jerry shook his head. "Global warming is a ruse, Bucky. There's been research."

The ice in the glass clicked against Bucky's teeth. "How about the human weather, then, Jerry? Conflicts and feuds breaking out, American against American, Christian against Christian, even Muslim against Muslim, though as I understand, that one's been happening for generations. All morality, all decency out the window. The homos getting married, for God's sake."

"Language, Bucky. No oaths."

"Sorry. My upbringing. At any rate, the world is unraveling."

"The beginning of the end," Jerry conceded. "Like in Revelations."

"Whatever, Jerry. No, I mean you're probably right. Very much like Revelations, or at least the part of it before the seals start to get opened."

Bucky filled his glass. The welcome splash of whiskey against the ice broke the density of silence, which seemed unbearably long, the space of half an hour. The ice down to slivers, like the melting icebergs Jerry Jeff denied. "It's no reason to stagnate, Reverend," he cautioned at last. "The signs may be there, but they been there for ages. The Vikings who give the names of things to this casino, they had visions of wolves swallowing the sun and moon, of huge serpents twisting their way from the sea to the shore, making hurricanes as they go. Of roosters crowing loud enough to literally wake the dead."

"Those were myths, though," Jerry objected. "They were just stories that people used when they didn't understand things."

"Whatever, Jerry. Because they talked about things we still are afraid of. Like earthquakes and floods and hurricanes. Oh, we may understand them more, but we aren't any closer to stopping them. And the human things we're no closer to stopping, either. The horns that summon us to battle. Like the trumpets of Revelation?"

Jerry nodded. "Against the New World Order. Our oppressors. And that myth about the wolves eating the sun and moon. It's like the third and fourth trumpets, isn't it?"

Bucky nodded sagely, wondering what he was getting into. "Whatever it is, Jerry, it's no call to inaction. You're supposed to clear the way, aren't you? To fight the good fight, even at the end of days? Because all the stories end in new heaven and new earth. Even the old pagan Vikings imagine a new world rising out of the flood, all of us washed clean by the waters."

It sounded good. He'd put Jerry to bed early and go back out to the bars. Bucky was good at talking: tomorrow he'd find a way to persuade his friend to roam the tables with him, once more before they made their way back to the city. Jerry was on about attending George Castille's funeral: he had a way—one that Bucky found admirable—of sticking by the people he knew. Didn't know how well it would work in the campaign, but it was good for now, good for a selling point.

Again Bucky almost felt bad over finagling an innocent like Jerry Jeff Pfeiffer. He marked it off as a hard, unflinching service to a better world, something he had learned on those Little League benches forty years ago, waiting for hippie parents who dawdled and smoked weed and placed him second. It's what he told himself. He wanted a world where those types didn't run things, didn't run them into the ground. And that was part of why Bucky loved folks like Jerry Jeff Pfeiffer, who would pick up their kids if they had them, who wouldn't let down the people who had to trust them in a pinch.

Having said that, he sure would like another day at the casino. Especially considering the run he was on and that his talisman didn't have work to return to, the theater having been closed for three days in mourning.

"So, we're headed back for Castille's funeral? If you're running for office, Jerry, you might consider that he ain't necessarily your kind of people. You know what I mean."

Jerry glared at him. "What are you saying, Bucky? Castille gave me that job. There was something in him that could of been saved. It just got lost somehow on the way. It's pretty much like the world you were talking about."

"I understand. That don't mean you have to attend the funeral, does it?"

Jerry shook his head and slipped into a flannel pajama shirt. Bucky checked his watch. Nine fucking thirty. Well at least he had a window of time for bourbon and amenities.

"I've got to go, Bucky. Some other lost folks are picketing the funeral. It's just a mess, and I have to be there to stand for George Castille against *them*, even if I don't stand with things about how he done."

18.

Prague was his golden city, its crumbling gothic towers, the Charles Bridge lined with the statues that came alive at night, if you asked the street vendors at the Winter Markets.

But by spring of 1945, the streets had lost their magic for Hauptsturmführer Florian Geist, along with the rest of Middle Europe. On the morning of May 8, garrisoned with an SS unit at the Barrandov, he heard about the Czech attack on the radio station at Fochova Street, Still, his cohorts held their ground, and Geist knew the weakness in the wind as Karl Frank vainly negotiated with the Allies.

It was complicated. Things were happening quickly. On the 5th Geist had joined a squadron of the SS sent to reinforce the soldiers at the radio station, and by late morning he was there, armed and holed up as the Czech policemen mounted their assault against the garrison and armed citizens rushed through the alleys and over the rooftops for a shot at the Germans who had held the town for six years.

Geist knew the situation was final. The Russians were barreling toward the capital from the east, and the American

Third Army was scarcely an hour west. Caught in the vise of hostile armies, they planned to keep the radio in hand, the communications center from which they might negotiate surrender and peace with the Americans.

Because they all knew what the Soviets would bring.

Hence the counteroffensive. Pistol in hand, Geist led his squadron north toward the city center. Before him ranged a trio of Jagdpanzer 38 light tanks—what the men called Hetzers. True to their nickname, they were baiters on this assault, sent out to draw fire from the alleys and rooftops. It was delay they hand in mind, holding the city long enough to cut the deal.

There was something exhilarating about such cleansing, about the march toward his beloved Old Town Square—the place that had shimmered in his memory for years. And it was the place to end all things, where his heart and work lay in residence, for he did not believe it was an ending.

Up Melantrichova Street he traveled, away from the radio station, into an uncanny stillness, as the old building leaned in upon him as though old Prague opened to receive him, then closed around him and swallowed him whole. Smoke from the square ahead began to filter through the air, first smelled and then as a kind of translucency as the Hetzers took the narrow street in column and the troops hastened forward to walk between them.

Like Zrcadlo in his film, Florian Geist stood on the threshold of great, transforming change. The muted light of a spring morning surrounded him, and he breathed in the mingled smell of gas and gunpowder, of smoke from Kozna Street, and it was as though he inhaled glory, he wanted to hold the moment— the acrid, elating taste of the air, the anticipation, the brink of fulfillment—like the climax of a great, transforming film, the images passing in silent essential light...

∞

Even he would have laughed at the irony of Anděl Musilová,

looking out a shattered window pane above the narrowing of Kozna Street as the column approached Old Town Square.

She, too, stood at the brink of change as she aimed the rifle between the Hetzers and marveled at her fortune.

She had taken back her maiden name early in the war, when her young chemist of a husband had sensed that a gentile name would mask Anděl and their children. Had the Germans held the town longer, the surname would not have protected her, and she might as well have remained Anděl Vesela. But hiding no longer mattered when she heard he was in the midst of his squadron, moving toward the old town square. She left the children in safe, responsible hands, and had rushed over three blocks and up the fire escape of the building, peering out the window just in time to see Hauptsturmführer Florian Geist, dressed formally for the occasion, the black Totenkopf apparent at his collar as he stopped, looked back down Melantrichova Street, and shot his cuffs as though he were bound for a dance.

She aimed, said a prayer to a God she no longer believed in, and squeezed the trigger slowly as he dropped to the cobblestones before even she heard the solitary shot. And Anděl Musilová knelt at the window, resolved and cleansed, as the soldiers return fire and the world sheared away.

∞

The protest was the topic when Max and the Vitale twins returned to the city.

They all gathered shaken at a Huntington's table. Dominic was there, to Max's disappointment, and Leni had invited herself along. She sulked in the booth, miffed that the waitress had told her that Huntington's was a "No Smoking Establishment".

So there were five, and Todd was blistering outrage at the picketing. Mahanaim Evangelical Church, grabbing the heels of several fundamentalist churches nationwide, had begun picketing funerals and all kinds of public mourning, blaming all death and disaster on America's "acceptance of the gay lifestyle."

"George's sister oughta hire armed guards for the funeral," he proclaimed. "George never hurt anyone, and we all owe him."

Max sighed. It was difficult, the physical resemblance between the twins, when you saw the shape into which Todd could turn Ellen's benign and lovely features. He stirred more sugar into his coffee and waited for the storm to pass.

But Dominic seemed bent on making it worse. He was on about the First Amendment, how it was best to ignore those types, that they weren't after righteousness as much as they were attention. They were like the mobs with torches and pitchforks in the Frankenstein movies—extras, he said, not the main story. Just part of an atmosphere of meanness that we should rise above as we honor our friend.

It became too much to take, and Max finally spoke out. "Excuse me, Dom, but that's such bullshit. The high ground gets flooded, too. Especially by these assholes. No, I don't think we should go so far as armed thugs, like Todd says, but it's time to face down that bunch at Mahanaim before they become another Westboro and start getting all kinds of press."

The two men glared at each other. Leni leaned back and smiled, a shark's precision in her expression. Max noticed, and it angered him even more. He sniffed shook his head, and muttered something about *fuck this ahinsa posing, anyway.*

Then Ellie rose abruptly and left the table. All eyes followed her as she covered her face and rushed out of Huntington's, crossing the street to the theater right in front of a passing auto, its brakes shrieking and its driver shouting at her with an oath sealed from hearing by the windows of the car and the restaurant. She waved apologetically, distractedly, and unlocked the theater doors to enter its healing and solitary darkness.

"Poor child," Leni murmured, so tenderly that the three men looked up in astonishment. "She needs some girl talk," she said as she stood and followed the vanished girl, lighting a cigarette as she stepped outside and crossed to the theater. Todd blurted a brief, soft laugh in her wake, and for a moment the tension between Max and Dominic seemed to waver, almost to dissipate, until both of them recognized who they were, what the stakes were, and that it was not about free speech nor funerals, nor even about George Castille.

∞

Ellie surprised Dominic by insisting that they still visit the monastery, even though George's funeral had been set for the very afternoon when they had planned on meeting John Bulwer. Dominic suggested that it would be thoughtless, even rude to miss the ceremonies, but Ellie pleaded with him. Said she had to get away again.

That she didn't mind unfamiliar ghosts, but that she wanted to set behind her those spirits she had known and loved.

It seemed cold to Dominic, the grandchild of a semi-professional Irish mourner. Mary had always hoped the widow would keep the dead man above ground an extra day so that the wake would last longer, and Dominic had learned almost genetically the comfort and quiet humor of the funeral time. But the girl he might be about to choose was more modern, it seemed: a brief burst of mourning followed by a retreat from memory, driving off from the departed with no glance in the rear-view mirror.

She picked him up at the theater. He came out the front doors into the morning light, found Ellie parked at the curbside, animated in talk with Max Winter, who glared at Dominic as he rescued Ellie from righteous attentions, from Max's passive-aggressive talk about the funeral. Scarcely speaking to Max beyond a muttered *hey*, Dominic climbed into Ellie's Volkswagen Beetle and she gripped the wheel as she steered onto the interstate.

The first leg of the journey was every bit as nerve-rattling as Dominic had been promised. He'd heard about trips when Ellie drove—speeds twenty miles over the limit, the sidle and weave through lanes of traffic. So at the first rest stop outside the city, he offered to drive, claiming to know the way to the monastery.

From then on, the trip was smooth, even pleasant. Dominic asked her what she and Leni had talked about, and the reply surprised him—that Leni had suggested a day trip with him as company, letting on that she sanctioned and approved of the romance. The subject of funerals faded into talk about Buddhism and Bulwer. Then, at Ellie's insistence, Dom told her a little more about Peri Bathgate, guarding his words and emotions because he knew what an intense buzz-killer it could be to bring up one's exes.

The car coasted off the interstate and onto the state roads, winding through a country of beautiful, rolling yards, of expensive cars parked next to humble ranch-style houses and double-wide trailers. It was not alien country to a New Englander, especially a Vermonter, and Dominic caught the derelict landscape only peripherally, his eyes on the road, alert to the yellow "deer crossing" signs.

He smiled, his thoughts drifting, remembering a letter to the newspaper back when he lived in Vermont, in which someone had suggested that the signs be moved from a particular intersection where a number of deer had been struck by autos, because "surely we can find a safer place for them to cross."

He took a turn on a narrow county road, remembering Bulwer's scrawled directions, and Ellie was talking about her brother. How Todd had been strange all along.

Early, she claimed, they had actually looked alike. Her mother said that pink and blue had become mandatory when she took the twins on outings, because when she dressed them in the neutral colors of babyhood—whites and greens and cheery yellows—she was always stopped by friends who asked which was which, so the clothing had become a shorthand, saved her conversations about the kids she really didn't want to talk about that much.

Of course, as they got older, other problems had replaced the simple, early identifications of infancy. Ellie had felt, she said, that Todd was her gloomy and masculine shadow. In grammar school, he followed her at a distance just close enough to be discomforting, and when the changes of puberty came, that distance narrowed.

Dominic laughed nervously at the stories. Soon, though, he couldn't even laugh. Several times Ellie had seen Todd's eye through the bathroom keyhole, found her underwear in his tangled sheets. He was the evil twin people always joked about. The doppelganger, dark figure in the horror movie.

As Ellie went on about her brother, Dom tried to dismiss it all as characteristic drama, but his instincts told him that some things hadn't changed.

Dominic had seen Todd struggle against the young men who were potential suitors to his sister. In fact, there was probably a kind of barometer in the whole business: when Todd disliked you more than the other guy, it was a sign you were Ellie's preferred suitor for the moment. Or when Todd disliked you, it was a sign to Ellie that you were worth a look. The road ran both ways.

But it seemed that preference was a shifting and volatile thing. Here in the car, gliding through sunlit farmlands on roads hooded with trees, Ellie was the prize in the passenger seat: lovely and blonde and olive-skinned, a perfect storm of genetics and possibilities. If he could only be sure that she liked *him* and not his attentions. But then, this road ran both ways as well: Dominic wondered if he enjoyed her company more than his rivalry with Max.

Thoughts of Peri left him cautious and tired. Solitude had some advantages. And Ellie was turning out to be an unwieldy girl—bright and alluring and more than certainly a mess.

He was relieved to set aside the subject, to meet Bulwer at the bottom of a hill, where the steep, rutted gravel trail branched off from a county road to ascend toward the monastery. They parked their cars at the foot of the road and started the climb. Bulwer used a walking stick that neither Dom nor Ellie had ever seen, and they slowed their pace to accommodate him. Soon he outstripped them, though, and waited for them where the trail leveled, and together they stood and rested a moment, Dominic breathing the heaviest, as a wing of Canada geese passed overhead going south, their calls to one another like the creaking of rusty hinges.

"It gets easier from here," Bulwer assured them, and Dominic thought he heard teasing in the older man's voice.

They rounded a corner and in front of them lay a Buddha garden. Dominic wondered what they called it, sure there was a name. He'd heard *vihara* and *chaitya,* but from what he knew, the terms didn't apply to a grassy hill covered with statues. They walked through all kinds of Buddhas—the peaceful Abayha Buddhas, the Dhyana mudras with their hands cupped like alms bowls, Laughing Buddhas, which Bulwer explained were *bodhisattvas.*

One of them looked like the old homeless guy Bulwer had spoken to outside Huntington's. It was Ellie who pointed it out, and despite himself, Dominic smiled at the connection. It seemed like the monastery should not be a place for silliness, and yet there it was, along with peace and awareness, acceptance and the here and now.

He took Ellie's hand to help her over a gravelly crest on the road. Bulwer stalked tirelessly in front of them, claimed to be in better shape now than he was "at their age".

Made them smile at the criticism.

All the while Dominic wanted to feel like he was coming home, wanted a wave of peace that did not come. He wandered through the Buddhas and brought his thoughts back to the present, guided and counted his breaths, but he felt restless as he left the garden and crossed the road, ending up beside the little brook that brushed against the temple. Today the water was cloudy, and the banks littered with charred scraps of damp paper. There was something so sad about it that he sat down, tossed pebbles into the current as Bulwer and Ellie approached.

He drifted into their conversation as Bulwer explained the Ghost Festival to Ellie, who had never heard of the celebration.

"We're at the end of the Ghost Month, Ellen," Bulwer said.

"There are three big days around this festival. The gates to hell open on the first of the month, and right in the middle is the festival day. The gates close at the month's end."

Ellie laughed nervously. Nobody—not even skeptics—liked the prospect of hell's doors open.

Bulwer told her that it was an inauspicious time. There are other times in the calendar, he said, that people honor their ancestors, but this is the time when those ancestors return. In the Ghost Month, sometimes it was less an honoring than an appeasement of parents. You watch yourself on strolls. Some people don't swim during that time, for the ghosts are notorious for drowning swimmers. Few people travel or invest in business.

You bribe the ghosts. Those of your ancestors and those who have no living relatives. The solitary ghosts can be the most frightening.

So you burn counterfeit money in huge denominations. Set out food or tea for them. Leave empty seats at the dinner table. Sail paper boats down streams and rivers to guide them back. He gestured toward the wet scraps of paper, and Ellie sat down by Dominic, sat nicely close to him, her shoulder brushing softly against his as Bulwer went on about the festival.

At the end of the month, he said, the gates close, and the wails of the spirits can be heard as they return.

Hungry ghosts are sad and pathetic creatures, Bulwer told them. Their stomachs are huge and gaping, but their mouths are tiny and their throats narrow, so there is no way to satisfy their hunger. They got that way because of previous lives, when they were driven by greed, by envy and jealousy, by the simple, powerful cravings for things.

Dominic liked the way Bulwer explained things. Simple, but without condescension. And yet he thought of his mother, hollowed and bloated by the cancer and discontent that took her, IVs dripping pain killer under the pocked flesh of her hand. He lurched back to the present, watched as another tossed pebble broke the current. The sadness ebbed because Ellie felt good against him. Her shoulder was warm as it rose and fell with her breathing, and he ventured an arm around her as Bulwer finished talking and walked back up toward the Buddha garden.

The air suddenly vibrated with the ratcheting sound of cicadas, and Dominic stood, helped Ellie up, her hand firm and smooth in his. He held it as they ascended the bank of the creek and stood on the gravel road. Bulwer was some way ahead of them now, standing by the temple gate, in conversation with two slight, brown-robed figures. Ellie slipped her arm through his, and they walked toward Bulwer, who was bowing to the shorter of the robed men, steepling his hands in greeting.

Dominic started to speak to Ellie. He had words for her at last—nothing momentous, at least not yet, but for her ears alone—so he stopped on the trail, looked another time toward the temple, and steadied his nerves.

And then something passed across the road, a buckling of air that clouded his view of Bulwer and the monks, that hovered over the dusty gravel. It gathered solidity, and Dominic could see a head, shoulders, a slight frame. Neither a narrow neck nor a distended belly, but insubstantial nevertheless, at first like a brown-robed monk but translucent, the air brindled with a dusty wind. It reminded him of Peri's transparency through the long-ago apartment window until the shape of the thing magnified and passed from cloud into another strange familiarity, as Dominic stood at the brink of recognizing something else, someone else.

As Dominic and Ellen drew nearer, the apparition beckoned. Now a pinprick of a mouth opened in its muddy face, and an eddy of dust and dried leaves surged toward the aperture, as though the figure drew all air, all substance into its hidden core. And it took a shape more defined, as the imagined monk shifted and congealed, its skin pale and swirling now, the mouth closing like a hole in dough, and soundlessly the figure beckoned, taller now, and ruddy, bearing family resemblance but oh so altered.

Dominic stopped in his tracks. A voice—outside him or inside him, it was impossible to tell, but a deep voice, masculine and familiar—called his name. It took all his will not to follow, even though he was sure that if he did follow he would be snatched, drawn under, a drowned child in the currents of the Ghost Month.

And *Dominic* he heard again, and *Dom,* and *Dommie,* then Bud and *Boyo,* the last one a name he hadn't been called in thirty years, and his heart broke.

And as the tears surged like a subterranean current finding the surface and rushing to sunlight, bearing mud and leaves and the ashes of paper boats, and *Dom* the voice said, and again *Dom,* and *Dominic!* then, rising in pitch and timbre until he was back in the hot sun of early September. And it was Ellie's voice, and she was shaking his arm, and he coughed and bent at the knees and she crouched with him and hugged him and asked him if he was all right.

And he was, and he said so. Told her it was all this dust and wind and the goddamned heat.

And Ellie laughed and turned loose of him, and they stood. This time she helped him to his feet and he accepted the hand up, vaguely embarrassed by the gesture, by his own vulnerability.

"Where did Bulwer go?" he asked.

"Indoors, Dominic. We should probably join him. It's freaking hot out here and about to get the best of me, too."

They neared the monastery gate and Ellie held his arm tightly. She giggled. "You looked like you saw a ghost, Dom."

To which he laughed and shook his head, skirting the words that would affirm or deny or pin it down.

"If you did, I hope it wasn't hungry," she teased. "From the way Mr. Bulwer described them, I'd rather not run into one. In the Ghost Month or any time."

∞

They meditated in the still air of the Quonset hut that served the small monastery as a temple. Cheerfully and patiently, the monk explained to Ellie the concepts of mindfulness, of counting the breath. But during the short spans where they sat in silence,

Dominic heard her stir on the cushion beside him, could sense her restlessness, her desire to get going.

As they walked back down the hill, Bulwer was less lecturing, more conversational. He listened indulgently to Ellie's claims that meditation *might not be for her, at least not now,* and put up with Dom's strange shift of mood.

For his part, Dominic walked behind his friends, his thoughts still on the strange happenings by the creek. By now he had almost talked himself into believing it had been a brilliance of sun off the water, heat shimmer from the road. Anything but the unsettling figure that had shadowed the day and left him sad and sun-weary.

He knew that, by now, George Castille's funeral would be underway, and it pained him that he wasn't there. But something about the dead burying the dead, he remembered. It seemed to him better to be with Ellie and Bulwer.

For Bulwer, too, had been eager for this trip to the monastery. Had talked about it for days leading up to the disastrous news, and then respectfully backed away from planning the trip with Dominic because he thought that no doubt all at the Shangri-La would attend the funeral. When Dominic had told him otherwise, that Ellie needed to be out of town in the presence of weighty things, he'd pretended to understand, his pleasure that they were still coming overriding his surprise at the lapse in etiquette.

"Are you sure?" he had asked. And Dom knew that his *yes* would raise trouble, not with Bulwer but with those who stayed behind, those who attended the funeral. But now on the sun-dazzled gravel road, having left the dead to bury the dead, he felt better about his decision, especially since John had slowed again in front of him, was waiting for him.

"Since you're here," he began.

And then he explained how he was ready to hand over the store. He was seventy-five, he revealed. The daily duties of the store were resting on him more heavily. Something about the passion fading. The wisdom was there, but the body that housed it was tired.

And surprisingly, he wondered if Dominic would be willing to take over Salvages. It could be a slow transition between owners, he said. Six months, a year, in which he would show Dom how things operated, tune him more to the business side, the orders, the cash flow, all of the things that were as remote and inscrutable as hieroglyphs to Dominic's drifting mind.

"It sounds like a great opportunity, Dom," Ellie volunteered. He wished she would stay out of it. After all, they weren't a couple, so she shouldn't have a say.

He circled around an answer. Talked about how interesting it was. Appeared as touched and grateful as possible when Bulwer insisted he was passing it down, not selling it, that he'd be there to advise even when it was Dominic's outright. Felt he should be touched as well when Ellie took his hand, obviously moved by the moment.

"It sounds interesting," was all he could say. "Thank you for the offer. It's a good one." inwardly kicking himself because he knew it was not enough to say for any of them—for him, for Ellie, and certainly not what Bulwer wanted or deserved. For after all, there was still a search ahead of him—one that had floated back into his sights on the banks of that slow-moving, ashen creek.

Telemachus was on the move again. And Dominic feared that, as always, the lost boy traveled alone.

They reached the cars, and as Ellie climbed into her passenger seat, Dominic lingered with Bulwer and promised he would consider the offer. It could be something, he told himself. There was a small efficiency apartment over the tottering shelves of the bookstore—one that Bulwer rented out on occasion, but that would be ideal when the theater closed and he would be his own anyway, burnt out of his Ninth Street place, no longer housed in the theater, and unwilling to return to Grandma Mary's chaotic haven.

The sun was behind them as they took the exit ramp into the city. A left and a right, and he left her with a kiss at the curb before taking the back door up into the mournfully darkened theater.

19.

B ut it was far from irrelevant for Leni Zauber, perched in the projection booth, working feverishly, urgently over the Steenbeck, each frame coming into view as she found herself drawn in slowly by the inveiglement of Florian's art.

She had always been his advocate, champion of his genius as a special-effects innovator. Among her favorites was this: the meticulous frame-by-frame transformation of Geist himself, playing the actor Zrcadlo—the "mirror-man" who could adopt the appearance, mannerism, and voice of any person in whose presence he found himself—as he turned into Halberd, the fleshy, middle-aged Dr. Thaddeus Halberd, played by Emil Jannings.

The quality of the film here was grainy, despite her efforts. Nature of the beast, she told herself. There are some things restoration cannot rescue. But frame by frame, Zrcadlo changed, as through some cinematic sorcery Geist seemed to transform into Jannings, the handsome Aryan face slowly devolving toward the older actor's settled, heavy countenance. Usually, the director did such things by a series of jump cuts: a focus on the transforming face, then someone or something else, then back to the face, where the "changes" would register on the actor. Lon

Chaney had spoken of sitting still for hours, of even having his hands fixed by carpet nails to be completely motionless (though Leni had never believed that story, especially after seeing the great change come over Florian Geist).

And here, frame by frame, she stood in wonder at the master of guise and illusion. Geist's eyes were moving, his features as well as they blended impossibly toward the older, more corpulent features of Jannings. It was something the directors of here and now, the Peter Jacksons and Guillermo del Toros, would have had trouble doing, even with their soft and pampered access to computer graphics and their over-reliance on the green screen. It was something to do with Geist's performance, as Leni had always known: it seemed as though he was acting himself into the image of Emil Jannings.

Leni sat back in her chair. She would have given anything to see the filming of the scene. Whether he had done it before the camera or on a cutting-room floor in Prague (it was the Prague print of the film, after all, well preserved and handed over to her by a bundled archivist who seemed to sleepwalk his way to transfer the copy into her gloved hands), what he had done was magic—more by far than the shadowy occultists of Meyrinck's fiction. Quickly she moved the Steenbeck over the rest of the scene, shaking her head, muttering in German. Never again was Zrcadlo shown in a way that the character could be identified as Geist. Instead, the camera focused full face on Halberd, Zrcadlo glimpsed only from behind, as a shadow cast over the doubtful, meaty face of the older man, as a force or entity off-camera to whom he spoke, at whom he recoiled in wonder and fear.

Leni's thoughts were lurching over every alternative, discounting them one by one. It was a single take. She was certain.

And the man who seemed to tremble at the presence of the other was Florian Geist, who had transformed himself into the older, heavier, and infinitely more famous countenance of Emil Jannings. Now Leni understood Jannings' vehement disavowals in the late '30s, his claim that he had never been a part of *Walpurgisnacht.* She understood the incomprehension of the few who had seen the film on release, who had *wondered how could he deny what we see upon the screen?*

Florian Geist had played the role all along.

Leni did not know what to make of this. In a mixture of admiration and fear, she scrolled to the intertitle, translated the German:

I am the invisible nightingale who sits in his cage and sings. But it is not every cage whose bars resonate when the bird sings. I have sung to you often, so that you might hear me, all your life long you have been heedless.

There had been no Jannings in the film. Perhaps no Hermann Braun, no Hannes Stelzer. Only Dagover and Pema, but no longer was she certain of the women, either. Geist, in his shifty, transmogrifying fashion, might have played those roles as well. The only guarantee was that he couldn't be two actors, two characters at once, could he?

Leni exhaled. The world had just become permeable, slippery. She was no longer certain of where things were headed.

∞

At about that time, they were laying George Castille to rest.

The cortege passed down Villanova by Our Lady of Serenity, black vehicles in a shimmer of heat off the pavement. The sister had provided roses for the roof of the hearse, and six cars followed. George would have boggled at how conventional it was.

Max smiled to think that. Seated by Todd in the third car, he had exchanged whispers about how surprised he was—how surprised they both were—to ride with friends of the family. It was a little sad at first, but then they were heartened by the gathering at the gravesite.

Until they saw the signs.

Horrible *fag* signs, proclaiming God's hatred. Brandished with scowls and catcalls as the cortege approached.

"Motherfuckers," Todd whispered, and Max glared out the window at the pickets from Mahanaim Evangelical Church. The desire for a gun brushed against the outskirts of his thoughts, but he pushed it away, he was better than that. The pallbearers climbed out of the second car—a well-dressed bunch, he noted, and lined up at the rear of the hearse amid shouts and abuses.

The Reverend Billy Hightower was there, as they had expected. Saved (to hear him tell it) from a dissolute life that included "the sodomite lifestyle" by wandering into Mahanaim—in itself far-fetched logistics, given that the church was a mile off the nearest state road—Hightower had preached and demonstrated his way to the head of the congregation, and stood now in the middle of the crowd, blaring the worst of St. Paul through a bullhorn.

"God damn it," Todd hissed, tugging on Max's sleeve. "Look over there."

Many of the congregation of Heart Ministries had assembled in the back of Mahanaim's pickets. Jerry Jeff was there, and Aldo Wooters. The two dim-witted girls who hosted a ghost-hunting reality show on public access—Amber Jade and Jade Amber Landon, if he remembered correctly. Max looked around for a camera, expecting the cynical worst from such people, and at last he saw it, on an old-school tripod set up on a hill overlooking the gravesite, the cameraman bent between two statuary angels.

It didn't take long to recognize Dominic Rackett behind the camera, but before the incredulity and rage could rise in him, Todd had tugged at him again, was pointing out the window, back to the assembling crowd.

"There better be a good fucking reason for Pfeiffer to be here," he growled, as Jerry Jeff breasted his way through the masses, decked up in a shiny suit and a hideous bolero tie. Jerry passed between the rows of signs and stood in the no-man's-land between the protestors and the mourners, waving his hands for silence as the Mahanaim faithful shouted and menaced him with placards.

"Please," Jerry began softly, so softly that Max knew what he was saying only by reading his lips. From somewhere over by the Landon girls someone shouted for silence, and after a few roiling seconds of back-and-forth, the noise ebbed and Jerry Jeff began to speak.

"I know most of us come from different places," he said, his voice scarcely raised above a conversation, so that people in the back of the crowd shouted "What did he say?" until those in the front shushed them to silence.

"I know some of you come from Mahanaim and some from the theater. Some come all the way from out of town and some from the TV show."

Max looked back up to the stone angels. The camera sat alone on its tripod. No sign of Dominic.

"We come from different places in the world and from different places in the heart," Jerry continued. "But I expect we all mean well because I have to expect that to make it through this world. Because if we don't expect it, there's a part of us that is pretty much done for. A part of me, anyway.

"I confess I will always be puzzled by Mr. Castille's kind of love. He spoke of it without shame, which some might call shameless, though others might see a dignity in the speaking. As for myself, I wonder why, but I choose to remember him for other things."

An angry shout from the crowd went unfollowed, unanswered.

Pfeiffer raised his hand. "I remember him as a kind employer with a sense of humor I didn't always understand, but others did, and they laughed along with him, though never in a mean way I could figure. I remember him as a man who bent the rules to give me time to minister. As someone who listened to the youth in his employ, and without the judgment they may have needed, because they needed the listening more.

"And it's a question of degree for me. I'm puzzled by the kind of love, but that don't mean he didn't love someone. And

I'm talking about a love that looked after someone more than himself, a love for his neighbor that didn't have anything to do with the lust on your signs, but everything to do with his heart's mystery.

"Who am I to say when love isn't love? I'll jump in the direction that love is love, brothers and sisters. And I'll jump a little further and say that any love, even misguided love, trumps it all over hate."

Max scanned the crowd quickly, realizing that if it came to scuffles in the cemetery, he'd be enlisted. He wanted to punch Hightower, even at dire cost, but he figured on the numbers and hoped it didn't come to that. He guessed that Todd would be pretty useless in a fight, and the pallbearers seemed too refined for fisticuffs. Mr. Trabue had showed up, but he was off a ways, on a slope opposite the abandoned camera and tripod, and there was no telling whether he'd join in or even what side he'd take, and Max had given up on Dominic's help entirely, had written him off, had wondered why he had tried to like the fucker in the first place...

Then Aldo Wooters burst out of the crowd and rushed toward Jerry Pfeiffer.

Max pushed past a frozen Todd and hurried toward the encounter, not ten feet away when Wooters dropped to his knees and began, loudly and tearfully, to express sorrow and repentance for his many sins.

`It stopped them all. Hightower and his crowd moved back, a cautious distance from this bizarre altar call, as Wooters owned up to his anger at the unrighteous, at those who did not love this city or this country, that perhaps in his dream of a better, cleaner community, his hopes of taking back America, he had stumbled on the side of righteous rage.

Max rolled his eyes as the Landon girls hollered at the loud and tepid confession, as did a busty redhead over in the legions of Mahanaim, and by now Aldo Wooters was barreling down the road to repentance and heedless of those he ran over. Pfeiffer crouched in front of him earnestly, their conversation lost in the rising mumble of the puzzled crowd. Wooters wept, fell prostrate, and now Jerry knelt and prayed over him, his arms extended evangelically and the whole crowd falling into a kind of reverent silence.

They rose at last, to a scattering of tongues and *praise Jesus.* Both of them tearful, Jerry and Wooters stood at respectful distance as the words were said over George Castille, as Hightower and his followers dispersed almost abashedly, and Max's old boss and friend was laid to rest in the presence of a smaller but more loving audience than perhaps he had ever enjoyed in life.

But as they left the graveside, each mourner was lost in that kind of awkwardness that makes each funeral personal. Max shepherded a tearful Todd through the dispersing crowd, wishing it was the other twin instead, where an arm around her shoulders could both console and suggest a happier interest. He caught a glimpse of Bucky Trabue, sunglassed and hatless by the driver's door of a decrepit Volvo, Jerry Jeff leaning against the hood, the two of them locked in clandestine conversation. Then he looked back to the stone angels, not quite believing that Dominic could have been that cynical.

Max took it all in. He swore under his breath. Then he turned a last time to the grave, where the canopy was being broken down and a solitary, indifferent reverse hoe awaited its role in completing the burial.

∞

Bucky had seen the dark-haired boy, too. The cameraman standing at the rise by the tripod—slight, semi-Asian and distant, like an extra in one of the silent films at the Shangri-La.

But there was no time to connect the dots. He wished to Jesus that Jerry Jeff wouldn't tangle himself with that graveside altar call, but there they were at the funeral's edge—Wooters and Heart Ministries and the whole damn lot of them—and *it was what it was,* Bucky told himself in a phrase that he hated, that he didn't really know the meaning of, god damn it.

He had some big plans for Jerry Jeff. As of yet he wasn't too sure how standing up against this Mahanaim was going to pan out, but he would have given Jerry Jeff a thousand dollars of his personal pocket money not to stand up to them in the first place.

All in all it was a backwater of alliances. Fundamentalist churches and reality shows. Bucky longed for the days when money could buy a swing district, and in those that were largely black or working-class, where the Party didn't stand a chance, you could finance a candidate into respectability and transplant him to another district for the next last option. It didn't work that way anymore. You made pacts with the devils you didn't know rather than with the old, familiar devils, because there was something tidal and transforming at your feet, washing your ankles and climbing toward your knees with every ebb and flow.

"So, Jerry," he said, his greeting a kind of prelude to a question he couldn't frame in words.

Jerry grinned and replied, "So, Bucky," and stood upwind respectfully as his friend and advisor lit a cigarette and blew contemplative smoke rings into the still, humid air.

"The Wooters fellow? He picks today to come to Jesus?"

"Well, that's just it, Bucky. I ain't sure. This benefit-of-the-doubt business can wear me thin."

Jerry raised his hands and, to Bucky's surprise, they seemed to incandesce, to glow crimson in the backlight of the emerging sun. Bucky blinked, and suddenly things were normal, things were resolved. But there for a moment, this protégé, this prodigy, seemed larger than the custodial preacher or anointed janitor that Bucky had taken on, transforming like an old-time wizard into something he almost was but really was not. Bucky felt ignorant, called out, his hands gripped tight to ungovernable reins.

∞

And in the aftermath disputes and doubts and acrimony.

Back from the monastery, the passionate but strangely chaste kiss from Dominic Rackett still warm against her lips, Ellen Vitale was shocked when Max stepped in front of her car, slapped the hood angrily, and motioned for her to roll down the window. By reflex she locked the car doors as though the street behind the theater had suddenly become a dodgy neighborhood, then remembered it was Max, that things were all right, that if anything he liked her more than he should.

He leaned in the window when she opened it, a little more cool and serene by then, but he was on about something, about *how dare Dominic*. For a minute she thought he had seen them kissing, thought it was none of his damned business. But it wasn't that: it had things to do with George's funeral, with Dominic's standing in the crowd among the protesters. Which was impossible, and she told him so. But he kept on about how it had to be Dominic, he knew him when he saw him, and why was she covering for him, so Ellie said ask Bulwer if you think I'm lying to you but I am *so* over this and if you don't stop I am over you as well.

That shut him up. Whether it was mentioning Bulwer or threatening him with rejection she couldn't tell. Ellie closed the window on his emo foolishness and on his arms, almost catching them. Then she drove away watching him diminish in the rearview mirror. He looked all abandoned and sad, and for a moment she felt sorry for him, even though he was clearly the one at fault. This whole feud between Max and Dominic was out of hand, had just gotten real, and maybe it was time for someone to do something about it.

John Bulwer, perhaps. Or whoever. The mediator was irrelevant. She just wanted it over.

∞

On a night when everyone needed to be going somewhere, when the cast of characters stirred with a restless mortality, Todd ended up at Heart Ministries Outreach, where he was hoping he might find Jerry Jeff Pfeiffer. And sure enough, after only an hour's waiting, the minister's old car pulled to the front of the building. Secretive in the far end of the parking lot, his right hand twitching, Todd watched Pfeiffer enter the building.

He waited, smoked a cigarette, then followed inside.

The door lay unlocked in Pfeiffer's profound trust of the world, and the minister had gone back to his study. He had picked out Todd from the parking lot, because he didn't even startle at the knock.

Jerry sat at the desk, cleared except for an old tensor lamp and a Bible. He looked up, smiled wearily. "One of them rough days, Brother Todd."

"You made it rougher, Jerry," Todd said. "That whole sorry business with someone like Wooters. What the hell were you thinking? A man of God who could make a stranger's funeral all about himself. He didn't know George. He was there for the goddamned attention—yes, I'm sorry, I'll watch my language—in on this 'Just As I Am' conversion bullshit, and you played right into his game. What's *wrong* with you?"

Todd leaned forward and grabbed the tensor lamp, shining it in Jerry's eyes. Pfeiffer blinked, his pupils contracting to pinpoints, and with the light close to his face, the shadow diffused and grew behind him. His shoulders, already broad, seemed to expand and angle like spread wings, but his face looked exposed, almost endangered in the relentless beam of the lamp. He reached out, turned the lamp to the side.

"It's not that simple, Todd. Do you refuse someone who's headed to salvation? It's just…the opposite of this lamp here. The light. It's behind things and shines through them. We only see part of it. There's energies the naked eye don't take in, that we only know about from the scientists. But what I *can* understand is that light is always on the move, Todd. It's constant on the move. The scientists used to say it was a particle, or a wave. Now they imagine it's both a particle *and* a wave—I can't get my thoughts how it can be both, but there you are—but the thing is that it's constantly moving. And the windows, like them stained glass windows out in the worship hall, we only see on account of the light moving through them. They're steady, those windows. One image they give you—something from the Word, a single moment in time and eternity that freezes the light, that means things on account of the light…"

Todd nodded, pretending he got where Jerry was headed.

"But windows like that are products of the olden times," Jerry continued. "When we understood things different. And now in the modern age, light shines through the frames of a film, don't it? Each one a little different from the one before it, so it looks like the folks on screen are alive and moving, when it's really shadow and light, isn't it? Oh, Brother Todd, we see so little in the light we can manage, and what I seen at Mr. Castille's funeral was a soul departed to where only the Lord knew it was going, and another in need, in the here and now, or pretending to be in spiritual need. But pretending or genuine, in need of something."

He cleared his throat, turned off the lamp. The light from the hall outside the office fell over the edge of the desk as Jerry rose, guided Todd toward the door. "I don't save nobody, Todd," he said. "They save themselves. Or Jesus saves them, only they have to help Him do it."

"But Aldo Wooters, Jerry! He's…"

Jerry nodded. "He is that, too, isn't he? Like you and me. He's that and no more and no less."

Metropolis (1927)

It is probably the most famous film from the period. Expensively budgeted, still impressive for its use of special effects—its amazing creation of a world within a limited spectrum of film technology—Fritz Lang's *Metropolis* is more than simply a film. It is a cultural phenomenon that outlines the 20th Century's fears of mechanization, social inequality, and the revolutionary violence that might well be waiting in the wings.

Freder (played by Gustav Frölich) is the sheltered son of Joh Fredersen (Alfred Abel), mastermind of Metropolis, the dark, futuristic city in which the story is set. Having lived a pampered and drifting life, he is stirred from his pleasure-seeking by the beautiful Maria (Brigitte Helm), the spokesperson and mother figure of the city's underclass. Smitten, he goes in search of her, traveling into the depths of the city, where he sees the monstrous treatment of the workers in their desperate attempt to keep Metropolis' mysterious machinery in operation. Disguised as one of the workers, he descends to the city catacombs, where he attends Maria's inspirational homily and discovers that the workers await a Mediator—one whose understanding might bridge the hostile gap between the laborers and their overlords.

Meantime, things are not well in the upper regions of Metropolis. An old feud between Joh Fredersen and the mad scientist Rotwang (Rudolf Klein-Rogge), once rival suitors for the hand of Freder's mother, has resumed many years after Hel Fredersen's untimely death in childbirth, and Rotwang plots the undoing of Fredersen by deploying a robot to undermine the mogul's hold on the city. Clever and vengeful, he fashions his "Machine Man" in the image of Maria, thereby luring the workers into an ill-advised uprising and Freder into the chaos of the city in revolt.

Parts of the film have become a little hokey in the passage of years. Weimar Germany was terrified of Bolshevism, and the revolutionary workers (along with "Red Mary," Brigitte Helm's dark alter-ego) come across as mindlessly enraged, and Freder's role as the Mediator provides a bit too pat of a solution to the impossible problems of the city. Still, the sets and world creation are inventive and visually striking, Helm is radiant in her dual role—with the possible exception of Marlene Dietrich, no actress of the place and time is more blessed by the camera—and Klein-Rogge is delightfully (and suitably) over the top as the grandfather of all movie mad scientists. Two films-within-the-film, one on the Tower of Babel and the other on the Apocalypse, are ingeniously included, in some ways more stark and dramatic than the rather predictable story that frames them.

All in all, it is impressive. If you've been attending the film series since its beginnings in mid-August, you'll no doubt be impressed with how far film technology advanced in the mere eight years

from *Caligari* to *Metropolis*. Lang presents a visual poem about the modern city: his Metropolis is supposed to frighten the audience, but it ends up fascinating and impressing us. Machinery and the Apocalypse dance hand in hand, and it makes us wonder what a comparable nightmare of our own times might show on the screen. Would the technology have taken us over in a different way—smart phones and social networks sealing us off from the eye contact and face-to-face interaction that for millennia served as the soul of communication and perhaps the communication of soul? Or could the foiled creative fire of our own spiritual yearning, used almost as a plot device as Lang's film played to the secularized Weimar Republic, have found its way back into our imagination with force, the new millennia in which we live bearing the fruit of modern anxiety by picking up where the old religion left off, by returning to the old forms of faith with a kind of unquestioning fury?

Whatever the case, these questions are not the movie's to answer. *Metropolis* continues to provide its own spiritual satisfactions: Freder's process of growth is moving, taking us from a man whose clothing and mannerisms smack of pre-adolescence to a repurposed hero, young father to the city's waifs and orphans. It makes you think about our own delayed maturity, how so much of it is wrapped up in cloudy ideas of who we are or who we are supposed to be. And the subtle pairing of our hero with the mad inventor—both of whom have issues with the distant, almost removed Joh Fredersen—suggests at a kind of dark psychology, of withheld approval and generational struggle. But again, these are issues that someone else might address at length: it is up to us to enjoy Lang's grand masterpiece, its startling images and epic scale.

The version of the film we show has 25 minutes of restored footage, film discovered in 2007 at the Museo de Cine in Buenos Aires. As always, and especially during this "Geist-haunted" month, we wonder how German things found their way into Argentina, but we are nonetheless thankful for the additions, as they develop and almost complete Lang's warning vision of a future toward which we all too well might still be headed.

--Dominic Rackett

∞

The *Metropolis* article was the subject of their conversation, when Dominic returned from the monastery.

He walked through the lobby of Shangri-La toward Leni's office, thinking of Ellie and the quiet of the weathered roads in the woods north of the river. But he was rushed back into business, into the little room blue with residual cigarette smoke and Leni Zauber's irritation.

She shook the pages at him and scowled. "What were you thinking when you wrote this, you idiot?"

Her accent was more prominent, almost a caricature, and Dominic thought for a minute how little he knew her.

"This goes to the printer this evening, and it is a self-indulgent piece of foolishness. How could you speak of 'Geist-haunted' and raise again the hysteria of August? We are close to the premiere of *Walpurgisnacht*, you negligent boy, and your words bring back a silly controversy?"

Dominic looked away. She sounded rehearsed, overstated, like a negative review online. But perhaps she was right. It was ad copy she had hired him for, not reporting.

But Leni was hardly finished. "And how can anyone think *Metropolis* is about the stupid and passive Freder and his father issues, not the doubling—*die doppelgänger*—you pick up on the last page only to let drop for the other nonsense."

Dominic tried to respond. Felt the tension and the rubbery-smelling smoke of Gauloises on his skin, as though both had gathered substance in the closeness of the office.

He let it go. Perhaps her words were close to home.

And he was haunted as well by the spectral form on the monastery path.

"It is all about *die doppelgänger*, Dominic," Leni continued, her voice softer now, more forbearing. "Just think about the films you have written about already. The sleepwalker and Franzis who pursues him, both in love with the same girl. And Orlok

273

the vampire, who is the rival of Hutter for the affections of the young man's wife. And even in *Waxworks,* the poet is both the hero of each story and the monster who opposes him. Do you see now? Do you see?

"For right you were about the doubles in Metropolis. Freder and Rottwang—Joh Fredersen's spoiled son and the mad scientist. But it is not a simple good and evil, the 'good cop/bad cop' duality of your American television, now is it? For it is the sleepwalker, the vampire, Spring-Heel Jack and the mad scientist who draw our attention. There is no place for the good boy, Dominic. The good boy does not please the father—nobody does—so the good boy must set out to please himself."

"Yes, ma'am," Dominic breathed quietly. He was surprised at the contemptuous look Leni gave him in return.

"And which do we remember," she continued. "Saintly Maria who preaches in the catacombs to Metropolis' workers? Or Red Mary, who drowns the city?"

The image of Maria, the incomparable Brigitte Helm, had glowed in his memory's recesses through the dark weekend and through his visit with Ellie to the monastery. Leni saw the bad girl as the winner, but the robotic Red Mary had failed: twitching and mugging, proclaiming, "Let's all watch as the world goes to the devil," she had burned at the stake on celluloid for ninety years as a testimony to the fate of fanaticism and calculation. But Leni was right about this: something in the audience humanized Red Mary's inhumanity. We enjoyed her dressed as the Whore of Babylon perched atop a strange golden eye or lens. she was remembered for flooding the city and toppling the towering structures of Metropolis until it seemed as though only one structure was left standing—the weird, outmoded Gothic cathedral before which the final scenes of the film took place.

"She destroyed everything but the gargoyles," Dominic claimed, trying to cobble a joke into the argument. "But seriously, Dr. Zauber, five or six years later, when Hitler became Chancellor, the vision of Red Mary must have haunted Fritz Lang. I suspect the mobs she goaded on looked an awful lot like the Brown Shirts. Lang left Germany soon after, didn't he?"

Zauber sighed. "It took him a year. And only to France. Americans imagine him on a plane to Los Angeles as the Reichstag burned, but it took him a while, and he didn't plan on coming to the States. His wife became a Nazi, you know, and Lang probably wouldn't have left had it not been for his Jewish ancestry. And Red Mary was Red at the time, more Lenin's *doppelgänger* than Hitler's, who was yet on the horizon. And all through that time, they had seen countless rabble-rousers. All through any time, young man, and the line is thin between Red Mary and certain janitors I could name."

She pronounced the word "yanitor," and for a moment Dominic did not make the connection.

Then, "No, it's not the same. Jerry's good people. I'm hearing he went to George Castille's funeral and faced down the crazies."

"Heard and did not see?" Zauber asked. "I thought you were at the funeral."

It seemed a lot to explain. Dominic felt that he was supposed to apologize for his absence. Felt also that he could not, not really.

"I just think that Jerry…"

But she waved him away. "Some people," she said rather ominously, "rise too readily above their situation. For now there is a difference. But who is to say, Mr. Rackett? Best that he stick to the cleaning of lobbies, and you…"

She pushed the DVD across the desk to him.

"You to *your* matters at hand. Watch the film again. Look for its mystery, then write and rewrite. See what you will change. I will go to the printer tomorrow morning, in my hand your new copy. And watch alone: you are working tonight, not dating the employees."

∞

Two films were watched closely at the Shangri-La that night. One in Dominic's flat, the other in the screening room.

Still mildly irritated by Leni Zauber's reproaches, her slighting of both his work and his behavior, Dominic sat on his bed, intent on the sweeping, simplistic plot of *Metropolis,* trying to find something to say that he hadn't said already. As much as he hated to admit it, Leni had been right: he was missing something in the film.

Through the Maria/Red Mary scenes he raced, fast forwarding with the remote, pausing when things struck his eye, for whatever reason or for whatever motive beneath reason. Was there something in the towering buildings? Something in a specific slant of light on the set—those backdrops in which you couldn't tell whether the interplay of shadow was caused by lamps or skillfully rendered by matte painting? Dominic let his intuition stop the film, hoping that some subterranean turn of his brain would bring to light the elusive thing that Leni had ordered him to find.

To be *ordered forth in search of mystery.* It struck him as particularly German, like the Himalayan expeditions that the Nazis had sponsored back in the 1930s, the adventures in Nepal and Tibet that apparently had haunted Florian Geist.

He had almost reached the end of the movie. Atop the cathedral, among the gargoyles, Freder and Rotwang struggled hand to hand for Maria, a fight scene almost comical in its inelegance, punches thrown rapidly and clumsily, the actors reeling from what seemed to be disturbances in the air rather than bodily impact.

Below the two, Joh Fredersen watched in suspense and agony, as his son battled at mortal heights. Stripped of his authority, his mastery of an imploding city, Frederson was a mournful old man, dropping to his knees in a throng of rioting workers, who circled him briefly and then stood still: after all, they had almost lost their children minutes before, and the common ground of that near-tragedy seemed to strike a curious peace among adversaries.

Kneeling there before the cathedral, his face uplifted and caught by a sliver of light, the actor Alfred Abel seemed iconic and haunted, like a face in a cathedral window beholding the Last Judgment.

Dominic leaned forward. The remote slipped from his hand onto the bed.

It was the face of Indy's Nazi. Weathered and fragile, but with no doubt the image he had pursued across decades and countries and miles of film footage.

But even as he concluded this, Dominic began to doubt. He stopped and reversed the DVD, his hand shaking too much to be reliable, and the sequence lurched awkwardly back to the fight on the cathedral arcade. He reversed, and went too far in the reversal. Again Freder and Rotwang—Froelich and Klein-Rogge—staggered through their silly fight, Gottfried Huppertz's music swelling dramatically.

Dominic groaned and fast-forwarded, this time fixed on Abel's face in closeup. But he was no longer sure. Now he had lost it, as though a last frail hope was making him see things.

The next day he would visit the library. According to the search engines, Alfred Abel was long dead by the filming of *The Last Crusade*. Dead, it turned out, by 1938, which was when the scene in the Indiana Jones movie was supposed to take place.

Not that the dates mattered. It was a vestigial silliness, a grasping at straws, which had made Dominic search in the first place. By then he had revised the article, scrapped his revision, and given the original, unedited copy to Leni Zauber.

Who, preoccupied now with some other agenda, some trouble he could not figure, did not even notice.

∞

Because that night, as Dominic fell briefly into the world of *Metropolis*, Leni's work on Geist's film continued, her astonishment rising as sequence by scene by frame passed through the Steenbeck. A setting once recognizable as the Prague of her youth became, as the reel moved on, more abstract and indefinite. Buildings became angular, asymmetrical, receding into soft focus and mottled shadows like sets being torn down after the closing night.

She had no idea how Geist had achieved the effect. Today, she figured, such a thing would be possible, if still ambitious, with CGA and a whole technological arsenal at the director's command. But what was available to Geist was the camera and the cutting room: Leni had already watched dumbstruck the scene where the actor Zrcadlo transformed into Dr. Halberd, easy enough through the techniques available at the time, but now she knew that Geist had conceived the transition in another way, that before the camera he had transformed his own appearance to that of the much older, much heavier Emil Jannings. Character had metamorphosed not because of makeup or cinematic illusion, but because the actor had changed his face to that of...another actor.

"*Aweysha*," she whispered, and crushed her cigarette dangerously close to the inflammable film as it turned slowly through the viewer.

And Geist was everywhere. As the actor Zrcadlo, he appeared in virtually every scene. He occupied sight, at one time leaning against a statue on Charles Bridge, at another standing beneath the huge astrological clock on the Old Town Square as the procession of figures marched above him, commemorating the change of a long-vanished hour. The city was a haze behind him, Geist's choice of shallow focus suggesting not only that the story was going on largely inside Zrcadlo's head (which, of course, was what shallow focus almost always did) but also that the world around him was shifting, unstable, a dependence of light and shadow that could at any moment open into another world.

So, for the most part, the eye was fixed on Zrcadlo, recognizable as Geist, of course, but his appearance fluid and inconstant on the screen: he appeared as a kind of strange and pliable hybrid, his face somewhere between the handsome Aryan features she remembered, and those of another young man, hair tousled and darker than Geist's, a countenance strangely familiar to Leni as she ran the same sequence, time and again, through the Steenbeck. For a minute Geist's Zrcadlo seemed to age: he looked like Alfred Abel as Joh Fredersen, the middle-aged master of Metropolis, then meatier, like Emil Jannings. And yet in all these shapes and incarnations there was that other young man, a face inconstant under all those faces, visible in the lightning's-breadth of a frame and then vanishing again, becoming Abel or Jannings or Geist.

Carefully, Leni reviewed a string of a dozen frames—the moment in which her eye had caught the elusive face embedded in the quick transitions of this part of the film. Finally, two frames isolated a man in early middle age—early forties, perhaps—disheveled hair and darker eyes than Geist's.

She knew she had seen him, or a photo. And not long ago. The face jarred a recollection she associated with curiosity, with prying into something probably not her business—at least not until now. She cursed her age and the frays in her memory, stepping back day by day in a kind of theatrical memory palace, imagining each room of the Shangri-La (because it was here she had seen his image).

Not on the ceiling in the lobby. Not Dante, not Chaplin. Leni's thoughts traced slowly over Castille's office, the head shots of Paramount and Universal actresses, then through the bar where stills of the great movies—*Citizen Kane, Casablanca, Vertigo*—formed a quiet part of the décor.

Nothing there. Nor was he the Apollo, the Prometheus, or the Hymenaios on the landing. The face was hardly that of a god, nor even a good-looking actor, but more like an everyday sort, plucked from real life behind a counter or the wheel of a Chevrolet, from a small room at the top of the stairs…

Her thoughts rushed immediately to the topmost room of the theater. In her memory she prowled through Dominic's room, the poster of the Buddha, a photo of a weary-eyed Asian woman who was no doubt the boy's mother. To the book and the jacket photo, the man at the edge of promise, his eyes in black and white anticipating a success that would elude him in this world.

Even then, his picture on the back of his first and only novel, Gabriel Rackett had been on his way out.

21.

They had seen him pass through their gray country. An amorphous blade of flame like their own, but that was the only way in which he was familiar. They longed to know his name, his destination—mostly to know why he was there.

They were hungry, feeding on curiosity. In the space of a summer (though they had no idea it was summer, living beyond the passage of seasons) their hopes had risen and fallen, only to rise again with the new one's arrival.

Florian had told them not to mind. Told them that this flame was hiding something.

So the six of them—Ombrade, Orlac and Orgon, Marie and Maria and Magdelein—were left in the brindled dark to fashion their prospects from persistence of vision. There were six of them before there were four. Then there were three, then five, then six again, then two, as the flames and thoughts commingled.

This much they could gather, pieced together by Ombrade, who had been a monarch more than once, a wrestler, a professor, a diabolical emissary—in all his time a plotter and discerner of plots. Something had been recovered—a missing part of the story, a window in memory was nudging them all even closer to completion.

Maria knew how such things worked. Knew that this part of the story intersected with her own. Had felt the conversation center on her from somewhere Over There. Knew also that the story was out of her hands and in the control of another— another female, at least—but things moved slowly Over There, she also knew. And having been a queen once herself—of an underground kingdom, she seemed to recall, one fraught with danger—she knew that any promised restoration might be a long time coming.

They had no choice but to trust in Florian. And for her this was difficult: he was a nexus of zealotry, charm and corruption. He would not keep his word if it deflected him from purpose. But sometimes treachery could be the mother of good. Or so the story went, and some of its versions in which she had found herself.

He had told them to watch the girls. It was sleight of hand, she suspected. A misdirection when her eyes should be elsewhere. But nonetheless she watched, catching glimpses of the story as a shadow growing in a wide field of light, hard to make out—like a photographic negative—but visible in outline, where it seemed to be the same old story of love and rivalry.

∞

Ellie had no idea why she consented to go out with Max Winter to begin with. She had seen him mooning at the margins, had gone with him and with Todd that time to the Runic Legend Casino. That had been when he was safer, though. When he had seemed like all the other boys, tobogganed and sparse-bearded, skinny jeans and Buddy Holly glasses. She never minded the look, but mistrusted the posturing that usually went with it.

But Max was mildly spoken, friendly by default. A little shy about pressing his interests, which had bored her after a while. She knew he disliked Dominic, and she suspected rivalry had something to do with it. But only now had the hostility become vocal, as he followed her to the parking lot behind the theater and went on about how Dominic had betrayed them, angrily majoring on his presence with all the fundies at George Castille's funeral.

He was wrong about the facts, but the whole business gave him an edge that she did not quite dislike.

"I know better, Max," she had said, lighting a cigarette only to have him pluck it from her mouth and drop it to the pavement, grinding it under his shoe in a quick, emphatic gesture that both alarmed and excited her. Now her voice quivered. "Dominic was with me all afternoon. Took me to the Varhana Monastery because it was George's funeral, because he knew I couldn't stand it."

Max pushed his glasses back on the bridge of his nose. "You're covering for him, Ellie. I saw him at the edge of the crowd. Todd and Jerry Jeff saw him, too. You can ask them."

"Why do I need to ask them, Max? Dominic was with me across the river."

Max looked away disgustedly, and despite herself Ellie grabbed his arm. He tensed at her touch but did not pull away, and she was surprised to think how wiry he was, how the thin arms were muscular and hard, actually, and that she liked this bristle about him, liked basking a little in his anger.

"John," she said after a pause, as though retrieving the name out of some dusty archive. "John Bulwer. You can ask him. He was with us."

"I know what I saw, El. You're sweet on him, so you're making things up."

She bristled a little at that. "I'm not making things up. And I'm not sweet on him. Jesus. Even if I was, Max, none of that is your business."

Now Ellie walked toward the back door of the theater. For a second or two, she heard no footsteps behind her, then Max followed, his pace slow.

She wheeled to face him. "Ask Mr. Bulwer," she snapped. "You won't believe me, so ask your freakin' hero. He took us up there, guided us around the monastery. And on the way back, he practically handed Salvages to Dominic. Told him he wanted a book guy to carry on. Thought Dom was the one to do it."

Max flushed scarlet, and Ellie realized she had told him this for damage.

"Stick with your story, Ellie," he muttered. "We both know, even if you won't admit to it."

All of a sudden she was frightened. And beguiled as well.

The mildness in Max that she had taken for granted was frayed around the edges. And yet there was courage beneath it. A kind of resolve that shook out his aimlessness and left a residue. Neither of them could quite believe it when, after a brief silence by the theater back door, he asked her to dinner—not the Peaceable Kingdom this time, he insisted, but just the two of them to "settle some things," as he put it.

It was even less believable when she still accepted.

∞

It was strange watching the others straggle into the theatre across the street as the Shangri-La prepared for the Saturday matinee showing of Metropolis.

Max had arranged things carefully, but it already seemed like a compromise. An afternoon showing was the only time that Leni could spare two workers, and even so, she put Max on call in case more help was needed at the counter. So the date would be in broad, unromantic sunlight, and at Huntington's rather than the quiet little Italian place across the river, which he had chosen for atmosphere and wine.

Nevertheless, she had consented to meet him. And as they ordered lunch, Todd entered the theatre without noticing them, followed about ten minutes later by Dominic, who saw them through the window, paused and waved, then headed for the lobby. A brief, adolescent feeling of triumph surged through Max as he ordered beers for Ellie and himself, told a skeptical Marlene that they needed a minute with the menu. Then, as his favorite sullen waitress carded Ellie (who was still young enough to be irritated by it), he looked out the window at the Expressionist poster under the marquis. The golden Heinz Schulz-Neudamm lithograph, long and geometrical, the Machine-Man dwarfed by the city.

"It takes a good mad scientist," he mused. Then, to Ellie's look of puzzlement, explained that the Machine-Man, created in *Metropolis* by Dr. Rotwang, ends up being a little too much to handle.

"Haven't seen it yet," Ellie admitted. "Sounds like one of those 'future is scary' films."

She was still a little combative. He understood that. So he explained that it was kind of like the Frankenstein films, where the scientist creates the monster for one thing, then it ends up with a mind of its own and does something else entirely. He could sense her turning the words in her thoughts, making them about her, about them.

He was relieved to see Bucky Trabue wander into sight, because he could switch the subject. Say that was what he meant all along.

And Ellie seemed to soften. Together in a kind of conceded silence they watched quietly through the glass as Trabue lingered under the poster like a disheveled tourist, then disappeared through the lobby doors.

"So, Bucky's a mad scientist these days?" she asked him at last, teasingly, as the beers came to the table, and Marlene set hers down diffidently, Max's with a bit more courtesy.

"Oh, yes," Max said. "You should've seen Jerry at the funeral."

He knew it was a bit of an accusation. They sat quietly for a moment, sipping Huntington's watery beer, both wondering how they would swim through this current of discontent.

∞

He knew he had seen *Metropolis* back in his college days. But this time there was restored footage, a sharp DVD printing, and new subtitles that came close to passable English.

Bucky found himself drawn in by the visual poetry of the film: the workers as pistons in a huge, tiered machine that transformed into a hungry, demonic face through a convergence of stop motion, mirrors, and multiple exposure. But as the workers were led to the sacrifice, driven over a precipice through an array of cogs and gears into a doorway of thick, bedazzling light, he forgot all he knew about cinematography and film editing, imagining himself on the stairs with the marching workers as they trudged toward their immolation. Holy hell, but it felt real: you could almost feel the heat emanate from the screen, and Bucky held his breath until the scene cut back to Freder, terrified and white-garbed, who he watched as the holocaust unfolded before him.

This was our hero, Bucky remembered. The pampered rich boy transformed in a moment by the image of a girl standing at the border of his cloistered garden. He had an epiphany, this Freder, and the glowing blonde hair and wide asymmetrical eyes of Brigitte Helm would lead the boy through the perils of mechanization and corporate capitalism to the steps of Metropolis' medieval cathedral, where he joined the hands of his robber baron father with that of the dimwitted chief worker, making accord among the haves and the have-nots.

It was still what we needed, Bucky told himself. For the workers in this city were like Jerry Jeff's congregation, barely able to read above a fourth grade level if they chose to read at all, and the powers that be, like that sumbitch Rausch, using willful ignorance to make money for their families and rich friends. We needed a hero like Freder, Bucky believed, but he wanted that hero to stand up for the right things—the nuclear family and small businesses and the church, and stories where the good guys won.

Which was why he hated Rotwang, that schemer in a house dark and gabled, his laboratory an arcade of glass and light and liquid, forerunning the labs of Frankenstein in the Universal monster films. Rotwang was all brilliance and drama, making his robot resemble Brigitte Helm's gentle Maria in order to stir the workers toward Bolshevism, thereby undermining both them and the masters who governed them. Not even the dreadful fall from the heights of the church—like that Starr boy had done on Fourth and Fellini a few years back—was justice enough for a mad scientist.

And yet.

It was hard to see Rotwang anguish at the tomb of his one love, stolen from him by Freder's father. Bucky knew the poisons of the past, how sometimes a good deed takes root when you have sowed vengeance. And Metropolis seemed to veer from focus as he stared at the screen, setting down his bag of untouched popcorn as he thought of Jerry Jeff Pfeiffer, who, like Wegener's golem or Lang's Maria or any Frankenstein's creature, had gone rogue on intentions in ways that Bucky did not—could not—possibly understand.

∞

"I think I'm losing ground at the theater, Grandma Mary."

Dominic sat on her sofa, listlessly swirling the instant coffee she had rustled for him on short notice. In an outrageous hot pink sweat suit, his 80-year-old grandmother kept glancing at the treadmill and at Sean Hannity on the television in front of the machine. He had interrupted her afternoon, but she had called the theater several times while he had been up at the monastery, leaving messages on the answering machine in hushed, dramatic tones that she had to see him. Something to do with his father, she claimed, and so he had walked in the heat of the day to her place, down past the corner the locals called "Fourth and Fellini" for its cast of derelicts and characters, then past a more seedily elegant strip of Fourth Avenue, old town houses on his left, the park and the outdoor theater to his right.

Another theater lay in his plans for the evening.

At the Southland 4 Cinemaplex was an Indiana Jones Retrospective. It started at 4:00, and if Dominic didn't stay long at his grandmother's, he could arrive just in time to catch the beginning. And in plenty of time for the *Last Crusade.* Having seen *Metropolis'* old treatment of fathers and sons, of Alfred Abel kneeling in the square, years away from the Nazi in the Indy movie, Dominic yearned to arrange things again, to watch again the film that had haunted and defined him for 25 years.

For a time it seemed as though his whole plan was headed for disruption. Running into Todd, who was just arriving as he left the theater, Dominic caught the latest in the series of angry glares he was drawing from his fellow workers. Todd passed him, did the old high school belligerent shoulder-bump that pretended at actual collision when everyone involved knew that it wasn't. Irritated, tired of Todd and Max as his pair of adversaries, Dominic spun on his heels and glared at Ellie's brother.

To find Todd glaring back.

"Ellie don't want you," he growled, brushed his hair back, and headed toward the theater door.

"She doesn't want you, either," Dominic replied calmly.

Todd stopped. For a moment his shoulders bunched, then he paced off fuming, the revolving door to the lobby whirling at his passage.

So Dominic continued, his anger calming as he approached the city's main public library, its towering statue of Lincoln crusted with verdigris and neglect.

It was like a journey into the collective past. He had been waiting for Mary Lull's wisdom as regarded his father's story— whatever she could provide about Gabriel's attraction to the house across the street, his history with the folks who lived there, and the circumstances surrounding the Christmas night when he had vanished for good. It was part of Dominic's imagined quest, and he had loaded the meeting with anticipation, only to find out, with some disappointment, that his grandmother wanted a box off her hands.

Stuff from his father's room at the old place. The Barbara Remington poster for the old edition of *Lord of the Rings*, fragments of a plastic Wolf Man and of Frankenstein's Monster, possibly worth something if they had still been in their boxes, along with the rest of the old Revell model kits. Baseball cards, of course, mostly St. Louis Cardinals, all too weathered to be collectible.

And of course the manuscripts. Some handwritten, so that if Gabriel Rackett had been Tolkien or George Martin or Ursula LeGuin, the pages would have been worth something on the market.

Not that Dominic would have sold anything in the box. That was what he told himself, anyway. Because Grandma Mary was telling him so little.

"I'm sorry, Dommie," she said, and he wondered why it was "Dommie" now, rather than the usual "Dominic" or "Dom".

"I'm sorry, but your father was a mystery to me. I loved him, mind you, but I don't believe I was cut from the cloth of motherhood, and there are times that I regret I couldn't have been more nurturing. We were like cohorts in the early years over on August Street. I think if he was around he'd tell you I made for an interesting mother, but as for a good one, I doubt it. And then when he went away and became Northern and married that horrible woman, I know she was your mother, but she was no good for him, then who am I to say, having been to the altar three times myself, the first two failed marriages and the last one when I settled and weathered it out…"

Her voice dipped in and out of the audible, and when Dominic could hear it, it was something he had heard before. He wished he didn't have to lug the box all the way to the Cineplex by bus, but it was too late to go back to his place and drop it off. Idly he looked through its contents, thumbing through handwritten character sketches and haiku, finding at last the typescript of a short story. And for a while he listened, or pretended to listen, to Grandma Mary, then let her give him bus fare (though he could afford that, at least, though he already had it with him).

He took the 18 bus south over the run-down corridor toward his father's childhood home, the box awkward on his lap, reading the story.

∞

Ere Babylon was Dust

A story by Gabriel Rackett

...It may be easily conceived that my progress was rapid. My ardour was indeed the astonishment of the students, and my proficiency that of the masters. Professor Krempe often asked me, with a sly smile, how Cornelius Agrippa went on, whilst M. Waldman expressed the most heartfelt exultation in my progress....Every night I was oppressed by a slow fever, and I became nervous to a most painful degree; the fall of a leaf startled me, and I shunned my fellow creatures as if I had been guilty of a crime.
--Frankenstein.

Ere Babylon was dust
The Magus Zoroaster, my dead child,
Met his own image walking in the garden.
--Percy Shelley, Prometheus Unbound

Two old men in a lonely study.
Waldman and Krempe, Krempe and Waldman. Science

faculty at the University of Ingolstadt. Counsel to generations.

Together, having walked the Danube banks, returning north to the school.

Waldman alone sensed the absence. Krempe was occupied in the hard, empirical flux of things, the decay of leaves, the brittle growth of amaranth spreading at the cemetery margins. Waldman alone noticed the light tilting over the sad rigor of the tombstones: a light that almost takes substance, shimmering in regret and spoiled vegetation.

Seven Octobers have passed since Victor Frankenstein's melancholia and fever. His had been a strange course of study, shunning lecture halls for private tutorial and visits to professors' quarters, walks along the Westfriedhof, philosophy and science caught on the move. Frankenstein was a man too solitary: both Waldman and Krempe should have recognized the signs, especially when the seizures began, the behavior veered, and even tutorials became less frequent. Then they found Frankenstein in the town cemetery, forlorn among the tombstones and charnel houses like some distracted ghoul.

Frankenstein lay by a fresh graveside, dank earth under his fingernails: the mound above the grave was cratered, its dirt scattered hysterically, a coffin lid shining dully in stunned moonlight.

The cloth and brush of Krempe had washed the stain from the boy's hands, but not his confusion.

It is your doing, Waldman, Krempe hissed.

And Waldman knew, in deep intuition, that his colleague was right.

Waldman regrets his earlier advice, his indulgence for Frankenstein's studies in alchemy. When the boy had mentioned Agrippa and Paracelsus, Waldman had played the more popular professor, encouraged Frankenstein by saying that hermetical reading was not wayward, not at all. That such magic was the ancestor of Franklin, Galvani and Volta. That it *mocked the invisible world with its own shadows.*

But now, in the study with Mrs. Shelley's document, regret

has become more poignant, more acute.

We all make monsters we neglect, Waldman tells himself.

It is just that some have to answer for them.

On that cemetery night, walking together, Krempe hauling the lad on his back and Waldman traveling ahead, his guidance vague, they had removed Victor Frankenstein to the university surgery, where the young man slipped in and out of coma, subject to violent seizures in his waking moments. It was the *falling sickness,* the *sacred disease:* the patient sniffed and sipped the air, his eyes rolling in terror at something unseen over Waldman's shoulder.

Waldman followed the young man's gaze to Krempe, framed in front of a window where candlelight reflected onto glass, onto the outer darkness eased only by a vexed and wavering moon.

You wanted them to love you, Waldman, Krempe whispered. *That love without demands on you, toward which they flock in youth and uncertainly. You blessed their errors for that affection, and they singed their hopes in your banked and dwindling flame.*

Bad poetry, Waldman replied. *Bad poetry and worse wisdom.* But sitting helpless as Krempe attended to Frankenstein's agony, something within him urged him to give way, to follow the guidance of his more sensible colleague.

Sometimes, Krempe claimed, the worst of epileptic symptoms—the fits, the fainting, even the rare hallucinations—can be eased through direct stimulation of the brain. For it is the brain, not the mind that suffers, Krempe said, and the soul hungers for the body's healing. Neural impulse, as Galvani's work suggested, was electric, and the findings of Flourens and Rolando showed that the brain lit with energy like the bulbs of Davy and Swan. A stimulation of the left temporoparietal junction had produced stability in the patient and could perhaps affect some remedy—if not for the disease, at least for its most miserable symptoms.

His hand guided by Krempe's suggestion, Waldman affixed electrodes to the young man's cranium. In the sputtering light of the charge, Victor's eyes fluttered, his countenance livened, even as his arms spasmed upon the operating table.

The first time he lay still, insensate.

The second time.

At the third and most powerful jolt, his entire body convulsed. A shuddering intake of breath, and his eyelids opened.

Victor was alive, sentient. Waldman wanted to shout the news.

The spasms calmed. The patient was dazed but aware of surroundings. Waldman he recognized (his memory still hazy, though, when it came to Krempe). Victor spoke of lurid dreams: of windswept Alpen crevasses, the desolate Irish Sea, of ice-turgid northern waters, and always something dogging him, walking together with him, in the mist he inhaled at twilight and exhaled at dawn, tasting of sweet decay.

Such was their conversation three days before the thunderstorm and Victor's strange vanishing into the Bavarian wilds. That morning he was hale enough to travel, promising he would attend Waldman's lecture the following evening.

Waldman did not believe him. But he did not expect this departure. This flight to solitude and the terrible creation, of which only recently Waldman has learned. For that night of seizure and galvanism was the last time the two spoke, the last they crossed paths.

Krempe claims to have seen it coming. Of course, he is the hard scientist, as he often reminded his colleague. But Waldman suspects that Krempe had been surprised as well, that his was the scientist's way of "knowing all along". For when the packet of letters arrives from Mrs. Shelley, Frankenstein's biographer and widow of the great poet, both professors read them with rising horror. The correspondence of the young ship's captain who carried Victor across the Arctic waters is a mix of admiration and revulsion, as though two opposing states could occupy the same space. The misdeeds of their former student dance between commission and omission, venture and cowardice, and like the good scientist he is at times, Waldman reads the evidence with amazement, a hypothesis forming in his thoughts.

This creature, he begins…

'*This monster*', *you mean?* Krempe interrupts.

I prefer '*creature*', *Krempe. To call it* '*monster*' *is too severe, too damning. Too harsh to that young man we had come to admire. For he gave the creature breath and volition without giving it flesh.*

Krempe scoffs, for how, of course, was *there breath and volition without flesh?*

Then falls silent, his squat and homely features resembling at last Waldman's own. He nods in agreement, but more reluctantly as Waldman traced down the list of the creature's outrages: the murder of Frankenstein's little brother, in which Victor himself was complicit by failing to stand up and speak in defense of the poor serving girl who was executed for the crime; the death of Henry Clerval, Victor's closest friend, found strangled in a coracle; and most horrible, the murder of Elizabeth Frankenstein, fiancée and bride (though referred to as 'present', as 'cousin' and even 'sister'—one can see in her very naming the forbidden ground Victor skirted). All so outrageous that he wonders whether the ship's captain has made it up, or Mrs. Shelley, or whether Victor himself lied to one of them through the other….

Lied before his solitary trek toward ice and oblivion…

Or if…

And in that moment a sudden flash, like a storm above the Westfriedhof.

Not solitary. The monster… Krempe begins. Rights himself. '*The creature*', *that is. The creature drew him away into wastelands. So the two might die together.*

Waldman shakes his head. *Still wide, Doctor Krempe. Frankenstein was alone.*

Alone? But the monster…

'*Creature*', *Krempe. A figment. A figment of mind brought to life by seizure and wild hope. For the mind is a garden of ghosts, and the brain a Voltaic Pile of latent energy. Perhaps it was the charge we applied to the temporoparietal junction…*

You applied, Krempe corrects. *No. I applied.*

He pauses, as if remembering one last thing. As if he was

the last man, whose task is memory alone.

He stands framed by the window. The light shines through him.

And so it was, in the capsized afternoon, that Waldman guesses at last the dark secret of Victor Frankenstein. Not only the creature, alone on the heath, reading its *Paradise Lost and Parallel Lives,* had been brought to life by Frankenstein's imagination. There was also Krempe, borne of fever, ignition, and the falling disease, and from a young man's desire for foil and adversary.

The professor vanishes into sunlight, and Professor Waldman, who until this time had imagined himself as substance, breath and volition and flesh, now feels the beams pass through his fingers, their source an indefinite spark in some creator's febrile brain.

22.

While Dominic's bus crept southward, John Bulwer lit a cigarette and put Coltrane on the turntable. It had been Mendelssohn all morning until the spirit changed path. Now the slinky sinuousness of the cymbals and opening bass of *Love Supreme* on parade under the scratch and patter of the old record.

Lifting himself a little slowly from behind the counter, he went down the SF aisle, ducking the police tape and laughing quietly at the *Nyarlahotep* warning, as he always did. It had been a quiet afternoon at Salvages. Two guests an hour previous— guests, not customers, because this pair never bought anything— and he figured he might close the shop early, seeing as traffic was dying down on the sidewalk and also at the usually busy intersection.

He thumbed over a copy of *Dacia*. He hadn't read it himself, and as Gabriel Rackett's champion against the academics and snobs, he dreaded to dive into the book, fearing that after years of advocacy, he might not like it, might in some way estrange Dominic, who was touchy when it came to his father, and would no doubt intuit any dip in enthusiasm.

Bulwer heard the door to the shop open, and emerged from the shadowy shelves to find Max Winter leaning on the counter, watching the Coltrane disk in its hypnotic spin.

"And Winter arrives early," Bulwer proclaimed, already knowing that Max had heard all the puns, would laugh or smile out of mere politeness.

But he wasn't smiling. "Got a minute, Mr. Bulwer?" he asked plaintively, his red-rimmed eyes meeting Bulwer's full on.

"What's up, son?" he asked, and when Max asked him about the trip to the monastery, told him the truth, how both Dominic and Ellie had found George Castille's funeral too hard to bear, the prospect of mean-spirited fundamentalist picketing too angering to abide. That a short trip, planned days before George's sudden passing, had been a blessing in disguise, starting a healing for two of them—a healing that all who knew the old impresario would have to undergo in their own times...

He caught himself mid-lecture, seeing that Max had expected the facts far otherwise.

"I suppose I can throw righteous anger out the window, John," he allowed, and Bulwer noticed they had returned to first names.

Max lifted himself to sit on the counter, stared in front of him at the hard-bound bestsellers, and recounted the long story of how Dominic had disappointed him. He claimed to have been all about the friendship when Dom arrived, but then things had shifted away from that, had made it impossible to be his friend.

"Do you know the Prodigal Son story, John?" he asked, and at the quiet nod of the older man, launched into a self-pitying account of how he hated that fucking parable now, because he was the son who had stayed. He'd done all that was expected: gone the extra distances at Shangri-La, made friends with Todd, treated respectfully the erratic Ellie. And then when Leni Zauber came onto the scene, dragging with her this vagrant from nowhere, everyone seemed to be in a contest as to how far they could bend over to kiss Dominic's ass. And he had stayed silent, then, through the mediocre film articles and the favor Dom had curried among George and Leni and Ellie, now Ellie.

But he could have sworn, Max claimed, that he saw Dominic up on the cemetery knoll, not as a mourner but as a kind of ally for the Reverend Billy Hightower and that bunch of bigots at Manahaim.

He told this urgently to John Bulwer, who realized how desperately Max was trying to convince himself.

Then he brought up the store, which, of course, was why he had come here this afternoon, why he was unburdening his history to the old man. The store. How Bulwer was handing it over. The last unexplainable indignity in a long list, he said, then glared at Bulwer, as though there were something that could speak to the vast indifference of the universe that he felt encroaching on Salvages, the neighborhood, the whole way he was seeing the world around him.

"Max...Max..." Bulwer said at last. "How could you have expected..." Then let it drop, flipping the disc on the turntable to let in the second half of Love Supreme. The track called "Pursuance," Elvin Jones' climbing, visionary drum solo resolving into the bass and sax, so magnificently that Bulwer's thoughts followed it away from Max's complaints. When he returned to mindfulness, the boy at the counter seemed less desperate, as though he had passed through chaos and strife and illusion, finding at last his own way out.

"So this is what I plan to do, John," Max announced, still probing for approval. "I'm going to pursue her. Not in a creepy way, mind you, but as her suitor."

"You mean Ellie?"

"Yes, Ellie, of course. Who were we talking about? She's gone out with me before, John, and if her brother hadn't tagged along, and if George hadn't killed himself on our second date night, for God's sake, I swear we would be further evolved, we'd know each other better and she'd have started to see that I am much better for her than...than others."

John nodded. Max was convincing himself, was rehearsing

his motives aloud but John was pretty much convinced that the kid was dead in the water if Dominic had decided to court the girl. Then again, he wasn't altogether sure whether Dominic was pursuing, or pursuing something else, or when it came down to it, being pursued himself.

"So I think it's pedal to the metal, as my old man used to say," Max continued. "I'm more her age, we grew up in the same town, with roughly the same background—not some gypsy weirdness that roams through the whole northeast looking for ghosts...."

John was surprised. Max was brushing against the edge of insight, but he wasn't sure the boy would reach it. But if he did, from there it was not all that far to compassion, to his understanding that Dominic was passing through dark country. To realize that however this rivalry turned out, none were evil, all wished good for themselves and the girl and the world.

With Coltrane as his celestial soundtrack, Bulwer reminded himself of the Lotus Sutra, of the Buddha of Compassion:

> *If sentient beings are in great adversity,*
> *And immeasurable pain afflicts them,*
> *The wonderful power of his wisdom*
> *Can relieve the suffering of the world.*

He resolved to listen, but as Max went on, Bulwer had no idea whether the "immeasurable pain" was life with the girl or life without her.

"Max," John began, "I can't see that you have another choice. I'd want to see this out if I were you. They tell this story in Tibet about Gesar, the great warrior king. His adventures form the greatest epic of Tibetan literature. His name means "unconquerable," means someone who can never be put down. So, how did he get to be that way? From the moment Gesar was born, his evil uncle Trotung tries all kinds of means to kill him. But with each attempt Gesar only grows stronger and stronger."

Max's phone rang. He glanced at it and set it on the counter.

John slipped away from a brief and sudden irritation. "For the Tibetans," he continued, "being a warrior is a spiritual thing. To develop a special kind of courage, one that is innately intelligent, gentle, and fearless. Yeah, you'll still be frightened, but the warrior is courageous enough to undertake suffering, to relate clearly to the most basic of his fears. Gesar sets out to learn the lessons Trotung teaches. *'Trotung tro ma tung na, Gesar ge mi sar,'* is what they say. If Trotung were not so evil and scheming, Gesar would not rise so high."

Max frowned. "Are you saying that Ellie is scheming? Because from what I've seen…"

"No, no, Max Headroom. It's about adversity. How resistance makes us stronger."

The phone rang again. Max muttered something about "having to take this" and removed himself to the shelves, dangerously close, Bulwer noticed, to the menacing SF/Fantasy aisle. From the shadows came the sound of hushed agreement, and shortly Max emerged with the news that he had to be going, he was sorry, but it was a work thing.

"But before I go, John. Are you saying that I have a chance with El? Is there something you know?"

Inwardly, Bulwer despaired. The kid had pretty much missed it all.

"What I'm saying is that the result doesn't matter. Nor what you encounter on the way there. It's more about the resolve to take the journey. About that first interior movement toward what you are becoming. Toward each movement, truth be told…"

Max had half an eye to the door. John realized he was being boring, struggled for the agreeable words that would pass on the truth of this thing.

"There was a girl once," he said quietly, with hesitation. "A girl in a troubled time."

"And I'd like to hear about her, John. The next time I will. But before I go—and there's no other way to do this but to ask it straight up—is it true that this store is going to Dom on your retirement? Because I have heard…"

His voice trailed away, and John realized he had only skimmed Max Winter's great adversity. It was hard, he figured, to be supplanted at twenty-two? twenty-three? So much loss in that, a floor so flimsy and shifting that it makes light of great Nyarlahotep's lair. He was glad, now, that the conversation had not made its way to the girl, to Toshiko Collins, because suddenly, sharing that memory seemed dangerously close to betrayal.

∞

Dominic nursed his father's manuscript halfway down the highway, getting out of the bus at the Cineplex and carting the box into the near-empty theater, slipping uncomfortably into an aisle seat in the first few minutes of *Raiders*.

Indy had already made his way into Nepal, where he would meet Marion Ravenwood, played by Karen Allen and still the only one of the movies' heroines that Dominic took a shine to. Todd's "Ellie don't want you" still haunted him, Dominic smiled to think that it would take years of films before it became clear that Marion had wanted Indy all along. He was not sure he could wait like that for Ellie.

Knowing the movie by heart, Dominic realized he had missed nothing important to his search: everything hinged, he told himself, on the third film, on the one scene in Berlin, still hours away. And yet he paid attention, as he had so many times, looking for a clue, an insight, a variant.

Indy and Marion make a warring truce and head for Cairo, but Dominic's thoughts came back again and again to *Last Crusade*, to his memory of father and son first seeing a film on father and son, a kind of harmonic convergence in his memory which he would mine until he found its answers. Or until the end of his days, whichever came first.

Still, he was distracted this time. His father's unpublished story was rushed and rough, but troubling to his son, strangely moving years after the old man must have written it. The whole idea that, by the end of the story, everyone dissolved into the fictions they were—that was hard to take, as though Gabriel had abandoned the characters entirely beyond the cluster of words they were, that you knew they were but that in reading you chose to be otherwise, fashioning flesh and blood out of sentences.

He didn't like it. It was too meta, too self-consciously postmodern. He hadn't seen that part of his father, and it almost seemed like Gabriel had been trying too hard to be young. But his thoughts traced through the idea until *Raiders* was half over, until Indy had reached Egypt and been lowered into the snake-infested Well of Souls.

So what if the characters on the screen—even the intrepid Indy himself—were only captured gatherings of shadow and light, propelled across the screen by our own persistence of vision? So what if every film depended upon our being fooled? And what was more, to consenting to the foolery, because to do otherwise was to ruin everything?

Dominic sat distracted through the linked chases and action scenes that livened the Egypt section of the film. Watched, with the usual excitement, as Indy slid beneath the Nazi truck, holding on by whip alone. It was a scene pirated from the great stuntman Yakima Canutt in John Ford's Stagecoach, but Dom knew that Harrison Ford himself had spent a few rib-bruising frames beneath the vehicle, and he figured there was a stamp of experience in that.

Before he knew it, the film had reached the "face-burning scene" in which the villainous René Belloq, Nazi collaborator and Indy's chief adversary, opens the Ark of the Covenant in the presence of what seemed like half the SS in Egypt. As the lightning flashed over the seared and melting faces, the cold theater warmed with the sheer intensity of the images. Dominic clutched the box in his lap, for a moment absorbed by the bonfire of light and animation, almost forgetting the horror of it all in the conflagration of lights—the heads melting and exploding, but with a flash and incandescence more like fireworks than holocaust, waves of ghosts coursing over the screen like lights glimpsed underwater.

And for a moment, behind the whirling phantoms, he thought he saw a deeper movement of light, something like a current of fire and water intermingled, neither element extinguishing the other, as the blaze flowed across the screen, carrying with it apparitions afloat on a surge of something that passed from element to vital, breathing force. It was something like yearning that carried the ghosts, and they turned on the crest of its negligent current like corpses raised from a shipwreck.

Dominic had not seen this before. He wondered about restored footage, but only for a breath as his father's face surfaced and sank in the burning tide. He must have cried out. He thought he heard his voice erupt over the soundtrack, the soft slap of the box as it tumbled to the floor at his feet.

"Da," he whispered. And was gone.

∞

Two rows behind where Dominic was seated, an older man, intent on the film, happened to glance toward the aisle and notice, with surprise but not too much concern, that the young man had vanished.

He could have sworn there had been a noise. But then he had been caught up by the movie. With no further thought, the man turned back to the screen, where Indy and Marion are being briefed by Army Intelligence, who explain that the Ark is safe, that *we have top men working on it now.*

∞

Dominic could not breathe. Smoke filled his lungs, and the path he walked or thought he walked was on fire beneath his feet, but giving off no warmth and all too little light.

He tried to pull himself away from where he was, if he

was indeed there. *Hypnogogia* or *dip-non*—he tried to name it, thought that by naming it he could harness it in—something pressed against his chest as he tried to orient, and again he saw Gabriel ahead of him, half cloud and half father, moving in and out of the red light, assembling and reassembling, but like a mirage always the same distance before him.

The ground beneath him was strewn with cable and wire. Something scuttled through the shadows, barely beyond the visible, and Dominic strained to catch sight of it. Once he even stopped, peered apprehensively into the darkness, but the very act unmoored his bearings, and when he looked back, Gabriel was far from him, almost invisible in the tangle.

For some reason, he could not call to his father. It was more physical than a reluctance: the very air seemed pressed back tightly into his chest, so he had trouble breathing, never mind emitting a sound. He picked up his pace, stumbling over narrow tracks and ducking underneath unsteady scaffolding until Gabriel seemed closer, the red light under his feet bleeding away into a white light that framed his retreating figure. It was like the light at the end of the tunnel that you hear of in all the accounts of near-death experience, and for a moment Dominic wondered if he was dying, if he'd had a seizure or heart attack in the Cineplex and if Gabriel, like the legends generally went, was the loving family member sent to guide him home.

$$\infty$$

Too much like Dominic Rackett for the resemblance to be accidental, the figure walked into Seventh Heaven and took a seat near the stage. Dressed in a gray suit, his wire-rimmed spectacles masking his eyes as though he saw everything from behind mirrors, he regarded the girls with a surmising, directorial eye.

The time had long past since he had been aroused by such things. In fact, it had been years since he had been even remotely interested in the turn of a dancer on a pole, the coarse vibration of American music. He took in the solitary girl on the stage, flooded with light in a sea of prevailing shadow.

Chantelle, he guessed. Because at Seventh Heaven, three of them were named Chantelle.

And there was a Destiny, as there always was. And Monika with a "k" because that spelling was invention, a "k" that made her special. And, to his great delight, a black girl named Vendetta, who he had decided was missing a dictionary when she made her choice.

It was not like when veils and sheer silk masked the anatomy. And after all, the Chantelle on stage would have been too old for his liking, even in those days.

She leaned back, one hand gripping the pole, and looked down at him. He returned the gaze, waited for her to flinch and avert her eyes.

There. Now he could watch and think in undisturbed peace.

Pour some sugar on me, the song urged. Then *hot-blooded, a fever of a hundred and three.* He did the Celsius conversion quickly, focused his gaze behind the girl, where faintly, in the shadowed mirror of the bar, a light, glimpsed faintly like a window high and remote in winter fog, staggered from one end of the glass to another.

Another Chantelle leaned toward him, offering drinks. Perhaps more. He had forgotten most of that long masquerade. He waved her away, again delighting in the slight recoil of her shoulders as she slipped between tables toward a pair of leathered bikers.

Slowly and almost undetectably, the dodging light in the mirror stilled for a moment, then swelled, filling a corner of the glass with its approach.

23.

It had been Leni on the phone to Max, summoning him back to the theater and telling him to pull the car around.

The final edits of *Walpurgisnacht* were complete. The film was primed, its jaws open. As far as she could tell, Dominic had taken the first steps in its direction. Each pass through the final minutes of the film revealed a darker shadow in the deep focus. Leni knew enough not to attend to it, to give it free rein frame by frame until it gained solidity and density. But already the shadow was gathering substance, a kind of palpability. As it drifted over the Charles Bridge you could see the light buckle around it, the Baroque statues along its pathway bowing in curiosity and deference.

Now she stood a floor above the theater, above the landing and the downturned faces of the immortals. Dominic, she figured, was deep in the other country. It would be days until he got out. In the meantime, there was enough for her to do. Let the shadow cross the bridge in the film: she would burn bridges in this newer and daylit world.

She could not imagine the boy would return until shortly before the filming. So the article on *Walpurgisnacht* would serve two purposes: it would estrange the writer from everyone around him, and it would make the audience look the other way.

Leni slipped on her black gloves, regarding herself in the boy's sad dresser mirror. It was glass without the furniture that once had framed it, leaning against a wall by the window. It had seemed a strange salvage for a young man: such creatures were notably undergroomed, especially in these times, but Dominic had proven an exception. He was involved with his self, the depths of its regions, and that alone had drawn him into reflective spaces.

Absently, she remembered lines from an old English poet. *And a crack in a teacup opens / A lane to the land of the dead.* The bottom corner of the mirror was smirched, melted and scorched by the fire from which the boy had retrieved it. Above the cloudiness, however, the reflection was clear but distorted, like a funhouse mirror or a trompe l'oeil. She remembered the painting of Rossetti's, the woman emerging from a gallery of identical women who lined her passage down a corridor of receding images, as though she were running the gauntlet of her innumerable selves.

In the back of the dresser mirror a kind of recessive darkness seemed to pool on the wall, a shadow behind her like something she ought to remember but couldn't. She turned to see it full on, and caught in the corner of her eye the reflected darkness expanding in the mirror, herself at the center of it, darkening as well and growing younger in a breath, a small necklace aglow at the hollow of her throat.

But she turned again to confront the apparition, and it was gone. And yet the woman before her looked somehow younger, restored from the wreckage that had only minutes ago climbed the stairs to Dominic's room. Still, she figured, she could not have competed with the pretty, brainless thing who had ensorcelled all of the young men at Shangri-La. Leni pushed from her thoughts a vague and patchy recollection, as Ellie took shape in her speculations as a kind of roadblock, a blonde whirlpool that could drown the boys in frivolous conflict.

Once Ellie was out of the way, there would be less to tie Dominic to this town, to the life he had to give up before he picked up the new one. It would free him for a mission. Spurred on by a theatrical sense of destiny, Leni turned to the door. She was tempted to look back, but gathered her thoughts and descended the steps to the lobby and the girl.

"Max is pulling around the car, Eleanor," she said. "What you're doing can wait, dear. Something is afoot that you'll need to see, but we have to drive so that I can show you."

∞

She could have passed for forty.

It astonished Max, who had never been able to guess Leni Zauber's age beyond George's suggestion that she must be well into her seventies. There was so much he wanted to ask her now, but she was all business, all directions and backseat driving.

Her backseat driving from the front seat, unfortunately. Leni had slipped into the passenger side of the car, taking the seat that Max had hoped would be Ellie Vitale's.

Because all of this was for Ellie's benefit, Leni insisted. Because it was time she knew a thing or two.

Driving the two women past the university, beneath a railroad bridge where seasonally semi-trucks tried and failed to navigate the low passage (probably because, as George had often insisted, the sign painter had mislabeled its height by a foot or two). Max kept his eyes on the road, not daring to look in the rear-view mirror at what he hoped would be a look of disappointment on Ellie's face, or at the seat beside him, where, with the briefest of sideward glances, he had noticed that Leni's skirt had slipped precariously halfway up her thigh.

What could he be thinking? How wrong was any of this?

He had often taken refuge in being the one whom people didn't notice. He had floated through a Humanities major in the university, positioned himself anonymously in the company of hipsters downtown and in the older neighborhoods of the city, wearing the obligatory fedoras and skull caps, ironic t-shirts and plaids, trying and failing at the beard. An army brat, though, he knew better when his comrades talked about the "mindless conformity" of the military, knew it was more complicated than that.

For him, the alternative city was a place to hide, to assimilate. To rebel in the way that everyone else was rebelling.

But in this summer, and especially during this festival, Max Winter had worn his namelessness with less ease. It was harder to be overlooked than unnoticed, he decided, though he wasn't quite sure why this was, nor quite sure at the difference between the words.

From the moment that Dominic had come on the scene, Max had been the overlooked one. He may not have played by *the* rules, mind you, but he had played by *some* rules: had taken the Film Studies classes, had written genuine essays instead of haiku and nonsense, had courted the girl respectfully, starting at a distance and working politely toward asking her on a date. Dominic had walked on the scene late and untutored, got the job because Dr. Zauber knew his grandmother, the friendship with Bulwer because the old man knew of his daddy's novel and they had that Buddhist thing between them. And he seemed to be getting the girl, most importantly, though he was too old for her and because God knows why.

It was like the parable. The undeserved grace that happened to someone who was not you. And though it didn't seem that Dominic had conspired against him, not really, Max felt conspired against by destiny, by a kind of cosmic grudge, and he wasn't surprised that Leni and Ellie talked over and around him as the car crept by the university bus stop, the art museum in its last stages of construction and restoration, and on beneath the railroad overpass and its deceptive signs.

Beyond that bridge was the South End of town, working-class and (Max had always thought) pretty much immune to false surmises. Leni directed him past the typical suburban litter of fast food drive-ins and trailer parks, auto salvage and Pentecostal churches. The famous track was on the left, its gates locked and barred until the autumn season revived the place and the South End bustled with gamblers, hot walkers, and hucksters.

"Turn right here," Leni demanded a second too late, and Max crossed lanes quickly, perilously, sliding in front of a shrieking BMW and down the chosen road, indistinguishable from the one he had just left, except a hulking white bear crouched near the curb in the distance, startling him at first until, on approaching, he recognized it as an advertising statue reminding passers-by of their need for air conditioning, as if they needed reminding on a late summer day in the upper south.

"There it is," Leni whispered, pointing to another statue, a thoroughbred perched atop a garishly purple building.

Max knew Seventh Heaven from the anecdote: after the World Trade Center attack, the club had joined the expression of nationwide sympathy by posting a sign almost mythically American.

We remember 9/11. God bless America. Lap Dances.

So there it was, in its purple glory. Max had seldom wandered beyond the interstate to this part of town, and it was like those in-car safaris, he figured, regarding the lions from behind the safety of metal and unbreakable glass.

The terms changed, though, when Leni told him to slow the car. Finally, his glacier creep annoying the drivers behind him, Max gave up and dipped into the club parking lot, just in time to see three figures emerge from the doors of Seventh Heaven. And now he knew why Leni had been so insistent.

Out of the club came Dominic Rackett, ducking the sun as though he had been submerged in darkness for months. His wire-rimmed glasses brimmed and glowed, as though a spotlight had been trained upon his entrance. On each arm was a tired girl possibly once beautiful, attentive to something he was saying and laughing at a joke.

"It can't be," Ellie whispered from the back seat.

Leni shrugged. *"Sei's drum.* Now left here, Max."

And dutifully Max turned out of the parking lot, bound on the same road they had just taken, wondering why Leni had brought them all this way for a kind of prying revelation, as though your grandmother had dragged you down an unlit hall to peer into a keyhole.

But Leni was hardly a grandmother, sitting there beside him, smooth legs crossed and her gloves removed and placed almost daintily, triumphantly on the seat between them. Max kept his eye off the high ride of her hem and looked ahead, Ellie beginning a soft, bitter litany from the back seat.

"It *can't* be. It just...*can't*. It was so...*Hefner*. So fuckin' *Rat Pack*."

"*Goodfellas*," Max added with a smirk before realizing his comedy was unwelcome. He tried keeping his eyes on the road now, but was distracted by a crowd assembling up ahead, fat men in suits directing traffic through a makeshift intersection, cars trickling into a church parking lot where someone had set up scaffolding and a legion of the faithful was gathering on a Wednesday afternoon.

∞

Among that number was Bucky Trabue, not long from the casinos and the funerals, counting until he lost count the places he would rather be.

Jerry Jeff Pfeiffer's ass was dragging, Bucky had concluded. The spirit of the evangelical janitor was finding the road of ambitions a rocky one to follow, and George Castille's funeral had changed the road map somehow, when Pfeiffer had found himself in a deeper place—somewhere Rausch and his cohorts had never intended to send him, because it would mean defeat of the party and another four years of DeMoyne Troubles. And yet, in this unsettled country with its perplexity and complexity, Pfeiffer had set aside the political goals that he might never really have entertained in the first place, and in the setting aside he was finding a kind of resolute peace. He was on his own now. He had kicked free of things,

Bucky Trabue was god-damned if he could figure out what the fuck he was doing at this rally anymore, or for that matter why he was hitching his wagon to Jerry Jeff's fading star. There was something to Jerry Jeff Pfeiffer, that was sure. He had gathered a whole mess of creatures into his following, and swelling crowd was a signal that if something in him switched into gear, he could drive this train to local office and maybe beyond. Rausch and Pete Koenig had that part right: a whole generation of mouth-breathers was available to support him, from Deacon Aldo Wooters to the ghost-hunting dimwit girls, half the congregation of HMO, bouffanted Evangelicals from across the river who couldn't vote here but could make others vote, and all the marginalized from a couple of black people who held on to the illusion that the Republican Party gave a shit about them through the Campus Young Republicans too schooled for the crowd and too unhip for the university they tried every once in a while to lead toward the political light.

If they only knew what he thought of them, they would tie him to a tent pole and float him downriver.

Even the spangled one. The heavy, big-haired derelict they called T. Tommy, who was showing up every time Bucky turned around of late. It was like allegiance to the fringe had brought the Elvis impersonators out of the woodwork, and there he was again at the back of the crowd, pungent and glittering.

Jerry began to speak now, thanking Koenig and Rausch and some of the Party, his voice low and roundabout and drawling. He just couldn't get the hang of the politician's energetic *glad-to-be-here!* warm-up. His stump speech was still ministerial, the first few minutes of the talk with the same kind of slow, hushed ease that the preacher read the Bible passage for this Sunday.

Bucky had stopped listening. Jerry Jeff was headed nowhere. The campaign was already floundering because the Bible could stir them up until the one in charge started thinking about it, and then the one in charge had two choices: he could keep talking Bible and do as he pleased, or he could take Bible seriously and drop away from the dog and pony show.

There's probably a place in hell reserved for me, Bucky thought. Then looked beyond the ripe audacity of T. Tommy Briscoe toward an approaching party of three, a gray-suited man escorted by a brace of strippers.

He had seen this fellow somewhere before. Dark complected, slight of build, not the kind you expect to be escorting working girls in this time. Bucky searched his memory for some connection: he'd seen the boy previously, and it was only a matter of a minute or so, with his ward heeler's gift for names and faces, that he recalled the figure at the margins of Castille's funeral.

As Bucky approached the young man, the connection unfastened in his thoughts. This was and was not the same young man. Something in the skin's texture, a translucency about the jaw line and a vagueness of features, as though Bucky glimpsed him in a dream or underwater or through sun-dazzled eyesight. Whoever he was, the gray-suited man was occupied with the speech and the girls, heckling Jerry Jeff with soft, conversational tones at first, until his volume rose with the girls' approving laughter.

It was part of Bucky's job to put a lid on these things, always a dance between firmness and downright disrespect. Given the heat of the day and Jerry Jeff's slow unraveling, he figured he wouldn't be at the job too much longer, so he might as well go out with decency. God knows he'd done shameful things in the service of the Party, but this, he decided, would not be one of them.

"May I help you?" he asked. "I'm with the campaign."

The girls turned to him, their contemptuous stares unrehearsed, Bucky reckoned, because contempt was precisely the emotion they weren't allowed to show on the job. Nevertheless, it caught him off guard, and he felt exposed, diminished, like all three of them were looking through him and finding the unstitched portions, the strain at the seams.

Bucky had always been shy around the girls who attracted him. It was why work for the Party had been easy, its entitled women and their severe hair like a double vodka laced with salt petre to his middle-aged sex drive. But these two would vote Democrat, attractive in their disheveled, last-call late thirties, down on their luck and still miles above his grasp.

Bucky introduced himself, still feigning good company. The girls, it turned out, were both called Chantelle. The trespasser introduced himself as Dominic.

"Well, Bucky," this Dominic observed, saying the name like it was an alias, like nobody could go by such a label. "I guess they don't do fascism like they used to."

Over the suppressed giggles of the Chantelles, Bucky glared at this new adversary, knowing the type from thirty years of knocking heads against them. "I guess that's too bad for someone who likes his lines clearly drawn, ain't it, Mr. Dominic?"

He would have liked to see Dominic's eyes, to see if the laugh had any sport in it or whether he was only pretending he didn't mind being argued with. Bucky liked drinking with lefties when they liked whiskey and weren't the primpy, sheltered kinds that almost all of them were nowadays. He couldn't tell which group this Dominic would fit with, not with the pools of light in his wire-rims, so to be on the safe side, he asked if the three would *keep it down a little, seeing as this was church property and that the speaker was a man of the cloth and all...*

But of course this set Dominic about some church-state slyness, the kind of tired thing you heard all the time from people whose party launched most of their campaigns from AME churches, and Christ if Bucky wasn't tired of it all, tired of the same expected arguments, his and his opponents', and maybe Jerry Jeff was right, maybe this was just the thing that a man needed to set aside.

Maybe it was time to call in the dogs and piss on the fire.

All of this while, on the podium, Jerry Jeff Pfeiffer was going on about how *all things, when you seen and understood them truly, how they touch upon and relate to each other, don't stand apart but they stand together.* He said it was *like we lived in a big net woven out of each other, each of us a net and each of us connected, he said, and each of us watching the others from a distance and from up close. And he said the Lord had come to him, and likened us all as a net of brilliant jewels, each with a countless number of facets. Each jewel reflects in itself every other jewel in the net and is, in fact, one with every other jewel...*

"Like the jewels in my sequined raiment," someone said behind Bucky Trabue, and he turned to see T. Tommy approaching, the air around him abuzz with body odor and stale wine.

Dominic stiffened at the approach, and the two regarded each other across a short space bristling with light.

"Then a fashionable net it must be," the younger man conceded, his glasses taking on a glow more brilliant and surreptitious. "Because god damn, just look at you…"

Bucky found himself on the side of the drunken Elvis impersonator, especially when Tommy smiled at Dominic.

"Yes, we are both kind of a pair," Tommy conceded. "Aren't we, old buddy? I think we have met before, in the dark backward and abysm of time."

Puzzlement leaked from under the glow of Dominic's glasses, and for a moment his grip on the Chantelles loosened.

"I expect that we met on the night of the preview. You and a younger man come to the balcony, brought me out to the lobby, and effected rescue from my seizures. Or at least you resemble my hero, sir, and if you are, upon your deeds the gods themselves throw incense."

"Why don't you go away, old man?" Dominic asked, his request cold and polite, more of a demand than a plea.

Bucky knew this kind of tension. Knew where it might head. Stepped between the men in intervention, but T. Tommy was unmoved, whether by threat or by courtesy.

"It's like a film, ain't it, son? Like the whole body of cinematic endeavor was one film and one only, all plots and sets and actors and characters connected in a huge tapestry of stories, kind of like the preacher was saying when he talked about the glittering net. So that the Duke is a cowboy and a Marine and a fighter pilot, simultaneously and in sequence, because space and time get jumbled all together in this film, you see…"

"You're crazy, old man," Dominic muttered, stepping back, wrestling to remove his jacket lest it come to blows in the August heat. Bucky moved to stand between them, but Tommy stood ground and smiled, muttering something about *risings and sensations,* for all Bucky could make of it. Something about a *dancer and a dance.*

"Why, you're my own son," he whispered at long last to the stunned and suited Dominic, as the Chantelles looked on. "You're my own, ain't you?"

"*Sei's drum,* old man," Dominic hissed. "Whatever." He turned away, leaving the girls perplexed and disconnected, standing shabbily in the church parking lot, the taller Chantelle still holding his gray jacket as he stalked off into the crowd.

And as was so often the case of late, Bucky Trabue did not know what to make of things, but as was so rarely the case, he did not know what to say.

∞

Tommy watched the man until he lost him behind a young family, a happy father holding his son on his shoulders, the boy laughing and lifting his face to a rain that was slowly beginning to fall over the south end of the city. The child pointed to the sky, and for a moment Tommy fought back tears.

"You sentimental old drunk," he whispered. "You big old glimmering crybaby." The strange gray man had almost slipped from his memory, and what remained was an unmoored welling of emotions.

The rain picked up, and Tommy stepped away from the crowd, headed toward the back of the church and the stairway to its basement he had noticed on arrival. Sometimes you could still find a trusting pastor who'd leave the basement door open, and a man in Tommy's state could find shelter there, and, given luck and the right denomination, a nip or two of the communion wine.

He stood at the top of the stairs as the rain swelled from sporadic drops to a slow drizzle. Down there it would be dry, he told himself, but at the first step of his descent, he clutched the railing, his heart fluttering and a harsh, dizzying rush undermined his feet. He lowered himself to the stairs and sat down with a wheeze, watching the still dark of the cellar spread out before and below him, inviting him toward a place he dreaded to go but was fixing to go regardless.

∞

Their car had reached the underpass and was speeding back by the university toward the theater, and in all that time Ellie had not stopped talking.

She listed reason after reason that the gray-suited man could not be Dominic Rackett, that she knew for a fact he was in another part of town, helping her brother move some boxes from their mother's house, how he planned to go to an Indiana Jones revival at the Cineplex, she had heard him say it, she was positive it was today…

All the while Max's grip tightened on the steering wheel and his vision blurred. The simultaneity of Dominic Rackett—his talent to be in several places at once—was wearing thin. It had been a long morning already, and the heat of the day, the strange events, and the tiresome tension between Ellie and Leni had pretty much gotten on his last nerve.

Leni herself was bending under the constant harangue. She was turned away from them, looking through the passenger window as Victorian town houses flashed by and the car rushed north toward Broadway and the theater beyond.

"I wrote the article for him," Leni said at last.

Ellie's eyes widened. "Excuse me?"

"All of this was for his grandmother, you know," Leni confided, still looking out the window as the car snaked into the alley behind the theater. "It wasn't my fault that the boy fell short of expectation."

"But how do you mean, Dr. Zauber?" Ellie's questioning was taking on a bit of backbone, Max noticed. For all her disappointment in Dominic—because she couldn't doubt that was him in the parking lot, who could?—Ellie was fully aware that the master of slackers had at least never slacked on the movie articles, that he had given his best.

Even Max was forced to admit as much, though he still figured he could have done better with the project. Now he could kick himself for not having offered suggestions, not lending a hand when Dominic's articles had spiraled downward, whenever that was. For not having read the articles to begin with.

Max had held off, kept silent when Leni had lit into Dominic over the *Waxworks* article. He could have stepped in, could have settled a peace between the two of them and been the bigger man. Perhaps Ellie would have looked at it as maturity, and perhaps it would have even won her favor. He had held off because he figured that a critical word would have been taken as resentment, the good son saying to the prodigal, *I told you all along, now see what this has gotten you,* and Dominic would have seen it for what it was, really.

His thoughts made pockets to contain his other thoughts. The buildings rushed by the window, the shimmer of heat on the old city blocks conjuring mirages, as the street before the onrushing car seemed to pool and liquefy, the brownstones taking on angular, geometric irregularity, as though something in their upper stories had been fractured by relentless sun. All the while, Max's thought dwelt on Dominic, on Dominic's peculiar troubles, and he realized that, regardless of stepping forward or stepping back, what he saw and what he felt would have been unmasked for the envy it was.

All the while, Leni was going on about Dom, her judgments

harsh and, as far as Max could tell, entirely just. The boy was lazy, yes, and indirect. Too old to be called *a boy*, certainly too old to be thought of as one. His charm entitled him, and his gifts had made easy the first steps of things, so that when the harder steps lay before them, when the competition was others as gifted as he was, Dom had not developed the gumption, the muscle to scale those steps.

Perhaps Dominic was, as Leni claimed, a talented failure. Max wondered about such things, about his own supporting role as a creature of limits and industry. And though he found it hard to sympathize with a gifted and variable rival, found it impossible to support such a character, he could at least, he figured, take a noble way out. He could step back from Dominic Rackett and speak no evil, especially in the presence of Eleanor Vitale.

24.

Dominic wandered deep in shadow. At first he passed readily through a kind of backstage littered with dollies and cable, following the faint light ahead of him, held like a lantern above the retreating form of Gabriel Rackett.

The back of the concrete studio opened into a long arcade. Dominic stepped around a camera tilted against a cinder block wall and made his way along a gloomy cloister walk, an arcade stretching to the edge of sight. There, near the vanishing point of the long gallery, his father carried a candle into the rising shadow. But the sight was no longer encouraging or paternal: it just seemed cold and far away.

Dominic still believed it was his father ahead of him. But now a suspicion that it might be a projection of Gabriel, a screen image cast into the unending dark tunnel behind the theater, rose in his mind, though he wondered how this could be, why he suspected it, and how they both had found themselves there. He saw his father in outline, then briefly substantial, almost solid in the light he carried, but mostly as the light itself, a floating candle, a pale species of foxfire.

The suspicions grew, and Dominic stopped out of caution,

imagining all kinds of perils and traps. But the light ahead of him continued to move: it receded deep in the corridor and passed from sight, leaving him in darkness. Now he was afraid, afraid of losing the light, his father, everything, and he began to run, slowing when he saw the light again, when he could follow it through the gloom at a walker's pace.

Again Dominic felt that he was no longer moving, at least not in any way that counted for movement. His feet pressed the spongy earth, and the candle floated ahead at a measured and unchanging distance, as though its bearer was keeping intentional pace with the one who followed him. It was like the light reassembled from memory rather than emerging from the fog ahead, and for a moment Dominic wondered at how internal this was, supposing that he might be dreaming, perhaps. Especially when the arches on either side of him seemed to keep pace as well, moving forward in accompaniment and just beyond the reach of his extended arms, no matter how close to them he moved.

Tall buildings towered behind the colonnades—skyscrapers, their tops vanishing into shadow and mist. They were beautiful, geometrical, streamlined like architect's models. From what he could see, though, there were no ground entrances: the buildings rose white and marmoreal, as clean and flawless as new tombstones, Dominic thought, both pleased and unsettled by the thinking. For a moment he almost lost the light ahead of him, almost forgot that it was there or that somehow he was being guided.

In a rising panic, it occurred to him that he might be here forever.

And with that thought, he glimpsed the light again at the vanishing point of the long arcade, and beside him the arches began to move, slowly at first, but more swiftly when he gathered traction and strength. Now it felt like movement, like walking, like running, as Dominic began to sprint toward what he thought might be his receding guide.

As suddenly as it began, the arcade ended. Now the streets

began to curve and tangle. He was in his town, which was not his town. And if he had left behind a city in the abstract, a metropolis half residing in the mind of its architect, what he approached was something fallen, convoluted and fractal, the peaks of the houses wavering like tongues of dark flame, the windows of the buildings distinguished from the outer walls only as quadrilateral, deeper darkness.

Dominic inhaled, and followed a bend in the alley before him, hopeful because he glimpsed (or thought he glimpsed) a faint pooling of light at its farthest recess.

At last he realized he had wandered into Holstenwall. Caligari's town. Site of the fair and the somnambulist murders. Suddenly the windows, the recessed doorways seemed like simmering dark surfaces: the shadows gathered shape into the swell of a retreating shoulder, into eyes that watched him back.

It seemed easy enough. Follow the light ahead. Don't let the movement at the corner of your eye distract you from the journey, from passing through.

Now the corridor began to rise and narrow, and the light ahead seemed to climb the surface of a tower, small and tightly focused, like a spotlight in a catacomb. It settled on an upper-story window, and bathed the glass in borrowed light, receding into the room behind the open shutters until it revealed shadow of a thin, almost gaunt woman holding something toward the window, as though the outdoor shadows illumined the thing in her hand.

Then a subterranean voice—one that had welcomed him out of the chorus of flames at the womb's door of this uncanny place—began to intone his own words, changed by the years and an unexpected revision and the shadowy climate:

> *Neither wind nor air*
> *in this terrible valley*
> *that devours its young*

that once, my father
you had come to visit
the sentence of years

making you unfit
for poetry for vision
for the unmasked truth

Better to die young
better not to be born
than to be born here.

And of course he knew the voice, changing beneath sound into the inflections of someone he had almost wed, someone who now slept with others in a gifted house, in sinecure offered by a big university, honored for his words, for almost his words only ("unmasked truth" was too dramatic and stable for his language, he would give her that), claiming they would always be her words because they had shared a bed when he wrote them.

But what of that? In some ways, once uttered, the words were no longer his. They floated in a dark woods, waiting to be grasped by the next passer-by.

Already Peri Bathgate was translucent, her frame blending with the frame of the window, the light above him cloudy and going dim.

It was like the cops when they put up the yellow tape. *Nothing to see here. Move on, people.*

So Dominic moved on, passing the window until her words—and his—tumbled out of earshot and memory. But the light was gone as well, and Dominic cursed his own stupidity, felt in the darkness for walls, turning back and groping his way toward the tower…

Until he hit solid surface. Again a kind of cinder block, as much as he could tell by touching. There was so much down here, an architecture and terrain that seemed to be unsteady, shifting and dissolving as Dominic moved, his hand pressed to one wall until he collided with another and turned, steering by touch as though he was navigating a labyrinth. A whisper of sound somewhere in the maze, and he waded toward it.

Soon he despaired of a firm place to stand. On occasion the floor seemed to tilt, and Dominic misjudged the distance to walls, bumping against them in the pitch-black. He remembered the scene from *Indiana Jones and the Temple of Doom*, the contracting room, Indy about to be crushed in a trap that seemed designed for no purpose except an exercise in villainy. He pushed the thought away, and when it returned, concentrated on the brush of his fingers against the concrete, on listening. He knew the saying about the blind compensating with other senses, and he wished the compensation would kick in, god damn it, because he had no idea where he was, and no idea within that idea.

Perhaps he *was* dead, as his first, panic-stricken thoughts had whispered. Perhaps it was that light, after all—the steering of the soul toward whatever afterlife was in the works for someone like him. Nguyen Van Yen had told him to avoid the lights, to travel on in the darkness and avoid the temptation to pursue lights strangely colored, the guidance into a new incarnation, to resist and resist until you passed out of samsara, the horribly recycling of life that goes on through eternity until enlightenment breaks the pattern, the ordeal…

But for right now he was hungering for light, for purchase, for a release from the closeness and entanglement of this journey. He pushed away these thoughts of entrapment, settling into touch and hearing, only what the senses had to offer, taking it in without judgment or reflection. Wherever he had come to in this warren of shadows, it was now within earshot of music: "The March of the Gladiators," it was (though how he knew the title was beyond him) played on a calliope.

Calliope. The steam-powered organ Dominic remembered from State Fair midways. And the Muse of Epic Poetry, as he recalled.

So, was this an epic journey? Or simply a sideshow act? Feast or famine, Dominic told himself. It was funny, when you came down to it. He was too lazy for epic heroism, too vain to take a supporting role. The music was no longer ahead of him, but under him, riding little jets of steam through the hairline fractures of the floor.

There was a world under this world, and a crack in the floor let light ascend, crazing the path ahead of him, which stopped at what seemed to be the lip of a crevasse.

It was all traps down here. Like one of the worst of Indy's adventures, every step mined in some diabolical pulp-fiction snare. But what seemed to be a ledge ended up to be a stairwell instead—steep and without railing, spiraling down into the heart of something. Layers upon layers, it seemed. And from somewhere deep in the coiling descent, another light, dim and banked and edged with scarlet. Dominic followed the sound, descended...

Twice he almost lost his footing, felt the sudden, vertiginous lurch in his chest as he thought he was going over, head over heels into who knew what depths of darkness. He remembered the head of the stairs in the old Bell House, twenty years ago, his father's last backward glance before Dominic lost him in shadows. But it was not that night, and this time he was the man, the responsible one, the one alone in undiscovered country. He regained balance and composure, and as he went downward on a path that seemed eternal, the steps gathered light, his footing was more secure. Eventually he reached level ground, in a region gloomy but less dark, ahead of him an encampment of lights crowned by a huge, rotating wheel.

It was the carnival the music promised, seen from a distance. Human life, human contact—something to relieve the terrible shadow and loneliness of this place where he had wandered for...

For how long?

The wheel spun slowly in a midway crowded with flames. The gray lights Dominic had seen in his first moments in this strange, slipstream passage—the people or creatures or entities who had welcomed him—were now in the hundreds, each a tongue of silver, each hovering a space between spicules of jagged energy and something resembling a human form. Faces around and above him, like the bas-relief on the lobby ceiling at Shangri-La, as Dante became Offenbach became the less recognizable Cocteau, images becoming more current and less recognizable as Dominic approached them. Some milled around him, some rose and descended on the rotating arc of the imposing Ferris wheel.

Then he saw his father, there in front of a sideshow booth, bent to the edge of recognition, suddenly and for the first time frail in Dominic's eyes. This was not even the Gabriel you would expect to see after the stretch of years since his vanishing in the Bell House: it was, instead, a man decades older—maybe sixty, as though he aged here as he would have in the world outside, and yet Dominic knew him instantly, and moved toward him to greet or comfort or take his arm and balance him in the sparks and the dodging light of the carnival.

But on his approach, the woman beside his father moved slowly into the light. Dark hair scattered with gray, becoming at once familiar, her delicate hand extended toward his father as Gabriel leaned and rocked and hurled the baseball in the diminished sling of his left arm. It struck the target with a festival ringing, and his mother laughed with delight and Gabriel's arm encircled her waist, and for a moment it was the way Dominic had always yearned for it to be, and he quickened his steps to join them at the booth.

But Gabriel was turning from him, accepting the stuffed bear from the carnie and handing it to Jasmine, and the two of them ambling through the crowd toward the Ferris wheel as Dominic wrestled through insubstantial bodies, then ones with more heft and solidity, trying to get to them, calling out *daddy* and *momma*, then switching to their names, but all the time unheeded as the couple boarded the gondola, the midway gliding away from them.

Dominic shouted again. His hands dropped limply to his side as he watched his parents ascend and crest above the turbo lights, where they were lost in the permanent night and he lost track of which gondola, hurrying to the base of the wheel to greet them on their way down.

He was almost sure of the car, lifted his hand to wave...

And it was Ellie and Todd who rode in his parents' place, looking up into the geometry of spokes and drive rims as their car ascended again, Todd reaching across the back of the seat to brush Ellie's blonde hair with his pale, nervous fingers, but she was laughing, pointing at something, as the wheel kept turning and they rose into the dark. Only now did Dominic recover his voice, calling vainly after them and, hearing no reply, he crouched apprehensively and waited for the wheel to revolve and descend.

Lost in the night, the gondola rocked unsteadily, and Dominic peered into the gloom, the artificial lamps of the carnival. He felt as though his childhood had just vanished, and in one turn of the wheel he had been taken from the a six-year-old's dreams of his father—a dashing Southern novelist who needed only a lucky break or two to reunite with a woman who still loved him, who had not forgotten him really—to the image of a girl he halfway courted, fastened in a circling cab with her disquieting brother, in need of rescue when the wheel had turned.

And now the slow rotation of the ride was slower still, the topmost gondola descending until it was at last eye level, opening for the uniformed man and the very young girl to alight. The girl he had never seen—Asian, and in her mid-teens at the oldest—but her escort, a man clearly Dominic's age, dressed in the black death's-head uniform of the S.S., clearly the elusive figure from the Berlin colonnade in *Last Crusade*.

The officer looked directly at Dominic, beckoned. All this distance, the long, obsessive search: it had come down to an encounter in a throwback amusement park. Dominic met the man's gaze, the girl slipped away into shadow, and the next gondola descended and stopped, the couple getting out who might or might not have been Ellie and Todd, because now Dominic could see nothing but the man before him, stalking through the midway, looking over his shoulder, certain that Dominic would follow.

∞

The carnival behind them now, they moved with the speed of a cinematic jump-cut to another place—a dense woodland, where the uniformed man moved elusively through trees and undergrowth, Dominic following cautiously, losing track twice, but guided back to the path as the man re-emerged from the forest and motioned him to follow.

The danger of this pursuit was not lost on Dominic. He couldn't think of a circumstance in which a Nazi uniform boded well, and yet almost twenty-five years—from a movie theater in his childhood to a world behind a screen as an adult—had brought him to this juncture, and as frightened as he was by the darkness, the wilderness, the spectral figure he pursued, he figured he would have to stick it out now, regardless of the perils.

But no matter his resolve, Dominic startled when, bursting through undergrowth, he came face to face with his quarry.

The man regarded him mildly, quizzically, his shape gathering hue in that strange, abstractly washed way of colorization. Nowhere ever had Dominic seen eyes that shade of blue. It was like a porcelain color, like it was fashioned out of air and water in an artist's studio, because it did not occur in nature. Dominic caught his guard dropping, then realized that the landscape around him, once blanched and colorless, had changed to brilliant dark palette, greens mingled with the black and red of the officer's uniform, the Meissen blue of his eyes.

Meissen?

"You're Florian Geist, aren't you?" he asked, the whole search becoming clear in a sudden epiphany of fear and memory and light. And embarrassment that he was obviously the last to know.

And you could have been so much more, was the answer, the words like tremors in Dominic's inner ear, intuited rather than heard, their source the man who stood before him, though Geist did not speak as much as set forth intimation.

You have been looking for me for some time, nicht wahr?

Dominic nodded dutifully, his mouth half agape, and Geist grinned.

Would it surprise you to know that I have looked for you even longer? Though now, alas, I am thinking that I have looked to the wrong one altogether.

"The wrong one?" Despite his nerves in the presence of the notorious Geist, Dominic was drawn in by the mystery, miffed at being second choice.

Geist slipped behind the barely substantial bole of a tree, his black uniform visible through the translucent gray column of bark.

I am not sure why Zauber chose you now. Perhaps an accident.

He peered around the tree and smiled, and now Dominic could sense the charm, the taunting composure, could understand how this man had inveigled women and men and those in scarcely approachable power.

Then again, you saw me in the recesses of that silly film. So something in you was chosen.

Geist regarded him quizzically, and Dominic knew he was supposed to be flattered, to bask in being singled out. He knew the rules had changed, that the boyhood search for adventure and the sentimental search for his father had suddenly turned serious, perhaps deadly. That now he was in over his head, but that part of him did not mind.

You really have no idea, do you? Geist's unspoken question, inferred on Dominic's nerve endings, made him wonder again whether he had left the seat in the theater, or whether this whole adventure, fitfully spun from light and shadow, took place in the screening room of his own jostled mind.

"I know it's more than film history, if that's what you're asking."

Geist's laughter was melodious. He defied the Movie Nazis of Dominic's memory, seeming instead to be a normal guy, roughly his dad's age when Dominic last had seen him.

That much is true, Geist conceded. *Though something in*

Zauber clings to that, and it speaks well of you that you did not fall for her "art for art's sake" Weltanschauung.

"She's in love with you," Dominic suggested, for the first time glimpsing the pain and long-suffering of that flinty, abrasive woman.

But she is…past her prime, Geist teased, his eyes on the strange dappling cast by the blanched light on the leaves. Forever would I love, were that she fair. But that is history now, as much as the other things—as Ufa, as Heydrich and Prague. But you still have no idea.

There was no way to respond to him. Confused over the roundabout musing, the reference to unknown things, Dominic kept silence. He was hoping for that moment—like the ones in a Bond movie—where the arch-villain maps out his sinister plan while 007 is strapped to a laser-powered drill or dangled over a school of frenzied sharks. The moment where it all was clear, the long arc of the story resolved in a simple explanation.

But aweysha, Geist said. As though that answered everything. The thing the novel got right was aweysha.

There was a time I was in your place. A theater, I was all of fifteen. Not much older than you when you were drawn forth by Indiana Jones in all his silliness.

For me it was Caligari. Werner Krauss ambling over the set like some crabbed and visionary creature. He looks into your eyes as the iris of the camera closes, out through the darkened theater to you alone, his gaze beckoning. Because I knew, from that fractured city, the buildings arrayed like shards of broken glass along twisted alleys and cul-de-sacs, I knew that it was…the insides of my world. Of Germany broken apart by a long war and perfidious leaders. Holstenwall was where our souls lived, and the doctor had come to mend us.

There is the scene, early in the film, you remember? where Franz and Alan—fools the both of them—go to the sideshow of the Holstenwall fair, to where Caligari has set up his booth, promising to the crowd that he will reveal the somnambulist. A whole generation of us knew—I was too young, admittedly, but the boys scarcely five years my senior had come back, those that did, from the gas-addled trenches, the barbed-wire imprisonments, the abattoir of machine gun and field artillery—and they knew too well what it meant to be a somnambulist, a sleepwalker. Commandeered by elders, shell-shocked and drained with dysentery and influenza, four out of five of them damaged, they went through the motions of living, dying as men before their bodies died, as the poet said.

I knew Cesare the Somnambulist, knew him from the faces of Potsdam when I was a child. Knew him in Berlin, and all the sleepwalkers, would see them again and again in the theater and on the screen. But in the dark that day, it was Cesare's haunted eyes that found me out, and I was changed. The film set forth a power that passed through me like an electric surge, and I knew then what I had been called to do.

"So…it was like Hitler's ambition, your own," Dominic concluded. "To recover for your people what was lost in the Great War."

Geist frowned. *Oh nothing that political and earthly, little man, though a beautiful ambition that was. The Fuhrer stopped at the threshold of the soul, which was where aweysha begins, you know. My ambition is less broad, but deeper. I intend to rescue the lost.*

Walpurgisnacht
(1936)

Dir. Florian Geist

Starring Emil Jannings, Hermann Braun, Hannes Stelzer, Lil Dagover, Tsering Pema.

This is the film you have been waiting for, the moment for all film aficionados to gather and celebrate. Now is your chance to see the signature film by Germany's greatest unknown director, Florian Geist, and to be the first audience anywhere to see it.

Geist was one of those generational rare geniuses, perhaps the Orson Welles of his time and place, though far less hungry for publicity, scandal, and sensationalism than the American impresario. One might say his career passed "under the radar," while his death in 1945 Prague went virtually unnoticed by the world at large, though not unmourned by a small but knowing film community who revered him.

Geist's political affiliations have been aired in this community earlier in the season, and yet its vision is more complex than its detractors (who have yet to see the film) have framed it. *Walpurgisnacht* speaks to desires more universal than those of a particular place and era, and its message, like the characters who people its story, is timeless.

Based on a World War I German/Czech novel by Gustav Meyrink, *Walpurgisnacht* is set in the castle district of Prague during that disastrous conflict. The aristocratic inhabitants of the district don't view themselves as residents of Prague, and they are oblivious to the brewing civil unrest and their obsolete political order. Their complacency is unsettled by the arrival of an actor, Zrcadlo, who possesses the uncanny gift of assuming the appearance and nature of whatever character he portrays. Geist himself, who plays Zrcadlo in *Walpurgisnacht*, was suspected of this talent, and indeed Emil Jannings was to insist that he did not act in the film, that the role of Dr. Halberd was played by Geist as well. Oddly enough, Hermann Braun (Ottokar in the film) is said to have charged Geist with the same masquerade, though Braun's disappearance on the Russian Front in 1941 made corroboration impossible. Lil Dagover cameos as the Countess Zahradka and the prostitute Lizzie the Czech, but she is scarcely recognizable through the layers of makeup it took to age a 40-year-old woman well into her seventies. Only the exotic Tibetan child actress Tsering Pema (1921?-?) is recognizable in this her only feature role.

Walpurgisnacht is an apocalyptic novel. By that, we mean a story of ends and beginnings, of the collapse of the old and of the renewal that must necessarily follow. The book ends with a millennial procession of the downtrodden, defeated and disenchanted, toward the crowning of a new emperor in the Prague castle district—a troupe of beggars, servants, and revolutionaries, at the head of which a man made of smoke marches, beating a drum-head of human skin. Geist, it is said, was

at his greatest genius in displays of illusion and ceremony. The one-eyed general Zizka, iconic in Prague's heritage, may or may not have come to life in the humble figure of Ottokar the violinist, and the ancestor of the young Countess Polyxena may or may not have stepped from a painting to re-inhabit her descendant, and the devil himself may or may not have visited the middle-aged court physician who, by a kind of strange accident, becomes the hero of the film. Magic dominates Geist's cinematic world: double exposure reveals ancestors and forerunners behind the actors, and present actions intersect with patterns and connections established in an historical and spiritual past. We are all ghosts, the director tells us, bound to one another by power and desire.

Unscreened as of this printing, *Walpurgisnacht* is described by its restorer, Ms. Leni Zauber, as "grand and magnificent chaos." It is is the ideal film of the period, embodying all the obsessions and concerns of the 1930s, all the yearning and desire that would end—or seem to end—in the ashes of Middle Europe. Magic and mayhem mesh perfectly with Geist's images of revolution on all levels— those of the body, of the body politic and also of the spirit that informs them both.

--Dominic Rackett

∞

To rescue the lost.

Ambition that left Dominic speechless.

But it was the announced purpose of Florian Geist, what had brought him back out of wreckage and nothingness to this place and time.

Then again, what had brought Dominic into the recesses of this undefined country beyond his own desire to be a hero, to reunite with his father…to rescue the lost.

Geist moved out of the undergrowth and onto the path, standing in the way like a wolf in a fable. *It was in Tibet,* he continued, *where I made association, where I learned the way of the mountains and of beliefs far older than the ones with which I had come of age. My own instruction—the tepid Lutheran fare of youth—paled against the stark, ghost-haunted wisdom of the lamasery. You know this yourself, Dominic: it was why you were one of those we called, though it would seem you stand on a cliff's edge now, ready to set aside the mantle of your possibility for some sentimental and personal quest.*

Dominic started to object. He had always seen himself as generous, even altruistic. But Geist looked through him, or rather into him, and he began to wonder whether the search for Gabriel was anything more than the self-pitying adventure of an entitled son, or a way to prolong childhood, because, as long as you sought your father, you didn't have to stand on your own.

They were ideas he had not considered. He wondered if others had considered them for him, had been too polite to say.

Too polite, perhaps, Geist agreed. *Most people live by their desires, by their karma. You know that.*

Dominic nodded stupidly, increasingly sure he was in over his head. "We are born into this world," he said, "with our desires. We might spend all of our lives acting on reflex, reacting and responding to those desires, to the karma that rides along with us. Am I right?"

But what does the bodhisattva do? Geist asked, and it felt like catechism. Dominic wished he had the answer, but it seemed that Geist was not expecting it, not really, as he turned away and headed down the forest path, beckoning over his shoulder like a squad leader, and whether from perverse curiosity or from nowhere else to go, Dominic felt compelled to follow.

Now the air smelled of astringent, of alcohol, but beneath that, of things in subterranean decay. They were indoors again, Geist leading Dominic down a corridor of sputtering light: the lamps that lined the hall were bare bulbs, half of them burned out, and the walls were covered with graffiti bombs, slogans in what Dominic guessed to be a bastardy of Italian and German, untranslatable üchen script, and wall art in which the carnival wheel they had only recently left behind underwent a series of renderings, each one more abstract and colorful until the last one verged, as Dominic had known it would, on a mandala, as the wheel passed from the world into a painted rendering of the afterlife, of the land of the dead.

There it was, the six realms, a Bhava Chakra, a wheel of life laid out in Krylon and Spanish Montana, in a middle ground between a graf piece and a meditative sand painting. The figures in the drawing vibrated with provisional life, shifting in and out of representation before Dominic's sight—at first the monks robed in saffron, wearing the ushnisha topknot, bent beside stylized Japanese streams, evolving, as the drawing seemed to change and shift, into T shirts and baggies, the bodies of water at curbsides, streaming into storm drains, carrying with them generations of litter, tangling the flow as the water pooled and rose around them.

Geist cleared his throat, motioning Dominic onward. He turned and followed, feeling like a pilgrim in some medieval poem, a traveler through a symbolic land where the key to interpret is missing. There was no choice but to follow, although he feared that Geist was the worst of guides.

So the life that flows through each of us, Geist explained, opening a door and motioning Dominic through, *is all connected.*

But you know that, ersatz Buddhist. You know all about the dependence of one thing on another, do you not?

Dominic knew he was being mocked, reduced. To say *yes* was as much a lie as saying *no*. He had learned some of these things from his books and from Bulwer, but *all about them?*

"Who knows *all* about them, Captain Geist?" he asked elusively.

Geist shrugged, and filed in place behind him.

I do.

"Well, I certainly don't," Dominic conceded. "Not all, at any rate."

Geist's laughter echoed brittle in the corridor.

Of course not all. Perhaps not any. Your fevered animal life, like a cattle prod spurring you on from one sensation to the next, your whole way of life a reaction, a response...no will, no incentive, no autonomy...

This in contrast to the one who lives gansho no bosatsu. Do you know it?

A deep and dramatic sigh at Dominic's silence.

"According to vow." The one who lives according to vow. Who I really am is inseparable from all things. All things dwell in my life. My purpose, my path, is different. People such as you—or such as you so far—think only about the narrow, personal scope of their lives. But I live according to vow. Because of that, my life and its importance are not the same. The fate of humanity lives within me, and I have survived this form, the form you see before you—the form of my emanation body...

My vow has taken substance and form, has survived my earthly embodiment, the disasters of the War and Prague...to descend on you. But...

Dominic had enough. This was crazy. This was poisoning everything. But Geist kept speaking.

Oh, it is this search for your father...he is long gone, and so easily replaced. You're no Telemachus, no Parsifal, no Luke Skywalker...

And the figure in front of him began to roil and flicker, the death's-head uniform dissolving into gray flame, wavering slowly, taking on a new form…

As Gabriel Rackett stood, or seemed to stand, before his son.

See? Geist whispered tauntingly, taking on the accent and inflections of Dominic's lost father. Even the smile was bona fide, and Dominic almost called out to the figure in front of him, almost rushed to him. Then stood back, appalled by the cruelty of the whole thing.

The man before him laughed, the antiseptic smell rising until Dominic almost choked on it.

Oh, it's just beginning. You can give up now and save yourself the rest.

"Give up and *what?*"

I think you know.

Now they were in the hospital room. Jasmine Mountolive lay in the bed, her eyes unfocused, bright but milky as opals. Geist or Gabriel faded to a silvery, guttering flame in the back of the room, and Dominic approached the bed, as he had done years before on that wintry day in Boston.

"You managed to visit," his mother observed, her voice dry and indeterminate, seeming to float all around him, anchored not in the cancer-diminished woman lying there, but in the air itself and the resonances of his thought.

"Of course I did. Why wouldn't I?"

"Because you're chasing *him*. And you will never catch him."

Dominic sat on the edge of her bed, moving aside the I.V. tubes, the monitoring wires.

"You've set aside everything for him. A career. An education. Peri. The new girl."

He started to object, but her hand, weakly raised, waved away the words.

"You left her with her brother in the wheel, didn't you? You followed Geist. Because you thought—"

"I thought he would take me to Da. Yes, I did."

"I hated that. *Da.* Your grandmother put you up to it."

"Gramma Bowers?" He couldn't help himself, because he kept remembering all this was staged for him.

"You know better," his mother whispered dully. "Grandma Rackett, Conroy, Lull...whatever name the old harridan goes by."

"But Ma," Dominic replied. "You're...gone. Passed ten years ago."

"So you think I'm a figment, Dommie?"

"Yes, but more as well. I don't know *what* more...but you're more real than a figment."

His mother looked beyond him, dark eyes glazed, the cacophony of tones and buzzes from the monitoring machines, and the lurid lights flickering blue and green with indecipherable numbers.

"You never called me that," Dominic said at last.

"You do know I did the math wrong, after all," the woman on the bed insinuated, her stomach swollen, the pale pipe of her throat constricted by the cancer he imagined. "It was Ben and not Gabriel."

Dominic shook his head. "No. You may have done the math, but I did the mirror. A hundred times after he was gone. I read it like his manuscripts, read it as inheritance. And yes, looked in the mirror for signs of them both, but it's my father only I see there, not your Ben. And you never called me 'Dommie': only *he* did."

"Then perhaps you are his boy, after all," she conceded, her voice a rattle he barely heard over the continuous tone of the flatline. "Perhaps it is genetic, this capacity to fail. It was there in his father, whom you didn't know...a hillbilly ne'er-do-well that left his mother for a shiftless young thing..."

Dominic shook his head, trying to picture his Grandpa Rackett. His father had never said...

"Can't stick with a girl, either, can you? Floated by a few in college, in and out of that almost-marriage...and you just left the new one in the hands of her brother—you know he isn't right, but you were too busy being a son to be a man, weren't you? They're afloat on a wheel somewhere—mandala or Ferris, it makes no difference—and you abandon what's in front of you to chase ghosts and shadows.

"But then, how could you have been otherwise, Dommie? A narrative poem in haiku? Why, Gabriel himself could not have imagined anything more useless…"

The laughter was harsh and mocking, but it suddenly struck him funny as well. Smiling at your mother's deathbed seemed vile and forbidden, but he was about to do it, about to send her off in laughter returned, but then the world changed around him and he was in the Park. At the theater, its geometric sets halfway between Caligari and the brick town houses that lined Fourth Street behind it.

∞

Dominic stood center stage, alone. There were people in the tiered seats—a dozen, no more. An audience ranging from Peri to George Castille to the strange Tibetan girl he had seen with Geist in the Ferris gondola. There were the two girls from the ghost-hunting show, Reynardo Rosa, Nguyen Van Yen, the spangled T. Tommy Briscoe, and some others indiscernible behind the floodlights and the shadowy tongues of flame that fluttered like witnesses at the margins of his sight, gradually taking on bodily form until they stood at the back row of the amphitheater, beautiful and cold and sad.

Dominic looked for his father, but failed to find him among the living or the dead.

Geist's voice echoed off-stage. Dominic wondered if it was in earshot of the audience, if it were part of the play or a stage direction.

So you have come this far. It shows resolve. It shows bravery, I suppose.

But in the service of some entitled vision-quest, isn't it, after all? A little bit of bourgeois adventurism, isn't it?

The audience seemed closer than it should ever have been, crowding the bottommost rows of the amphitheater. Dominic was penned in on all sides. The Tibetan girl and Castille stared through him, as though they had found out something about him he had yet to discover on his own. Nguyen and Rosa and T.Tommy looked upon him more sympathetically.

Just through the door behind you, Geist urged, his voice palliative and kind. Over the threshold. Exit stage right. There is a whole world that needs your rescue, Dominic. It is you alone that can do this, can make all right the hesitations and the indirection of thirty years...

Drawn to the voice and its prospects of rescue, Dominic turned and opened the door. He could feel everyone's eyes on him as he looked down into the darkness. Something glowed and rattled under his feet, and for a moment he almost lost balance, almost fell forward into the gloom. He gripped the door frame, looked down at the white, almost liquid shuffle of the stage, and light from somewhere caught the boards, its reflection tilting into his eyes and momentarily blinding him.

The light shone through the tiered crowd and Dominic saw them as shapes behind shapes, as though he looked toward the promenade through layers of glass. The shapes receded into the shadows until only the gray flames remained out by the statuary lining the walk—flames that were wavering, dwindling, becoming transparent themselves.

Dominic turned from the door, stepped off the stage into the shadows, and the amphitheater was empty again. *No,* Geist commanded behind him, but still he kept walking. Tendrils of mist reached up to embrace him, and somewhere in the gray recesses he heard T. Tommy again.

"Are you back now, Dommie?"

And again Geist said *No,* then *Nein* more loudly, and Dominic couldn't breathe. The gray flames dissolved before him, and there were two ways to go: further into darkness, or toward a light he could still glimpse above the rise of the park grounds and the colonnade beyond it and a copse of mulberry and water maple—a wheel of lights, faint and stationary, the bulbs on the drive rim winking out one by one, the colors dwindling to monochromatic white. Todd was with Ellie back there, wasn't he? And strange though it might be, something not quite brotherly in his love, it was surely a love Dominic could leave her with for the time being, while T. Tommy's voice still echoed improbably, calling him away from her and into annealing shadows.

∞

He wandered toward the voice as the mist thickened around him, as it gathered warmth and heat and substance, and it was even more difficult to breathe now. Smoke filled Dominic's lungs, and the path he walked or thought he walked was on fire beneath his feet, but giving off no warmth and all too little light.

He tried to pull himself away from where he was, if he was indeed there. *Hypnogogia* or *dip-non*—he tried to name it something pressed against his chest as he tried to orient, and again he saw or thought he saw Gabriel or Tommy ahead of him, half cloud and half father and half homeless and glittering Elvis impersonator, too many halves moving in and out of the red light, assembling and reassembling, but like a mirage always the same distance before him.

For some reason, he could not call to his father. It was past reluctance: the very air seemed pressed back tightly into his chest, so he had trouble breathing, never mind emitting a sound. But now the spectral figure before him began to speak, an inveigling summons that Dominic more intuited than heard.

This is the way out, it whispered. *Follow me.*

He started to obey, then stood still. Was it Geist or Tommy or his own missing father?

Follow me, it said. *The light is this way. Take the steps and let go of everything behind you.*

Like Orfeo in the old story, like the boy who was the subject of Ben Mountolive's long-ago and deceptive article, Dominic picked up his pace, stumbling over narrow tracks and ducking underneath unsteady scaffolding until the shape in front of him seemed closer, red light under his feet bleaching into a white light that framed a glittering, retreating figure.

Above all, Dominic wanted to look back. He wanted to see if Geist was in pursuit. Though the very thought horrified him, worse was the prospect that the shape in front of him might turn out to be the selfsame thing he fled. It was a voyage in the dark, thoughts undermining other thoughts until Dominic was mindful only of movement, of the soft pad of his feet against a smooth hard floor.

The passage brightened into a long, cluttered corridor, like the one in the government warehouse, where the Ark was stored at the end of *Raiders*. And yet a few steps toward the light told Dominic that no, he had not fallen into the film like in some amateurish movie script, not gone woodenly meta like the professors in his father's Frankenstein story. Instead, his path took him toward a steep industrial stairway, where his father or Tommy or someone entirely other was ascending, wearily, shoulders bunched with the gravity of age.

Dominic called out finally, something bursting in his lungs, drowning in light. He rushed to the foot of the stairs, but his guide had vanished above. Clambering quickly toward the high opening, he struggled onto a broken wooden floor, onto terrain half-shadowed and musty and familiar.

He lay on the shattered back aisle of Dry Salvages, in the country of great Nyarlahotep, struggling for air and balance.

∞

While scarcely a mile away, lying on the ground in the cemetery, Tommy Briscoe awoke to a dazzlement of starlight, wet with dew on his trenchcoat and under him, breathless and a bit battered from a journey he barely remembered.

It was like he'd been dropped from a distance—tugged aloft

and hurled through shadows and dropped, a feeling that was, surprisingly, not unfamiliar to a man with a history and with backroads of alcohol. Tommy smiled painfully, remembering fragments of a dream: how the whole world had vanished and switched on him, only to reappear and discover him at the exact spot where the one adventure among many had begun for him days ago…

Or at least what he thought was days…

He remembered his wounding, his healing in the flickering shadows of the balcony. Remembered someone beside him like an insubstantial companion at the corner of his vision. He thought of hard rain, of tornadoes, of a quiet pool deep in the woods of his childhood. Oddly, of a corn-shuck doll his little girlfriend had given him, back when the world was wondrous, and then her face, glimpsed through a window as the remembered glass blurred with his tears.

He wiped his eyes, laughing at what a sentimental motherfucker a bottle of Richards could make a man.

∞

Seven of them stood in the foothills, the gray flicker of their flames commingling.

It was time to move. Six of them embraced, by now no longer quite aware who they were, but clinging to the understanding that something had once connected them in brilliance and nearness, in the light of which they were only shadows, a baseless fabric of vision.

Goodbye, they whispered. *Auf wiedersehen.*

Angrily the seventh urged them not to go, the Totenkopf on his gray hat flickering in and out of a borrowed light. Not yet, he told them, when their roles were hardly over.

But they trailed away one by one. First Orlac, then meaty Ombrade, looking for all purposes like a defeated penguin. Then Orgon followed, and only the women remained, gray blades of fire, warm across the glitter of his death's heads.

Come with us, they pleaded. Then Marie and Magdelein turned from him, and only Maria was left—the most beautiful of all, the one whose residual energy kept the last bond to earth.

She coaxed and urged, reminded him how other adventures awaited them. That it was easy to dissolve, embrace the calm, recur. But he would no longer listen, and soon her persuasions grew faint, receding into the silence out of which they had first arisen. Then, she, too dissolved, and standing in a littler of pearlescent beads, he looked back toward the abandoned theater, toward justification and purpose and release.

26.

ominic's phone was bristling with messages. But he recognized few of the numbers.

He was tired. Confused by the events of the day. He had walked out of Salvages into a misty September rain that only intensified as he walked toward home. Drenched by what soon became a downpour, he left wet tracks on the stairway to the theater loft, closed the door of his apartment behind him, stripped and wrapped a towel around his waist and fell backward onto the bed, his hair still dripping, letting it all go.

He picked up the phone almost as an afterthought, thumbing through the received calls with a rising sense of dread. He didn't get this many calls in a week. None were from Ellie, nor Bulwer, nor even Grandma Mary.

The first call was from Leni. He had seen the programs in the lobby, readied for tomorrow's debut of *Walpurgisnacht*. He wondered why she had given him the byline, but he figured he knew the gist of the call.

He had never really unpacked his suitcase, which lay under a pile of clothes by the apartment's one window. Just close the damn thing, crash with Grandma Mary, and see if

Bulwer could give him some more hours. The festival ended with *Walpurgisnacht,* anyway, so he was being cut loose only a weekend early.

He shrugged. It wasn't as if the job with the theater was the most pressing thing on his mind. He'd listen to it later. Who cared, after all?

He called up the next message and listened to Todd's flat intonations.

Where is she, motherfucker? I told you to leave her alone. If she isn't back by tonight I'll put a GPS on this phone and track both of you down, god damn it.

Dominic sighed, having no idea what that was about. The next number in the message queue had dialed him three times. It turned out to be Max, with roughly the same news, though in Max's urgent but managed tone rather than Todd's hysteria.

Hey, dude. You seen Ellie? She hasn't been home for, like, goin' on the second day. Todd's freaking, and her parents aren't much better. Call me at…well, you have the number right in front of you.

By now he was weary of disembodied voices. He set the phone down beside him. It rang almost immediately.

Max again. Who had no doubt thought Ellie was with Dominic, but, finding this was not the case, filled him in with what little was known about her disappearance. It was a long enough absence—given phones and Facebook and the whole network of her contacts, not to mention that she still lived with her parents—to raise concern, though not alarm.

Furthermore, he was addled by the country through which he had just passed. Both Dom and Max knew Ellie well enough to mistrust a silence, and so it seemed like a good idea to begin with her haunts. There were coffee places she liked, and a vegan food café she visited on moments of penitence and moral resolve between hamburgers. Max thought that this might be one of those times: after all, she was missing, wasn't she? And sometimes, Max said, going missing was a sign of the reconnoiter, the questioning of the grounds where you stood.

Dominic could not agree more. And yet he couldn't keep

the girl in focus, his thoughts on the country he had just travelled. His conversation did not rise above grunts and monosyllables, and when Max offered to pick him up, he declined, saying they could probably cover more ground if they searched separately. Max's enthusiasm hit a speed bump; he trailed off in muttering as well, then said that, whatever the case, they could meet tonight and trade notes at the premiere.

It was only after he hung up that Max's parting words registered with him.

A brief look at the time and date on the phone confirmed it.

Dominic had lost a day in his strange passage.

∞

"I have no idea what's up with him, Mr. Bulwer," Max confessed, as he turned left onto one of those steep, brick-cobbled streets that still lined the north-south thoroughfares of Moon Hill. "I try to give him the benefit of the doubt, because you all like him—every last one of you. He's like...*charismatic*, I suppose."

Bulwer smiled, drew the cigarette packet out of his shirt pocket, looked at Max and raised an eyebrow.

"The car's not mine, Mr. Bulwer. Dr. Zauber rented it, and she smokes in here all the time. Can't you smell it? But like I was saying..."

Bulwer cracked a window and lit up, turning away from Max to blow the first plume of smoke. "He is charismatic, I suppose. But it's more than a simple magnetism, Max. There's a kind of hopeful residue in Dominic. It doesn't look as though he's headed anywhere, but whether it is a woman or a job, he is *not yet* where he really wants to be. So indirection is all right, because he understands it as the next step. What is consistent— and I think it's what draws everyone to him—is that he believes he is headed toward *the real thing*, That it's on the way, that it *will* come about. He's the type of man who's afraid to be bound to anywhere or anything whatever."

"So...you think he's not really my rival for Ellie, John?"

"I think we should find the girl, Max," Bulwer replied, glancing quickly back over his shoulder as Max turned onto smoother pavement. "Those Moon Hill incline streets are hell on the suspension, son."

"Not my car, John," Max muttered through clenched teeth, reminded of Bulwer's neutrality to the rivalries of younger men. "You know...I was thinking about *Caligari* again this morning."

Bulwer, in a wave of non-mindfulness, flicked his cigarette butt out the window. "*Caligari?*"

"Yeah. Mainly Franz and Alan. Remember how they make a pact early in the film? How their rivalry for Jane won't change their friendship?"

"The friendship that doesn't have a chance," Bulwer observed. "Alan is dead five minutes later, as I recall."

"I know, right? I told Todd that Alan was there to die and give Franz a reason to hunt down the killer—to go after Caligari and the sleepwalker. But now I'm thinking there was more of a reason to have Alan in the film than just to kill him off."

Bulwer stared out the window. "Look over there. Another one of Pfeiffer's rallies."

"John, I know why they included Alan now," Max insisted. "To be the promise of something. To foretell the Peaceable Kingdom."

John's outburst of laughter tumbled into smoke and coughing. "You're still on that Peaceable Kingdom, Max? You're old enough to know better. Look at that assembly we just passed in another church parking lot. Every last one of them indifferent, or blinded by religion and resentment. "

"Not Jerry," Max objected. "He's just a good man I disagree with."

He changed the subject immediately, but Max kept thinking about it as he let Bulwer off in front of Salvages and made his way back toward town. No sign of Ellie in Moon Hill, nor in the shops or cafes that surrounded Salvages and Vinyl

Solution, the ill-named record store two blocks closer to the city center. Someone in Smokers Accessories already made the standard "milk carton" joke over the counter display of bongs, proving once again that high minds might be too high to mind. It seemed like everyone he and Bulwer had asked was either indifferent or flip about the whole situation. Too stoned or self-absorbed to care.

Max had one more stop before he made it home. After all, he had promised Jerry Jeff he would be there.

He remembered his first real talk with Dominic. How their ghosts of fathers had haunted them both—Max's through distance, and Dom's through downright absence. He had liked Dominic then, though cautiously, and he had to admit that the whole thing soured when Bulwer seemed to play favorites. But it wasn't about Bulwer, this rivalry, he thought as he parked by the curbside next to the church and drew out his phone, scanning its screen for missed calls though he had it in his pocket all the while.

It was about Ellie, of course. It occurred to Max that, outside of a few hipster-leaning shops in the town's most hipster-leaning districts, he had little idea where to find the girl. But still he seemed one up on Dominic, whose strange disaffection on the phone not three hours earlier—the grunts and short answers—suggested a kind of removal, that somehow he was drifting away.

∞

It was a larger crowd than the last one, Bucky noted.

He felt awful about it. All because of Jerry Jeff's dream, he now looked into bleak prospects, just as the Pfeiffer campaign seemed to be gathering steam.

Bucky's had always been a history of waiting for the other shoe to drop. Sometimes, though, it dropped before he knew it. He and Jerry had weathered the trip to the casino together, which Bucky should never have planned for the straitlaced and pious potential candidate. But aside from Jerry's silence on the way back to the city, it had been successful enough, he figured: the two of them had become closer, which would be great for the coming campaign, and Bucky himself had won four hundred dollars, somehow relating this to Jerry Jeff's disapproving presence over his shoulder at the blackjack table.

Because Jerry Jeff drew down serious mana. What was it that the charismatics said about charisma? It was charisma if Bucky had ever seen it: a godly gift lavished on a humble creature. There was something in the janitor's speaking that was both vulnerable and powerful, like you wanted to guard him from the very world that people like him were put on this earth to transform, to take the harshness out of it and put decency in its place. Bucky didn't know how to describe it, though he felt it in the man's presence.

The Spirit, they claimed, gave folks the word of wisdom and the word of knowledge, healing and miracles, discernment of spirits, tongues and interpretation of tongues and prophecy—Bucky could recite the passage he remembered from the Vacation Bible School he sneaked off to against his parents' wishes. But since then he had knocked around the world long enough to wonder if those gifts were around at all. When his constituents thanked Jesus for a parking space, or much worse, seemed to gloat over things like George Castille's suicide, it made Bucky wonder why the Lord would hand out charism anyway. But just when you had given up, someone like Pfeiffer would come along, who believed in the good and decent country where the wolf lay down with the lamb.

It put Bucky in mind of the painting in the Shangri-La Theater—the old 19th century primitivist one that looked like a kid had done it. Surely when Jerry Jeff cleaned over there, he would have dwelt on that painting and those things.

It was like Jerry Jeff Pfeiffer was a perfect candidate for his district and his party. He played to type. What had fucked it up was that he wasn't playing.

I am no cynic, Mr. Trabue, Jerry had said, as the two of

them drove toward a rally that had held such promise but was now headed toward disaster. *I know that Jesus is coming again, and whether it's in my time or someone else's, it don't matter, because there's a surety that it will happen indeed.*

"Amen," Bucky had answered, knowing this part of the routine.

The showers had started as a soft drizzle that morning, but had picked up considerably, as though the weather itself was a warning of some impending disaster, some mishap, of the other shoe dropping at last. Jerry Jeff's windshield wipers rattled and whined over the rush of the rain. It boded ill, and Bucky knew more was on the way.

And if I'm being honest, Mr. Trabue, I'm still wondering why you took me to that boat. I don't hold with games of chance, and a smart man like you should have been able to figure that out. It was like you brought me there as a luck charm and so it made me think what kind of talisman I was supposed to be when you got me up on that podium.

It wasn't like that, Bucky insisted. But he was damned if he could offer what it *was* like, with Jerry Jeff staring over the wheel at horizons, with that earnest choirboy look and the clip-on tie like he was headed to church or a speaking engagement.

Bucky didn't like where this was headed.

Either way, Jerry Jeff said. *Whether you were exploiting me or whether it was genuine and true but misguided, I heard from a higher authority once I come back. There was this dream I had, Mr. Trabue...*

Bucky knew it was over. Jerry Jeff recounted the dream, and Bucky realized he had lost out to a subconscious Jesus. It was the Son of God Himself, all robed and compassionate, rising, Pfeiffer said, like he was surfacing through glass or a mirror. He had shown his wounds to the janitor, the marks of the nails, the great injury inflicted by the Holy Spear. And Jerry Jeff was all about these things, having taken the dream as a revelation.

He was older than I had reckoned, Mr. Trabue, Pfeiffer said. *He hitched his shoulders and slipped his hands out of the folds of the robe and shown me the scars. Not to ask for pity, but just like he was saying that this happened, that it was the way of things. He came as the crucified Jesus, not yet resurrected, though of course we knew where the story was headed like you do in the middle part of the movie. And I knew as well, and also without him telling me, that I was to set aside secular things and return to the ways I had known and loved, that serving him was doing humble work, out in the world and in the church. And that such work was blessed by its freedom from the ambitions you had set before me, because though I share your hopes for the city, for America, and for the world, those hopes rest, he seemed to be telling me, in the hands of other men.*

Bucky was on the phone to Rausch and Koenig almost before Jerry Jeff parked the car, hating himself as he dialed and feeling more like an informant, a snitch, than the public servant he assured himself he was despite his growing doubts. But Rausch, after a flurry of profanity and a huge, embarrassed silence on the Reverend Koenig's end of the conference call, mapped out an alternate plan, tersely and urgently, and, having spelled out the next quick and vital steps of the campaign, demanded that Bucky hand the phone to Aldo Wooters.

∞

It was breaking Bucky's heart that he had to be the one to tell them. But it was one of the unpleasant things in an increasingly unpleasant job, and he was the man who did the dirty work, the man who carried the weight. He tapped the microphone, thinking that it would be just his luck if the rain was to leak through the umbrella held half-heartedly over his head, short out the wiring and electrocute him in front of an expectant audience.

Dead man walking, he told himself. And began to tell the assembly that Jerry Jeff Pfeiffer had, after long deliberation, decided that perhaps the world of politics was not *his* world, that he could be of more use to his community and, more importantly, to his Lord, by staying put—just where he was, and just doing the things that God had wanted him to do to begin with.

There were some outcries from the crowd. It was, Bucky knew, a church group, and a Holiness group where folks were used to talking back to the preacher. There was an angry turn at the beginning, like some of them had thought it was his idea, the Party's agenda, and if they could have only known how much it pained him to introduce their next councilman, Deacon Aldo Wooters, who had a lot of catching up to do but would hit the ground running and come out on top with their help and their prayers, and it made Bucky sick, made him like to puke when he could sense how the wind had left them, that Wooters was dead in the water if the fundamentalists weren't behind him.

So Bucky offered his services, claiming his years of experience would stand behind a fine and capable citizen like Aldo Wooters, and all the while he was hoping the storm had subsided and no big divine bolt of vengeful lighting was going to descend and evaporate him on the podium. But it went well, and Wooters—and Pfeiffer right after him—shook hands with Bucky Trabue, and then the three of them lifted their hands aloft, grips linked in that famous American sign of political solidarity, and Bucky heard the cheering begin and started to forget about the rain and the setbacks and his own self-loathing, thinking that maybe they could pull it out after all, that it was still eight months until the May primary, and that Rausch could see to it that Wooters was unopposed, and that when all was said and done, that the sound of hoofbeats he imagined drumming in his ears might not be as dire as he figured, that it might just be telling him there was plenty of time for all kinds of cavalry to come to the rescue.

∞

Max had arrived as the rain lapsed and Bucky finished, and the sodden crowd, wet past grumbling and impatience, had begun an *Aldo! Aldo!!* chant raising homemade signs, the ink already running, watching the podium where Aldo Wooters waved at them awkwardly.

He had to hand it to Jerry: not many people could keep a crowd waiting on a gloomy day, but here was an everyday working joe who had the power, had the message, which—though Max did not and could not agree with its particulars—was peaceful and decent and readily handed over to another man for carrying it on, and he was glad he knew Jerry Jeff Pfeiffer on that sullen morning. He admired principles in anyone, and seeing Jerry on the podium, endorsing Aldo Wooters in the rain, was tempered a little bit by knowing that Jerry Jeff was headed toward what he believed to be a higher calling. And Bucky Trabue wasn't half bad, either: Max's bird colonel father had taught him at least that reprehensible politics could attach themselves to decent men, and it surprised him that he was thinking that, as he climbed the steps to his apartment, stopping at the mailbox, thumbing through and discarding a copy of The Watchtower and a pizza ad, checking his phone for Ellie's number, though as always it had been in his pocket all along.

He was still worried about Ellie—of course he was—but there had been something in the rainy afternoon that had settled Max Winter, that had made more benign his slant on the world and on the people he knew in it. Maybe John Bulwer was not the guru everyone wanted him to be, and could stand some lessons from his own school: maybe the simple fact that we were all in this together would end up saving us from each other.

Max imagined the old bookseller rolling his eyes at such innocence. He stood at the landing and looked back through the barred glass of the apartment security door, where a gray light let him believe that the rain was coming to an end. He would go to Salvages tomorrow, just to touch base with the old man.

The package in front of his door surprised him a little. Only his name on it, and no addresses—neither a return nor his own. Max shrugged, picked it up and tossed it to the bed, noticing it lifted and hit heavy, and deciding that weight alone was a good reason to open it right off.

The note that wrapped the pistol was in block print, simply

phrased and meticulously written down.

Here. I trust you'll do the right thing. —DR

He stood beside the bed, holding the gun, his consternation turning quickly into a dull, cold anger.

27.

The rain did not let up. Sweeping over the rooftops, leaving the streets awash with the effluvia of the city's late summer dry season, it cast gloom across the eight o'clock premiere night, and the staff trailed into the Shangri-La drenched and dispirited.

All except Leni Zauber, who sat exultant in the projection booth. Around six o'clock she looked down to see Jerry Jeff Pfeiffer, his hair matted and rat-tailed by too long in the rain, begin the meticulous task of sweeping the tiered chairs of the house. She wasn't surprised to see him return, although rumors had spread that he planned to resign and devote himself to the campaign.

Leni knew better. Pfeiffer was one in a line of disappointments. His star had dropped from an imagined heaven, and his too-scrupulous nature had cost him dearly. Only two days before he had brushed against the edge of power—small-time for now, admittedly, but a place of purchase, a spot from which he could have climbed quickly and gracefully to a place far beyond his station. And chances were that enough of him would have remained to enjoy the ride, to have been grateful for where it had taken him once that moment came and he found himself cheering on the next in line, who would vault over him because of wealth and family and the place on a coast or in a central and major city, where the next in line always comes from in America.

It would not have hurt him to rise with that tide, but in the end his ignorance had reduced him. And now he would sweep out lobbies and call on Jesus, calling more loudly, Leni suspected, when the theater closed and he found his way, undereducated and disconnected, into the unemployment lines of the city.

It wasn't long until Max peeked in. He and Jerry exchanged courtesies, and Max returned to the lobby. Leni gave it a moment, then came down from the booth and followed him, standing by the Peaceable Kingdom mural as Max set up the popcorn machine and opened the concession till.

She knew it was morbid to wait for the next arrival, but then *schadenfreude* was part of her mother tongue. And no sooner had she thought it than there he was, as if on cue. Stylish even in jeans and a rain-darkened oxford shirt, greeting Max, who glared at him. Then something of an exchange, Max's voice rising, Dominic frowning abstractly, and Leni moved from her place on the wall, passing between them to remind them they were in public now, that whatever quarrels had started between would-be alpha males needed other places to finish—places that were not the Shangri-La on her opening night.

Then Max showed Dominic a piece of paper. Dominic held it at eye level, declaring oddly that it wasn't his writing, that everyone these days was writing under his name.

He looked dully at her. Puzzled and a little annoyed, she turned toward the Peaceable Kingdom.

Then decided to let it be, as the boys took positions like sentries, Max staying where he was behind the counter, Dominic setting up, oddly, by the street entrance, a place they usually put the girl.

After all, Leni Zauber had more to attend to.

She returned to the booth, played a while with the projector. The old reel-to-reel she had brought from her flat. The theater should go out with a flourish, she had claimed disingenuously. Walpurgisnacht was yet to go to disk, after all, and we should add to its silence the faint flutter of film through the projector, the authentic and historical experience of a film never shown yet, presented as its creator had planned to present it. The board had balked at the additional cost, until she assured them that she had the projector with her, an old Motiograph. The Steenbock editor she had sneaked past Castille. Then, meticulously, she had grafted the salvaged and added scenes onto the Prague master print, so that in the end, she had come up with a version not unlike the one Geist had intended, but perhaps unlike the one he would have approved. Castille had backed her on the Motiograph, still trusting her before their association fell apart. For a moment she felt grateful to the old invert, who had stood for things even when he stood in the way.

In short, the film was ready. Now the world would meet Florian Geist, whose genius had been so long overlooked. Leni leaned back in her chair, thought twice about lighting a cigarette. Did so anyway.

After all these years she still adored him. And now, as the film came to light and life in this recessive little town, Leni wondered again if she should have begun her mission in a larger and more glamorous city, coastal or northern, more inclined to the visible and the celebrated. But no, they had discussed this in the long years when Geist was making the film—that in obscure country an idea is allowed its shape, its evolution, its sense of the home-grown that would make it attractive to those who would take it up. No rallies in Berlin, Geist had told her, where the people were too many and too variegated. Best to begin small, like a seed in hidden ground.

Leni stubbed her cigarette. Seven o'clock: an hour until the curtain rose. And an anxiety, anticipatory and at the same time gleeful, filled her as she rose from her seat and headed back to the lobby in a slow, extended version of pacing. They would all show, she knew: they would all convene for this event, and Geist would speak through her after decades, his artistry manifest on the screen at last, changing through light and shadow the lives of all who set eyes on his work.

∞

Dominic watched Dr. Zauber settle under the bas-relief mask of Milton, and wondered if things could get even stranger in his world.

Something was eating Max. He guessed it had to do with Ellie Vitale, because there was a part of Max in which Ellie had everything to do with everything. But the aggression had been pure middle school playground, Dom asking if he had heard from Ellie, but Max moving too close to him, the tilt of his chest changing the subject from concern to aggression, muttering something about *who the hell you think you are, Rackett,* calling him out by his last name. And though it had been years—perhaps even back to middle school now that he thought of it—since Dominic had been in a genuine fist fight, he had seen it seconds away in Max's direct stare, in the way he occupied space. So Dominic had looked at the note, denied it, accepted Max's perplexing comment that he *hadn't brought the damn thing, anyway.* Then backed off, hating to be unmanned in that ancient dance of slow burn and testosterone, and Leni had passed between them, and the bristle in the air had subsided. He had gone to the door, then, figuring they were both still at work after all, and that what needed settling would be settled once the film was over, and that what would be needed now was someone to man the gate at Ellie's absence.

So they had set position. Jerry Jeff had greeted them as he walked through the lobby on his way to the downstairs bathrooms, and maybe half an hour later, Leni had come out of the house, and there she was under Milton when Ellie walked in out of the rain.

The girl was a holy mess, drenched and shaking as though she had walked miles through the rising deluge. Instantly she rushed to Dominic and embraced him, and part of him knew that this would not help matters with Max at all, while another part of him kind of liked it, felt the stir that Ellie had always given him, wanted more though now he knew that was unwise, maybe impossible—not only for now, but also in the months to come.

"You have no idea, Dom," she whimpered, and started to say something about Todd, but he shushed her and ever so gently pushed her back to arm's length.

"There's towels up in my place," he said softly, handing her the key. "And if you want, my shirts are probably not big enough to swallow you. And, if you aren't too partial to fashion, there's some sweatpants at the top of the suitcase. Bulky but warm.

I'll sell the tickets till you get back. No rush, Ellie. It'll all be here."

Ellie frowned and shook her head, then dropped her gaze. She turned and started to walk away, then stopped and rocked slowly on her heels, her back to Dominic, her shoulders bunched. Then she turned again, and without lifting her head, her eyes veiled beneath sodden hair, snatched the keys and headed for the stairs. Max called for her as she passed, extended an uncertain hand, but she was by him and on the landing, and he glared at Dominic as though he was angry at forgetting something.

∞

It was a crowd of some stature, Leni noted, as almost the last of the invited guests straggled into their seats. She had decided not to speak before the film, to reserve time for talk and questions after it was shown. But people were there from all factions in the community, from Congressman Rausch and the Reverend Koenig all the way to those poor, dimwitted girls who starred in the ghost-hunting reality show on public access television. The university president was there, and the pizza magnate who had lent his name to the downtown sports facility, and Councilman

365

Troubles was reputedly on his way, as was his freshly minted opponent in next year's general election.

Leni saw the bedraggled Ellie Vitale come in and sit down, dressed like an urchin and escorted by Max Winter. She wondered who was taking the tickets, then remembered that Dominic had been there when she left the lobby. No need to worry about the trivialities, she told herself. Now what was left was the premiere: it had all led up to this, over a sweltering summer and over unimaginable years preceding that summer, wearisome years of patience and editing, of patching the Prague master print with the few excerpts she could gather from archives in Berlin, Moscow and Bologna. And of course from the film that Geist brought back from Tibet.

The audience had settled into their chairs—perhaps a hundred people, but the premiere was an elite event, and tomorrow the general admission would no doubt fill the theater at both showings.

But what after that?

It dawned on Leni Zauber how decades of work—more decades than she could remember and more than those around her could possibly believe—had come down to this showing. *Aweysha*, she reminded herself. This was when she was supposed to stop working and start to exult, to bask in the victory, as the whole scarcely credible enterprise launched itself onto the screen and into the imaginations and spirits of those attending.

There comes a moment in a movie theater when an audience intuits and acknowledges that it's time to begin, and the conversation shambles away into silence moments before the lights go dim. Leni recognized it had come, and exhaled gratefully when someone—Dominic, she guessed—had seen to the light and the curtain. Not a bad boy, Mary's grandson, but too distracted to be worth much at this time of his life, and as his mid-thirties would soon tilt toward forty, perhaps too distracted too late to be worth much at all.

The credits came onto the screen now, and Leni was glad she had preserved the fraktur font of the titles. Then to the initial scene: a sunlit drawing room inside the Hradčany Castle, the aristocrats in various postures of louche thick-headedness. The portly Dr. Halberd, played either by the fleshy Emil Jannings or by Geist himself—Leni was no longer certain—leaned against a mantle, pretending to listen to what seemed to be the witless chatter of the Countess Zahradka, played by Lil Dagover, who denied her part in the film a decade later, when the Russian tanks still occupied Potsdam and Berlin.

Leni steepled her fingers, reclined in the projectionist's chair. Geist was no fool, placing his major stars on camera first. The intertitle read Conversations of No Importance, and Halberd rolled his eyes broadly and mugged in the style of the cabaret clown, and the scene lingered just enough to create a restiveness in the audience but not the boredom that would dampen the film before it began.

Because then came the announcement: *A Strange Man Sighted.* Someone was loitering on the walls overlooking the Moldau River—a vagrant, they said. A public disturbance.

Seize him, the Countess ordered, and with an immediate parallel cut, the film moved to the wall, where for the first time Florian Geist appeared as himself, as the actor Zrcadlo.

Leni heard the intake of air from the audience, for as always there was something rapturous about the man. His saunter over the narrow allure behind the crenellated wall was pure Geist, a mixture of sentiment that she had often compared to the dance of two great American silent stars, but where Chaplin mixed comedy and pathos while Keaton mixed comedy and melancholy, in Geist's demeanor was a hint of menace, the tentative to and fro of his steps not quite free of a swagger. Zrcadlo shot his cuffs, letting the stage light catch the glitter of the links as the white sleeves flashed for a moment in the arms of his black jacket; then he turned to the crowd, and you could feel the palpable force electric, as for a moment he left or seemed to leave the ground like that beautiful but talentless Reaves boy had done in the Matrix movies with computers and special effects. But this was one camera, one simple dolly shot, one actor afloat on magic and sheer will as the house of the Shangri-La filled with the barely audible rumble of people moving back in their seats, of hands taking hands in a moment of silent invasion.

Leni wanted a cigarette. She rested her chin in her cupped hands and stared dreamily into the screen and those eyes.

∞

Dominic slipped into a back-row seat. Weary and disjointed, willing to write off the last few days as fatigue, hallucination, anything but what they seemed to him as the film began, he approached Walpurgisnacht as though it held a last revelation. Watching it through would give him a sign, he thought.

He stood near the back and watched the nobles primp and saunter on an eighty-year-old set. Jannings was there, and the ageless Lil Dagover, and at first it was a drawing-room scene like the ones he had seen before—the Expressionist, jagged sets of the Weimar Republic, and he began to wonder what the fuss was in the first place. Then the cross cut, the bridge, and Zrcadlo afloat among Baroque statuary.

Dominic knew at once who it was. The pale countenance, the dark suit, the lean man hovering, and shapes emerging from the roil of gray and black that defined Zrcadlo and his slow, dramatic hang above the Moldau.

It was the Geist of his nightmares, his ghostly counselor and guide and adversary. Slowly, dreadfully, Geist turned to face the camera. His eyes were pale, light gray on the film stock, though Dominic caught in their depths a trace of impossible blue. Geist met his gaze across the span of years and distances, the fluid borders between the living and the dead, and of course it was the same overpowering stare he had set forth years ago in the arcades of Indy's Berlin. It was confusing: Geist's floating image slowly became translucent, and out of its misty light another image struggled to emerge, a double exposure that Dominic knew instantly was not on the film but nonetheless behind it.

Out of the light and shadow his father seemed to rise.

Dominic would never remember taking the stairs. He found himself on his bed, staring at the ceiling, as though startled from deep sleep or shaken from a fugue state or seizure. Later he would figure that only a few minutes had passed—five? ten?—but at the moment it seemed longer, like his recent vanishing into Geist's carnival of tunnels. He turned on his side, felt a cool dampness on the bedspread. Ellie's wet clothes were draped over the chair.

His trunk was open, its contents stirred. One of his shirts was missing.

He had no idea what would come next. But he knew what would not, and for a moment he lay in the bed he would never share, his thoughts on the closing of the Shangri-La and on the uncertainty that lay before him.

∞

Thirty minutes into *Walpurgisnacht,* Todd Vitale stepped onto the rug, his boots and black raincoat dripping. The lobby was empty, the concession stand unmanned as well, and the plaster mask of Goethe gazed down at him, blank-eyed and white, from unfathomable height, though Todd could not tell him from Isaac Newton or Wordsworth.

It was all over. He could not keep his sister to himself any longer. She was in there by now, probably telling Rackett all of what had transpired, gaining his sympathy, turning family against itself and leaving her one reliant friend, her brother her twin in the cold the cold

the world the beautiful world had rushed by him and he had grasped in vain for the hem of its garment while the faceless corporation had taken his theater his Shangri-La and then Leni Zauber walked on to take the festival to ruin *Caligari* and *Nosferatu* and *Metropolis* and if that was not enough she had pushed him aside for Max when he knew more about these films than any dimwit passive-aggressive hipster and if *that,* mind you, *that* was not enough she replaced Max with Rackett who had come from god knows where, a haiku poet for the love of Jesus, and if *that…*

if *that*

He thought of his sister and tumbled into rage.

At least Jerry Jeff had stood for something, or so he thought, at least Jerry but not now, not anymore, he had backed away from it all and that sweaty nonentity, that sanctimonious prick Aldo Wooters had taken poor Jerry's place, and it would seem they had that much in common but he had tried to stand for principles while Jerry had backed off backed the fuck away out of cowardice sheer cowardice and they all stood for nothing now and if you stand for nothing you will fall for anything

and a wild and desolate wave swept over him and something was knocking at his heart it was pounding like a trip hammer for the love of Jesus what was wrong with him it was time to do this to get it on to get it over

and the pistols both rode easy and light in his hands' assurance and he wondered if Max had read the note, had brought the gun, though probably not, given the passive-aggressive pussy he was…and Todd crossed his wrists like Keanu or Neeson imagining *Cinema Paradiso* and *Inglourious Basterds* and the burning the burning and before he entered the dark arena imagined himself riding the air as he aimed at the Kingdom the Peaceable Kingdom at the assembly of Quakers and Indians and pivoted to take in the seated girls the livestock and at last long last he aimed at the little child that would lead them

∞

And now the moment came in the film where the devil himself visited Dr. Halberd.

In the book, of course, Lucifer had delivered his manifesto

as *the god who grants all wishes,* standing dark-skinned and clad only in a leather loincloth, wearing a black miter that glinted with gold.

Leni chuckled wickedly. For the granted wishes were the wishes of the spirit, not the wishes of the thoughts.

We tell ourselves the things we want that are proper and kind, Florian had told her. As though we want those things and not their dark counterparts.

But in our depths, disturbing spirits muster like an evil army. They are Lucifer's legions, and we join them willingly because they speak to a deeper value, he had said. To the world we want and the world for which our spirits yearn.

He had tried, she knew, to express this on the screen. To lift the concept, beautiful in its horror and glory, out of words and into image and light.

And the scene was coming. The scene that, of all those living, was known only to Leni Zauber, who had found it in a Prague archive, had raged over it when first she saw it, then set it aside and brooded over its place in the story and the film

It had surprised her, the documentary footage of the sky burial Geist had lodged in this sequence. She remembered the day, remembered Geist trying to console a young German girl when they both knew that his even younger Tibetan mistress waited for him somewhere nearby, so yes there was anger, yes there were hot tears rising, but the sequence on screen was beautiful, in soft focus and lifted from the horror and pain, forefronted by a time-intensive traveling matte. In essence, Geist had wedded the two moving images: at the bottom of the screen, Lucifer, with a wave of his diabolical hand, showed the *Tomden* on the mountain and the vultures descending, hopping in anticipation. And then, seamlessly, he had cut to the hazy burial scene, where an actor (Hermann Braun, perhaps? Geist himself?), crouched above the shadowy body, tugged at something, and lifted a less substantial shadow, translucent, gray and whirling, like a torn fabric held to the light.

The audience gasped. "His skin!" someone whispered.

So they knew.

Rapt in what followed, Leni did not hear the noise in the lobby. For her the only sound was the rapid rattle of the film feeding, the only sight the girl crouched in the foreground of the scene, naked and dark and Asiatic, her boy's haircut belying the new blossom of her woman's breasts, her face now obscured in the brilliance of the Klieglight.

And Lucifer stood behind her, dark and glittering. And depending on when your eye caught his face he was Ottokar and Zrcadlo, or he was Florian Geist, the image double-exposed uncannily so that layers of skin and countenance overlay each other, and the devil was a chaos of faces, all things in shadow and light.

He stood naked behind the girl, who bent intently over a drum, binding a glowing drum-head to the shell, and his darker hands on her shoulders began to knead and massage her roughly, and the soft focus intensified until you could not tell (because you were not supposed to know for certain) whether he caressed or strangled her, or whether, far more intimately and unspeakably, he entered her on the screen.

Down in the audience, a woman cried out. In the booth Leni gasped, as unseen hands began to tighten on her shoulders, as she knew that Florian Geist was behind her. The face of Tsering Pema resolved into a far more familiar image, and she fitted the skin on the drum as the devil embraced and entered her and Leni looked into the screen and saw herself at last.

And it was this scene that Todd Vitale first saw as he burst open the door to the house of the Shangri-La, holding a brace of pistols and letting in light.

∞

From the landing, Dominic watched it begin.

He saw Todd enter the darkened house, thought nothing of it until he heard the first shot, the screams and commotion, and the first rush into the lobby as the bedlam began. He took the stairs two, three at a time, stumbled in front of the Peaceable Kingdom, and recovered balance.

∞

For a moment Todd stood at the back of the theater, steering his gaze to the flicker of film light. He saw the image on the screen, the devil behind the Tibetan girl, but he barely took in the scene, his eyes scanning the crowd for his sister, his co-workers.

He saw someone stand, recognized Dominic's shirt, took aim. Then the light from the screen swelled to reveal his sister, and he jerked the pistol toward the artificial stars.

So the first shot was wild, striking the starscape on the house ceiling, which cracked and opened a bolt of simulated lightning over the stage. The Reverend Koenig lurched across his chair and covered his wife Maraleese, while Congressman Rausch ducked between rows and the rest of those present wavered, some standing, several lurching through the aisles toward the screenside exit, one short woman rushing toward the front before she realized she was headed toward the gunman, then dropping to the aisle and screaming something incoherent about *who I am* and *don't you know...*

∞

Dominic burst through the door on the other side of the theater. He rushed down the aisle, headed for Ellie. Max had grabbed her, though, and pulled her down, and Dom could see the two of them crawling, Ellie clutching Max's shoulder as they made for the alcove and the statue, so he figured he was the one now, someone had to stop it.

He turned and headed toward Todd, who fired once with each gun—one at the screen and the other at the projection booth, whooping like a desperado. He was not aiming, was whirling in the aisle then backed toward the screen, menacing one man back to his knees and firing again at the image of Lucifer as the film stalled and the black figure hovered behind him.

Todd fired again as Jerry Jeff grabbed him from behind. For a moment they locked, like the devil and the girl, then in a muscular, slow embrace Jerry Jeff wrestled down Todd and another shot rang from the apron, a flash masked by the first row of chairs.

Dominic raced toward the screen, where the projected figure of Geist as the devil seemed to open in an iris of brown bubble, like one last special effect, and later he would remember shouting for someone to *get the booth* to *go there* but it was reflexive, it was a shout in chaotic dark, and he smelled smoke as he stumbled to the apron and found both Todd and Jerry gone.

∞

Leni was reflecting on the delicacy of things—how a small nudge of the structure can send a whole building tumbling—when Todd's stray bullet struck her full in the chest.

She was knocked from her chair. For a moment the pain knifed through her, then almost immediately changed to a numbness, a weariness. She tried crawling to the table but slipped in a strange, sticky wetness, and the paused image on the screen was that of Florian Geist.

Of course it was. Florian had ruined everything.

Ten minutes ago she had known who she was. And now, the life draining from her on the floor of an obscure projection room in an obscure American city, she was passing from knowing into nothing, dissolving into images and associations.

The memory of the mountain slope and the *Tomden*. The faint pressure and burn in the hollow of her throat where once the pendant rode, crafted by an ancestor from a *ringsel* strung on wire, the stone a relic of a *bodhisattva*, of a saint.

Which he still was to her, in her reverie, despite his betrayals.

No wonder the cast of her memories never featured the girl. Like the old conspiracy questions of why you never saw two people together.

When all was said and done, Leni had shared Florian with herself. She knew that now. But in a sudden, final rush of impulse she decided he was hers alone, that she would share him with no other. Resolved, she sang softly the passage from Wagner. The one near the end of the world.

> *Fühl' meine Brust auch,*
> *wie sie entbrennt;*
> *helles Feuer*
> *das Herz mir erfasst,*
> *ihn zu umschlingen,*
> *umschlossen von ihm,*
> *in mächtigster Minne*
> *vermählt ihm zu sein!*

It was from the *Götterdämmerung*, Florian's favorite opera, Wagner and his mad apocalypse, where Asgard bursts into flame and the Norse gods burn away. Brunhilde casting herself into fire and singing one last time to her lover Siegfried. Feel my breast, she sang, as the world slowed and the fire rose higher. How it burns, how glowing flames lay hold of my heart. Fast to enfold him, embraced in his arms, made one by the might of our love.

She sang and she thought this as the world slowed, as she drew herself painfully up to the table on which the projector sat and the chaos and cacophony receded in the world below her. Pistol fire ricocheted at the edge of her hearing, like something remembered rather than sensed, and time seemed to tilt and drag as she plucked the smoldering cigarette from the table and placed its glowing end directly beneath the projector gate, expecting a holocaust of nitrate and gun cotton, Brunhilde's immolation at the gods' end, but starting the slow melting of the acetate stock, fire-resistant and developed in Prague to prolong the life of what

Geist told them was *an immortal film.*

∞

Bucky heard it on the radio as he and Wooters approached the theater.

Shots fired at the Shangri-La.

"Not again!" he exclaimed, veering the car into oncoming traffic on Broadway, turning the wrong way entirely down Third , his old Plymouth fishtailing to a stop behind the theater.

"It's not the guns, Bucky," Wooters began, launching into the talking points they used after the mass shootings, as Bucky slammed the car door and rushed toward the shouts, the sputter of radios, police voices rising above panic and discord, trying to manufacture order in a place that would never be the same.

Bucky knew one of the police lieutenants, but he was not much better for the knowing. An APB alert, it seems, had been issued for the shooter, who had vanished, along with the theater janitor who had last been seen trying to restrain him. The professor was the only casualty: one of his men, the lieutenant claimed, had found her dead in the booth, the projector and film blackened by a localized burning. Congressman Rausch claimed to have been hit by stray gunfire, but it seemed to have been the back of a theater chair that had bumped him at a particularly difficult angle. Fortunately, the rest of the audience was unharmed though shaken, which was a good thing all around, the lieutenant confided, because if the shooter had set forth on an effective killing spree, it might not have lowered the city I.Q. all that much, but it sure would have put a dent in the cash flow, if you knew what he meant.

Bucky knew perfectly. He thanked the lieutenant and rushed to find Rausch, who was attended by two former staff members while he awaited an unnecessary EMS trip to the hospital, the police having left his side to attend to serious calls for help.

"It's a good thing we're taking this building, Trabue," Rausch said. "Some of the arts people are nice enough, but there's a real cotillion of wackos in that community."

"So, they know who done it, sir?"

One of the staff gophers looked up from his manufactured concern for the congressman. "One of the theater employees, they're saying. Goddamn disgruntled loners."

"World's full of 'em," Bucky agreed. "They oughta band together. Be less lonely and probably less disgruntled."

The Congressman glared at him. "Mr. Trabue, it's been my job to make damn sure they don't."

Bucky nodded and backed away, wondering what the fuck he was supposed to do with such knowledge.

∞

He was kind of flattered that the Winter boy had introduced his girl.

Bucky met the young couple out on the street in front of Huntington's as the police evacuation of the building went from opening floodgates to a mild, meandering trickle.

The girl was pretty, and settled on Max's arm, her head leaned against his shoulder. Bucky had seen her before, and figured this was a kind of "office romance." Figured as well that it was the principal reason boys Max's age got jobs to begin with—to meet girls, because boys like Max were good kids but not worth much of anything else.

When he found out later that the girl was the shooter's twin sister, he couldn't do much more than shake his head. *Life's a funny old dog, ain't she?* he thought to himself, and not for the last time.

Because Bucky'd been sure they would have caught this Todd Vitale by now, but the boy eluded authorities, as the police liked to say. He couldn't believe the suspicion that Jerry Jeff

Pfeiffer had aided Vitale in his escape: it wasn't in character, he told his lieutenant, and beyond that, it just didn't make horse sense.

Epilogue

llie Vitale moved in with Max Winter at the turn of the year. They didn't talk much about the last night at the Shangri-La, because their knowledge and experience had never quite settled into words.

Max suspected he was second choice. That he might always be. It was nothing he could ever pin down, but the thought preoccupied him through the damp autumn as he picked up part-time work at Salvages, hoping that his hard work and eagerness would suggest to Bulwer that when the time came to hand over the store, there was a likely candidate at hand. But Bulwer was evasive, and one day, standing near the Nyarlahotep Aisle, Max looked down at the ruptured floor and suggested, "It might be time for us to fix it."

To which Bulwer replied, and not without kindness, that there was something about that crevasse that was worth keeping, at least until he retired, when he would probably take the books on the road—a traveling library and emporium, he called it, with a mild irony. Everything is a form of letting go, Bulwer told him, then laughed at his own pronouncement, saying it was something you said at the end of a movie.

Max tried in the few months at Salvages—before he returned to school and things changed in himself and in the old world he left behind—to get Bulwer's take on the subject of Ellie. The old man insisted that it wasn't *his* take that mattered, that even what Ellie thought was not as important as where she was, and the sooner Max got that into his head, the happier he would be.

Eventually he got that into his head, and Bulwer was right: Max Winter became happier.

In December, Max and Ellie both registered for classes at the university: Ellie to put some requirements behind her for a major she planned to declare someday, and Max for graduate school in the humanities, because he figured the best thing to do with an Art History major was to prolong it.

The application for graduate school had been, like many of Max's ventures, rushed at the last moment. His undergraduate grades were mediocre at best, his test scores little better, but the grad school was, as a former professor confided, in need of warm bodies. So Bulwer had written a reference, and oddly enough, Mr. Trabue had dropped a word to Congressman Rausch, who was on the Board of Trustees like he was on the Board of Everything. So there was a kind of provisional sense in Max's admission—half tuition and again a feeling he was on trial until he proved himself.

∞

Before these "life events" (as Ellie had announced them on Facebook), the couple were the ones to see off Dominic Rackett.

They had questioned him after the shootings, of course. Everyone connected with the Shangri-La and with Todd Vitale had been brought in, and the police kept Dominic busy longer than they did most others. When it turned out he was in the dark on most everything, they sent him to his grandmother's for a few days, after which they told him he was free to go if he "kept them informed of his whereabouts."

Dominic informed them that, if he was free to go, he figured that meant he was free to go to Vermont. And they, in turn, figured why not.

Max remembered the day of departure as a series of escalating frustrations. They stood on the loading dock of the bus terminal and made fun of the departing passengers, who with rare exceptions had the look and the whiff of vagrancy. Dominic said that when he was a kid, he had taken a long bus from Boston to Michigan to visit his old man, and that the people on board were generally nicer than they looked.

They saw the old glittering derelict there—Tommy, as Max recalled. Dominic knew him some, and went over to talk to him while Ellie and Max sat on a lobby bench, holding hands and watching the board that announced arrivals. When Dom came back, he assured a questioning Ellie that the old man was harmless, really, but he moved down the bench and looked at the old vagrant for a while, until they posted the loading dock for Dominic's bus. The three of them stood, and Dominic gave Tommy a slow, almost childlike wave, and the old man turned away quickly and went out through the main entrance. And it was then that Ellie kissed Dom goodbye, chastely on the cheek like it was a kiss that she had saved up for Todd if she ever saw him again, but Max still felt a sharp twist of jealousy between his shoulders.

∞

But the day of departure was not happy for Dominic, either. The Greyhound would take all night and most of the next day. The last stop before Burlington would let him off in the middle of Vermont, not far from the old schools his father had attended, but even closer to the little college town where he had worked in a book shop downstairs from a café that overlooked Otter Creek.

That was all ahead of him, but for now he was hungry, sleep-deprived. Nevertheless, he had landed on his feet with a good-sized wad of cash courtesy of Grandma Mary. And there was a trust fund still managed by his stepfather he could dip into if things became overly dire: maybe he had relied on that in his imagining, though he hoped he hadn't, he hoped he had grown up some.

The talk with the old homeless guy at the Greyhound station had kept him awake through twenty hours of travel. Dominic had remarked to T. Tommy how they *had to stop meeting like this,* and Tommy had nodded, had played dumb and laughed. And he said you must be *midway in your thirties by now, son,* and Dominic confessed he was but that people usually guessed him younger.

Dominic wanted to ask Tommy about that day at the amphitheater, about seeing him in the audience to the strange play of shadows. But he held back because there was still a part of him that figured he could have dreamed it all, and another part that figured a guy in Tommy's circumstances might lie or elude or embroider. So they said their goodbyes, and again the exchanged glance lingered like it had when he and Max had rescued T. Tommy from a panic attack in the first showing of *Caligari* at a time that seemed so long ago that it was almost coeval with the film.

He had kind, sad eyes, did T. Tommy.

He told Dominic he might want to cease his travels and settle down. "After all, I took to wandering when I was about your age," he confided, "and I liked to never made a name of myself."

Dominic said he'd consider the advice, and rejoined his friends, where Ellie kissed him goodbye and this time he felt nothing but brotherly, as he did when he hugged Max, waved at them both at the bus entrance then climbed aboard, looking back to see the glittering T. Tommy Briscoe standing in the entrance of the terminal, drawing light from the waning September sun.

∞

And that very evening, as Dominic changed buses in Toledo for the last long leg of the journey east, Bucky Trabue sat on the front row at Heart Ministries, the well-dressed but uncomfortable Congressman Rausch and Reverend Peter Koenig present for the official, bona fide announcement of Aldo Wooters' campaign for a seat in the United States House of Representatives.

The other announcement—the one in the church parking lot under the driving rain—had come too late for the City Council elections. Jerry Jeff Pfeiffer's name was still on the ballot, but Demoyne Troubles, scandals and all, was running essentially unopposed. Bucky had pitched the congressional campaign, saying that it gave them until the next primary in May to get the wheels oiled, that the seated Congressman was even more unpopular than Troubles, that they had a good to excellent shot of turning the district in the fall.

And Rausch, in the comfortable home from which he influenced politics in another district, another state clear across the river, found himself in agreement and in support. In agreement, he said, no matter what. In support as long as it didn't involve his attendance at more than a handful of those goddamned tent revivals that passed for Party meetings these days.

Bucky couldn't have agreed more. He was in all kinds of discomfort at the company, the tambourine and gospel, the dark wool suit that was lightweight but itching like steel wool armor. He wanted it over until Wooters began to speak.

Out of somewhere the sweaty little moon-faced fatboy had found a voice for his grievances, and his kickoff speech was incandescent, at least for the hardcore party members who loved his tune of guns and Jesus, of family and free enterprise and our boys in uniform and of taking back America because someone is fixing to take it away without our constant vigilance.

And Wooters knew when to stop and get the ovation, would first lean back at the podium and then, when the cheering started, would fold his arms and step away, letting the volume of love and outrage swell over him, then shoot his cuffs, raise his hands, and motion the people to silence. Then on he would go about immigration and marriage being for one man and one woman, and how neither the government nor interest groups had a right to, and applause would swell again, and he worked them like a revivalist, and as he brought them to silence once more, Rausch leaned toward Bucky and whispered, *I think something just dropped out of heaven.*

And Bucky Trabue thought in his deepest heart, as he signed himself on for another campaign, *that, or maybe we just fell into something.*

∞

All of this while Dominic drowsed upright in the bus seat, as he wakened to transfer in Cleveland, then took the long trip in silence across the northern edge of Ohio, bound for Erie and Buffalo, Rochester where he was conceived if he could believe the stories, then Albany and up into the Green Mountain State.

He would startle awake now and then and look out on the deep night along the interstate. It was a tamer part of the country, he supposed, than the city he just left: the landscape got...softer in the eastward roll. He remembered that past Albany the roadway would rise into more rugged country, through the Adirondacks and into the Green Mountains, there at the northernmost margins of the Appalachians.

The new bus climbed on to the interstate now. There would be one more transfer, and Dominic would be headed home. The nodding passengers in the seats in front of him looked like the audience to a strange show of light in the windshield of the Greyhound. Dominic watched the green signs pass and slowly lost track of the mile markers.

About the Author

Over the past 25 years, Michael Williams has written a number of strange novels, from the early Weasel's Luck and Galen Beknighted in the best-selling DRAGONLANCE series to the more recent lyrical and experimental Arcady, singled out for praise by Locus and Asimov's magazines. In Trajan's Arch, his eleventh novel, stories fold into stories and a boy grows up with ghostly mentors, and the recently published Vine mingles Greek tragedy and urban legend, as a local dramatic production in a small city goes humorously, then horrifically, awry.

Trajan's Arch and Vine are two of the books in Williams's highly anticipated City Quartet, to be joined in 2018 by Dominic's Ghosts and Tattered Men.

Williams was born in Louisville, Kentucky, and spent much of his childhood in the south central part of the state, the red-dirt gothic home of Appalachian foothills and stories of Confederate guerrillas. Through good luck and a roundabout journey he made his way through through New England, New York, Wisconsin, Britain and Ireland, and has ended up less than thirty miles from where he began. He has a Ph.D. in Humanities, and teaches at the University of Louisville, where he focuses on the he Modern Fantastic in fiction and film. He is married, and has two grown sons.

CPSIA information can be obtained
at www.ICGtesting.com
Printed in the USA
BVHW03s0940081018
529524BV00026B/48/P